Homeplace

Pocket Books by JoAnn Ross

JoAnn Ross

Homeplace

Pocket Books

New York   London   Toronto   Sydney   New Delhi

Pocket Books
An Imprint of Simon & Schuster, Inc.
1230 Avenue of the Americas
New York, NY 10020

This book is a work of fiction. Any references to historical events, real people, or real places are used fictitiously. Other names, characters, places, and events are products of the author's imagination, and any resemblance to actual events or places or persons, living or dead, is entirely coincidental.

This Pocket Books paperback edition September 2019

POCKET and colophon are registered trademarks of Simon & Schuster, Inc.

For information about special discounts for bulk purchases, please contact Simon & Schuster Special Sales at 1-866-506-1949 or business@simonandschuster.com.

The Simon & Schuster Speakers Bureau can bring authors to your live event. For more information or to book an event, contact the Simon & Schuster Speakers Bureau at 1-866-248-3049 or visit our website at www.simonspeakers.com.

Manufactured in the United States of America

10 9 8 7 6 5 4 3 2 1

ISBN 978-1-9821-2186-0
ISBN 978-1-4165-4068-7 (ebook)

During the writing of *Homeplace*, I've had reason to be grateful for a number of special people: Caroline Tolley, for her keen eye and thoughtful editorial advice; Lauren McKenna, who smooths the way and is a joy to work with; Damaris Rowland, the wisest, most supportive agent in the business; as well as the terrific members of RWA—Online.

Also—my son, Patrick; his wife, Lisa; their wonder daughter, Marisa; and the newest family miracle, Parker Ryan Ross, who handled early obstacles with a great deal more aplomb than his elders.

And, once again, and always, to Jay, the grand love of my life.

Homeplace

❧ 1 ❧

Coldwater Cove, Washington

It was a damn three-ring circus. And Olympic County sheriff Jack O'Halloran had gotten stuck with the job of ringmaster. Despite the cold spring drizzle, the hillside was covered with people, many carrying cameras. Some bolder, or more curious, individuals pressed as close as they could to the white police barricades. Kids were running all over the place, laughing, shrieking, chasing one another, having themselves a dandy time. The mood couldn't have been any more electric if a bunch of TV stars had suddenly shown up on Washington's Olympic Peninsula to tape an episode of *NYPD Blue*.

Ignoring the rain dripping off the brim of his hat, Jack scowled at the vans bearing the names and logos of television stations from as far away as Spokane. Which wasn't all that surprising. After all, Coldwater Cove had always been a peaceful town. So peaceful, in fact, it didn't even have its own police department, the city fathers choosing instead to pay for protection from the county force. Crime consisted mainly of the routine Saturday night drunk and disorderly, jaywalking, calls about barking dogs, and last month a customer had walked off with the ballpoint pen from Neil Olson's You-Pump-It Gas 'N Save. It definitely wasn't every day three teenage girls barricaded themselves in their group home and refused to come out.

Meanwhile, Dr. Ida Lindstrom, their court-appointed guardian and owner of the landmark Victorian house, had apparently set off this mini–crime wave when she'd been taken to the hospital after falling off a kitchen stool. Although the information was sketchy, from what Jack could determine, when a probation officer had arrived to haul the unsupervised kids back to the juvenile detention center, Ida had held an inflammatory press conference from her hospital bed, adding fuel to an already dangerously volatile situation by instructing the girls to "batten down the hatches."

Having grown up in Coldwater Cove, Jack knew Ida to be a good, hardworking woman. Salt of the earth, a pillar of the community, and unrelentingly generous. During her days as the town's only general practitioner, she'd delivered scores of babies—including him. Since lumbering was a dangerous business, she'd also probably set more broken arms than any doctor in the state, and whenever she lost a patient—whether from illness, accident, or merely old age—she never missed a funeral.

She'd inevitably show up at the family's home after the internment with a meatloaf. Not one person in Coldwater Cove had ever had the heart to tell her that her customary donation to the potluck funeral supper was as hard as a brick and about as tasty as sawdust. Ida Lindstrom had many talents, but cooking wasn't one of them. Six months ago, when they'd buried Big John O'Halloran, Jack's father who'd dropped dead of a heart attack while hiking a glacier on nearby Mount Olympus, Jack's mother had surreptitiously put the heavy hunk of mystery meat and unidentifiable spices out on the back porch for the dogs. Who wouldn't eat it, either.

Jack admired the way Ida had taken to opening her home to at-risk teenagers at a time when so many of her contemporaries were traveling around the country in motor homes, enjoying their retirement and spending their children's inheritances. But the plan, agreed to by the court, the probation officer, and Ida herself, dammit, had been for the retired doctor to provide the kids with a stable environment, teach them responsibility and coax them back onto the straight and narrow. Not turn them into junior revolutionaries.

"I still think we ought to break down the damn door," a gung ho state police officer insisted for the third time in the past hour. Jack suspected the proposed frontal attack stemmed from an eagerness to try out the armored assault vehicle the state had recently acquired at a surplus government military auction.

"You've been watching too many old Jimmy Cagney movies on the *Late Show*," Jack said. "It's overkill. They're only juveniles."

Juveniles whose cockamamie misbehavior was proving a major pain in the ass. The standoff was entering its sixth hour, television vans were parked all the way down the hill, the satellite systems on their roofs pointed upward, as if trying to receive messages from outer space. Jack figured he was a shoe-in to be the lead story on the six o'clock news all over the Pacific Northwest. Hell, if he didn't get the girls out pretty soon, they may even make the national morning programs. And while Eleanor O'Halloran would undoubtedly be tickled pink to see her only son on television, the idea didn't suit Jack at all.

"They're not just your run of the mill juveniles," the lantern-jawed officer reminded him unnecessarily. "They're juvenile delinquents."

"Minor league ones. The most any of them are guilty of is truancy and shoplifting. Want to guess how a bunch of grown men wearing combat gear staging a military assault on three little girls would play on TV?"

"Crime's crime," another cop from neighboring Jefferson County grumbled. Although the standoff wasn't occurring in his jurisdiction, that hadn't stopped him from dropping by for a look-see.

He wasn't alone; Kitsap, Island, Clallam, and King counties were also well represented. Even the Quinault and Skokomish reservations had sent uniformed men to offer backup and gain experience in hostage situations. Not that this was exactly a hostage situation, since the girls were all alone in the house. The assembled cops were having themselves a grand old time. Jack was not.

"He's right," another cop agreed. "You may not consider shoplifting a punishable offense in your county, Sheriff, but in my jurisdiction, we view teenage malfeasance as a slippery slope to more serious crimes."

"Got a point there," Jack agreed dryly. "One day a kid's swiping a tube of Mango orange lip gloss from a Payless Drugstore and the next day she's toting an Uzi and holding up the Puget Sound National Bank."

He took the cellular phone from its dashboard holder and dialed the Lindstrom house again. The first time he'd called, the oldest girl, Shawna, had informed him that Ida had instructed her not to speak to him. Then promptly hung up. From that point on, all he'd gotten was a busy signal, suggesting they'd taken the phone off the hook. And dammit, apparently still hadn't put it back on.

"There's always tear gas," one of the Olympic County deputies suggested.

"In case you've forgotten, one of those girls is pregnant. I'm not willing to risk harming any unborn babies."

"So what do you propose to do?" a grim-faced man asked. His belted tan raincoat with the snazzy Banana Republic epaulets on the shoulders made him stand out from the local crowd clad in parkas and Gore-Tex jackets. He'd introduced himself as being from Olympia, an assistant to the governor. Unsurprisingly, the state's chief executive was concerned about the public relations aspect of this situation.

Jack shrugged and thought of his six-year-old daughter. He imagined how he'd want the cops to respond if Amy took it into her head to barricade herself in their house.

"They aren't going anywhere." They'd also refused to speak to anyone but Ida. Deciding the contrary old woman would only get them more stirred up, he'd instructed the hospital to remove the phone from her room. "The way I see it, the best thing to do is wait them out. For however long it takes."

No one argued. But the grumbles from the assembled lawmen told Jack that he was all alone, out on an increasingly risky limb.

New York City

The mob began to gather early. The senior citizens chanted slogans and marched in circles, holding their placards high. One of their leaders bellowed through a bullhorn, reminding them that this was a war. They all cheered. Some waved their signs, others their fists.

By the time Raine Cantrell walked out of the federal courthouse a little before noon, the protesters were primed for battle. Anxious for blood.

"I think I've just discovered how it feels to go diving for sharks without the metal cage," she murmured.

She'd been warned there'd be a demonstration, but given the demographics of the plaintiffs in the class action lawsuit, she hadn't expected such an unruly mob. The cacophonous chants echoed off nearby buildings; catcalls and belligerent shouts rang out over the blare of car horns.

The street was jammed with illegally parked vans bearing the insignias of all three major networks, along with CNN and various local television stations; thick black cables snaked across the sidewalk and the crowd of reporters, photographers and cameramen jockeyed for position.

"Christ. Every reporter for every half-assed paper and television station in the country must have shown up for this circus," her client, Rex Murdock, muttered.

During the months they'd worked together preparing a defense, the CEO and principal stockholder of Odessa Oil Company had revealed himself to be a man accustomed to controlling everything and everyone around him. He was brash, rough-mannered, impatient as hell, and handsome, in a rough-hewn way. All the women at Choate, Plimpton, Wells & Sullivan would inevitably cease work whenever he strode through the offices, the wedged heels of his lizard skin cowboy boots tapping a purposeful tattoo on the Italian-marble flooring. Even sixty-four-year-old Harriet Farraday, who'd worked as comptroller at the law firm since the Stone Age and had a dozen grandchildren, had taken notice.

"Why, he's a man's man, dear," Harriet had explained one day when Raine had questioned the effect her client had on seemingly the entire female staff. "You don't find many of those anymore in these so-called enlightened years." She'd made a little sound of disgust as she looked around the office. "Especially around here."

"You'd think the bastards would have better stories to chase than this half-baked, bush-league case," that man's man was grumbling now.

"Perhaps we should go back into the building and try leaving by the rear door," a second-year associate attorney from the firm's investment division suggested. His face was pale, his anxiety, evident. Raine wondered if he was rethinking his decision to enter the glamorous world of big-city corporate law. She also decided that as bright as he admittedly was, he wouldn't pass Harriet's male litmus test.

Raine's legal team was made up of a clutch of associate attorneys, a paralegal whose job it was to hand over briefs with the precision and speed of a transplant-team surgical nurse, and various dark-suited minions who'd been at her client's beck and call during the past three weeks of the trial.

Standing between them and the elderly crowd was a reassuring wall of blue. The police were grasping riot sticks she suspected none wanted to use. After all, video of burly cops beating up Grandpa and Grandma headlining the nightly news would definitely undermine the mayor's effort to refurbish the city's image.

"Slinking out the back way would make it look as if we were ashamed of our case," she said.

Okay, she may have made a slight miscalculation regarding the emotional impact of what, had it not been for the millions of dollars involved, should have been a routine contract case. But her Grandmother Ida had taught Raine that nothing could be solved by sticking your tail between your legs and running away from a problem. "Perhaps I should stop long enough to answer some questions."

"No offense, Raine. But I'm not real sure that'll calm them down," Murdock warned.

"They're definitely in a feeding frenzy. But avoiding the issue won't make it go away. We may have won in court, but believe me, Rex, the media's going to play this as a David-and-Goliath story. And from the average person's point of view, you're going to be cast as a malicious, greedy giant."

"Remind me once again why I should care?"

A low burn began to simmer just below her ribcage. Raine ignored it. "Do the two little words *Exxon Valdez* ring a bell?"

His scowl deepened.

"I'll just try to defuse the situation a bit," she said, taking his nonreply as begrudging consent. "Before it gets totally out of hand.

"Hell, you've handled this case damn well so far." He did not add, as Raine suspected he might once have—*for a woman*. "Might as well let you ride it out to the whistle."

Raine realized this was a major concession on his part. A wildcatter who'd struck it rich back when the gushing black gold could put a man on easy street for life, Rex Murdock did not surrender the reins easily. In fact, there'd been more than one occasion in court when she'd seriously wished the bar association guidelines allowed attorneys to muzzle their clients.

They'd reached the police barricade. *Show time*. Raine willed herself to calm as she faced down the crowd. The motor drives of the still cameras whirred, sounding like the wings of birds fighting against the wind that was ruffling her chin-length brown hair.

It was a cold day that gave lie to the fact that according to the calendar, spring had sprung; atop the building the flags snapped loudly in the wind and the taste of impending rain rode the brisk air. Foolishly believing the wake-up forecast predicting sunny skies, Raine had gone to work in a lightweight charcoal gray suit and white silk blouse that allowed the wind to cut through her like a knife.

"Ms. Cantrell!" A sleek blond woman sensibly clad in a black trench coat shoved a microphone past one of the cops. Raine recognized her as an attorney turned legal correspondent for CNN. She also occasionally showed up on *Nightline.* "What is your response to those who say your client is snatching bread from the mouths of the elderly?"

Raine looked straight into the camera lens. "I would simply reiterate what the court has decreed. The plaintiffs' claim was rejected because my client adhered to United States law by properly informing all employees, upon the signing of their employment agreement, that the company reserved the right to alter or terminate their retirement benefit package at any time."

As her response was answered by a roaring tidal wave of boos, Raine's attention drifted momentarily to an elderly woman sitting in an electric wheelchair. The woman was dressed in a navy blue fleece warm-up suit and high-topped sneakers bearing a red swoosh. Her white hair had been permed into puffs resembling cotton balls and her apple cheeks were ruddy from the cold. A black helium-filled balloon bearing the message *Shame* in bold red letters floated upward from a white string tied to the back of the chair.

Strangely, as Raine looked down at the elderly protestor, the white curls appeared to turn to salt-and-pepper gray, and the apple-round face morphed to a narrow, more chiseled one that was strikingly familiar. Impossibly, Raine could have sworn she was looking down at her grandmother.

She blinked, relieved when the unsettling hallucination vanished. It was not the first such incident she'd had in the past few months. But they seemed to be getting more vivid, and decidedly more personal.

"Excuse me?" she asked a reporter whom she belatedly realized had been speaking to her.

"Jeff Martin, *Wall Street Journal.*" The intense young man wearing wire-framed glasses impatiently reintroduced himself. "Would your client care to comment on the Gray Panthers' latest press release claiming that by cutting off access to health care for retirees and their spouses who are not yet qualified for Medicare, the defendant—and you, by association—are risking the lives of our nation's grandparents?"

This question was followed by a roar from the crowd. When the fanciful vision of Ida Lindstrom's disapproving face wavered in front of her eyes again, Raine shook her head to clear it. Then forced her uncharacteristically wandering mind back to the reporter's question.

"No offense intended to the Gray Panthers, but not only is that accusation an overstatement of the facts of the case, it's blatantly false, Mr. Martin. My client"—she purposefully avoided using the reporter's negative term *defendant*—"offers one of the most generous retirement packages in the industry."

The boos intensified. Protesters shouted out rude suggestions as to what Odessa Oil—Rex Murdock in particular—could do with its retirement package.

"But Odessa Oil also has a responsibility to its stockholders, many of whom are those same retirees." Determined to make her point, Raine doggedly continued, fighting back a drumming headache as she raised her voice to be heard over the crowd. "The decrease in crude-oil prices worldwide has left the company with no option but to discontinue free health-care benefits to those who opt for early retirement. As a federal court has determined today they are well within their rights to do."

The boos reached the decibel of the jackhammer that had begun pounding away inside her head. The placards were waving like pom poms at a football game. Someone in the crowd threw an egg that broke at Raine's feet, spattering her black suede Italian pumps with bright yellow yolk and gelatinous white. The attack drew enthusiastic applause from the coalition of protesters even as two of the cops waded into the crowd to find the assailant.

"You've given it your best shot, Raine. But these folks are flat-out nuts." Murdock had to yell in Raine's ear to be heard. "We're like Crockett and Bowie at the Battle of the Alamo. Let's get the hell out of here."

The icy wind picked up. The adrenaline rush of her courtroom victory had begun to wear off. Fearing that the next egg—or something even more dangerous—might hurt more than her shoes, Raine was ready to call it a day.

With two of New York City's finest clearing a path, Raine and the others began making their way to the black stretch limousine double-parked in the street beside an *Eyewitness News* van. They were pursued by the pack of reporters who shouted out questions like bullets from automatic rifles. Without waiting for the uniformed driver to get out of the car, one of the minions rushed to open the back door.

The limo, boasting two televisions, a fully stocked bar, and wide leather seats, was the height of comfort. The first time she'd ridden in the lush womb on wheels, Raine had felt exactly like Cinderella on her way to the ball. Today, although she'd never considered herself even a remotely fanciful woman, Raine imagined she could actually hear her grandmother's voice.

"Never forget girls," she'd instructed Raine and her sister on more than one occasion while they'd been growing up under her Victorian slate roof, "it's a lot easier for a camel to get into heaven than a rich man."

The saying was only one in her grandmother's seemingly endless repertoire of malapropisms. The last time Raine had heard it had been six years ago, the weekend she'd graduated from law school, when she and her grandmother had shared a grilled-portabello-mushroom-and-feta-cheese pizza at Harvard Law's Harkbox Café.

She glanced out the tinted back window at the protesters, watching them grow smaller and smaller. While the men rehashed the trial, Raine wondered why she didn't feel like joining in the conversation.

She should be jubilant. After all, she was the one who'd brought Odessa Oil into the firm in the first place, which had bolstered her reputation as a rainmaker. Today's verdict should put her on the fast track for partner in one of the largest, most prestigious law firms in the country. It was precisely what she'd been working toward for years, ever since she'd grabbed hold of the brass ring that had landed her a summer intern job at Choate, Plimpton, Wells & Sullivan. It was her personal Holy Grail and it was finally in sight.

She was intelligent, articulate, a former member of the oldest, most respected law review in the country, and currently a successful litigator who'd put the tiny northwestern town of Coldwater Cove, Washington behind her. She was a winner in a city that lionized victory. She had a three-thousand-dollar-a-month apartment furnished in sleek Italian leather, brass, and marble, and since the firm paid the tab for hired cars to drive their attorneys home at the end of the admittedly long workdays, she hadn't stepped foot on the subway since her arrival in New York.

Life was nearly perfect. So what the hell was wrong with her?

Raine rubbed her cheeks to soothe tensed facial muscles and sat up straighter in an attempt to untangle the knots in her back muscles. When the simmering flames began burning beneath her ribcage, she took out the ever ready roll of antacids and popped two into her mouth.

She'd become more and more restless these past weeks. And, although each night she'd fall into bed, physically and mentally exhausted, she'd been unable to sleep. She'd conveniently blamed it on the gallons of coffee she'd drunk while preparing for the trial, but if she were to be perfectly honest, her uncharacteristic distraction and anxiety, laced with a vague feeling of discontent, had been stirring inside her even before she'd begun preparing Odessa Oil's appeal.

As she chewed on the chalky tablets, which were advertised to taste like mint but didn't, Raine decided that her only problem was that she'd been working too hard for too long. After all, one-hundred-hour workweeks were common for those trudging along the yellow brick road to partnership.

Especially litigators, who tended to do the lion's share of the firm's traveling.

At first, after escaping the grinding poverty of law school, she'd been excited by the prospect of seeing the country at the firm's—or, more precisely, the clients'—expense. She'd looked forward to the frequent-flier perks attorneys at smaller firms could only dream about: being met at the airport gate by a uniformed driver holding a sign bearing her name, automatic hotel upgrades, and first-class airline tickets.

In reality, most of the time the only part of the country she was able to see was from thirty-thousand feet in the air. During visits to clients' cities, she tended to spend her entire time in airports, hotels, and office conference rooms and jet lag had become a way of life.

But life was filled with trade-offs, Raine reminded herself with a stiff mental shake as the limousine wove its way through the snarl of midtown traffic. And unlike so many others, hers came with a six-figure salary, health, life, and disability insurance, a 401(k) plan, bar association dues, and in the event she were ever crazy enough to try to juggle a demanding career and motherhood, paid parental leave.

She just needed a breather, she assured herself as she felt the familiar steel bands tighten around her head. She reached into her briefcase, took out a bottle of aspirin and swallowed two of them dry as she'd learned to do over the past months. On afterthought, she swallowed a third.

A short break to recharge her batteries would be just what the doctor ordered, she considered, picking up her thoughts where she'd left off. Perhaps it was time to take that long-overdue vacation she'd been planning—and putting off—for years. The one where she'd spend several sun-drenched days lounging beside a sparkling blue tropical lagoon while handsome hunks delivered mai tais and rubbed coconut oil all over her body.

This time the image that floated into Raine's mind was not one of her grandmother, but of herself, clad in a floaty, off-the-shoulder sundress emblazoned with tropical flowers. Not that she owned such a romantic dress, but this was, after all, a fantasy, so Raine wasn't about to quibble. She was strolling hand in hand with a drop-dead gorgeous man on a romantic, moonlit beach.

Music drifted on the perfumed night air as he lowered his head to kiss her. His mouth was a mere whisper away from hers when the rude blare of a siren shattered the blissful fantasy.

This time she was really going to do it, Raine vowed as a fire engine roared past the limo. While the others continued to gloat, she took out her Day-Timer and made a note to call a travel agent.

As soon as she cleared her calendar. Sometime in the next decade, she amended as she skimmed the pages filled with notations and appointments. If she was lucky.

❦ 2 ❧

Coldwater Cove

The continual drizzle finally drove the reporters back into their vans and the cops into their units. The sky over Puget Sound was as dark as a wet wool blanket and fog curled thickly around Ida Lindstrom's house. Jack telephoned the girls again, as he'd been doing every thirty minutes. When the only answer was a busy tone, he figured the damn phone was still off the hook.

It was nearly supper time. Concerned that they might be getting hungry—who knew how much food they had in the house?—Jack had decided to try to talk them into answering the door again when the cellular phone inside his Suburban trilled. Hoping it was Shawna Brown, who appeared to be the spokesperson for the trio, he scooped it up on the second ring.

"O'Halloran."

The silence on the other end told him what he already knew—that his tone had been too brusque. He dragged his hand down his face and tried again. "This is Sheriff O'Halloran. Is this Shawna?"

"No," the young female voice answered after another hesitant pause. "It's me, Daddy. Amy," she added as if he had another daughter he might possibly confuse her with.

A jolt of parental concern struck like lightning. "What's wrong, honey?" She'd gone over to his mother's house after school as she did every day. Having called earlier to explain his situation, he knew his mother wouldn't be letting Amy call unless it was important. "Where's your Gramma?"

"She's in the kitchen. Making cookies." Another pause that tested his patience. "The kind with the M&Ms in them."

"I see." He looked out the rain-streaked windshield at the house. The lights that had been turned on inside were blurred by the filmy curtain of fog and mist. He kept his voice mild, even as concern was replaced with mild exasperation. "Is there some special reason you're calling, Amy?"

"Yes."

Jack told himself that he should know better than to ask a six-year-old a *yes* or *no* question. "Can you tell me what it is?"

"I was calling about Puffy."

"Puffy?"

"My Nano Kitty." Unlike her father, Amy didn't attempt to conceal her exasperation. "The one you said you'd take care of for me," she reminded him.

Since the electronic pet had been banned from the first-grade classroom yesterday, Jack had agreed to keep it in his pocket. He'd also promised to tend to it while Amy was at school. If he'd known ahead of time just what that entailed, he might not have been so willing.

"Puffy's doing just fine, darlin'."

"Have you been feeding him?"

"You bet." If today was any example, the damn virtual cat ate more often than any real cat.

"Did you play with him?"

"Yep. We played chase the mouse not more than ten minutes ago." According to the instructions, a neglected Nano Kitty was a sad kitty; a sad kitty could become ill, requiring even more attention, including regular doses of virtual-kitty antibiotics.

"Oh. Good." Her obvious relief made him feel guilty for having considered, on more than one occasion today, tossing the damn gizmo into Admiralty Bay. "I was worried you might forget and accidentally let Puffy die."

"I promise, Amy, I won't let Puffy die." Since he hadn't been able to make that same promise when her mother had been diagnosed with ovarian cancer four years ago, Jack had every intention of keeping his word now. Even if his surrogate parenting of an electronic kitten was proving a source of vast amusement for his fellow cops.

"Okay." That matter seemingly settled, she turned to another. "Uh . . . I was wondering, Daddy . . ."

Yes, Amy?" He managed, just barely, to keep from grinding his teeth.

"Well, I was wondering . . . if I could maybe watch one of the tapes. Not the whole thing. Just a little bit."

He suspected she wasn't referring to *Pocohantas* or *The Little Mermaid*, but rather one of the videotapes Peg had made when she'd accepted the fact— long before he had—that she was going to die. What had begun as a simple love letter to the child she'd be leaving behind had evolved into a legacy of maternal comfort and advice.

The tapes—an amazing one-hundred-and-six hours of them—were tucked away in Peg's cedar hope chest with other personal memorabilia as a legacy for the daughter she would never see grow to womanhood.

"I was thinking maybe Gramma and I could drive over to our house after we finished baking the cookies. Just for a little while," she cajoled prettily when he didn't immediately answer.

"You know the rules, honey. You and I always watch the tapes together."

It had been what Peg, concerned about her daughter's possibly fragile emotional state, had wanted. And Jack was not about to let her down.

He couldn't count how many times during the past two years he'd wanted to tell his first and only love about some new event in Amy's life—like when she'd lost her first tooth and had left cookies and chocolate milk out for the tooth fairy, or last December when she'd played the part of a reed piper in her kindergarten's performance of *The Nutcracker Suite* and had insisted on keeping her stage makeup on while the two of them had celebrated afterwards with Ingrid Johansson's blueberry waffles at the Timberline Café.

Her first report card; her first sleepover, which he'd discovered was ill-named since the four little six-year-old girls certainly hadn't done much sleeping—so many firsts Jack knew Peg would have given anything to share.

"But Daddy—"

"Don't whine, Amy," he said automatically. It was

a new stage she'd entered into, not nearly as appealing as the previous ones and he hoped it would be short-lived. "I'll tell you what. Why don't you practice reading your new Dr. Seuss book, and I promise we'll go out for burgers, then watch a tape together tomorrow night."

"Okay," she agreed with an instant acceptance he sure would enjoy receiving from the teens inside Ida's house. "I'll go read it to Gramma while she bakes the cookies."

"Good idea," Jack agreed. "Hey, Amy . . . whose little girl are you?"

She giggled as she always did whenever he asked that question. "Yours, Daddy," she answered on cue.

"Love you, Pumpkin."

"I love you, too, Daddy." She gave a smacking kissing sound.

Jack gave one back, then hung up and dialed the house again, only to receive another busy signal. Next he called Papa Joe's Pizza Emporium and ordered two pepperoni-and-mushroom pizzas—a large for the girls and a medium for himself. He didn't know what they'd prefer, but figured since they were still refusing to talk with him, they could damn well eat whatever he ordered.

Then, frustrated, and fearing he wasn't going to make it to his mother's house in time to pick up his daughter, take her home and tuck her into bed, he went back out in the slanting, icy rain that was now falling like needles and strode toward Ida's front door.

New York City

The victory celebration took place high above the city, in a mahogany-paneled conference room overlooking Central Park. The mood was unrestrained, bordering on jubilant, as the cream of the legal profession celebrated yet another battlefield victory.

Champagne flowed, Waterford decanters of Scotch and brandy had been brought out, and even Oliver Choate, senior partner and founder of Choate, Plimpton, Wells & Sullivan, who usually remained ensconced upstairs in his executive suite, had joined the revelry.

"To the little lady of the hour." Murdock lifted the glass of Jack Daniel's the firm had begun stocking when he'd first become a client. "The toughest—and prettiest—litigator in the business," he boomed out. "The sharp as barbwire lady who managed to save our collective hairy asses."

"You have such a way with words, Rex," Raine murmured, earning a laugh from the others.

"Well, now, darlin', that's why I pay you the big bucks to do the talkin' for me."

More laughs. More corks popped, more brandy poured, more martinis shaken.

It was Oliver Choate's turn to toast. "To Raine. Choate, Plimpton, Wells and Sullivan's Wonder Woman."

"I'm hardly Wonder Woman," she demurred. "It was, despite the dollars involved, an uncomplicated case." Since much of litigation consisted of smoke and mirrors, Raine had become adept at setting up smoke screens to protect the firm's clients. But the *Retirees v. Odessa Oil* suit had been a text book example of the Golden Rule taught in her second-year Law and Economics class: He who has the most gold rules.

"You're right," Murdock agreed. "Wonder Woman's not quite right. Linda Carter looked real cute in that skimpy red, white, and blue outfit, but she didn't have your ball-busting, take-no-prisoners attitude." He skimmed a look over her, from the top of her head down to her egg-stained Bruno Magli pumps. "I know. That spunky gal on the TV show set back in olden times. The one with the big—"

"Breastplate," Oliver cut Murdock off before he could use the *T* word they all knew he'd intended. "And the *gal* you're referring to is Xena," he said, revealing himself to be a man of surprisingly eclectic tastes. "Warrior Princess."

"You got it," Murdock agreed.

Oliver lifted his glass again. "To our very own Warrior Princess."

The others followed. Even, Raine noticed, Stephen Wells, managing partner of the firm, which was mildly surprising since she and Stephen had bumped heads on more than one occasion. Raine had been at the firm less than a week when she'd realized that Wells was one of those stuffy dinosaurs who, if given the choice, would have never permitted women to enter these hallowed legal halls.

But that was before today. Before she'd proven that she could do anything any of the male attorneys could do. And she'd done it wearing high heels. Breathing in the heavy ether of admiration, Raine took a sip of the champagne. In contrast to the rain that had begun to fall, it tasted like sunshine on her tongue. Outside the floor-to-ceiling windows the entire city appeared to have been laid at her feet.

It was a moment to be savored. To tie up in pretty ribbons and tuck away in her memory, like the prom photographs and dried corsage petals her sister Savannah had Scotch-taped into floral-covered scrapbooks back in high school. Raine had never gone to a prom. The closest she'd come to teenage romance was the snowy December night her junior year of high school right after she'd gotten her braces off when she and Warren Templeton, a worldly senior and president of her debate team, had been parked out by Lake Quinault. It was the memorable night Raine had learned how to French-kiss.

Cigars were pulled out of a Honduran-mahogany humidor and passed around. Smoke filled the room as the conversation shifted from a rehash of the court case that had taken months of twenty-hour-days to prepare and a mere three weeks to present, to where to eat lunch. They were arguing over which steakhouse to go to—the mood was unanimously carnivoristic—when Raine's secretary stuck his head in the door.

"I'm sorry to interrupt, but you have a phone call, Raine."

"Tell whoever it is that Raine's off the clock until tomorrow morning," Stephen Wells instructed curtly, not giving Raine a chance to respond.

"The caller says it's an emergency."

"Who is it, Brian?" Raine asked.

"She refused to give her name." Having worked long enough at the firm not to be intimidated by the managing partner's irritation, Brian Collins ignored Wells's scowl. Raine suspected that being the only one who understood the Byzantine filing system he'd set up didn't hurt, either. "But the area code on the caller ID is from Washington."

"Perhaps it's the President," James Sullivan suggested.

"Calling to offer Raine the Attorney General's job," Rex said.

More laughter.

Raine found nothing humorous in this news. Especially since she suspected the call was coming from Washington State, and not the nation's capitol.

"I'll take it in my office." As her headache spiked again, she put her glass down on the table. Promising to return as soon as possible, she escaped the smoke-filled office. The heels of her pumps sank into the plush pewter carpeting as she made her way down the curving staircase to her office.

"I smell like a damn pool hall," she muttered. "The only problem with winning is it gives the partners an excuse to pull out the stink sticks."

"It's a guy thing," her secretary said. "You may be able to hold your own on the playing field with the big boys, Raine, but there are some things you'll just never understand."

"I prefer to think of myself—and all women who are sensible enough not to want dog breath and smelly hair—as a superior life form."

"You probably are. But I'll bet you don't have nearly as much fun. By the way, your caller is a kid. She sounds like a teenager, perhaps sixteen, seventeen. She wouldn't tell me what the problem was. All she'd say was that it was an emergency and she had instructions to call you. I didn't think you'd want me to share that with the others upstairs."

"No." A chill skittered up Raine's spine. Her grandmother wasn't a young woman. If anything had happened to her . . . "Thank you, Brian." Raine managed a vague smile for the young man who kept her life so well organized.

She went into her office, sank down in the swivel leather chair she'd splurged part of her end-of-the-year bonus on, and took a deep breath as she looked down at the blinking orange light. Then, spurred by apprehension, she pressed the button. "Hello. This is Raine Cantrell."

"Raine?" The voice on the other end of the phone sounded young and extremely nervous. But not hysterical, Raine decided with a modicum of relief. "This is Shawna Brown. I'm one of your grandmother's girls—"

"I know. She told me all about you." Raine couldn't remember which of the teenagers Shawna was, but decided it wasn't germane to the point. "Is my grandmother all right?"

"Well, that's not an easy question to answer."

"Why don't you try, dear?" Nerves made her want to snap at the girl; years of courtroom experience allowed her to keep her voice calm.

"Well, she says she's fine and dandy, but the doctors, they don't seem so sure. So they're making her stay in the hospital for tests, but—"

"Hospital?" Forgetting everything she'd ever learned about questioning a witness, Raine abruptly cut the girl off. "My grandmother's in the hospital? What happened?"

Visions of Ida Lindstrom driving her ancient Jeep off the twisting wooded road into town flashed through Raine's mind, followed on close order by the possibilities of a stroke or heart attack.

Her grandmother had always seemed as strong as one of the towering Douglas firs surrounding the Washington peninsula town. But then again, Raine reminded herself, it had been more than five years since she'd been back to Coldwater Cove. Some quick calculation revealed that somehow, while she hadn't been paying attention, her grandmother had edged into her late seventies.

"It's probably nothin' real serious," Shawna hastened to assure Raine. "She just had herself a little dizzy spell this morning when she climbed up on a kitchen stool to get the cornstarch. She was going to make a boysenberry pie.

"I've told her not to get up on that rickety old stool, that if she wants something on the top shelf of the cupboard, I'll get it down for her. She's so short, it's a real stretch for her to reach. I don't know why she even keeps things up that high, but you know your grandma. Told me she'd set things up that way when she first came to Coldwater Cove from Portland after her divorce, and didn't see any reason to change."

Just when Raine was about to scream, the girl stopped for a breath. "But I guess you already know that story."

"Yes. I do. So, if you could just get back to this morning, I'd certainly appreciate it."

"Oh . . . Sure. Well, I was out bringing the clothes in off the line because it was looking like it might rain, you know how iffy the weather is this time of year and—"

"Shawna." Having spent years learning to organize

her thoughts, Raine was growing more and more frustrated by the way the teenager's explanation kept wandering off the subject. "Why don't you please just tell me what exactly happened to Ida? Without any embellishments."

There was a pause. Then Shawna said, "I'm sorry I'm not tellin' this good enough for you."

There was no mistaking the hurt feelings in the girl's tone. *Nothing like badgering your own witness.* "And I apologize for sounding impatient," Raine immediately backpedaled. "I'm just trying to find out what happened."

"Mama Ida fell off the stool and, like, hit her head on the floor."

"I see." And she did, all too clearly. Raine's heart clenched as she imagined her grandmother—all four-feet, eleven inches, ninety-eight pounds of her—sprawled on the kitchen floor. "Did she knock herself unconscious?"

"She says no. But we called 911, anyway. Which really riled Mama Ida up, but Renee was scared. And so was I."

"Renee's another one of the girls?"

"Yeah. She's my sister. We ended up in the system after our mama and daddy died in a car wreck over by Moclips. For a while we were put in different homes, which is why Renee started running away. To be with me." She paused as if trying to decide how much to reveal. "I wanted to take care of us, but I'm underage, and after I got busted at a kegger on the beach, the judge said I wasn't responsible enough, so we had to stay in foster care. But things got better after we moved in with Mama Ida."

"I'm glad to hear that." Nice little boarding school

her grandmother was running, Raine thought acidly. Whatever happened to sponsoring a Brownie troop, where your biggest concern was the annual cookie sale? "So, you called 911. And the paramedics came?"

"Yeah. Though she was spittin' like a wet cat, they took her off to the hospital in Port Angeles. Which was when all the trouble started."

Raine pressed her fingers against her temple, where the jackhammer had been replaced by a maniac who'd begun pounding away with a mallet. The fire that had died down a bit during the conference-room celebration flared again in her chest. Higher. Hotter. "I'm almost afraid to ask."

"Our probation officer—that's Ms. Kelly, who Mama Ida always calls Old Fussbudget—was at the hospital checking on some guy who robbed a 7-Eleven a few years back. He'd been in a bar fight and was gettin' a cut on his head stitched up when your grandmother was brought into the emergency room.

"Ms. Kelly called the house, and Renee, who's too young to know any better, admitted we were here all alone. So, Ms. Kelly right away called Mrs. Petersen. She works for the county. In social services. She's found Renee foster homes the other times she's run away. Gwen, too."

"Gwen?"

"She's the pregnant one."

The thought of three delinquents alone in her grandmother's antique-filled home was not the most encouraging thing Raine had heard today. "I don't understand. You said it happened this morning."

"Yeah."

"Why isn't my mother handling things?"

"Oh, Lilith's on the coast with her friends, preparing for some sort of return-of-the-sun celebration, or something. It's like one of the coven's most important gatherings."

"Coven? My mother's a witch, now?" Despite her ongoing concern for her grandmother, Raine couldn't help being sidetracked by this little news flash.

"Not exactly. At least I don't think so. I mean, I haven't seen her waving a magic wand or boiling up toads and lizards in the Dutch oven or anything. It's Mama Ida who's always callin' it a coven. Mostly it's just some of your mama's New Age stuff. She's a pagan now," Shawna added matter-of-factly.

"I see." Raine poured a glass of water from the carafe on her desk and took a long drink, hoping it would put out the inferno blazing in her gut. It didn't.

"I don't care if the sun's coming back, sucked into a black hole, or explodes, Shawna. I want you to call my mother right now and have her get back to Coldwater Cove."

Not that Lilith would prove that much help. During her lifetime, Raine's mother had been a flower child, a war protester, an actress usually cast as the soon-to-be-dead bimbo in a handful of low-budget horror films, as well as a rock singer with a pretty but frail voice who'd managed to stay in the music business because of her looks. Which were stunning. Unfortunately, she could be selfish, like beautiful women often are, and in Raine's opinion, habitually behaved like a foolish, willful schoolgirl, mindless of the consequences of her actions. But at least she should be capable of preventing the kids from stealing the silver before Raine could get back home.

"I tried calling the lodge where they were supposed to be staying, but the lady who answered the phone said they all left to go camping out in the woods. She said Lilith said something about a ceremonial bonfire. But maybe the sheriff's sent someone out—"

"The sheriff? How exactly did he get involved in all this?"

"Oh. That happened after we locked ourselves in the house."

"You did what?" Raine jumped to her feet. At the same time she reached into the drawer for her plastic bottle of Maalox. "Why on earth would you do that?"

"Because Mama Ida told us to batten down the hatches and barricade the doors. She quoted something—you know how she does that all the time, right?—about free fighters and defenders of old homes and old names."

"And old splendors," Raine murmured. "It's from *Cyrano de Bergerac*." But, like everything else her grandmother quoted, it always came out twisted.

"Oh. That's the guy with the big nose, right? Mama Ida brought home the video last month. Gwen thinks Steve Martin's really funny. For an old guy, that is. Ever since then, she's been thinking of maybe naming her baby Steve. If it's a boy, I mean. Renee is voting for Leo. After Leonardo DiCaprio? I kinda like Denzel."

"They're all lovely names," Raine said. She ground her teeth, making a mental apology to Ida, who'd paid for years of expensive orthodontia. "Now, if we

could get back to why my grandmother told you to
barricade yourselves in the house—"

"Oh, sure. That's easy. She said there was no way
she was letting any government bureaucrat take us
away from our home just because we didn't, like,
have a responsible adult present in the house."

"I see." Personally, Raine thought that they'd be
in the same fix if her mother *had* been home. No
one, in her memory, had ever used the words "responsible adult" to describe Lilith Lindstrom Cantrell Townsend. "And I suppose it was when you
wouldn't open the door that the social worker called
Sheriff O'Halloran?"

"Yeah. Along with half the police in the state, it
looks like," Shawna said. "They're all outside. The
TV stations are out there, too." She paused. "Mama
Ida also told us that we weren't to bother you. And
I've always tried to do what she says, but there are
a lot of men with guns in the driveway.

"And I don't want to scare Renee or Gwen, but I
think you'd better get here as quick as you can. Before they send in a SWAT team to break down the
door or something."

Her knees grew weak. Raine sank back down into
her chair and tried to ignore the movie hostage
scenes flashing through her mind. The rain streaking
down the window blurred the view of the tulips and
spring green trees in the nearby park.

"I'll be there as soon as I can. Meanwhile, do you
have a phone number for the sheriff?"

"I can look it up. He's called the house a couple
times, but after I saw Mama Ida's news conference
on the television—"

"My grandmother gave a news conference from her hospital bed?"

As she twisted open the cap and chugged the Maalox, Raine told herself that she shouldn't be surprised. Her grandmother was a lifelong firebrand. Ida had even gone to jail back in the fifties for setting up a mobile vasectomy clinic in the parking lot of the annual Sawdust Festival and offering two-for-one bonus pricing during the three-day event.

"Yeah. She looked real good, too," Shawna said. "For a lady her age. Though I don't think the sheriff is real happy about her callin' him a storm trooper . . . Gwen taped it so she could watch it when she got home.

"Anyway, Mama Ida told us—on the TV—not to talk to anyone until she managed to escape the jackasses at the hospital. Those were her words, not mine," Shawna added, as if afraid Raine might not approve of the vulgarity. "So I took the phone off the hook."

After assuring Shawna that she'd take care of matters with the sheriff, Raine asked Brian to book her on the first flight to Seattle's Sea-Tac Airport. From there she could rent a car and take a ferry to Coldwater Cove. Fortunately, she always kept a suitcase packed with essentials in her office, which would prevent having to waste time by going to her apartment to pack.

She was anxious to call the hospital to check on her grandmother's condition, but along with marshaling her thoughts before speaking, law school had taught her to prioritize.

Raine vaguely recalled Sheriff John O'Halloran to be an intelligent, easygoing man who continued to generate enough good will in the county to get elected year after year. She couldn't imagine him attacking a house inhabited by three unarmed, frightened teenage girls.

Still, it didn't take Clarence Darrow to realize that the most critical item on the agenda was to prevent any one of the other cops Shawna had mentioned from deciding to play Rambo.

Olympic National Park, Washington

Cooper Ryan had received three calls in as many hours regarding the strange goings-on near Heart of the Hills. The third call, and the one that had captured his attention, had begun the same as the others—an illegal campfire, discordant music, and eerie chanting. However, a new wrinkle had been added: several women were reported to be gallivanting around the forest, as naked as jaybirds.

Ascribing to a live-and-let-live philosophy, normally Coop wouldn't have been all that bothered by the reports. However, a Boy Scout troop was scheduled for a nature hike through that area tomorrow and he doubted that their parents would be thrilled if the usual environmental ranger talk was replaced by an up-close-and-personal demonstration of the differences between boys and girls.

Coop drove out to the trailhead nearest the site of the reports and began hiking through the old-growth rainforest. They couldn't be far, he determined when the scent of burning wood and silvery flute music drifted through the fog-shrouded tops of towering fir and hemlock trees. Mist rose off a cushioned forest floor that was a mosaic of countless shades of green. Starflowers were just beginning to blossom amidst the interwoven ferns and mosses, bright harbingers of summer. Except for the distant music, the occasional chirp of a bird, and the sound of water running over rocks, the ancient old-growth forest was as silent as a cathedral.

When he reached the edge of a clearing, he saw them: a dozen women, all as naked as the day they were born. Hands linked, they'd directed their attention toward a woman who stood atop a pyramid of stone between twin fires. Her hands reached skyward, her voluptuous body outlined by the light of dancing flames. Long waves, topped with the woven band of red and white flowers that encircled her head, streamed down her bare back like molten silver. Despite the fact that her hair was no longer a rich, tawny blond, Coop instantly recognized her.

She was half chanting, half singing, while a heavyset young woman with her hair braided in colorful ribbons sat cross-legged in front of the stones, playing a flute.

"Ancient ones, trees of ancient Earth. Older than time can tell. Grant me the power at your command to charge my magic spell."

Coop wasn't all that surprised to discover Lilith Lindstrom had grown up to be some sort of witch. After all, she'd never really fit into the hard-working community of loggers and fishermen. Flighty, harebrained, and frivolous had been a few of the descriptions he'd heard over the years. Jealous wives or worried mothers of sons were more likely to call her dangerous.

Coop, however, had always thought her magnificent. And as elusive as quicksilver, as out of reach as the moon. Deciding that she wasn't really going to escape, not dressed—or undressed—the way she was, he folded his arms, leaned back against the gigantic trunk of a red-barked Western cedar and waited for the show—which included several provocative references to fertility—to come to a conclusion.

When it did, Coop began to slowly clap his hands. Heads swivelled toward him and female faces drew into tight, disapproving scowls. All except Lilith's.

"Cooper!" Bestowing a smile as warm as a thousand suns upon him, she stepped down from the stones and ran toward him. "What a lovely surprise."

With her usual impulsiveness, she flung herself into his arms and touched her smiling mouth to his. The kiss was light and brief. But it still sent a jolt straight to his groin.

"Imagine seeing you here," she said when he'd lowered her back to the mossy ground. "Do you know, I was thinking about you just last month. It must have been a foreshadowing. When did you get back to Washington?"

"A couple weeks ago." Around them, the other women were wrapping themselves in capes or pulling on sweats. If Lilith felt at all ill at ease about her nudity, she was sure hiding it well, Coop thought.

"I wish I'd known. I would have thrown you a huge blowout of a welcome-home party."

"I'm not going anywhere."

"Well, then there's still time." Seeming pleased with that prospect, she nodded. "What brings you out here?"

"I work here. In the park."

"Oh. Well, isn't that a coincidence? You being out here, and us running into one another—"

"It isn't exactly a coincidence. I received some complaints."

"Complaints?" She lifted a brow and combed a hand absently through her hair, causing it to drift over her breasts. Her still-magnificent naked breasts. "Whatever for?"

"To begin with, there's the little matter of an illegal fire."

"It's Beltane. We couldn't possibly celebrate without our fires. In the olden days the druids passed cattle through the flames to ensure prosperity. Since that seemed a bit impractical, we reluctantly decided to forego that portion of the ceremony."

Practical had never been a word Coop would have used to describe Lilith Lindstrom. And it sure wasn't now. "It's still not in a prescribed campground," he pointed out.

"Well, of course it isn't, darling. If you've received complaints about us celebrating our festival all the way out here in the middle of nowhere, can you imagine what would have happened if we'd held it in a designated campground?"

"Look, I'm willing, for old times sake, to overlook the illegal campsite and the nudity, but the fires are another matter. You're going to have to put them out."

She lifted her chin, changing from some ethereal woodland sprite back into the headstrong young girl who'd once driven him to distraction. "Not until we've concluded our celebration."

"Dammit, Lilith—"

"You can curse all you like, Cooper, but we are not

extinguishing those fires until tomorrow morning. I still have to draw down the moon tonight, after all."

"You can draw down the entire Milky Way for all I care, but the fires have got to be extinguished, and you all have to move to a designated campsite. And I want you dressed. Now." He feared if he told her about the Boy Scouts, she'd refuse to put her clothes on just to aggravate him further.

"Gracious, that's a great many orders." Her midnight blue eyes sparked with barely restrained temper. "I remember you having such wonderful potential, Cooper. What a shame you've turned out to be a narrow-minded dictator. And a governmental one at that."

Refusing to rise to the bait, Cooper pulled a narrow notebook out of his jacket pocket, scribbled a few lines, ripped the ticket from the book and held it out to her.

"What's that?"

"It's a citation. For the fires." Because she'd gotten under his skin, he flicked a quick gaze over her from the top of her head down to her crimson-lacquered toenails. "Though I may be a narrow-minded dictator, I decided to give you a pass on the lewd behavior."

"Lewd?" She plucked the ticket from his hand, tore it in half and dropped the pieces at his feet. "I happen to know for a fact that I'm not the first person to enjoy these woods sans clothing." Her pointed gaze reminded him that he should damn well know that, too. "Obviously, you've also turned into a puritan. Which is even worse than a dictator."

"I'm just doing my job." Because he was really

starting to get pissed, he scribbled out another ticket and shoved it toward her.

"And what a nasty, small-minded job it is, too." Lilith tore this one into four pieces and tossed them to the ground along with the others.

"Dammit, if you'd just agree to put the fires out and put some clothes on—"

"Not until we're finished with our ceremony."

He furiously scribbled a third. "This is your last chance, sweetheart. Tear this up and I'm going to have to take you in."

"I am very disappointed in you, Cooper." That stated, she grabbed the entire citation book from his hands, ripped the pages into confetti, then flung them into his face.

"Goddammit, that's it." Coop pulled the set of handcuffs from the back of his belt.

"What do you think you're doing?"

"What does it look like? I'm taking you in." He snapped the cuffs around her wrists, receiving a perverse pleasure at the sound of the metal clicking shut. After tossing his khaki jacket over her shoulders, he turned toward the others.

"I would advise you all to extinguish those fires. Now. We're a little short on holding cells down at park headquarters, but if you don't cooperate, I'm sure I can manage to squeeze you all in for a day or so. Until I can get the paperwork processed."

Without their leader, the coven, or whatever the hell it was, crumbled. Coop watched with satisfaction as the flute player retrieved a bucket of water and threw it onto the fire, which caused the flames to hiss and sputter. The others followed suit.

"Where the hell are your clothes?" he asked Lilith.

"That's my business." She looked amazingly cool for a naked woman whose wrists were handcuffed behind her back.

"Since I'm going to be booking you into my jail cell, I figure it's just become *my* business."

They were standing toe to toe, nose to nose. Coop reluctantly gave her credit for not flinching at either his tone or his glare.

"You're too uptight, Cooper," Lilith said with a toss of her silver head. "I happen to embrace nudity. It is, after all, our natural state." She skimmed a disapproving look over him. "You certainly weren't born wearing that uniform. Which, by the way, is not at all flattering. And the color is wrong for your eyes."

He hated that he cared what Lilith whatever-the-hell-last-name-she-was-going-by-these-days thought about him. Hated the fact that he had to resist the urge to suck in his gut, which while not as hard as it had been in the days they rolled around on a blanket in these very same woods, wasn't bad for a guy who was about to hit fifty.

"You can tout the universal appeal of nudity all you want, but if that squall that's out over the Pacific hits, you'll be embracing frostbite," he said.

"I happen to have it on good authority we're scheduled to have mostly clear skies with some high cirrus clouds, and a possibility for scattered showers come evening."

"See that in your crystal ball, did you?"

"Actually, it was the forecast on the Weather Channel."

"Well, don't look now, sweetheart, but I think your forecast is wrong. Because those black anvils gathering overhead sure as hell look like they mean business."

"So? Even if it does rain, the human body is waterproof."

Coop felt his jaw lock and realized he was clenching his teeth. He stabbed a finger toward a twenty-something young woman now dressed in a Seattle Seahawks sweatshirt, leggings, and sneakers. "If you don't want to be next, go into whatever tent belongs to this throwback to the sixties and fetch her some clothes."

"Go get my pack, Annie, please," Lilith said when the young woman hesitated. "Before Dudley Doright here decides to put us all in shackles."

The Seahawks fan ran to a nearby tent, returning with a dark blue backpack decorated with silver stars. Coop stuffed it under his arm and began dragging his prisoner down the trail.

"You're a bully, Cooper Ryan," Lilith said scathingly. "A horrible, rude, misogynist bully."

"Sticks and stones, darlin'." Now that he'd restored order, Coop was actually beginning to enjoy himself. He couldn't remember another time when he'd had the upper hand where this woman was concerned.

"I can't believe this is happening."

"I warned you about the consequences."

"Oh, I understand all about consequences. After all, I have been arrested before." Coop recalled those days all too well. While he'd been slogging through a goddamn jungle, trying to stay alive, she'd been throwing red paint on army recruiters and sleeping with long-haired, pot-smoking, hippie draft dodgers. "I know the drill," she continued. "What I cannot believe is that you would actually arrest a woman who gave you her virginity the night of high school graduation."

They'd both been virgins. But since Coop hadn't admitted to that back then, he saw no reason to set the record straight now.

They were still about two hundred yards from the trailhead when the dark sky overhead opened up, dumping buckets of icy rain that hit like needles down on them.

"It figures," Coop ground out as he ran toward the truck, dragging her along with him. "It just goddamn figures!"

Lilith Lindstrom had always been trouble with a capital *T*. Nothing had changed there. She was also still a knockout. Coop figured that having the woman rumored to have been the inspiration for the Stones' *Ruby Tuesday* back in his life again was proof positive that Fate had one helluva skewed sense of humor.

❦ 3 ❧

The Delta jet was streaking westward, managing to stay just ahead of the setting sun. Raine sat in seat 3A in first class, a yellow legal pad on the laptop table, making a list of things that would need to be taken care of once she reached Washington.

Obviously, a visit to her grandmother was high on the list. The doctor she'd spoken with on her cellular phone while waiting at the gate for her flight had informed her that Ida appeared to have suffered merely a fleeting case of vertigo. If the additional tests failed to reveal any serious underlying condition, Raine's grandmother would probably be discharged and allowed to return home tomorrow afternoon.

Although that didn't give her much time, Raine had every intention of getting those three delinquents out of the house before then. She understood all too well her grandmother's strong sense of social responsibility, but if she'd begun endangering her health, it was time for someone to put a foot down. And from Lilith's latest disappearing act, it was more than obvious Raine couldn't count on her mother for any show of responsibility. So, what else was new?

That left it up to her to set things straight. Fortunately, Raine thought, she was up to the job. Hadn't one of the wealthiest, most powerful men in America called her a warrior? If she couldn't handle one elderly woman and three teenagers, then she might as well resign from the bar.

One piece of good news she'd discovered was that it turned out Shawna and Renee had an aunt no one had known about. Child protective services was currently conducting an investigation, but according to the caseworker Raine had spoken with, the woman and her navy husband should be receiving custody of both girls within days. Which left only the pregnant Gwen to deal with.

She debated calling her grandmother from the plane, then decided that there was no point in risking a confrontation. Although the doctor's diagnosis had been encouraging, she didn't want to get Ida wound up and risk something far more serious than vertigo. Although her grandmother would probably never admit it, even to herself, Ida Lindstrom was, after all, a senior citizen. Not unlike the ones who'd been demonstrating against her client earlier. Had it only been two hours ago? The recent courtroom victory seemed as if it had happened in another lifetime.

Sighing, she took the phone from the back of the seat in front of her, swiped her platinum AMEX card, and dialed the number she'd already memorized.

"Well, hello, Ms. Cantrell," the now familiar deep

voice drawled. "What a surprise to hear from you. Again."

All right, so she'd called twenty minutes ago from over Ohio. Since when was it a crime to be concerned about a possible life-threatening situation taking place in the very home where she'd grown up?

"I was checking to see if there were any further developments.

"Well now, that depends." He dragged the subsequent pause out, as if he'd guessed how such delays irritated her.

"Depends on what?"

"Whether or not you think finding out Renee's a vegetarian is a development."

Renee was Shawna's runaway sister, Raine recalled. "I fail to see how that has any relevance in this case."

"She didn't like the pizza."

"Pizza?"

"The one I had delivered. Mushroom and pepperoni."

"That was a good ploy," she allowed. "Feeding them to create a bond." Raine had seen much the same tactic used on an episode of *Homicide* last season.

"Actually, it wasn't a ploy. I was starving and figured they might be hungry, too."

"Well. Then it was a very thoughtful gesture." Raine wondered how many New York cops would bother to think of such a thing. Then again, she decided, standoff situations in the big city were probably a great deal different than in Coldwater Cove.

"It wasn't that big a deal." She could hear the

shrug in his voice. "Shawna—she's the one you spoke with," he reminded Raine, as if she could have forgotten such a call—"was willing to pick up the phone long enough to call and tell me that the kid was refusing to eat it."

"Couldn't Renee just take the damn pepperoni off?"

"Now, you know, that's pretty much what I suggested." Raine heard the renewed humor in his tone and wondered if it was meant to be at her expense. "Turns out she's one of those absolutely pure sprout eaters who won't touch cheese, either."

Although she'd pulled every legal string she could from across the country, Raine still feared for the girls' safety. Her earlier reassurance regarding the sheriff's ability to pull this off without bloodshed had evaporated when she'd discovered, during their first conversation, that it wasn't Big John O'Halloran outside her grandmother's house, but his son, Jack, infamous high school make-out artist and jock extraordinaire.

Jack O'Halloran had been legend around Olympic County for both his athletic achievements and the stunts that kept him in judicial hot water and were particularly inappropriate for the son of the county's chief lawman. He'd been the quarterback of the Coldwater Cove Loggers High School football team, state all-star pitcher for the baseball team, and his senior year had been voted student-body president by the widest margin in the school's history.

He'd subsequently had the office taken away from him six weeks later during homecoming weekend when he'd led a raid to kidnap the mascot of a rival school. The members of the Fighting Beavers varsity football team had not found the ransom note's instructions—that they parade down Coldwater Cove's main street wearing only their jockstraps and helmets—all that humorous. Neither had school authorities.

From what Raine could remember of his antics, the term *hell-raiser* could have been coined with Jack O'Halloran in mind. He drank too much, drove too fast, and just about every female in the county between the ages of eight and eighty had found him irresistible. Including, dammit, she thought now, her. Not that he'd ever noticed her, four years behind him, skinny as a lodgepole pine, with bark brown hair as straight as rainwater and a mouthful of braces. The idea that such a man could actually grow up to be sheriff was incredible.

Putting aside an adolescent feminine pique she was vaguely surprised to discover lurking inside of her, Raine returned to business.

"I'm assuming that you were informed I've filed a TRO to stop the police from using violence against my grandmother's wards."

While she'd been on the way to the airport, Oliver Choate had telephoned a friendly judge he played golf with every Wednesday morning. That judge, in turn, called another in Washington State, who hadn't hesitated issuing the temporary restraining order.

"Yeah." For a man who'd been handed a court order, Sheriff O'Halloran sounded less than impressed. "Wally called a little bit ago with the news."

"Wally?" Not at all encouraged by the familiarity in the lawman's tone, Raine reminded herself that the legal good-old-boys club was not limited to New York City.

"Wally Cunningham. Judge Wallace Cunningham," Jack elaborated. "You might remember him. He played a little baseball before a torn rotator cuff had him taking up the law."

Damn. Wally Cunningham had been Jack O'Halloran's catcher on the Loggers baseball team. Raine vaguely remembered hearing he'd gone on to play Triple-A ball in Tacoma.

"That's all very interesting," she replied, her courtroom-cool tone suggesting otherwise. "But I'm more interested in whether the injunction was issued."

"Oh, sure. Wally and I had ourselves a pretty good laugh over it."

The easy, masculine dismissal in his tone had Raine grinding her teeth for the second time today. "I fail to see how either you or *Wally*"—her use of the judge's first name was tightly edged with sarcasm—"could find any humor in the potential use of force against three teenage girls."

"What we found humorous is the idea that anyone would think I'd stoop to using force against three teenagers in the first place. . . . Although," he added, as if on afterthought, "I can't deny being tempted on more than one occasion today to take my hand to those kids' backsides."

"If you so much as touch a single hair on those children's heads, Sheriff, I'll have you hauled in front of the bench on charges of police brutality."

"Threat noted, Ms. Cantrell." His tone suggested weariness with both their conversation and the situation in general. "Now, if you don't mind, the pizza guy's back with the veggie special and I have a dinner to deliver."

Before Raine could object, he ended the call.

Jack climbed out of the Suburban and, despite his continuing aggravation, grinned at the pizza delivery man.

"Things must be pretty rough down at the law offices, if you're taking on extra work delivering fast food," he drawled. "What's the matter, run out of ambulances to chase?"

Dan O'Halloran grinned as he handed his cousin the red-and-white box. "Why should I bother to go to all that trouble, when all I have to do is hang around here and wait for you to tromp all over those little girls' civil rights. Then sue the county for millions."

"Good luck. If my salary's any indication of Olympic County's assets, you'd be lucky to get peanuts." Jack lifted the lid, assuring himself that both meat and cheese had been left off the pizza, which appeared to consist of crust, red sauce, mushrooms, onions, and green peppers. He hoped to hell this would satisfy the finicky vegetarian delinquent. "So, I guess Mom called you?"

"Your mom, my mom, along with half the folks in town. But by then I'd already caught the promo on the early news when I dropped into Papa Joe's to pick up my dinner. I gotta tell you, Cuz, you didn't look half bad. I was thinking that if Hollywood got hold of this story, they might even want to build a new cop series around you. How does Jack O'Halloran, Hunk Cop with a Heart, sound?"

"Like you've been smoking the kind of funny cigarettes you can't buy in machines. . . . Jesus, and here I thought taking over Pop's office would be a walk in the park after being a city cop. Right now I think I'd rather be taking my chances with one of your everyday drug dealers wielding a Street Sweeper."

He began walking up to the front porch, his cousin and best friend, Daniel Webster O'Halloran falling in step beside him.

"I also heard that Wally signed a TRO to keep you from storming the house with a SWAT team." The humor in Dan's voice echoed that of the judge when Wally had called with the news of the temporary restraining order.

"Yeah. One of Ida's pit bull granddaughters has gotten her teeth into this and won't let go."

"That'd be Raine."

"Yeah." He climbed the steps to the porch, placed the pizza on the white wicker table and rang the bell. There was no answer, but out of the corner of his eye he saw the lace curtain on the front window move just a little.

"Veggie pizza for one!" he called out. Then waited. And waited some more. Realizing that they weren't about to open the door while he was standing there, he cursed and turned back toward the truck. "So, what do you know about her?"

"Not much. I took her half sister, Savannah, out once in high school." Dan's lips curved into a smile at the memory. "God, she was one gorgeous female. Masses of wild red hair that smelled like strawberries, curves that would make a *Playboy* centerfold look like Olive Oyl, and wraparound legs that went all the way up to her neck."

Since Dan was four years behind him, Jack hadn't

known Savannah. He also had no memory of the granddaughter that had been driving him nuts all day. "Only one date? What happened? Did she dump you?"

"Nah. She didn't get the chance. I just never called her again after that first date."

"Why not?" She definitely sounded like Dan's type. Actually, Jack considered, if looks counted for anything—and they sure had back in those hormone-driven teenage days—Savannah sounded pretty much like any guy's type.

Dan's grin was quick and abashed. "Because she flat out scared me to death."

They shared a laugh over that. "Sounds like I've got the wrong sister in my life. Can you remember anything about Raine?"

For a man who'd always enjoyed women, Jack had had about his fill of females today. Ida and the kids were damn aggravating, but the lady lawyer, with her constant phone calls, writs, injunctions, restraining orders, and sundry other legal threats, was turning out to be a herculean pain in the ass.

"Well, thinking back on it, we were on the debate team together my senior year. I remember her as being skinny, with braces and a chip on her shoulder as big as a Western cedar."

"The braces are undoubtedly gone by now. But if the phone conversations are any indication, I'd say the chip is still there. Larger than ever."

"Guess that means she still hasn't gotten her dad's attention."

Since Raine Cantrell's mother, Lilith, had been providing Coldwater Cove with gossip for years,

Jack recalled that Ida's granddaughters each had a different father. "And her dad would be . . . ?"

"Owen Cantrell." When that didn't seem to ring a bell, Dan elaborated. "He was the lawyer for the Sacramento Six."

"Is that supposed to mean something?"

"They were counterculture revolutionaries back in the 60s. Along the lines of the Chicago Seven, but they didn't get as much press. They were accused of firebombing a selective service office in Sacramento and conspiring to blow up others all over the West. Cantrell pulled a lot of magic legal rabbits out of his hat and got them acquitted. The case study was required reading in my criminal law class."

"Were they guilty?"

"I told you—"

"Yeah, yeah, I know," Jack interjected impatiently. "A jury let them off. But did they do it?"

"From what I've read of the testimony, yeah. But Cantrell was brilliant in revealing some of the government's heavy-handed tactics. So, the guys walked and he went on to become a hired big gun of the legal profession. In fact, I read in this morning's paper that he's heading up the team representing that TV sitcom star. You know, the one arrested the other day for stalking his ex-girlfriend, then slashing her throat."

"Cantrell sounds like a dandy guy," Jack muttered. "So his daughter is trying to live up to his lofty legal reputation?"

"You have to remember that I haven't seen her for years. And I'm no shrink. But yeah, at least back in high school, I'd say that was definitely the case."

"Terrific." Jack's curse was rich and ripe. That was

all he needed messing in this: a mouthy woman with an Oedipus complex waving her fancy Harvard law degree in his face. As the door to the house opened and an arm, clad in a pink sleeve reached out and snatched the pizza from the porch table, Jack wondered if his father had ever had days like this.

Finally, her long journey almost over, Raine was standing at the railing of the ferry *Walla Walla* that was making its way across Elliott Bay. The stiff wind, carrying with it the pungent bite of green fir and the softer scent of pending rain, cut through her suit and tore at her hair. But needing to clear her head after her long flight, and to prepare for battle with that small-town sheriff who'd been the bane of her existence these past hours, Raine resisted the lure of the ferry's warm interior.

Although night would have already fallen back in New York, here on the West Coast the sun was just beginning to set, turning the choppy waters a shimmering copper. Behind the white boat, the glass towers of the Seattle skyline faded into the distance. On the top deck, two suit-clad businessmen—obviously commuters—were taking advantage of the stiff breeze to fly kites that soared like colorful dragons overhead. On any other occasion, Raine would have enjoyed the carefree sight. But not today.

Perhaps it was the emotional roller coaster she'd spent the day riding, but her feelings were veering back and forth like an out-of-control pendulum. Visions, like isolated snapshots, flashed through her mind: a vague memory of a little girl holding tight to her mother's hand as they crossed these very same waters, excited at this new adventure, but secretly worried that they might be swallowed up by a huge killer whale, just like Pinocchio.

Another memory, from two years later, sponging Savannah's face with a wet paper towel after her younger sister, seasick from choppy waters, had thrown up the hot dog, barbecue potato chips, and Dr. Pepper Lilith had fed them for dinner.

And then there'd been that painful day when she was a beanpole-skinny thirteen-year-old, desperately wishing for some magic word that would make her invisible while her glamorous mother leaned against the railing, her hair flying out like a shimmering banner in the crisp sea breeze as she flirted with a trio of lovesick sailors who were drooling over Lilith like three chocoholics raptly gazing upon a giant Hershey bar.

During those childhood years, part of Raine had looked forward to coming back to Coldwater Cove. It was, after all, the closest thing she'd ever known to home, the only place she felt safe. Secure. But always, deep inside the most secret places in her mind and heart lurked the fear that this would be the time Lilith would leave them at their grandmother Ida's house and never return.

A young, obviously pregnant woman came out onto the deck with a little girl who was about the age Raine had been the first time she'd taken this ferry ride. As the woman pointed out the kites brightening the pewter sky and mother and daughter laughed together, obviously enjoying each other's company, Raine experienced a sharp feeling of loss for a childhood she'd never known.

Less than twenty minutes after leaving Seattle, she caught her first glimpse of Coldwater Cove in the

distance. The turreted, gingerbread Victorian buildings perched atop the green bluff overlooking Admiralty Bay were backlit by the setting sun in a way
that made them look as if they were on fire. A
slanted gray curtain between the water and the town
suggested rain. A suggestion that was borne out
when a random drop carried on the salt-tinged wind
hit her face. Then another. Then more, finally driving Raine inside.

As the ferry approached the pier, she sipped from
a foam cup of espresso that provided a much needed
burst of caffeine and watched a brown pelican skim
along the coastline in search of fish, the ungainly,
awkward looking bird surprisingly graceful in flight.
More pelicans perched on wooden pilings. When the
docking call sounded, Raine tossed off the last of
the espresso, left the glassed-in observation deck and
took the metal stairs to her rental car.

She'd no sooner driven off the ferry when she
found herself immediately engulfed in the wet, gray
curtain she'd seen from the railing. Rain sheeted the
windshield as she made her way through town,
headed to her grandmother's home. She hit the
search button on the car's radio, stopping when she
landed on what seemed to be a news station. She
listened to the weather forecast, which predicted
rain.

"Now there's a newsflash," she muttered, turning
the wipers to high as raindrops hit the glass in front
of her like bullets, obscuring her view.

The Pacific Northwest hadn't gotten these towering green trees that rose into the silvery mist like
shaggy arrows, or the seemingly endless supply of
crystal creeks and tumbling waterfalls, without re-

ceiving a lot of precipitation. Most residents considered the tradeoff worthwhile.

Coldwater Cove, originally founded a century ago by a Swedish lumberjack, remained a town of Nordic cleanliness, where shop owners still swept the sidewalks each morning and the streets were as clean as a Swedish kitchen. There was one theater, and churches outnumbered taverns three to one. The crack of Little League bats could be heard on Saturday mornings, the chime of church bells on Sunday.

She paused at the only stoplight in town where a wide, grassy town square at the end of Harbor Street served as the centerpiece of the town. A fountain bubbled at one end of the green; a horseshoe pit claimed the other. A clock tower, made of a red brick that had weathered to a dusty pink over the century, could be seen for miles. Raine wondered if each of the four sides of the clock still told a different time, and suspected, given the way the town seemed frozen in time, they probably did.

"We've just received an update concerning the ongoing crisis in Coldwater Cove," the male voice announced as she continued through town. "Stay tuned for the latest development following this word from Timberland Bank, neighbors serving the Puget Sound community for fifty years."

Raine dove forward and began twisting the dial. Having no doubt what the crisis referred to, she didn't have the patience to listen to a commercial pitching debt-consolidation loans.

After skimming through various country, jazz, religious, rock, and oldies stations, she gave up and returned to *K-SOUND—More News, Less Chitchat*.

"How about less commercials?" she suggested acidly as the bank commercial segued into one for a franchise fish restaurant, then a break for station identification. Then, finally! The news update she'd been waiting for.

"This is Patrick Christopher, with an update on the crisis in Coldwater Cove. Sources tell us that fire trucks from neighboring Port Townsend and Port Angeles have been dispatched to the Lindstrom residence. Although the weather has grounded K-SOUND's *Eye in the Sky*, we have our pilot, Captain Jim, in the newsroom, monitoring the situation. . . . Jim, what are you hearing from your sources?"

"Well, Patrick, there have been several confirmed reports of smoke coming from inside the house. We've been told that whatever fire may have been started seems to be under control at this time. Although that hasn't been confirmed by either Sheriff O'Halloran or any involved fire personnel."

"A fire?" Raine echoed, her blood going even colder than the rain lashing against the car.

"What about the three delinquent girls, Jim? Have you received any word regarding them?"

"Something's coming in now, Patrick. If you'll just wait a minute . . ." There was a moment of dead air. "Yes, the sheriff has reported that all three girls escaped the house unharmed."

Raine let out a long breath she hadn't even been aware of holding.

"Any word regarding a possible cause of the fire, Captain Jim?"

"Nothing's been confirmed as yet. But speculation seems to be that the police may have grown tired of waiting for the girls to surrender their standoff and shot an incendiary device into the house to smoke them out."

"A bomb?" Raine shouted at the radio. "He bombed three teenage girls?" The sheriff was going to pay for this, she vowed. She was going to keep the hick Lone Ranger wannabe in court until doomsday.

"Thank you, Captain Jim," the voice on the radio was saying. "Of course we'll keep you informed on further word regarding this potentially dangerous situation. Meanwhile, this is Patrick Christopher, K-SOUND Radio, returning to our weekly *Focus on State Government* with moderator Jane Kendall, in progress."

By the time she reached her grandmother's house, Raine was fuming, scheming the legal revenge that would not only cost the sheriff his job and whatever good reputation he may have inherited from his father, but everything he owned. Everything he might ever own. She was Xena, Warrior Princess. And she wasn't going to put away her weapons and cease fighting until she had Sheriff Jack O'Halloran's ass nailed to the courthouse door.

The bubble lights on top of the fire trucks were flashing through the mist, creating a surrealistic red glow as Raine plowed straight through the yellow police tape and pulled up behind a state police cruiser.

Fortunately, Raine noticed, the house was still standing, with no outward sign of fire damage. Normally, the sight of the weathered gray gingerbread house with its wide front porch and fish scale-roofed tower would have given her a sense of homecoming. Today, however, her mind was on other things.

She threw open the driver's door, then heedless of the rain, little caring that the heels of her suede pumps were sinking into the mud, she marched toward the group of uniformed men gathered together beside a black Chevy Suburban bearing the Olympic County insignia.

She stopped in front of them, dragged a handful of wet hair out of her eyes, then splayed her hands on the hips of her soon-to-be-ruined Donna Karan suit. "So which one of you cowboys is Sheriff Jack O'Halloran?"

Conversation came to an abrupt halt. All eyes shifted toward her before returning to the rangy man who seemed absurdly tall, standing literally head and shoulders above the others.

"That'd be me." Rainwater dripped off the brim of his—wouldn't you just know it? she thought scathingly—black Stetson. He was wearing a black Gore-Tex jacket that carried the same insignia as his ridiculously macho truck. "And you must be Ms. Raine Cantrell. The New York lawyer who's kept our county judicial system so busy the past few hours."

His half smile was obviously feigned, his gunmetal gray eyes offering not an iota of welcome. The tinge of sarcasm in his baritone voice frayed Raine's last nerve.

"If I weren't an officer of the court, I'd hit you for what you did to those girls." Her voice was tight with anger.

He gave her a bland look. "Since *I'm* an officer of

the court, if you were to hit me, I suppose I'd have no choice but to haul you in for assaulting an officer." He shrugged. "Looks as if we're at a stalemate, Counselor."

Raine thought about that. But not for long. "Not exactly. There's still the little matter of you bombing a house with three innocent teenagers in it, *Sheriff.*" She heaped the same amount of sarcasm on his title as he'd used on hers.

"A bomb?" His dark brows crashed down toward his nose. A nose that looked as if it had been broken at some time in the past. "As an *officer of the court*"—there it was again, Raine thought, that damn sarcasm—"you, of all people should understand the power of an accusation. I didn't do any such thing."

"And I assume that fire just started by itself?"

"No." He skimmed a look over her. Then turned away. She was about to demand to know where he was going, to insist he not walk away while she was talking to him, when he opened the front door of the truck and retrieved a school bus yellow rubberized poncho. "And it wasn't really a fire. Just a lot of smoke. When the storm knocked out the power lines, the heat went out. Of course, since they were refusing to talk with me, I had no way of knowing that. Until they got cold and decided to light a fire in your grandmother's old wood stove. Unfortunately, no one ever mentioned the advisability of opening the damper first."

She caught the rain gear he'd tossed toward her with a murmured, reluctant "thank you," yanked it over her head, then followed his gaze to the back seat of the truck, where the three girls seemed none the worse for their experience.

"And now that we've settled that, Counselor," he said wearily, "I think I'll leave the logistics of straightening out this mess to you and the juvenile-court system. Because it's been a long day and my patience is hanging by a very thin thread."

"I have a Swiss Army knife in my bag," she said with a blatantly false smile. "Would you care to borrow the scissors?"

He rubbed his jaw and gave her an appraising look. "You know, I didn't see the family resemblance at first. But now I do. Your grandmother's a smart ass, too."

Before she could think up a scathing response to that remark, they were interrupted by a woman wearing a belted tan raincoat, clear-plastic rain boots over sensible shoes, and a frown. She was carrying a clipboard.

"Ms. Cantrell?" she asked.

"I'm Raine Cantrell," Raine confirmed.

"I'm Marianne Kelly. I'm a probation officer for Olympic County."

Old Fussbudget, Raine remembered. "It's a pleasure to meet you, Ms. Kelly," she lied. "I only wish it could have been under more pleasant circumstances."

"Yes. Well." It was the probation officer's turn to glance toward the truck where the teenagers were watching the proceedings with glum expressions. "It's getting late and I need to ensure that my probationers are settled for the night. If there isn't an adult available to take responsibility for them, I'm going to have to transfer them to a juvenile-detention facility."

Raine could just imagine her grandmother's reaction if she stood idly by and allowed that to happen. "Isn't that a little harsh, Ms. Kelly?" she asked mildly. "Under the circumstances? After all, they're just young girls."

"Perhaps you haven't been kept apprised of the situation, Ms. Cantrell. These *girls* created a crisis today—"

"There wasn't any crisis," Jack interjected. "That was just the stupid word the media came up with to boost ratings for the six-o'clock news."

A nerve twitched at the corner of the probation officer's left eyelid. "That may be your view of matters, Sheriff, but the fact remains that their behavior was highly unacceptable for probationers. And they cost the county a great deal of money."

He shrugged. "I get paid a straight salary, Ms. Kelly. Which doesn't make allowances for overtime. The most I can see that they cost the county was the price of a couple of pizzas, and if it'll keep them out of the pokey, I'll spring for them myself."

"That's a matter you'll have to take up with the county treasurer," the woman said briskly. "My concern is what to do with these delinquents."

"Girls," Jack corrected.

"Girls," Raine said at the same time.

They exchanged a look.

"What about my mother?" Raine asked, directing her question at the sheriff. "Has Lilith been found?"

"Yep. But I don't think she's going to prove a solution to this problem."

"Why not?"

"Because she's currently incarcerated."

"*What?*" It had been a long day for Raine, too. She decided that Sheriff O'Halloran's patience wasn't the only one hanging by a very thin thread. "You arrested my mother?"

"Not me. Cooper Ryan. He's a park service cop. Seems your mother was breaking a few fire regulations."

Talk about your small worlds. Raine remembered Lilith once expressing regret that she'd let her high school sweetheart get away. Coming from her mother, who'd never been one to admit to errors in judgement, that was definitely saying something.

"Well." Her mind, dulled by the long day and a touch of jet lag, went into overdrive, attempting to come up with a solution. She looked over at the Suburban again, viewed the expectant expressions on all three girl's faces, and knew that what they were expecting was to be thrown back into the system.

"Would the court find me an acceptable temporary adult guardian?"

"I believe that would be satisfactory," Ms. Kelly said after a moment's hesitation. "Until the hearing."

"When will that be?"

"The juvenile-court calendar's extremely crowded at the moment, but since this is a special case requiring immediate attention, I could probably find a judge to hear the case in say, three days?"

Three days. It wasn't that long, Raine assured herself as she took the clipboard Marianne Kelly was now holding out to her. It was more than enough time to get Lilith out of jail, Ida out of the hospital, the two sisters off to their aunt's custody, and determine whether the pregnant shoplifter posed a risk to her grandmother.

Ignoring Jack O'Halloran's challenging grin, Raine signed her name at the bottom of all three guardianship forms.

❧ 4 ❧

"Well, that makes it official. They're all yours." From Marianne Kelly's grim expression, Raine did not find the words at all encouraging.

That matter settled to her satisfaction, Old Fussbudget marched back to a tan sedan. Both Jack and Raine watched her go.

"That was a nice thing to do," he said finally.

Somehow, the compliment, laced with obvious surprise, irritated her more than his earlier sarcasm. "It wasn't as if I had any choice." Her words were clipped, designed to forestall any further conversation on the subject. "Now, where did you say I could find my mother?"

"I didn't." Just when she was certain she was going to grind her molars to dust, he added, "But she's at the ranger station on Hurricane Ridge."

"I didn't realize they had jail cells in federal parks."

He shrugged again, drawing her gaze to his shoulders, which were wide enough to gain him a position on the Giants' offensive line back in New York.

Not that she could ever picture Jack O'Halloran living in New York City. He was absolutely country, from the tip of that black Stetson down to the pointy toes of his—what else?—cowboy boots.

The fact that she was even the slightest bit intrigued by the steely, Clint Eastwood glint that occasionally appeared in his narrowed gray eyes only proved how exhausted she was.

"Unfortunately, bad guys show up from time to time even in federal parks," he said. "Although mostly it's just drunk and disorderly, that sort of thing."

"And breaking fire regulations."

A wry twitch that hinted at a smile tugged at one corner of his mouth, momentarily drawing her attention to a faint scar bisecting his top lip. "That, too. Coop said something about teaching her a lesson."

"If he can pull that off, he's a miracle worker." Along with flaunting rules and regulations, Lilith had a knack for ignoring the little morality lessons most people learned from life. "But there's no way I'm going to allow him to keep her locked up in a cell all night."

"It's not like she's doing hard time."

"I realize that," Raine said stiffly.

It was the principle of the thing. After all, she used her education every day to defend individuals far less deserving than Lilith. If she couldn't help her own mother, she might as well have stayed in Coldwater Cove, married some logger or cowboy cop like Jack O'Halloran right out of high school, and had a passel of kids. She wondered about her chances of getting a writ of *habeas corpus* to get her mother out tonight.

"But surely disobeying fire regulations is a misdemeanor. Besides"—she glared up at the rain which continued to pelt down on the hood of the borrowed poncho—"we're obviously not in fire season yet."

"True. And if it were just the fires, Coop might have been willing to give her a pass." He rubbed a square, clefted jaw that suggested a stubborn streak. "Not that I'd claim to know his mind, but as a fellow cop, I'd have to guess that it was the lewd and lascivious behavior, along with indecent exposure and assault and battery, that landed your mother in the pokey."

"Lewd and lascivious behavior? Indecent exposure?"

Forget *habeas corpus*. Raine was forced to consider her chances of insisting on a competency hearing for her mother. If past behavior were taken into account, she doubted it would be all that hard to win a finding of *non compos mentis*. Although her mother might not be certifiably insane, anyone who took the time to have a serious discussion with Lilith for more than five minutes could easily judge her incompetent to stand trial.

"And assault and battery," he reminded her.

"Damn." Raine rubbed the back of her neck, where strands of hair clung like seaweed. "I don't suppose you'd happen to know whom, exactly, she's accused of committing this battery on?"

"Actually, I do. It was Coop."

Her heart sank all the way down to the toes of her sloshy, egg-stained pumps. "My mother assaulted the arresting officer?"

"Well, it was more like a slap, to hear Coop tell it. But I suppose, technically, he could hit her with a resisting arrest charge, too."

Even worse. She just didn't need this. Not now. She'd been running on caffeine and adrenaline for weeks. Now that the buzz from the espresso she'd drunk on the ferry was beginning to wear off, she could feel the physical and mental letdown sneaking up behind her.

"You know," he suggested mildly, "the park jail isn't exactly Folsom Prison. It won't hurt her to spend a night there. And it just might give her time to think about behavior and consequences."

Raine's answering laugh was flat and humorless. "It's obvious you don't know my mother." She looked back at the Suburban. "Since there's no way I'm going to risk leaving those girls alone in my grandmother's house, I suppose I'll just have to take them to Hurricane Ridge with me."

He swore under his breath. "You are definitely Ida's granddaughter." Seemingly mindless of the rain, he yanked off his hat and raked his fingers through his thick dark hair. "Neither of you women know the meaning of the word *quit.*"

Raine tossed up her chin, bracing herself for another skirmish. "Oh, I know the meaning all right. I just don't believe in it."

He jammed the hat back down on his head. Then closed his eyes and pinched the bridge of his crooked nose. Then sighed heavily. And cursed again. It was, Raine considered, the most emotion the man had shown thus far.

"That road to Hurricane Ridge is tricky enough in

the daylight in dry weather. If you insist on bailing your mother out tonight, I'll drive you up there."

He seemed torn between aggravation and pity. It was the pity that Raine hated.

"That's not necessary." Unwilling to surrender to his unblinking cop stare, which she had no doubt had earned him a dandy confession rate during interrogations, she straightened both her back and her resolve. "I'm perfectly capable of taking care of my own family, Sheriff. Legally and personally."

"You're dead on your feet," he countered. "No offense intended, Counselor, but you kind of remind me of one of the walking zombies in all those horror flicks I used to like as a kid.

"And although I've no doubt that you're a real go-getter back in New York City"—he drawled the name of her adopted city with an unmistakable lack of respect—"this just happens to be *my* county. And there's no way I'm going to spend the rest of tonight out in this damn rain picking up the pieces after you drive off that cliff. Because as bad as you look right now, you'd look a helluva lot worse dead."

His granite face tightened into harsh angles and dangerous planes; his expression turned as uncompromising as the jagged, snow-spined Olympic mountains jutting up behind him.

It was at that moment, as he looked down at her, arms folded across his chest, that Raine knew for certain what she'd already begun to suspect. Jack O'Halloran's outwardly easygoing facade and good-old-boy behavior concealed a granite will that might actually prove more unyielding than her own. Oh yes, she thought grimly, Choate, Plimpton, Wells &

Sullivan's comptroller, Harriet Farraday, would definitely approve of this man.

"Well." She stared up at him. "No one can accuse you of mincing words, Sheriff."

When he didn't say anything, just stood there, his brows and his mouth both drawn into an unrelentingly unyielding line, Raine experienced a renewed spark of competition.

"You realize, of course, that you have no legal authority to keep me from driving anywhere in this county I wish to go."

"I wouldn't bet the farm on that one."

Proving to be just one unpleasant surprise after another, he turned on a booted heel, strode over to her rental car, and while Raine watched in stunned shock, this man wearing the badge of authority—a sheriff who'd taken an oath to uphold the law!—took a huge black flashlight from his wide belt and smashed the car's left taillight.

All her verbal skills abandoned Raine. She was still sputtering in protest when he returned to where her feet seemed to have been nailed to the driveway.

"Although you may be a little rusty on Washington State law, having spent all that time back east, even in New York City, it's undoubtedly illegal to drive without two working taillights. Especially at night.

"You move that car five feet out of this driveway, Counselor, and I'm going to have to pull you over. And, perhaps, just for good measure, I'll impound the car. As evidence."

Coldwater Cove may not be the big city, but it had always been a civilized little town. At least it had been when she'd last visited, three years ago. Of course back then, this man's father had been sheriff.

"Surely you don't think you're going to get away with that?" Raine hated the way her fractured voice sounded like a stranger's. Her elocution had always been one of her best courtroom weapons.

"I can sure as hell give it the old college try. If push comes to shove, I'll throw myself on the mercy of the court."

The trace of renewed amusement in his voice reminded her that the court in question just happened to be presided over by his old high school baseball team catcher, Wally Cunningham. *Hell*.

Knowing when she'd been out maneuvered, Raine tried to remind herself that the key was to keep her eye on the prize. How many times had she had to remind clients of that little truism? So long as you remembered what you wanted to achieve, the road to that end could take any number of unexpected twists and turns along the way.

And Jack O'Halloran was definitely the most unexpected and unwelcome detour on a very exasperating trip.

Unable to throw in the towel without having the last word, Raine glared up at him. "If breaking my taillight was your idea of upholding the law in your county, Sheriff, I'd love to know how you got elected. What did you do? Threaten to drag out the truncheons and rubber hoses to anyone who didn't vote for you?" The scowl was replaced with a blatantly false smile. "Or did you simply stuff the ballot boxes?"

"Neither one."

If he was at all wounded by her sarcasm, he didn't

show it. His grin was one she remembered well from high school days. The dangerous, cocky-as-hell grin that had undoubtedly coaxed more than one buxom cheerleader into the back seat of his Batmobile black Trans Am.

"I simply relied on my devastating good looks and legendary superhero crime-fighting abilities. Oh, and of course my natural O'Halloran male charm," he tacked on with an exaggerated display of that alleged charm.

The man really was impossible. "I suppose being the son of the former sheriff didn't hurt either." Her tone was as dry as a legal brief.

"No." The grin faded at the mention of his father. Shutters came down over his eyes. "I suppose it didn't." He rubbed a broad hand down his face, and when he took it away, Raine realized that he was as weary as she was.

Which wasn't all that surprising, she supposed, given the fact that the day undoubtedly hadn't been a picnic for him, either. The sensible thing to do would be to just bury the hatchet and get on with springing Lilith from jail so they could all get to sleep.

"Since I don't want to explain to Hertz why my car was impounded, I suppose I have no choice but to let you drive me to Hurricane Ridge."

"With such a graceful acceptance, how could I possibly refuse?"

Raine ignored his sarcasm. "But first I need to call the hospital and check on Ida."

"You can call from the truck. So, now that we've settled that, let's get moving, Harvard. Your mother isn't getting any younger. And neither am I."

Raine wasn't all that surprised that he knew where she'd gone to school. After all, Ida had always enjoyed bragging about her granddaughters accomplishments. Although he certainly didn't seem at all impressed by her Ivy League credentials.

When he put his fingers around her waist and lifted her into the bucket seat of the Suburban, she had the uncomfortable feeling that she was being taken into custody. Because she wasn't honestly certain she could have made it up there in her snug skirt and high heels, Raine didn't object.

A call to the hospital revealed that since the doctors had decided her grandmother's fall was merely a passing case of vertigo compounded by a rickety stool, Ida could be released in the morning. Her concern eased, Raine turned toward the three teenagers who were sitting as stiff and silent as stumps in the back seat of the Suburban, as if afraid they'd be thrown back into juvenile hall if they breathed a single word.

"Well, I suppose, since we're going to be spending the next three days together, we should get acquainted. As you've undoubtedly figured out, I'm Raine." She attempted a smile that didn't quite work.

Still acting as spokesperson, Shawna introduced herself. Then the others. As she greeted them all, accepted their uncensored gratitude, and lied a little by professing to be pleased to meet them, Raine reluctantly decided that none of them looked all that dangerous.

Shawna was already a beauty. With her long swan's neck and high cheekbones, she reminded Raine a bit of Tyra Banks. Her face was framed with a mass of beaded braids, her earlobes each adorned with three gold hoops.

Sixteen-year-old Gwen, with her wide eyes and freckled face surrounded by carrot-hued curls, resembled a pregnant Orphan Annie. Or, Raine thought, taking in the red-and-white boat-necked polka-dot top she was wearing over black leggings, Lucille Ball, just before she'd given birth to Little Rickie.

Renee—Shawna's vegetarian runaway sister, Raine remembered—would have looked like any other thirteen-year-old girl poised on the threshold of womanhood. Had it not been for the terrified look in her Bambi brown eyes.

"Are we going to jail?" Gwen asked, casting a nervous glance toward Jack. Raine watched her place a hand on her bulging stomach in unconscious protection of her child. "I don't want to have my baby in jail!"

Her high tone wavered toward hysterical, making Raine hope that the stress of the day—a day that already seemed forty-eight hours long—wouldn't have the teenager going into labor anytime soon. At least if such an unfortunate event were to happen, having Jack O'Halloran along might prove useful. Weren't all cops trained to deliver babies?

"Of course you're not going to have your baby in jail," Raine assured her, not honestly knowing anything of the kind. If looks were any indication, the child appeared ready to give birth to a ten-pound basketball at any moment. "By the way, when are you due?"

"In two and a half weeks."

"Oh, well then," Raine said airily, "you've plenty

of time. After all, first babies are always late." She was certain she'd heard that somewhere.

"But he's already dropped."

"Mama Ida said that's normal with a first baby," Shawna reminded the younger girl. "It's called lightening, remember?"

"As if," Gwen scoffed. "I still think that's a dumb thing to call it, because the baby hasn't gotten any bit lighter," she complained. "And I sure won't mind if he decides to come early, though I don't want him born in any jail cell."

"You don't have any reason to worry about that," Raine said again. "Because none of you are going to jail."

"Then where is the sheriff taking us?" Renee asked, speaking up for the first time.

"It's Lilith who's in jail. Sheriff O'Halloran was kind enough to offer to drive us to Hurricane Ridge to bail her out."

"Lilith's in jail?" Renee's eyes got even wider.

"I'm afraid so." Raine sighed. Although she should have grown used to her mother's antics by now, it wasn't always easy playing grown-up to Lilith's adolescent rebellions. "Apparently she got in a little trouble in the park, and—"

"I told her that she'd never get away with it," Shawna broke in knowingly. "I warned her that the rangers would spot those fires, and as soon as they did, they'd catch her prancing around naked."

"You knew what she was planning to do?" Raine asked.

"Oh, sure. Like I said, it was part of an old druid ritual. Or Celtic, or something like that. Anyway, she invited me to come with her, but Mama Ida put her foot down."

"Good for Ida."

"To tell the truth, Mama Ida didn't have to object all that hard," Shawna said with a grin. "Taking off my clothes and dancing around in the woods would be like, totally pathetic. Not that Lilith is pathetic," she said quickly, as if belatedly realizing she'd just insulted their savior's mother. "I didn't mean it that way."

"I know what you meant. And you certainly showed more sense than Lilith."

"That wouldn't be difficult," Jack, who'd remained quiet during the conversation, murmured.

Although she might criticize her mother, Raine was not about to let anyone else. Especially a man who'd broken her taillight. Vowing to make him pay for any extra damage charges Hertz might add onto her credit card, she turned toward him.

"What did you say?"

Before he could answer, he was distracted by a sudden sound that seemed to be coming from his shirt. One that didn't resemble any beeper she'd ever heard.

"Damn." He pulled off the road and cut the engine. As Raine watched in amazement, he pulled a small plastic device from his shirt pocket. "Wouldn't you just know it," he growled. "The damn thing took a shi—" He glanced back toward the girls. "Needs the litter box cleaned out," he amended.

"Is that what I think it is?" Raine asked. His hand dwarfed the green plastic egg-shaped gadget.

"It depends on what you think it is. If your guess

is a damn electronic cat, you'd be right on the money."

"I see." Actually, she didn't see anything, but Raine was perverse enough to enjoy his obvious discomfort at the situation. "Do you often take your toys to work with you, Sheriff?"

"It's not mine. It's my daughter's." With a deftness that seemed at odds with such powerful hands, he pressed a button on the front of the toy. "She's not allowed to have it at school, so I promised her I'd keep the damn thing alive for her."

"That's very admirable," Raine said grudgingly. "Especially since most men would undoubtedly leave any virtual-cat-box emptying to their wives."

"I probably would, too." The problem taken care of, at least for now, he jammed the Nano Kitty back into his pocket. "If I had a wife." He twisted the key in the ignition, bringing the huge engine back to life. "She died."

"I'm sorry." Raine was truly sorry his wife had died. She was even sorrier she'd brought it up.

He shrugged as he pulled back onto the road. "It's been two years. I've come to accept it." His soft, weary sigh was barely audible, but Raine heard it. "Most of the time, anyway. It's harder on Amy."

"Amy's your daughter," she guessed.

"Yeah."

Although her mother hadn't died, Raine knew, more than most, how difficult it was for a girl to grow up without a mother. How it felt to be abandoned by the one person in the world who wasn't supposed to ever leave you. "How old is she?"

"Six." This time it was a smile she heard in his voice. "Going on thirty."

"Ah, one of those children my mother would refer to as an old soul."

"Or just a kid who's just had to grow up a little faster than most. Peg got sick when she was still a toddler."

Raine did some quick mental mathematics. If his daughter was six and he'd been widowed two years, obviously his wife hadn't died quickly. Sympathy stirred, but suspecting that Jack O'Halloran was a man who preferred to keep his feelings to himself, she allowed the unexpectedly personal conversation to wind down.

As her thoughts drifted back to her reason for being in this truck with him—Lilith in trouble yet again—Raine felt just about as glum as Sheriff O'Halloran looked.

As he drove up the steep and winding road to the Hurricane Ridge ranger station, Jack mentally horsewhipped himself. What the hell had gotten into him? Spouting off about Peg that way?

It was the forced intimacy, he decided. This situation—two people driving through a dark and foggy night, with the rain hitting the roof of the truck—would tend to encourage conversation. Especially after they'd both suffered an exhausting day. It wasn't anything personal.

That idea had him feeling better for about two minutes. Until he slanted a sideways glance toward his passenger who seemed to have fallen asleep. The flourescent green glow from the dashboard lights illuminated features that, while a bit too strong for conventional beauty, were still damn easy on the eyes. Her nose could have been considered aristocratic were it not for the fact that it tilted up, just a bit, at the end. Her mouth was a tad too stubborn for his taste, but he remembered the way it had softened when she'd asked about Amy and decided it had possibilities.

He watched her lips part to expel a faint, shuddering breath. In sleep, her features softened appealingly. Too appealingly, he considered, forcing his mind to focus on all the unnecessary grief she'd caused him today as she'd wielded the power of the law like a cudgel. No, he decided, more like a dueling foil, flourished with the cool efficiency of those rapiers in the old Errol Flynn flicks that still showed up on late-night cable from time to time.

Efficient she might admittedly be. But cool? Although some might look at her severely tailored suit and cinnamon brown hair and believe that, he'd seen glimpses of another woman. A woman who wasn't nearly as self-controlled as the lady attorney would like people to believe. The passion surrounding her as she'd stood up for those three girls she didn't even know, had flared like a newborn sun. After the unsatisfying phone conversations they'd shared before her arrival in Coldwater Cove, Jack had been surprised by the display of white-hot energy. And, dammit, interested.

As he set his jaw and glared out into the dark night, he reminded himself that even if he was in the market for a woman—which he wasn't—a skinny, mouthy New York lawyer with an attitude the size of Puget Sound and chips the size of Mount Rainier on both shoulders wasn't his type.

Even as he reminded himself of that, her perfume bloomed in the heat of the car. Unlike the sweet floral scent Peg had favored, this was spicy and complex and caused a disturbing churning deep inside him.

During the last months of Peg's life, intimacy had been one of hearts and minds rather than of shared bodies. Even in the beginning, before physical lovemaking had become impossibly painful for her, Jack had understood that his wife had needed reassurance that she was still attractive. That he still wanted her. Which, of course he had. But whenever he'd tried to prove that to her, he hadn't been able to stop from treating her like spun glass, delicate enough to shatter at the slightest touch.

On such occasions he'd pull back, foregoing the earthy passion that characterized their precancer lovemaking. His touch turned more gentle—almost tentative—his kisses gifted rather than plundered, and on more than one occasion when she'd cried out in what he desperately feared might be pain, his body had betrayed him, deflating like a three-day-old balloon.

She had, of course, assured him that she understood, that it didn't matter. But as he'd lain beside her, feeling like the world's greatest failure, Jack had known that deep down inside, it did.

After she died, the responsibilities of juggling single fatherhood with the demands of the seventeen thousand residents of Olympic County, who expected him to keep their streets and homes safe, had blotted out all desire for sex.

Until now. When it was returning with a vengeance,

As if sensing his unbidden, unwelcome hunger,

Raine opened her eyes just in time to catch him looking at her lips.

Feeling a lot like he had back in junior high, when his mother had caught him sneaking a look at his first *Playboy* centerfold, Jack dragged his gaze back up to hers.

Her eyes were soft, nearly unfocused as they met his, leaving him to wonder if he was imagining the sudden spark of feminine awareness in those gold-hued depths. What would she do, he wondered, if he pulled off the road, yanked her out of that leather bucket seat and plundered her wide, lush lips with his own?

Damn. He didn't need this, Jack reminded himself as he pulled into the nearly deserted parking lot. Not now. And definitely not with her.

∽ 5 ∽

After instructing all three girls to remain in the truck, Raine braced herself for dealing with her mother. Which, even in the best of times, had never been easy.

"Darling!" Lilith burst into the room in a whirl-wind of her usual energy and flung her arms around Raine's neck. "I knew you'd come rescue your poor abused mother!"

Raine didn't think her mother looked all that abused. In fact, except for that ugly orange jump-suit, she looked as stunning as ever. Even more so with the edgy emotion glittering in the midnight blue depths of her eyes. Lilith Lindstrom was a daz-zling creature of the moment, a wild child, even at fifty.

"You know I wouldn't let you spend the night in jail."

Raine slipped free of this woman who'd given birth to her, this woman whom she'd never under-stood. Although on some abstract basis, Raine could think of Lilith as her mother, it had been years since she'd thought of her as *mother*. And never, not even in the secret privacy of her own mind, had she ever thought of this radiant, ethereal creature as *mom*.

"You're such a good girl." Lilith's voice was light and sweet and young. Then, as her bright eyes took another, longer look at her eldest daughter, the smile faded and horizontal lines formed in a porcelain-smooth forehead. "Although I'd hoped that living in New York would have taught you a bit more about style. Wherever did you get that unattractive rainwear?"

"You're not exactly a fashion plate yourself." Raine's tone was a great deal drier than the weather. "Shawna told me about the nude dancing. But didn't you take some clothes with you?"

"Well, of course I did, darling. Surely you don't think that I'd drive nude on the highway?"

"Quite honestly, Lilith, I never quite know what to expect."

"Join the club," the man who'd released Lilith from the cell, muttered.

Cooper Ryan was yet another surprise in a day— and now night—of surprises. Raine knew that a fifty-year-old man certainly wasn't old, especially these days when the baby boomer generation seemed determined to continue to shatter stereotypes. But she certainly hadn't been prepared for him to be quite so—well, stunning.

Unlike Jack O'Halloran, whose rugged features appeared to have been harshly hewn from granite with an axe, her mother's jailer was as classically beautiful as a Renaissance statue. Lines fanning out from riveting blue eyes added character, rather than age, and his dark blond hair was streaked at the temples with silver that somehow added to his patrician appearance. Although she did not consider herself a fanciful woman, Raine had no trouble at all picturing this man strolling down from the heights of Mount Olympus to dabble with the mortals.

No wonder Lilith had fallen in love with this man. The pertinent question, Raine considered, was how on earth she'd walked away.

"Was it absolutely necessary to force my mother to wear prison garb?"

Unfortunately, Cooper Ryan proved to be yet another Coldwater Cove male she couldn't intimidate. He met her censorious gaze with a level one of his own. "Why don't you ask your mother that question?"

Raine turned back to Lilith, who was now perched on the corner of the cluttered oak desk, legs crossed, appearing more like an empress granting an audience to a roomful of needy peasants than someone who'd been arrested.

"Well?" she invited.

"It's quite simple." As Lilith tossed her head, Raine considered grimly that *nothing* about this woman had ever been simple. "I'm making a statement."

"I see." Raine was aware of the sheriff's faint, annoying chuckle, but refused to look at him.

"I'm a political prisoner. That being the case, I may as well dress the part."

Oh, good Lord. Would this damn day never end?

"You're not a political prisoner, Lilith." Raine bit the words off with exaggerated patience. Another day like this one and she'd have to begin buying antacids by the case. "You were arrested for setting fires outside of a designated campground."

"It's Beltane. The fires were necessary. And, as I've already explained to Cooper, surely he couldn't expect me to conduct a nude ceremony in a public campground with unbelievers." Lilith shot a blistering look toward the Greek god who was leaning against the wall, arms folded across his chest.

"I don't suppose you could have conducted the ceremony with clothes on?"

"Don't be silly, darling. Clothing inhibits magic. Everyone knows that."

"Try telling that to David Copperfield."

"David Copperfield, as talented as he admittedly is, is merely an illusionist." Lilith lifted her chin. "I'm speaking of real magic, Raine, dear. As ancient as Earth itself."

"Well, we certainly wouldn't want to inhibit that."

Raine momentarily wished that her mother was back in her Greenpeace save-the-dolphins mode. Until she recalled an incident concerning a motorboat and a Japanese tuna-fishing fleet that had nearly caused an international incident.

"But I believe the unofficial report also mentions assault and battery. On a police officer. Not to mention that little charge of resisting arrest."

"Oh, pooh." Lilith waved the accusation away as if it were little more than a pesky moth. "The only reason Cooper arrested me was to get back at me for not marrying him."

"If today's performance was any example of what you've turned out to be, I ought to be on my knees, thanking God that we didn't get hitched." From Cooper Ryan's gritty tone, Raine guessed that Lilith's barb had hit its mark. "Because we wouldn't have made it to our first month's anniversary."

"You're undoubtedly right." Lilith's answering smile was dazzling. It was also blatantly false. "Since there's no way I could have possibly lived with an ultraconservative right-wing bully."

"And there's no way I would have lived with a witch," he countered with a flare of heat that nearly took Raine's breath away. And it hadn't even been directed at her.

She couldn't resist slanting a quick glance toward Jack, whose expression told her that for once, they were in agreement. Cooper Ryan and Lilith Lindstrom had left a great deal unsettled between them. Including a surfeit of sexual chemistry that almost had Raine on the verge of an estrogen meltdown herself.

Although there were times, such as now, when she was forced to view her mother as a sexual being, Raine had never liked the feeling.

"I can see you two have a great deal of catching up to do," Jack said. "If you'd like us to leave you alone—"

"No!" Both Cooper and Lilith spoke as one, at precisely the same time. They stared at each other for a long moment. Then, finally, he gave her a weary go-ahead gesture.

"After the horrid day I've suffered, I just want to go home," Lilith said, trying for an air of martyrdom that fell decidedly short of the mark.

"You're welcome to her." Coop addressed his words to Raine. "And if you promise to keep her under control, I'll drop the charges."

"You certainly will not, Cooper Ryan," Lilith spoke up before Raine could answer. She tossed her head with renewed spirit. "I fully intend to see you in court. Where your tyrannical behavior can become public record."

He shrugged, seeming to decide that further discussion wasn't worth the effort. "Whatever. I'm sick and tired of arguing."

"As am I." She eyed him with what appeared to be honest regret. "I am horribly disappointed at how you turned out, Cooper. Why, you may as well have become a Republican."

"As it happens, I *am* a Republican."

"Oh, dear heavens. That's so tragic. I have half a mind to stage an intervention."

"If your behavior today was any indication, sweetheart, half a mind might be overstating your qualifications."

Lilith surprised Raine by laughing at that. Then slid off the desk in a lithe, graceful movement and glided over to where he was still standing in the doorway.

"All the boys in Coldwater Cove used to throw themselves at my feet. And while such groveling was admittedly flattering, absolute adoration can get horrendously boring. But you always were a challenge, Cooper." She placed her hand against the chest of his khaki uniform shirt. "I'd almost forgotten how stimulating fighting with you can be."

"Dammit, Lilith—," he warned.

"Yes, darling?" She went up on her toes and pressed her lips against his grimly set ones.

Although the kiss was brief, if the fevered crimson color rising from his collar was any indication, it packed one helluva punch. Even as accustomed as she was to her mother's outrageous behavior Raine found herself worrying what Jack O'Halloran might be thinking.

She sneaked another glance his way, instantly realizing her mistake when their eyes met again and a jagged bolt of lightninglike desire shot through her body, all the way to her toes. The only thing that kept her from melting into a puddle right here on the ranger station floor was her impression that the sheriff was every bit as disconcerted as she was by the flare of sexual heat.

The drive home blurred in Raine's mind. She vaguely remembered leaving the park headquarters with her mother and Jack and, wanting to put a little distance between herself and the sheriff, insisting Lilith sit up front while she took the third back seat for herself.

Lilith grudgingly admitted that Cooper had informed her about the standoff and Ida's hospitalization and had even checked several times for updates on both conditions.

"That was very considerate of him," Raine suggested.

Lilith shrugged. "He and Mother always got along. I used to think the only reason she wanted me to marry him was so he could become the son she'd always wanted."

Raine had no intention of getting into a discussion about her mother's love life. "Well, whatever the reason, it was still nice."

Her mother didn't answer. Silence settled over the interior of the truck. The girls appeared understandably wiped out by their eventful day and even Lilith proved uncharacteristically subdued as they drove back through the rainy, foggy night to Coldwater

Cove, stopping once at the Port Angeles McDonald's for Gwen to use the restroom. Then they were back on the road.

The distance between Raine and Jack precluded conversation. But they didn't need to talk for her to sense that they were both thinking about that unbidden, stunning moment of awareness.

Unlike her mother, who could still cause grown men to walk into walls, Raine had never been the type of woman to inspire hunger in any man. She'd never wanted to be that type of woman. To her mind, lust involved surrender—of control, will-power, of self. And surrender was simply not in her vocabulary. It never had been, and as far as she was concerned, it never would be.

When she leaned her head against the truck window and closed her eyes, she recalled a dream she'd had sometime during her teens. She and Savannah had been riding in a convertible driven by her mother down a steep, winding mountain road in the rain. The top was down and they were getting soaked. They were speeding around the switchbacks, the car taking on more and more speed, until it was racing downhill out of control.

"Take the wheel, Raine!" her mother, who was now inexplicably in the backseat, called out to her.

"I can't," she'd shouted over the squeal of the tires. The convertible was going faster and faster; the rain was falling harder and harder. "I'm not sixteen, yet."

"Neither am I," Lilith had shouted back without missing a beat.

Shaking off the memory, Raine sighed. The gray fog formed a seemingly impenetrable wall outside the rain-chilled glass, that had her once more wish-

ing for that sun-drenched beach. The romantic vi
sion she'd experienced in the limo fluttered
enticingly back into her mind. Although this time
the phantom lover was no anonymous stranger. This
time his all too recognizable gray eyes were silvered
by the moonlight.

Raine was gazing up at him like a besotted teenager, mesmerized by the lips that were inexorably
lowering toward hers, when suddenly she was no
longer standing with her lover on a moon-spangled
beach, but all alone, knee-deep in quicksand.

No! She squeezed her eyes tight. This was ridicu
lous! She was not, by nature, an overly imaginative
woman. She was an attorney, for heaven's sake,
trained by Socratic method at what was arguably
the finest law school in the country. Perhaps even
the entire world. Intelligent women who'd spent
years studying the strategies of legal thought and
argument did not suffer from hallucinations.

As Jack turned off the road onto the long driveway
leading up the hill to her grandmother's house,
Raine worried that the stress of the past months
may have finally gotten to her. Wondering if this is
what a nervous breakdown felt like, she decided she
really needed to take that vacation. Three days, she
reminded herself. Surely she could stay sane that
long.

Since he hadn't wanted to drag a sleeping Amy
out into the rain, Jack had reluctantly agreed to let
her spend the night at his mother's. But only after
assuring her that he'd be by first thing in the morning so they could have breakfast together before he
drove her to school.

As he entered the kitchen of the ramshackle old farmhouse Peg had begged him to buy before her death, he felt an unexpected surge of anger at his wife. One he hadn't experienced for months. How dare she desert him? Hadn't she understood that he didn't know a damn thing about bringing up a little girl?

Oh, sure, he thought, as he pulled a bottle of Rainier beer from the refrigerator and twisted the cap off with more force than necessary, he'd learned a lot in the past two years. But it wasn't the same as Amy having a mother, dammit.

Peg should have stayed here where she belonged. With her daughter. With him.

And that, he thought as he threw his body onto the family room sofa, was the crux of the problem. He took a long pull from the dark brown bottle, momentarily wishing the beer was something stronger. A lot stronger.

"You're not thinking about Amy."

His words seemed to echo in the empty house. The falling-down house he'd tried to tell Peg was larger than they'd ever need. But she'd proven surprisingly assertive those last months of her life, insisting that after all those years living in a Seattle townhouse, they needed a "real home." When he'd realized that she wasn't about to give in, he'd reluctantly acquiesced, even though they both knew that she'd never live to see it properly renovated.

"It's yourself you're feeling so fucking sorry for." The gloom he'd thought he'd put behind him settled over his shoulders. The roof had found a new place to leak; rain was tapping an annoying rhythm on the hand-pegged wooden floor. "Shit, nothing like a goddamn pity party to cap off a less than spectacular day."

He pushed himself to his feet, unlocked the small cedar chest and chose a videotape at random from the stacks Peg had created. He shoved the tape into the VCR, moved the wastepaper basket he kept for such purposes beneath this new leak, then flopped back onto the couch.

It was one of the tapes Peg had made outdoors, on the rugged coastline strewn with piles of driftwood she'd claimed always made her think of Sasquatch playing a game of pick-up-sticks. She was laughing, with her gentle eyes and her generous mouth, as she related the legend of Big Foot, that huge, hairy Pacific Northwest version of the Abominable Snowman, to her daughter, who'd someday be watching this tape.

Groaning, Jack shut his eyes against the pain. Then, unable to resist, reluctantly opened them again and watched his wife as she strolled down the beach, pausing to point out the wonders found in tide pools. She could have been any mother taking a lazy summer day to share her world with her child. She could have had all the time in the world. But sometimes pictures lied, Jack thought. And appearances could definitely be deceiving.

In the background the rising tide roared, gulls and cormorants wheeled over the towering offshore sea stacks and although he couldn't hear it on the tape, Jack remembered the sough of the wind in the fir trees atop the cliff. That same wind that was ruffling the fiery auburn bob beneath Peg's Seattle Mariners baseball cap.

The hair was a dazzling flourescent red color

never seen in nature, too bright to be real, which it wasn't. Claiming wigs were too hot, but unwilling to go out in public looking like, as she'd put it, "a transvestite Yul Brynner," she'd sewn strands from a cheap vinyl wig into the cap. And somehow, on her, it had looked just right.

Jack found himself reluctantly smiling back at his wife. Just as he knew she'd intended when she'd begun the ambitious legacy in the first place. As if Mother Nature couldn't remain immune to such a warm heart, the sun swept from behind a low-hanging pewter cloud and lit the gunmetal sea to shimmering sapphire.

A dizzying tumble of images appeared on the screen, disjointed scenes of sky and surf that had Jack remembering dropping the camera. For a long time the unblinking camcorder eye stared at the gray sand. A crab scuttled sideways into view, then disappeared again. Iridescent bubbles sparkled, then winked out like fallen stars. The frothy white foam seemed to be growing closer with each succeeding wave that washed onto shore.

"Jack!" Her voice was breathless. With laughter, and, he remembered, lingering passion from the kiss they shared after he dropped the camera. "It's going to get wet!"

There was a disorienting image of Peg's slender hands scooping it from the sand. Her gold wedding band gleamed, reminding Jack of the until-death-do-us-part promise that had seemed so far away on that sun-blessed Saturday afternoon they'd exchanged vows.

"We should get that on tape," she was saying.

He grumbled in the background.

"No, it'll be perfect," she coaxed prettily, turning the camera on him, catching him in midscowl. "Let's show our daughter what a blissfully perfect kiss looks like."

In the end, of course, she'd won. After steadying the camera atop a stack of bleached logs, she held out her arms to him. And, as always, he found it impossible to resist.

The staged kiss wasn't all that long. Neither was it as hot as the earlier, unplanned one had been. But it was sweet enough to make his eyes burn as he relived it in heart-wrenching detail.

Then, without warning, memories of kissing Peg battled with unbidden images of taking Raine Cantrell on the rough wet sand, like Burt Lancaster rolling around in the surf with Deborah Kerr in *From Here to Eternity* that had been broadcast on The Movie Channel the other night.

It didn't matter that he didn't particularly even like the New York lawyer who'd riled up hormones he'd almost forgotten were lurking inside him. The fantasy had caused a painful stirring in his loins and Jack didn't need to look down to know that although his mind might not want anything more to do with Ida's mouthy granddaughter, another, more vital part of his body was literally throbbing with the need to bury itself inside her.

"Goddammit!"

He pushed himself up from the sofa, jerked the tape from the VCR and locked it away in the chest again. Then went upstairs and stripped off his clothes, tossing them uncaringly onto the floor since there was no longer anyone around to complain. Jack's last thought, as he drifted off to sleep, was a strict command to both his mind and body to forget about Raine Cantrell.

When he awoke the next morning stiff, sore, and painfully horny, Jack reminded himself that a man couldn't hold himself responsible for his dreams. But that didn't make him feel any better as he showered, the stinging, ice-cold needles of water designed to chill any lingering desire.

∽6∾

Raine awoke to the clear, sweet song of a morning bird. Momentarily disoriented, she lay in the tester bed, looking up at the dancing dots of water-brightened light on the white plaster ceiling. It was when her gaze shifted to the square of sunshine on the bedcover that she remembered where she was. The familiar quilt was a living history of her family. Raine remembered her grandmother pointing out the pieces of her own mother's blue-serge church going dress stitched next to the red-and-black-checked flannel shirt Raine's great-grandfather John had worn while logging.

There was a pink square from the dress Ida had worn to her first day at school, two dotted Swiss triangles from the dress she'd worn to receive her medical degree, and a piece of lace, once white, now aged to the hue of old parchment, that had been cut from her wedding dress. Raine thought it ironic that although her grandparents' marriage had ended in divorce, the memory lived on, along with others, the fabric of so many lives sewn into this brightly colored family quilt.

Pushing herself out of bed, she made her way into the adjoining bathroom, which seemed smaller than she remembered it, brushed her teeth, ran her fingers through her hair, and decided to put the coffee on before her shower. Before going downstairs, she paused to look out the bedroom window.

Last night's rain had moved eastward toward Seattle, leaving the air as clear as crystal and from her window, located at the very top of the house's tower, Raine had an eagle's-eye view of the jagged, snow-capped peaks of the Olympic Mountains in one direction, the town and bay in the other. In the distance, a white ferry chugged from the dock toward Seattle. Three small skiffs—one with an eye-catching red sail—skimmed over morning-still water like butterflies over rippled blue silk.

Closer to home, Raine could see Coldwater Cove waking up. Kathleen Walker, pharmacist and the third generation of Walkers to run the Walker Drug Emporium, was on the sidewalk outside her red-brick, brass-plaqued storefront, unfurling blue-and-white awnings. The Orca Theater's marquee announced a Mel Gibson festival while across the street, the smoke coming from the chimney of the Gray Gull Smorgasbord & Grill revealed that Oley Swensen had begun smoking ribs for the lunch and dinner crowds. Although some might not consider barbecue a traditional Scandinavian dish, faithful customers swore Oley made the best ribs on the peninsula.

Directly below her window, a flock of shiny black starlings strutted across the dew-bright lawn like an army laying claim to conquered territory. In the center of the lawn, a pair of nuthatches splashed in a white stone birdbath surrounded by daffodils; the scattered water from their energetic wing flapping sparkled like diamonds.

The house was quiet, suggesting the others were still sleeping off the effects of yesterday's events. Raine tiptoed down the staircase, avoiding the stair that had always creaked like a rusty hinge.

The country kitchen was blinding yellow—like the inside of a lemon. It had always been this way, at least as long as Raine could remember. The paint strip Ida kept in the kitchen junk drawer referred to it as *buttercup*, but it had always reminded Raine of sunshine. Winter on the peninsula could, at times, turn unrelentingly gray and wet; the color was an uplifting antidote for the gloom.

Although Ida's cooking talents were marginal at best, the kitchen had always been the heart of the house, the room where new days were greeted with fishing reports broadcast on the old tabletop radio and broken hearts were soothed over cups of hot chocolate made with Quick from the yellow can that had been a mainstay in the pantry for as long as Raine could remember. Her own kitchen back in New York was closet-size, certainly not big enough for people to gather, not that she had any time for entertaining.

She spooned some dark ground coffee from a Starbucks stoneware jar she found on the counter into the white paper filter of the coffee maker, and poured in water. While she waited for the water to drip through the machine, Raine sat down at the pine table in front of the window, intending to make a list of all the things she needed to do today.

It seemed so strange not to be rushing off for

work. Drumming her fingers impatiently on the tabletop, she glanced up at the copper-teapot clock. It was still too early to show up at the hospital. Last night she'd been informed that Ida couldn't be released until after morning rounds, which began around nine.

"Perhaps I'll just check in," she decided out loud as she compared the silence of the kitchen—disturbed only by the soft hum of the refrigerator—with the beehive of activity of her office. Undoubtedly a host of phone calls had been piling up.

Conveniently ignoring the fact that Brian ran their little corner of Choate, Plimpton, Wells & Sullivan with the efficiency of the joint chiefs preparing for an invasion, Raine called her office.

"You haven't even been away for twenty-four hours yet, Raine," Brian reminded her, amusement evident in his voice after she expressed concern about the work she'd left behind. "Don't worry, I'm certainly capable of holding down the fort."

"I know." What had she thought? That Choate, Plimpton, Wells & Sullivan couldn't survive three days without her? "Thank you, Brian. I don't know what I'd do without you."

After laughing at his assertion that he didn't know what she'd do without him, either, Raine hung up, feeling vaguely dissatisfied by the brief conversation. While she was grateful that things hadn't fallen apart without her, deep down inside, part of her wished that they also weren't going so smoothly.

"What did you expect? You've been gone less than twenty-four hours. No one's indispensable," she muttered into the stillness. "Not even a Warrior Princess."

Since the coffee seemed to be taking forever to drip through the filter of Ida's jazzy new coffee maker, Raine had just decided to use the time to go back upstairs and take a shower when something outside the window caught her attention. Grabbing a corduroy barn jacket from the hook beside the kitchen door, she marched outdoors.

"What do you think you're doing?" she demanded of the man hunkered down behind her car.

"Taking care of your taillight," he answered with bland innocence. He held up some broken pieces of red plastic as evidence. "I've just about got it replaced."

"That's not necessary."

"Sure it is." He tightened a couple of final screws. "Since I'm the one who broke it in the first place."

"Surely the rental agency has people to take care of things like that."

"They probably do. But if you tried to drive with that taillight, I'd have had to write you up a citation, which would involve you having to stop by the magistrate's office—"

"That'd be Wally."

"Got it in one." His smile suggested that she'd just given the correct answer for Double Jeopardy. "Anyway, while you can undoubtedly afford the fine, I figure we both have better ways to spend our time."

"I don't suppose you could just overlook it? For today?"

He rubbed his chin and appeared to be giving her question serious consideration. "Surely you wouldn't be trying to talk a law enforcement officer out of doing his sworn duty?"

"Not at all. I was merely suggesting that you must

have more serious crimes to handle than worrying about my taillight."

"Not really." He shrugged. "This is a pretty peaceful county."

"Except for the occasional standoff situation."

"There is that." Jack stood up. "Nice pajamas."

Irked by the laughter in his voice, Raine pulled the edges of the jacket together over the top of the men's styled pajamas where black lambs gamboled on a background of red flannel. "I suppose you'd prefer it if I'd come waltzing out here in some black lace nightgown from Frederick's of Hollywood?"

"Now, that's a real nice offer, and I sure wouldn't want to discourage you, if you've ever a mind to greet me some morning in a getup like that," he said. "But I've always been partial to black sheep. Being sort of a black sheep, myself."

"Since you brought it up, I have to admit I was surprised when I realized that you'd taken over your father's job. I always figured you'd end up on the other side of the bars."

He laughed at that. "My folks figured the same thing. Especially my dad."

"So, what happened to turn you around?"

"The same thing that happens to most black sheep, if they're lucky. The love of a good woman."

She studied him and decided he was serious. "Some women might consider that an outdated, chauvinist statement," she said finally.

"Some women might be right. But that doesn't stop it from being the truth."

Before she could decide how to answer that, the Nano Kitty beeped. She watched him press the buttons, handling whatever electronic-cat emergency had occurred this time. Although it didn't make any sense at all, as she compared Jack's behavior with that of her own absent father, who'd never acknowledged her existence, Raine found herself almost envying Amy O'Halloran.

"Got that taken care of," he said with satisfaction as he stuffed the flourescent green egg back into his shirt pocket. "When it gets sick, you have to make sure it gets its antibiotics on time," he explained. "Otherwise, you run the risk of it getting worse. Maybe even becoming catatonic."

She couldn't quite hold back the smile. "That's terrible."

Instead of defending his foolish pun, Jack gave Raine a slow, appraising study that warmed his eyes and her blood. "You know, Counselor," he said, "you really do have a nice smile." He tugged on the ends of hair curving around her jaw. "You should use it more often."

Before she could determine how that outwardly casual touch had affected her, he was headed back toward the Suburban. "See you in court."

Raine blinked away a new, distressing hallucination she'd become momentarily lost in. One that had her standing in the fog, the motors of a 1940s propeller plane droning behind her. She was looking up at Jack O'Halloran, who'd inexplicably changed last night's parka for a trench coat, and was desperately wishing he'd tell her that the fate of the world didn't mean a hill of beans when compared to a man and a woman's happiness.

Just when she'd been about to beg him to let her stay in Casablanca with him, the familiar word brought her hurling back into the 1990s.

"Court?"

"For the juvenile hearing. Old Fussbudget will un-doubtedly call me to testify in the kids' case."

"How did you know the girls call her Old Fussbudget?"

"Hell, everyone in the county calls her that. But as annoying as the woman can admittedly be, she's got a reputation for fairness. I don't think Ida'll have too much of a problem keeping Gwen. And the girls, for the time being."

He touched his fingers to the brim of his hat. Then climbed into the truck and drove away.

The coffee was finally done when she returned to the kitchen. Raine tossed the broken pieces of plas-tic taillight into the wastebasket beneath the sink, quickly downed two cups while standing at the kitchen window, then went upstairs to get dressed to go to the hospital for her confrontation with Ida.

"I'm not hearing a word of it." The elderly woman was sitting on the top of her bed, dressed and obvi-ously more than ready to escape the institutional confines of the hospital. The scent of talc floated over that of disinfectant and illness. Her salt-and-pepper hair was pinned up, looking like an untidy bird's nest atop her head, but her crimson lipstick was intact. "Those poor girls have been moved around enough, Raine."

She folded her arms across the front of a sweatshirt which read: *I can only please one person per day. Today is not your day. Tomorrow's not look-ing all that good either.* "Old Fussbudget assures me that Renee and Shawna's aunt and uncle will make good parents, but I'm not going to let anyone take Gwen away."

"Did it ever occur to you that your shenanigans yesterday—telling them to bar the door and not talk to anyone, for heaven's sake—didn't exactly endear you to the authorities? You didn't just hurt your guardianship chances, Gram. You caused some pretty serious black marks on those girls' juvenile records."

"Nothing would have happened if that Old Fuss-budget hadn't gone and called the sheriff," Ida grumbled.

"Well, she did. Which made things really serious."

"Lucky for me I've got a good lawyer."

"I suppose it slipped your mind that I'm not licensed in Washington?"

"Would you believe me if I said it did?" Ida hedged.

"Not in a New York minute."

"Well, then, I suppose there's no point in lying. Of course I realize you're not licensed in the state, Raine, darling, which, by the way, I've never been able to understand, since it is your home, after all—"

"My home is in Manhattan."

"Don't be silly. Manhattan is where people work. Not where they live. And while I understand your desire and your need to be independent, Raine, I think you're overdoing things a bit by moving all the way across the country and living with . . . with . . . ," she searched for just the right word, ". . . Easterners."

"Some of them can be quite pleasant. When they're not eating their young," Raine said, her tone as dry as a legal brief. "And you're not going to sidetrack me, again, Gram. My point is that I can't possibly be your attorney because I'm not licensed in this state."

"Don't be such a stickler for details, that's only a technicality. Besides, how will it look, you turning your own aged grandmother away when you're willing to work for those thieving oil company scoundrels?"

"That's unfair. A court declared that Odessa Oil didn't steal from anyone."

"Try telling that to those poor pensioners your filthy rich client left without insurance."

"I'm not going to argue the case with you, Gram," Raine huffed on a frustrated breath. "Besides, since when did you care what people think?"

"I don't. But I have to admit that I wasn't real thrilled to turn on the television and see my own flesh and blood turn traitor to an entire class of senior citizens."

The muscles in the back of Raine's neck knotted and the familiar iron band around her forehead tightened. "The case was open and shut. Those retirees who'd filed suit didn't have a legal leg to stand on."

"How about a moral leg?"

"I'm not paid to be Mother Teresa. I'm a litigator. I get paid a great deal of money to fight my clients' battles."

Which left her living in the most adversarial environment possible, Raine thought, but did not say. While the battle eventually ended for a client, she moved from case to case, remaining in a constant state of conflict.

"Ha." Ida speared her with still-bright dark eyes

that reminded Raine of a curious magpie. "As Orson Welles said in *Citizen Kane*, "It's not difficult to make a lot of money, if money is all you want."

Despite her rising frustration, it crossed Raine's mind that this was undoubtedly one of the few times Ida had actually gotten a quote right. Unfortunately, she'd tossed it into the argument like a verbal grenade.

"It's not just the money, Gram. I like my job. I love it," she claimed with a bit more force than necessary.

"Does it make you happy?"

"Happy?" Raine was momentarily stumped. Having achieved a level of success that most young attorneys could only dream of, she was certainly *supposed* to be happy. Wasn't she?

"Of course I'm happy," she answered briskly. "But we shouldn't be wasting time talking about me. Since you're the one with the guardianship hearing scheduled for tomorrow morning."

"So you *are* taking my case?"

Feeling as if she was juggling flaming torches while walking a tightrope blindfolded, Raine ignored the escalating headache and prepared for the argument her grandmother was bound to launch. "It's not that simple. Now, I don't want you to fly off the handle—"

"When have I ever done that?"

"Well, there have been a few occasions—"

"Don't be foolish." The elderly woman broke in again. "I've always been the epitome of gracious manners. Ask anyone in Coldwater Cove."

There was no way Raine was going to touch that outrageous assertion. The truth was, her grandmother had a knack for stirring up more than her share of hornet's nests. A firebrand Ida Lindstrom had been born, and a firebrand she'd obviously die.

"How old are you?" Raine asked suddenly.

"What the dickens does my age have to do with the price of tin in China?"

"It's tea."

"What?"

"It's tea in China. Not tin."

"Really?" Ida frowned. "They don't have tin in China?"

"I'm sure they must." Raine wished she hadn't allowed herself to get off track. "I was referring to the old adage. Which mentions tea. And to get back to your question, the court may well feel that your age has a great deal to do with your ability to care for three troublesome teenage girls."

"Pooh," Ida scoffed. "They're not at all troublesome. In fact, they've been a marvelous help around the house. And it's nice to have some companionship. It's no fun being alone. Especially at my age."

Raine was not going to let Ida make her feel guilty about not returning home to Coldwater Cove after graduating from law school. "You're not exactly alone. Lilith's back home again."

"I love my daughter dearly. But believe me, having Lilith living under my roof is not exactly all that peaceful."

Since there was no way Raine could argue with that, she didn't even try. "What's she doing home again anyway?"

"Finding herself. At least that's how she explained it when she showed up on the doorstep without any warning last month. If you want to know the truth,

I believe it has more to do with the fact that she nearly lost her shirt in some business down in Arizona. The way she tells it, she was getting tired of her singing life on the road, so she went into business with a friend conducting vortex tours. But the woman turned out not to be much of a friend, since she embezzled most of their assets."

"Surely Lilith filed charges."

"Actually she didn't. You know your mother. She believes that insisting on retribution causes bad karma and the embezzler will have to work toward redemption in her next life."

"We can only hope," Raine said dryly. "Now, getting back to your case, I really can't legally represent you. But I suppose there's nothing to prevent me from addressing the court as your granddaughter."

"Who just happens to be a hotshot lawyer. Even if you do sometimes lack judgment when choosing your clients." The bird's nest atop her head wobbled and threatened to tip over as Ida nodded with obvious satisfaction. "That should clinch a win for our side."

"I'm still not certain it's for the best."

"Gwen's a good girl, Raine. She deserves a chance to prove it."

"Not if the stress of dealing with a delinquent teenager puts your health at risk."

"I'm as healthy as a mule."

And as stubborn as one, Raine thought. "You nearly fainted yesterday."

"I was merely lightheaded for a moment."

Raine gave her grandmother another long, judicial perusal. She seemed so much smaller, so much more birdlike, than Raine remembered from her last trip home. Almost frail. Yet the determination in those intense dark eyes was, indeed, that of a woman at least half her age.

"You never did tell me how old you were."

"Didn't anyone ever tell you it's not polite to ask a lady her age?"

"You're not a *lady*. You're my client. Sort of," Raine qualified yet again. "So, how about it? I should know, in case the presiding judge brings it up."

"Let's just put it this way, darling . . . if you were counting in dog years, I'd probably be dead."

It was Raine's turn to fold her arms. "That's no answer. If you want me to represent you, you're going to have to do everything I say."

"Absolutely," Ida said with a conviction Raine didn't believe for a moment.

"So, for starters, once more, how about telling me how old you are?" Ida wasn't the only stubborn female in the family.

Her grandmother rubbed her chin, drawing Raine's attention to her hands. Once they'd been long and slender and strong, capable of delivering hundreds of Coldwater Cove's babies. Now the knuckles were swollen with arthritis, proving, Raine thought sadly, that life didn't stand still just because you might want it to.

"That's a bit hard to say," the elderly woman said slyly. "Since I seem to forget more often these days."

"Terrific. I'll simply claim early Alzheimer's. That should definitely gain you custody."

"Well," Ida huffed at Raine's sarcasm, "I see you still have a smart mouth."

"I suppose I do. But I also happen to be proud of

it. Since I inherited it from my grandmother, whom I love and admire more than anyone I've ever known."

Ida's bright eyes glistened at Raine's assertion. "Now you've done it." She pressed a finger beneath her eye to catch the single tear that had escaped beneath sparse lower lashes. "Gone and made me choke up."

"Too bad. Because I *do* love you, which is why I'm still not certain that those girls staying with you is a good idea."

"I'm not letting them go without a fight, Raine. No matter how much you try to soft-soap me."

"I wasn't trying—"

"Of course you were." Ida cackled with obvious satisfaction. "You're right about being a warrior, Raine. Maybe even more than me, which is saying something. And I know you'll use any weapon in your arsenal it takes to win. Which is why I need you standing up for me in that courtroom. I may be old, but I'm no fool. Without you, we'd be up a creek without a paddlewheel. But I know you can make the judge see the light at the end of the tunnel."

Raine sighed. It was emotional blackmail, pure and simple. "Talking about using weapons—"

"I'll use whatever it takes," Ida vowed.

"I can't promise anything." Knowing the futility of arguing any further, Raine threw in the towel. "But I'll do my best."

"That's all I've ever expected, dear." That little matter taken care of, she slid off the bed and pulled on a pair of beaded moccasins that looked nearly as old as she was.

"And for the record," Ida said as they walked out

of the room, "I don't have Alzheimer's. In fact, my mind is as tarp as a shack."

Terrific. Raine groaned inwardly and wondered how, exactly, she was going to keep her grandmother from testifying. Although everyone who knew her could attest that Ida Lindstrom had been the queen of malapropisms long before her hair had turned gray, a judge might just take a different view.

∽7∾

"So," Ida said as they were driving along the winding evergreen-lined road back to the house. "Have you spoken with your mother this morning?"

"She was still asleep when I left the house."

"I'm not surprised. After last night's antics."

Raine shot her a surprised look. "You know about that?"

"Coldwater Cove is a small town. A story as juicy as that one is bound to get around pretty fast. So, is it true what they're saying about Cooper?"

"What are they saying?"

"That he's as hooked on the girl as he ever was?"

"I wouldn't know about that. But there was definitely something there. Some spark." Hot enough to set the entire forest ablaze, Raine thought but did not say.

"Interesting." The shaggy green trees shot by the window as Ida thought about that. "He was always good for her. The boy had a quieting effect on your mother that none of the rest of us could manage."

"She didn't seem very quieted last night." And

nothing about Cooper Ryan had been at all boylike. He'd practically radiated testosterone.

"We can always hope," Ida said. "It would be nice to see Lilith settle down with a good man like Cooper Ryan."

Since she personally thought that about as likely to happen as her mother sprouting gossamer wings and flying to the moon, Raine merely murmured something that could have been an agreement.

After they returned home, Raine called a meeting. When Ida started to come into the sunroom along with them, Raine insisted she wanted to speak with the girls alone.

"It's my hearing, too," the elderly woman grumbled.

"True. But I don't want you coaching the girls on what to say. The worst thing that could happen for our case would be for them to get caught lying on the witness stand."

Ida stiffened her back, pulling herself up to her full four feet, eleven inches. "It's a fine kettle of cossacks when a woman's own granddaughter accuses her of advising children to tell falsehoods in a court of law."

"I was merely suggesting that you'd encourage them to be creative in their answers. I thought we agreed that if I was going to represent you, I'd be the one calling the shots."

"You really are a hard woman, Raine Cantrell."

"I'm also a damn good attorney."

They stared at each other for a long, drawn-out minute, both women aware that this was a deciding moment in not only the case, but their future relationship.

"I've got some laundry to do," Ida muttered finally. "Best get to it." Thus conceding defeat, she marched out of the kitchen.

Raine sighed. Mission accomplished, but at what cost? She knew that Ida was accustomed to ruling the roost. She also felt a bit guilty in forcing an old woman, especially one she loved, to back down that way. Reminding herself that the ends justified the means, especially when dealing with courtroom battles, Raine put her personal concerns aside.

The sunroom, on the first floor of the tower, looked a bit like a gazebo that had been glassed in. The pine plank floors had been painted a bright summer-sky blue and a profusion of bluebells, daylilies, and peonies bloomed on the cushions of the white wicker chairs and sofa. Clay pots filled with multicolor displays of ruffled tulips, trumpet-shaped daffodils, narcissus, and hyacinths had been placed about the room. The colorful blooms perfumed the air.

"All right," she said, "the first thing I'm going to need to present your case is a bit of background. I realize it might not be easy to talk about, and if you'd like to have these conversations one at a time—"

"No," Shawna broke in. "We don't have any secrets from one another. Like Mama Ida always says, we're all family."

Raine experienced a little tinge of jealousy at the idea of her grandmother considering these strangers to be members of her family. She tamped it down.

What kind of person could be jealous of three homeless children?

She turned to the others. "Gwen, Renee, do you agree with this?"

Both girls nodded.

"All right, then." Raine sat down in the wicker rocker, her yellow legal pad on her lap, pen poised. "Shawna, let's begin with you. How long have you been in the juvenile justice system?"

"Mama and Daddy died last September. So, that'd make it almost nine months. I was never in trouble before that party, but since we didn't have any relatives to take us in, we just got turned over to county."

"But you do have an aunt."

"She and my mama hadn't talked to each other for a lot of years. They'd had a fight back after Renee was born, then Aunt Jean got married to some guy in the navy and started traveling all over. She says she wrote to Mama last fall, and again at Christmas, but the post office sent the letters back, since we weren't living at that address anymore. Then, when her husband got reassigned back here to Washington, she decided to look Mama up and set things straight." She sighed and her lips turned down in a frown. "But it was too late. When she found out Mama and Daddy were dead, she petitioned for custody. We were all set to move in with her next week. Until the ruckus."

"I see."

"Do you think the judge will stop us from going to live with Auntie Jean now?" Renee asked in a trembling voice.

"No. I don't think that'll be a problem," Raine reassured the thirteen-year-old. "Considering the mitigating circumstances." She turned to Gwen. "How about you?"

"I'm pregnant."

"Unfortunately, lots of girls get pregnant, but they don't end up in the juvenile system."

"Okay. I'm pregnant and I shoplift."

Raine made a note on her pad. "Is that all?"

"Isn't that enough?"

"I don't know. I suppose it depends on what you've shoplifted. And how often."

"A bunch of stuff. A lot of times." The teenager thrust out her chin, challenging Raine.

"You sound almost proud of that."

"I'm not proud. It's just the facts. You asked what got me put in juvie. Well, there's your answer."

And not exactly an encouraging one, either, Raine considered. "When was the last time you were caught?"

"About five months ago."

"Before you came to live with Ida?"

"Yeah."

"So, are you saying you haven't shoplifted since you arrived here?"

"I wouldn't dare. Mama Ida'd probably take a switch to me."

"I'm not certain switching is exactly my grandmother's style," Raine said. "But I do agree that she can be a strict disciplinarian."

"She's the only person who ever cared about me enough to get on my case for my own good. Most of the other places I've lived, the folks just tended to knock me around for no reason. Or because they got off on it."

Hearing this had Raine feeling even more guilty about her random flash of jealousy. "How many places have you lived? And were these foster homes?"

"Yeah. And there've been too many to count. I landed in my first home when I was still a baby and my mama got arrested for dealing pot. After she did her time, she got me back. Then she landed back in jail for prostitution. And after that, she was in rehab, but she's never stayed straight. I guess I've been in foster care most of my life."

Sixteen years. The idea was abominable. "I'm sorry."

"It wasn't your fault," Gwen said. "Besides, some of them weren't so bad. And a couple were even pretty nice. But none of them ever made me feel like I belonged to a real family."

"Until here."

"Until Mama Ida," the girl confirmed.

A thought occurred to Raine. "These episodes of shoplifting wouldn't happen to be whenever you were about to be moved again, would they?"

"Mama Ida's right. You're real smart." The tinge of acid in Gwen's tone kept Raine from taking the remark as a compliment.

"So, I'm right?"

"Yeah. So what now, you gonna send me to a shrink?"

"That's not my place." Raine wondered if Gwen had ever received counseling.

"Yeah," she said when Raine asked her. "When I was a kid. The guy said I was acting out because of separation anxiety." She folded her arms over her stomach in an unconscious gesture of self-protection and directed her gaze out the wall of glass toward the rolling emerald lawn and beyond that, Admiralty Bay. In her bright green trapeze top and capri pants Raine thought she looked a bit like a pregnant Laura Petrie today. "Big deal."

"It would be to me, if I hadn't had a place to call my own. A place I'd feel safe," Raine said calmly. "Actually, I admire you for handling things as well as you have. Shoplifting, as serious as it is, is a very minor offense considering some of the trouble you could have gotten into."

Raine couldn't help comparing the young girl's upbringing with her own. Although her mother had been anything but reliable, at least whenever her life had become too unstable, Lilith had always shipped her daughters back to Ida, who provided not only the necessary shelter, but a haven.

As her eyes drifted to the driveway, a distant memory flashed back, as clear as if it had happened yesterday. Raine recalled the creak of the stairs in the predawn silence, the squeak of the kitchen door, the crunch of gravel underfoot. Looking out her bedroom window, she'd seen her mother walking toward her car, suitcase in hand.

Raine remembered tearing down the stairs and running out of the house in her nightgown, begging her mother, who'd gotten a tour gig opening for The Grateful Dead, not to leave. The commotion roused Ida, who came downstairs, then held a hysterical Raine tight as her mother drove away.

A shadow moved across Raine's heart, like a cloud moving in front of the sun. She shook off the sudden chill and dragged her mind back to the problem at hand.

"All right, I think we can finesse the shoplifting," she decided. "Especially since the psychologist's report should already be in your file. Do you have any plans for the future?"

"I always wanted to be a doctor. Like Mama Ida." The sixteen-year-old dropped her gaze to her hands, which rested on the shelf of her stomach. She was squeezing them together so tightly the knuckles had turned white. "But I guess now, with the baby and all . . ." Her voice drifted off, her shoulders drooped.

"So you're going to try to keep the baby?" Raine asked carefully.

"I don't know." Gwen sighed. "At first I was going to get an abortion, because that's what the guy who knocked me up wanted, so he borrowed the money from his cousin and we went to this clinic in Seattle where nobody knew us. Since I was pretty nervous, I wanted Randy—he was my boyfriend—to stay with me, but he doesn't like blood and gore and yucky stuff. He won't even watch *ER*. So, he waited at the Denny's next door."

"Creep," Shawna muttered.

"Yeah, well, I knew it wouldn't do any good to argue with him, so I just, you know, filled out the forms. Then the nurse took me into this cubicle, and told me to take off all my clothes and put on this paper gown, and someone would come get me when it was time.

"I sat on the bench and tried to read a magazine someone had left behind, but I couldn't concentrate. The curtain was still closed, but I could sorta see through the cracks, and every so often they'd call out a name and I'd see a girl going by my cubicle, and I'd wonder about her story. How she ended up there.

"Which got me thinking about my boyfriend. I hadn't wanted to go all the way in the first place. I kept telling him that I wasn't ready, but then one night he told me that I couldn't expect him to be satisfied just making out. That if I really loved him, I'd show him. By having sex with him. So I did. So I wouldn't lose him, you know?"

"I can understand why you might feel that way," Raine said mildly. "But if he truly cared for you, he wouldn't have given you that ultimatum."

"I sorta figured that out while I was sitting there. I mean here I was, dressed in this stupid blue paper gown, waiting to have my baby sucked out of me, and he was next door eatin' his way through a Grand Slam breakfast. It was like he got all the fun and I was stuck with the trouble."

"I'd say that's a fairly accurate assessment of the situation."

"So I was already thinking that maybe this was a mistake. But then the nurse called my name, and I told myself it was too late. That my boyfriend had already paid the money, so I'd have to go through with it."

Since the girl obviously hadn't gotten an abortion, Raine remained silent and waited for the end of the story.

"But then I walked into this room that was like something from *The X-Files*. The only furniture was a chair and a table with stirrups. And beside the table was a tray with all sorts of instruments that looked like stuff from some torture chamber."

Her eyes welled up. "I looked at all that stuff and

just freaked. Then ran out of the room, back to my cubicle, threw on my clothes and got out of that place."

When the tears that had been threatening spilled, the teenager scrubbed them away with the back of her hands, reminding Raine more of a little girl who'd just had her bright red birthday balloon burst on her than a young woman who was weeks away from becoming a mother.

She drew in a deep, gulping breath. "I threw up on the sidewalk outside. My boyfriend saw me out the window and he got really mad and told me that if I was gonna have the baby, I was going to do it by myself."

"He's still financially responsible," the lawyer in Raine felt duty-bound to point out. "In fact, there are laws—"

"I know. Old Fussbudget told me all about them. But he got a bunch of his friends to say they slept with me, so we have to wait until the baby's born for a blood test. Not that it's going to do any good proving it's his," she said, looking far older—and more defeated—than her sixteen years. "Because he'll figure out some way not to pay."

She drew in a ragged breath. "Anyway, if I keep the baby, at least something good will come out of all this bad. And I'll have someone to love me."

Raine wondered how many thousands of unwed teenage mothers believed exactly the same thing. "How did you end up here?"

"I was hanging out in Seattle and panhandling on the ferry. I asked Mama Ida for some change, and she gave me a long lecture about how danger-

ous it was to be living on the street. And how I owed
my baby more. Then she brought me home."

Home. Family. It could not escape Raine's notice
that these two themes kept popping up. "Well, we'll
do our best to keep you here," she promised.

Only yesterday Raine had been responsible for the
financial future of a multibillion-dollar petroleum
company. Yet somehow, that hadn't felt nearly as
weighty as the responsibility Ida had placed on
her—the future of this troubled girl who was obviously desperate for the stability of a loving, protective family. Which, it appeared, she and Ida had
already created.

"There's one thing I want to make clear." Raine's
voice and her eyes turned firm. "If I have any indication you're making life harder on my grandmother,
I'll do everything in my power to get you moved to
a new foster home."

"Mama Ida says that we've all been a real help to
her," Gwen said. "We've taken over most of the
cleaning and cooking."

"That was wise," Raine murmured. "Taking over
the cooking."

"It was kinda for self-defense," Shawna spoke up.
"And Gwen's been a whiz in the garden."

"I've always liked flowers," Gwen revealed shyly.
"But I never lived anywhere long enough to grow
a garden."

"You must be responsible for all these." Raine ges-
tured toward the cheerful displays.

Gwen ducked her head. "I ordered the bulbs out
of a catalog."

"They're lovely. In fact, I think I'll take a few pictures, showing all you've done."

"Do you think that will cause the judge to let me stay?" Gwen asked, openly dubious.

"I don't know," Raine admitted. She'd never lied to a client and she wasn't about to begin now. "But it's one more weapon in our arsenal."

"So Gwen has a chance?" This from Shawna.

"About a fifty-fifty one. But I'm going to do my best to raise those odds."

"You'll win," Renee said. "Mama Ida says that you're the best lawyer there is. That you never lose."

With that positive endorsement, a weight as heavy as a truckload of bricks landed smack on Raine's shoulders. When she saw Gwen's wretched, unconfident expression, it got even heavier.

This was turning out to be one helluva week, Jack thought, two days after the standoff as he pulled the Suburban up in front of Linda's Beads and Baubles, a small boutique located in the outlet mall a few miles outside of town. And now, after a less than spectacular day, it looked as if he and Raine Cantrell were due for another skirmish.

Timing, Jack reminded himself as he hauled himself out of the truck, was everything. He clicked the lock shut with a beep of the remote, and headed for the store.

Sure enough, the first thing he saw when he entered was one of Ida's girls, slumped in a chair while a tall red-haired woman stood guard over her. The store smelled like flowers, reminding him of the fragrant potpourri Peg had scattered around the house in pretty crystal dishes shaped like seashells. New Age music drifted from hidden speakers on the scented air.

It was a decidedly female atmosphere, which had him feeling like a bull elk on the loose in a crystal shop as he wove his way through the racks of bright silk scarves, summer straw hats, and sparkly jewelry.

"What's up?" he asked, already suspecting the answer. He'd run a records check on all three girls during the standoff and had discovered that this one had particularly sticky fingers.

"I caught her leaving the store with a pair of earrings." Linda Hanson held out a pair of dangling gold earrings set with colorful stones Jack couldn't identify.

"Had she actually left the premises?"

"Well, not exactly." The boutique owner's mouth pulled into a tight frown. He and Linda had graduated from high school the same year and Jack remembered how back in her cheerleader days, those cherry-tinted lips had been a lot friendlier. "After all, if I'd let her get away, I might not have caught up with her."

"So, she was technically inside the store?"

"Technically." Linda's frown reached her eyes and made horizontal lines in her forehead as she followed his train of thought. "If you want to split hairs. But I've been in the retail business long enough to recognize a shoplifter when I see one. And this kid had every intention of stealing those earrings."

"That may be, but a court just might see it a little differently." Irritated at the way she was complicating his life yet again, Jack speared the delinquent with his sternest look. "Is she right? Were you going to steal those earrings?"

Gwen shrugged. "I could have been."

"You realize I'll have to report this to your juvenile probation officer."

"Geez. Now there's a surprise." Her mouth pulled even tighter than the boutique owner's.

Shit. "Let's go."

"Where?"

"I should just haul you down to juvie, hand you over to social services authorities, and suggest they throw away the key until you turn eighteen."

"Might as well," Gwen countered. "Since I'm gonna end up back there anyway."

"Well, it just so happens that this is your lucky day, kid. Because I'm going to give you a break and take you back to Ida's."

He motioned her to her feet, grateful when she obeyed, placed a hand on her elbow, and began shepherding her out the way he'd come.

"Aren't you going to put handcuffs on her?" Linda asked, openly miffed that her case wasn't being treated seriously enough to suit her.

"I usually save the shackles for the serial killers and bank robbers."

"You don't have to use that tone with me, Jack O'Halloran. After all, you and I go back a long way."

Jack wasn't surprised that her voice indicated a past intimacy. They'd dated for a brief, carefree time, back when he was playing high school football and she'd been waving her green and white pom-poms.

"Sorry," he said, reminding himself that public servants weren't supposed to resort to sarcasm, no matter how provoked. "But I think I can handle one teenager."

"That's not what I heard. I heard this one and the other delinquents—" her scornful tone made them sound like mad dog killers—"had you over a barrel the other day."

"You heard wrong. And now that we've stopped this crime wave, I'd better get back to work. No telling how many miscreants are out there planning to bring mayhem to our peaceful little town."

As he led Gwen out the door, he couldn't miss the girl's chuckle. "Something funny?"

"I guess you put Miss High and Mighty in her place."

"Miss High and Mighty just happens to be the mayor's daughter. His *only* daughter. Not to mention being the youngest of five kids, the other four being boys, which makes her just about as spoiled as any pretty girl can be.

"Now, I don't see any point in putting you in a cell just because you're acting stupid because you're afraid you're going to be sent away again," he said as he opened the door and helped her up into the passenger seat. "But if you felt moved to return to a life of crime, you definitely picked the wrong store. If you were trying to get taken out of Ida's home and thrown back into the system, you might have succeeded. And you sure didn't help my day any."

She turned away and pretended vast interest in the towering trees flashing by the truck window as they drove back toward Coldwater Cove.

"I don't suppose I could talk you into not telling Mama Ida about this?" she asked finally.

"Sorry. If she's going to stand up and vouch for you in court, she's entitled to know what you've been up to."

Another silence. Then, "I know I'm fat right now. But before I got pregnant, a lot of boys thought I was pretty."

He slanted her a glance, afraid he knew just where this conversation was heading and hoping like hell he was wrong. "A lot of boys are right."

"Lots of them wanted to sleep with me. Even after I got pregnant. But I said no."

"Smart girl."

"And pretty," she reminded him.

"That, too." His fingers tightened on the steering wheel as he waited for the inevitable. Jack decided to try to sidetrack her before things got really sticky. "When you grow up, you'll probably be a heartbreaker."

"I'm almost grown up now," she reminded him. "So, maybe we could work out a kind of deal? You could forget this ever happened, and I could give you something—"

"Dammit, that's it." He jerked the wheel, pulled off the road onto the gravel shoulder, and cut the engine. "You listen to me, and you listen good, kid, because I'm not going to repeat myself. Understand?"

Biting her lip, Gwen nodded.

"I asked if you understood." His sharp tone could have cut diamonds. "When a law enforcement officer asks you a question, you damn well better answer."

"Yes, sir!" she snapped back, with a flare of spirit he suspected had kept her alive and reasonably sane during a lifetime bereft of any security or affection. "Sheriff."

She'd spat his title from between tight lips. Not

wanting to break her spirit, but needing her to understand exactly who was boss, Jack nodded his approval. "That's better. Now, a smart girl like you should realize that prostitution is a one-way ticket straight to the gutter."

"It wouldn't be prostitution, because I wasn't asking for any money. Besides, you're a lot nicer than the other guys I know."

"Which definitely suggests you need to find new friends," Jack said dryly. "As for not asking for any money, it doesn't matter. What you were suggesting was wrong, kid. Legally and morally. And damn dangerous, because some guys might actually take you up on it."

"But not you."

"No. Not me. Not in this lifetime. No way. No how."

"Well, I guess you made yourself real clear." She turned and began staring out the passenger window again, but not before Jack witnessed the sheen of tears that matched the strangled, frail voice.

Once again he was given an insight he could have done without. *Christ.* And here he'd fooled himself into believing that life was only nasty in the big city.

"Look at me, Gwen."

Apparently having learned her lesson, she obeyed, giving him a view of a face even more miserable than the one he'd seen when he'd put her into the back seat of the Suburban last night.

"Whatever happened to you in any of those foster homes, whatever anyone did to you, whatever you thought you had to do, it wasn't your fault." He wanted to touch her, just a soothing hand to her shoulder, but feared that a male touch right now was the last thing she needed. "Do you understand?"

She bit her lip and nodded. Then, remembering his instructions to answer his questions, managed a weak, "Y-y-yes."

But her bleak, dark eyes said otherwise. Jack cursed again, mentally this time. "Is he the one who got you pregnant?"

"No." She sniffled. "It was his son. Randy was my boyfriend for a while. Until he knocked me up. But it could've been his father. If I hadn't gotten away in time."

"Did you ever tell anyone at social services??

"Are you kidding? Hell, no. Not that there was all that much too tell." She sniffled. "It was the last home I was in, before Ida's. The guy kept trying to cop a feel whenever his wife wasn't looking. He always pretended it was just an accident, but I knew better.

"Then one day, when she was working late and I was fixing dinner, he caught me alone in the kitchen and said that he'd found out I was putting out for his son. And then he said that if I was that hot to trot, I oughta try a real man." She bit her lip and closed her eyes for a moment. "He pushed me up against the refrigerator, shoved his tongue down my throat and put his hand up my skirt."

"Son of a bitch."

"He sure was that, all right. But I took the butcher knife I'd been using to cut the chicken and threatened to cut off his balls."

"I imagine that had some effect."

"Yeah. He let go of me real quick and afterwards, he pretended that he'd just been kidding and that if

I knew what was good for me, I'd better keep my mouth shut. Which I was going to do anyway, because I knew that when it came down to my word against his, Old Fussbudget would believe him. Because he's a deacon at his church and he and his wife are always taking in stray kids. Back when I was staying there, he got an award for being foster parent of the year."

"Yet another example of how screwed up bureaucracies can get."

She gave him a long look, appearing encouraged by the fact that Jack seemed to believe her. "But the next day his wife's diamond ring went missing," she continued. "When it was found in the bottom of the hamper in my room, they yanked me outta that home and plunked me back into juvie." She shrugged. "When I found out I was pregnant, Randy wanted me to get an abortion. When I didn't, he told his dad about the baby. That's when his dad said he'd teach me a lesson I'd never forget."

She took in a deep breath. "So I ran away and was living on the street. Until Mama Ida took me in."

Unfortunately, during his time in Seattle, Jack had heard similar sordid stories. But he'd never gotten used to them.

"Okay, here's what we're going to do. First thing on the agenda is to get tomorrow's hearing out of the way. Then we're going to take care of that creep once and for all."

Any color that had returned immediately drained from her face again. "You're not going to tell anyone about this?"

"You bet I am."

"But it'll only be my word against his." Jack could

see the scared child beneath the street-hardened exterior.

"We'll work to get corroborating testimony." His tone and his expression were meant to reassure. "You undoubtedly weren't the first girl he tried to rape."

"But—"

"You've got to trust me, Gwen."

"Maybe I do. A little. I guess." Jack thought she sounded surprised by that. "But all that stuff happened before I came to Mama Ida's. I don't want to stir things up again."

"I can understand that. But I'm also willing to bet that you don't want any other girl to suffer what you did. Or maybe even worse. We have to make sure the county doesn't put any more kids in that dangerous situation."

This time the silence was long and strained. Jack could practically hear the wheels turning around in her head.

"I hate the idea of any other girl having to put up with that shit," she said finally. "Because most of them probably wouldn't be as tough as me, so no telling what he might do to them." She heaved a deep, resigned sigh. "Okay. I'll do it."

"Good girl." This time he went ahead, followed his instincts and patted her knee in a purely paternalistic gesture. "It's going to be all right. *You're* going to be all right."

"You don't know that."

"Sure I do." He twisted the key, bringing the engine to life again.

They'd gone about a mile when she asked, "How?"

"Because someone I knew went through the same

thing when she was growing up. Unfortunately, she wasn't as quick with the knife as you were. But she got past it. And so will you."

Gwen appeared to think about that for another long silent time. "Was she my age?"

"Not when it happened. But she was just a couple years older than you when she started dealing with all those feelings she'd kept bottled up. After she told me about it."

Despite Peg's tearful protests, he'd wanted to track down the bastard who'd raped a thirteen-year-old girl and kill him with his bare hands. Fortunately, he'd avoided prison when it turned out the guy had died in a hunting accident two years earlier. Jack's only regret at the time was that pervert's death hadn't been long and excruciatingly painful.

"She must have trusted you a lot."

"I guess she must have." Even as he felt that familiar, bittersweet tug on his heart, Jack managed to slant the teenager a faint smile. "Since she married me."

∾ 8 ∾

The minute she opened the front door, Raine knew that the sheriff had not come to the house on any social call. She drew back to study Gwen, who was standing a bit behind him. Guilt shadowed the teenager's eyes.

"Let me guess. Your fingers got a little sticky again."

The girl shrugged. If her downcast face were any longer, she'd be in danger of stepping on it. "I didn't mean to. It just happened."

"No," Raine corrected firmly. Frustration made her voice sharp. "It didn't just happen, Gwen. You made the choice to steal." She turned toward Jack. "What did she take?" *Oh, please*, Raine thought, *let it be something small.*

"A pair of earrings. The tag said ten dollars, which keeps it from being a felony," he said, answering her unspoken prayer. "And proving once again that God does indeed watch out over fools and kids, she got caught before she took them out of the store. Which doesn't officially make her guilty of anything. But it's sure not going to help your grandmother's custodial case any."

Raine had already figured that out for herself. "I suppose you have to make a report?"

"Yeah." She reluctantly gave him points for looking nearly as chagrined as she felt. "The call from the dispatcher was already logged. Also, the shop owner is the mayor's daughter. I couldn't sweep this one under the rug, even if I wanted to. So, the thing we've got to decide now is what we're going to do about it."

"We?" Brows knit, Raine shot him a suspicious look. Life in the city, along with her litigious occupation, tended to make her unwilling to trust anything. Especially something as seemingly out of nature as she and Sheriff Jack O'Halloran being on the same side of any issue. "It appears you've already done your job, Sheriff. When you took Gwen into custody."

"I didn't take her into custody, dammit. I brought her home. There's a huge difference. And believe it or not, Counselor, my goal in life is not to put every teenager in Coldwater Cove behind bars. The thing is, the kid's going to need representation at her probation hearing tomorrow morning—"

"So soon?"

"Olympic County's known for its rocket docket. As you've undoubtedly noticed, Coldwater Cove isn't exactly the big city. We don't get a lot of crime, which means the court calendar isn't as jammed up as you're undoubtedly accustomed to. Gwen's case will be one of the first on tomorrow's docket."

"Damn. You're right. She needs an attorney."

Gwen turned toward her. "Why can't you be my

lawyer?" Her eyes turned harder than any sixteen-year-old's should be. "Or maybe you'd just as soon have me in jail so I'd be out of your grandmother's house."

"Of course Raine doesn't want you out of my house. And don't worry, darling, none of us will allow you to go to jail." A familiar voice entered the conversation.

Biting back a curse, Raine turned toward her grandmother. Today's sweatshirt announced her to be *Director of Everyone's Life*. Raine thought that to be about the most accurate statement she'd ever read. "I thought you'd agreed to stay in bed."

The elderly woman's initial response to that was a grunt and a steely gaze. "You and the doctor agreed. I don't remember being a party to such a pact. Besides, when I looked out the bedroom window and saw the sheriff's truck, I figured I'd better come see what was up." She shook her head as she shifted her gaze to her young charge. "I thought we'd agreed that filching things was an inappropriate way of dealing with stress, Gwen, dear."

The girl's expression got even glummer. "I forgot."

"Well, I suppose, that's excusable, under the circumstances," Ida agreed with a consoling smile that frustrated Raine all the more. Surely her grandmother didn't believe such a blatant lie? "This has been a trying time for all of us. So, the best we can do is deal with it. And move on." She turned to Raine. "Of course you'll represent Gwen."

"Dammit, Gram," Raine flared, irritated by the way she was being steamrollered again. "I've told you time and time again today, I'm not licensed in Washington."

"But you're standing up for me."

"As your granddaughter," Raine reminded her firmly. "I'll only be speaking to the court as a family member."

"Gwen's a member of this family."

"Not legally."

It was Ida's turn to shake her head in disgust. "As much trouble as your mother gave me, there are times, dear, and this is definitely one of them, when I do find myself wishing you'd inherited a bit more of her free-spiritedness."

Raine lifted her chin. "I wouldn't be where I was today if I had." Her voice remained calm, belying the inner turmoil she so often experienced when compared with her glamorous, flighty mother.

"I'm not certain where you are is exactly where you should be," Ida grumbled.

"Not that I want to interfere in a family discussion," Jack interrupted mildly, "but may I make a suggestion?"

"What?" Raine and Ida asked in unison.

"What about my cousin Dan?"

Raine blinked. "What about him?"

"He's an attorney. With a private practice. I could give him a call."

"I don't know," Raine vacillated uncharacteristically.

There was always the chance that the country lawyer could do more harm than good. She recalled Daniel Webster O'Halloran from the high school debating team. He'd certainly seemed intelligent, despite his unfortunate habit of making out on bus trips to various competitions around the state. While he might not have been the hellion his cousin was back then, the sheriff's cousin certainly hadn't lacked for female companionship, either.

"Dan's not some hick ambulance chaser," Jack said, as if reading her mind.

"I didn't say he was." But that was precisely what she'd been worried about.

"Daniel wrote up my will," Ida volunteered. "Seemed like a real smart boy."

"Writing a will isn't exactly on a par with providing a criminal defense," Raine pointed out dryly. "Or dealing with a custody case. No offense intended," she said to Jack.

"None taken." He shrugged again. "Since it was my cousin you insulted this time. But if it eases your mind any, before he returned home to hang out his shingle, Dan was a federal prosecutor in San Francisco. I figure he should be able to handle a simple case of juvenile shoplifting."

"Well." Embarrassed at having been caught in an act of negative stereotyping, Raine vaguely wished they could begin this conversation over again.

"I think you ought to call him," Ida volunteered. "After all, dear, one should never look a gifted horse in the mouth."

"He does sound like a solution to our problem," Raine allowed. "But do you think he'd be willing to take our case?" she asked Jack.

"Sure. Just let me give him a call."

Five minutes later, after sending Gwen upstairs to her room to think about the consequences of what she'd done, Raine was with Ida in the kitchen, listening to one side of a telephone conversation that didn't begin all that encouragingly.

"I didn't realize you were out of town," Jack was saying.

Her spirits sinking even lower, Raine was forced to watch him listen to his cousin on the other end of the line, his occasional "uh huhs" and nods giving her not a single clue as to the direction the conversation was taking. "Just a sec," he said finally. "I'll ask her."

He covered the mouthpiece of the kitchen wall phone and turned toward her. "He's in Anacortes running down a deadbeat dad for a client. But he says it's just a matter of waiting for the guy to show up at his favorite bar after work. So, he could meet with us later this evening, if that's okay with you."

"That sounds fine." Evening meetings were a way of life in Raine's legal world.

"Terrific." He returned to the conversation. "She says that's fine. So, how about meeting at my place when you get back to town. Say around eight? Okay. See you then." He hung up, seeming satisfied with both the situation and himself.

"Your place?" Raine inquired coolly. "What's the matter with meeting here? Or at your cousin's office?"

"Because he wants me at the meeting for background."

"*Your* office, then."

"Your grandmother's problems have already cost me one evening with my daughter this week. I figure if we get together at my place after I put her to bed, I can kill two birds with one stone."

That was admirable, Raine admitted reluctantly. If any of the men she'd worked with at Choate, Plimpton, Wells & Sullivan had shared similar feelings, none of them had ever dared state them out loud.

"I suppose, since you put it that way . . ."

"Then we're set. In fact, if you're willing to settle for spaghetti, you can eat supper with Amy and me."

Mental warning sirens sounded. Raine folded her arms. "Are you accustomed to cooking dinner for people whose cases you're working on, Sheriff?"

"Not as a rule. Since most of the people I meet in my line of work aren't the kind I'd want to spend all that much personal time with."

"I've never believed in mixing business and pleasure."

"Now why doesn't that surprise me? And for the record, Harvard, I'm not planning to seduce you with pasta and a jug of red wine, then jump your bones the minute you let your guard down. The only reason I suggested you join us for dinner is that the farm's a bit of a drive out of town—"

"You live on a farm?" Raine was distracted by that idea. There was no way she could picture this man wearing denim overalls and tilling soil. Not that he didn't look strong enough to haul around plows, or bales of hay, or whatever farmers did all day. Farming just seemed too tame.

"A Christmas tree farm," he divulged. "And since it's off the beaten track, it can be difficult to find if you're not familiar with the back roads, which is why you'd be better off making the drive in the daylight."

"I grew up here," she reminded him. "I'm certain I can manage."

Another shrug drew her gaze to his shoulders, which seemed even wider than they had last night.

Even as she assured herself that she wasn't the slightest bit interested, Raine couldn't but help notice how strong and hard his chest appeared beneath that knife edge-creased uniform shirt.

"Well," Ida said, rubbing her hands together with obvious satisfaction as he sketched them a map to the farm on a notepad he'd pulled from his pocket, "now that we've got that settled, how about joining us for lunch, Jack? I was planning to rustle up some tofu chili and cold meatloaf sandwiches."

"Thanks anyway, ma'am," he said quickly. Too quickly, Raine thought. Obviously, he'd had occasion to sample her grandmother's infamous meatloaf. "But I'd best be getting back to the office. A lot of paperwork piled up during yesterday's little drama."

With that excuse hanging in the air, he escaped out the door. Watching him leave, and thinking about the upcoming lunch, Raine was tempted to follow.

"Such a nice young man," Ida enthused as they watched him walk across the driveway with a long, masculine ground-eating stride that Raine found reluctantly pleasing. "Did you know he's a widower, Raine?"

"He mentioned that." Instead of the traditional khaki uniform trousers, he was wearing a pair of Wrangler jeans. As he climbed into the truck, the denim pulled snug, causing Raine's mouth to go a little dry. "And, although I know you can't resist meddling in other people's lives—"

"I never meddle," Raine's grandmother protested on a huff of breath.

"Of course you do. But any ideas you might have

concerning Sheriff O'Halloran and me would be a waste of time."

"Ideas?" Ida feigned innocence.

"Matchmaking ideas."

"Oh, fiddlesticks," Ida scoffed. "That thought hadn't even occurred to me." She waited just a beat, then added, "But if a woman were interested in finding herself a man, she could certainly do a great deal worse than Jack O'Halloran."

"That's a matter of opinion. Besides, my life is already full enough. I'm not in the market for a man."

"Don't be silly," Lilith, who chose that moment to enter the sunny kitchen, stated. "Every woman's in the market for a man, whether she admits it or not."

"I'm not."

Lilith gave her elder daughter a long, silent appraisal. "If that's true, darling," she decided finally, "you're in even worse shape than I'd feared."

Not wanting to get into an argument with her mother, Raine managed, just barely, to hold her tongue.

Jack was irritated as hell at himself. It wasn't bad enough that he'd shaved twice today, when he found himself actually watching out the window for Raine, he knew he was in deep, deep trouble.

"She's still got ten minutes," his cousin, who'd arrived a half hour earlier advised.

"I wasn't keeping track."

"Of course you weren't." Barely repressed laughter thickened Dan's deep voice. "You just figured it'd be good exercise to wear a path in that rug."

"She could be lost."

"True enough. But from what you've told me, I'd guess that the lady travels with a cell phone. If she has any problem, she'll undoubtedly call."

"She might not have the number."

"So, she calls 911."

His cousin's grin was wicked and all too knowing. "You know, you can be every bit as much of a pain as you were when you were a snot-nosed kid," Jack muttered.

"And you're as much of a control freak as ever. When are you going to get it through that thick Irish head that even you can't control everything and everyone around you?"

"Believe me, I've already learned that. The hard way."

"Shit." Dan scrubbed a hand down his face. "I'm sorry, Jack. I wasn't thinking."

"It's okay. For the record, you're probably right." He glanced up at the grandfather clock again. The pendulum was still swinging, its slow back-and-forth arc revealing that it hadn't really stopped. "Although controlling Raine Cantrell would undoubtedly be like trying to capture mercury. Frustrating and ultimately impossible."

"So, the chips are still there?"

"Only about the size of Mount Olympus. But then again, every once in a while there are flashes of . . ."

His voice drifted off as he saw the headlights coming up the long driveway. If he'd been annoyed with himself earlier, he was downright disgusted at the sharp rise of anticipation he felt.

"Of what?"

"Huh?" As he watched her climb out of the driver's seat, Jack wondered why he hadn't noticed how long her legs were. An image wavered tantalizingly into his mind—a provocative picture of those long slender legs wrapped around his hips.

"You were mentioning flashes?"

He shook off the jolt of pure lust and reminded himself that he'd given up tumbling into the sack with every female who caused a spike in his hormones a very long time ago.

"I just get the impression that she's not as tough as she tries to come off."

She was wearing the same slacks and sweater she'd had on earlier when he'd taken Gwen to the house and as he watched her approach the house with a smooth, feminine sway of hips, Jack considered, once again, that Raine Cantrell was a lot softer than the tough big-city lawyer image she'd put on.

When he imagined burying himself in that soft female warmth, he decided he'd definitely been too long without a woman. Perhaps he ought to pay a visit to Jenny Winger. He and the former Miss Teen Olympic County had shared some good times back in high school. Now that Jenny had recently shed her second husband, she'd gone out of her way to make it clear that she wouldn't mind picking up where they'd left off so many years ago.

Reminding himself yet again that playing with fire only resulted in burned fingers, Jack assured himself that the only reason he was hurrying to the door was to keep her from ringing the bell and waking up Amy, who'd finally, after three readings of *Where the Wild Things Are*, fallen asleep.

"I see you found the house okay," he said as he opened the huge hand-carved oak door. He nearly groaned out loud at the pitiful opening line.

"Your instructions were very clear." It had begun to rain again, just a soft mist that sparkled in her hair like scattered diamonds. The spreading yellow glow of the porch light brought out red glints in that sparkling hair Jack hadn't noticed before. She was wearing those black-framed glasses again. Jack was surprised to discover that he was a sucker for a female in glasses.

"I'm glad." He was grinning down at her like some besotted kid. It was definitely past time he got laid. Jack made a mental note to give the newly footloose and still-sexy Jenny a call.

She glanced past him. "Are you going to let me see the inside?"

Shit. "Sorry." Damning the heat he felt rising from his collar, he stepped aside, letting her into the house.

"Oh, it's lovely," she breathed with what he took for honest appreciation. She glanced around at the cozy foyer, with its oak coatrack, oak floor, and cream wallpaper edged with a border of perfectly formed evergreens. "I like the way that border brings the farm indoors. I wish I'd taken your advice to come during daylight so I could see the trees."

"Perhaps some other time," he heard himself saying.

She gave him a brief look. "Perhaps," she agreed.

He led her into the living room, unreasonably pleased when she oohed and aahed over the cedar paneling and rustic beamed ceiling. At first he'd been dead set against Peg selling off her life insurance policy to get the down payment for the house and Christmas tree farm they couldn't quite afford. But when, during those final, horrific months, she'd gotten such delight out of refurbishing the place, he'd decided going into debt was definitely worth it, if it brought his wife pleasure at a time when so much of her life was filled with pain.

After she'd died—having managed to complete the tiny foyer, the living room, and gotten started on the kitchen—he'd given no further thought to the house. Amy, after all, was too young to care about such decorating details as carpet and paint samples, and his mother, if she did disapprove of the state of the rest of his home, was wise enough not to say so.

"I would have thought your tastes would run toward modern art, brass, and Italian leather," he said.

"Actually, you've just described my apartment." She ran her fingertips down the cedar wall that gleamed in the lamplight like burnished copper. "But this is more cozy."

Raine turned her attention toward the man standing beside a tall stone fireplace that looked large enough for some past homesteader family to have cooked in. Even if she hadn't recognized him, she would have taken him for an O'Halloran. His hair was more of a sun-bleached sandy brown than his cousin's, his eyes a morning-glory blue rather than gray, and his handsome face more smoothly sculpted, but there was no mistaking that square chin and the sublime self-confidence that radiated from every male pore.

"Hello, Daniel."

He smiled with his mouth and his eyes and held out his hand. "Hi, Raine. And, it's Dan."

When his long fingers closed around hers, Raine was more than a little distressed that she didn't feel that sensual tug that his cousin could instill with just a look. She'd been hoping that her uncharacteristic response to Jack O'Halloran had merely been the result of her celibate lifestyle.

"It's great to see you again," Dan said with genuine warmth. "I wish it could have been under more pleasant circumstances. You're looking terrific, by the way."

"Thank you. It's nice to see you, as well." That was the absolute truth. She knew it was ridiculous, but Raine was grateful for a chaperone, of sorts. Dan O'Halloran's presence would ensure that she wouldn't go completely over the bend and act out any of the crazy, sensual fantasies she'd been having about Coldwater Cove's sheriff. "So you became a lawyer."

"Yep. Though I'm not a high-powered corporate one like you. I run a family practice. And speaking of family, how's Ida?"

"She gave us all quite a scare, but the doctors say she's fine. Thank heavens."

"That's good to hear. She's a super lady."

"Even though she can be one gigantic pain in the ass from time to time," Jack muttered.

Raine turned back toward him. "I should be offended by that."

He lifted a dark brow. "But?"

"But it's hard to get up on my high horse when you're right."

They all had a little laugh over that. Then, after Jack had served a coffee that Raine found surprisingly tasty, they settled down to business.

An hour later, she'd been forced to reexamine her

feelings about Daniel Webster O'Halloran. "You're very good."

"You sound surprised." His smile held not a hint of annoyance at the idea she'd obviously misjudged him.

"I suppose I am." She ran her fingers up and down the barrel of her pen. "I have to admit that when Jack first mentioned you, I thought that since Coldwater Cove is such a small town—"

"I'd not only have a small practice, but a small, provincial mind, as well."

"Yes." There was no point in denying it. "And I'm sorry. As a litigator who spends a great many hours studying jury prospects, I should know better than to prejudge anyone."

He shrugged shoulders that were as wide as his cousin's. Another O'Halloran trait, she thought as her gaze slid to Jack, who looked even more substantial than usual in his black fisherman's sweater and dark jeans. And, dammit, more appealing.

"You don't have to apologize, Raine." Dan's easy voice drew her attention back to their conversation. "There was a time when I would have felt the same way. Which is why, after I graduated Stanford law, I stayed in the Bay Area. San Francisco might not be New York, but it sure seemed like Oz to a kid from Coldwater Cove."

Dan O'Halloran was not only intelligent, he was a genuinely nice man. The type of man any sensible woman would find appealing. Unfortunately, from her reaction to his more annoying cousin, Raine was discovering that she wasn't nearly as sensible as she'd thought.

"Jack said you worked in the prosecutor's office?"

"Yeah."

They passed a few pleasant minutes sharing war stories and lawyer jokes. For the first time since she'd arrived in Coldwater Cove, Raine relaxed and began to enjoy herself. Of course, she thought, Dan was a lot easier to talk with than his cousin.

"So," Dan wrapped up another story, "After we'd determined that my client had been unconscious when she was pulled from the car, I asked her what had happened next. 'Mr. Abernathy gave me artificial insemination,' she answered. 'You know, mouth to mouth.'"

Raine laughed at that. Jack, she noticed, did not. In fact, now that she thought about it, he'd barely said two words since they finished talking about Gwen's case.

"I guess I'd better get going." Dan stood up. "I still have a brief to write before I hit the sack."

Raine rose as well. Jack stayed sprawled on the overstuffed green-and-cream-dotted-chintz covered sofa. "Well, I certainly appreciate you helping out with this." She extended her hand to Dan. "I'm feeling much more positive about Gwen's case."

"You should." His fingers curled around hers. "Actually, there wasn't much reason to be too concerned in the first place." He glanced over at his cousin, who merely gave him a bland look in return. "I'm surprised Jack didn't tell you."

"Tell me what?"

"That we've got an in with the judge."

"Let me guess. Judge Wally will be hearing Gwen's case."

His eyes twinkled, his lips curved upward in another one of those woman-melting smiles that while appealing, failed to move Raine on any primal level. "None other. You know the old adage: A good lawyer knows the law. A great lawyer knows the judge."

He flashed a grin toward Jack. "Don't bother seeing me out, cuz. I know the way."

Jack's response to that was a grunt.

With that Dan was gone, leaving Raine and Jack alone.

"Well," she said. "I suppose I'd better be leaving as well."

"I suppose so."

His tone was gruff and he sounded definitely irritated. "Are you going to tell me what I did?"

"I don't have any idea what you mean."

"Don't you?" They were standing toe to toe, her looking up at him, him looking down at her. "I may have misjudged your cousin, but I can certainly tell when someone's ticked off. So, do you want to tell me what I did to offend you? Or are you going to just continue to sulk?"

"Sulk? I never sulk."

"Well, for a man who never sulks, you're certainly doing a pretty good imitation of it, Sheriff."

"You realize, that most women wouldn't be so quick to insult a man."

"I'm not most women."

"No. You're definitely not." He tucked her hair behind her ear, then slowly trailed his thumb around her jaw. "You and Dan sure seemed to hit it off."

The edge was back in his voice. *Could he possibly be jealous?* "He's a nice man. And we have a lot in common."

"Yeah. You both have incredible opportunities to screw up other people's lives."

"That's a rather unattractive accusation."

"You can't deny that you're always looking for the angle. The loophole. Any way of putting the facts together that'll make your case persuasive to the court or jury. Even if the truth gets lost in the process."

"I hadn't realized you'd attended law school, Sheriff."

"I didn't. But if you spend enough time in courtrooms you catch on pretty quick. Don't they teach you to argue both sides of a case in law school?"

"Well, of course, but the law is incredibly complex. Arguing both sides teaches the implications of using one rule, as opposed to another."

"Whatever, the way I see it, law schools are designed to turn out lawyers uncommitted to any ultimate personal values. The kind who can indulge in intellectual and moral acrobatics in the courtroom because clients want contentious, razor-toothed sharks who'll perform whatever distasteful deeds it takes to win. Lawyers willing to prostitute their legal skills and beliefs to represent clients they might have, at one time, before their heads got all screwed up with power games and courtroom battles, found repugnant."

Those were the most words he'd strung together since she'd met him. They were also decidedly unflattering. "Why don't you say what you really think, Sheriff?"

"Are you saying I'm wrong?"

She paused, giving the matter honest consideration. "I suppose that in some ways, your description might apply to some litigators I know. But it certainly doesn't fit me. And surely you don't believe your cousin's unethical?"

"Of course not. But Dan's the exception."

"Not the only one."

He skimmed a look over her face. "Point taken."

"Besides," she continued, "law doesn't come wrapped in neat, tidy little packages. Just because I can see shades of gray along with the black and white—"

"Now see, that's where you and I are different, Harvard. Because I tend to stick to the black-and-white view. Good guys and bad guys. We cops like to keep things simple."

"That may be true for some cops. But not you. You're more complex."

He lifted a brow. "Think so?"

"I know so. Despite all the trouble they've caused you, you treated those girls with kid gloves."

"Unfortunately, the courts and citizen review groups tend to frown on police brutality these days."

"That's not the reason. You didn't think of them as just delinquents, you thought of them as individual kids with problems. You saw the grays, Sheriff. Whether you want to admit it or not."

He appeared to think about that for a moment. Then, as his gaze settled on her mouth, Raine drew in a breath.

"Well, whatever our individual take on jurisprudence, Dan's definitely right about one thing."

"What's that?" Once again the atmosphere between them had become intensely charged. Raine imagined she could feel the electricity humming beneath her skin.

"About it being late. You probably should be getting home as well."

"I suppose you're right." From the way he was still looking at her, like a man looks at a woman he wants, she suspected it was not his first choice either. When she felt herself responding to that hot gaze, like a woman responds to a man she *wants* to want her, Raine tried to remind herself that giving into these feelings would not be at all wise.

A light mist that was not quite rain had begun to fall. All too aware of the man walking her out to her car, Raine barely noticed it. A foghorn tolled out in the foggy bay; somewhere a dog let out a long, sad howl.

"Aaron Olson's beagle-terrier mix," Jack murmured.

"What?"

"The dog. The night shift usually logs about three complaints a month about the mutt."

"Oh." Raine was amazed either of them could hear anything over the hammering of her heart. "Well," she said, trying for a briskly professional tone that failed miserably, "I suppose I'll see you at the courthouse tomorrow, then."

"I suppose so."

When she would have opened the driver's door, Jack curled his fingers around her shoulder and turned her back toward him. "No. Not yet." He skimmed a thumb around her uplifted jaw.

Unable to help herself, Raine shuddered in response.

"You shivered."

"I did not."

"Liar." Without taking his eyes from hers, he

slipped his hand beneath the back of her sweater, splaying his fingers on flesh that felt as if it was burning up. "You did it again."

"If I did, it's only because I'm cold." She lied again.

"Perhaps we can do something about that."

"Jack . . ." The sighed word was more invitation than complaint. She found herself leaning toward him, felt her lips part in anticipation.

Before Raine could remind herself, yet again, that this was *not* a good idea, Jack lowered his mouth to hers.

❧ 9 ❧

Prepared for power, Raine was surprised by the gentleness of what was more promise than propei kiss, as the entire world narrowed down to the drugging feel of Jack O'Halloran's lips against hers. It was as if he was the first man to kiss her, the first man she'd ever *wanted* to kiss her.

As Jack deepened the kiss, degree by intoxicating degree, Raine felt a golden heat flow through her, making her feel as if she'd swallowed the sun. They could have stood there in the cool night mist, Jack kissing Raine, her kissing him back for a minute, an hour, or an eternity.

Desire uncurled inside her and as she found herself wanting more, Raine struggled to remember that she'd never been the type of woman who indulged in one-night stands or brief sexual flings. She was only going to be here in Coldwater Cove one more day. Which definitely precluded giving into temptation where this man was concerned.

As if possessing the power to read her mind, Jack slowly lifted his head, breaking the exquisite contact. "There you go. Thinking again." He smoothed the lines in her forehead with a fingertip. "Trying to figure all the angles."

"I can't help it." Until meeting Jack O'Halloran, Raine had never regretted being so analytical. "I'm a lawyer. That's what I do."

"Not now." When she would have dragged her hand through her damp hair, he caught it and kissed her fingertips, one at a time. "Not with me."

Raine felt as if she were melting. "This is impossible," she complained weakly.

Was it so wrong to want order in her life? Rules? Structure? Until a few days ago, Raine wouldn't have even had been asking herself this question. And now, distressingly, she couldn't come up with a quick or easy answer.

"You're probably right," he surprised her by agreeing. "But that hasn't stopped me from thinking about it since you first plowed into my crime scene."

"You didn't like me."

"Can you blame me? You'd been going out of your way to make my job—and my life—harder on a day that was already rough enough. You were, Harvard, pretty much a pain in the ass, which was only one of the reasons why I didn't want to get involved with you. Hell, I'm not sure I do now."

Raine felt a prick of wounded feminine pride and tried to remind herself that she had been thinking exactly the same thing. "That's not very complimentary."

"You want compliments?" He leaned closer, bent his head again.

"I didn't say that." She backed up a step. "I was merely making an observation."

"You know," he said conversationally, "when I was a kid I used to like to walk along the coast and look for flotsam from old shipwrecks. I had a pretty good collection of Japanese glass floats, some bleached boards—one with the part of a ship's name on it— and when I was sixteen, I unearthed part of a ship's figurehead from a pile of driftwood that had washed up on shore near Cape Disappointment.

"It was just her head and shoulders, but I took her home and hung her up on my wall. Late at night, I'd lie in bed and think of all the sea tales about how, when a ship was about to go down, the sailors would hear singing in the wind. Of course it would turn out to be the song of mermaids, luring them to their doom."

His eyes turned weary, his voice resigned. "That's pretty much how I felt about you the other night while we were driving up to Hurricane Ridge."

Over the years, Raine had been described as opinionated, stubborn, argumentative, and, on one memorable occasion, a rebuffed would-be suitor had accused her of being encased in enough ice to cover Jupiter. The one thing no man had ever accused her of being was a *siren*. That description fit Lilith. Not her. She'd spent her entire life molding herself into a woman who was the polar opposite of her glamourous, seductive mother.

She drew in a breath, expelled it. "I can't decide whether to be insulted or flattered."

"Why don't you sleep on it?" When he touched his mouth to the palm of the hand he was still holding, on some distant level Raine was vaguely amazed that her skin didn't sizzle.

Then, when he ruffled her hair in a friendly, casual gesture, Raine decided that as devastating as those kisses had been, Jack O'Halloran was even more dangerous when he was being friendly.

She'd have to stay on her guard tomorrow, she reminded herself as she drove back through the deserted streets, her headlights shimmering on the wet asphalt. Her carefully planned life was on track. She knew where she was going and exactly how to get there. She'd worked hard from childhood to become the cool, logical, dispassionate woman she was; she was on the verge of achieving everything she wanted. Sheriff Jack O'Halloran, as sexy as he might admittedly be, was simply a complication she couldn't afford.

Without warning, she was spinning back in time, metamorphosing into a too tall, too skinny, too serious girl with heavy glasses, freckles across her nose and a mouth full of metal braces that would have foiled the most intrepid teenage boy from kissing her. Not that many had been inclined to try. Which had been just fine with her. At least that's what she'd always told herself. Until Jack O'Halloran's kiss had tilted her world on its axis.

Dammit, what was the point in being so strong and confident in the rest of her life, if she was going to melt whenever she got within kissing distance of this man? What had happened to Xena? Where was the intrepid, take-no-prisoners female warrior princess when you needed her?

Raine asked herself that question all the way back to Ida's house. Unfortunately, when she pulled into the driveway, she was no closer to figuring out the answer than she'd been when she'd escaped the surprisingly charming old farmhouse and a man who, if she let him, could disrupt her life.

By the time she climbed between the sheets that smelled of the Mrs. Stewart's bluing that Ida had always added to the wash, Raine was forced to admit that somehow, when she hadn't been paying attention, Sheriff Jack O'Halloran had already become a major distraction.

Go to sleep, she instructed herself firmly. *You've got to be sharp in court tomorrow morning. Forget him.*

Much, much later, as she lay on her back, looking up at the swirls in the white plaster ceiling while a soft predawn silver-and-rose light slipped beneath the window shade, Raine realized that forgetting Coldwater Cove's sheriff was a great deal easier said than done.

After a restless night, Raine met everyone downstairs. She was relieved that the girls had followed her instructions to dress as demurely as possible. Dressed in a stiffly starched black-and-white jumper, Gwen resembled a cross between a pregnant Flying Nun and Mary Poppins.

"You look lovely," she reassured the girl, who was worried that her obvious pregnancy might hurt their cause.

Raine then turned toward her grandmother who was dressed in a vintage cranberry-hued Jackie Kennedy–style suit that smelled vaguely of mothballs. A pillbox hat in the same color perched atop the upswept gray bun like an egret's nest crowning a Sitka spruce snag. "You look pretty snazzy, too."

"I had to get this out of the attic." Ida ran her

hand down the skirt, smoothing nonexistent wrinkles. Raine noticed that her hands were trembling. She couldn't recall ever seeing her grandmother this nervous. "Don't have much need to dress up in Coldwater Cove."

"Well, isn't it fortunate it's back in style," Raine said with a reassuring smile her grandmother didn't return.

"Did you call the school?" Gwen asked suddenly.

"The school?"

"To tell them we're not coming. I don't want to get an unexcused absence on my permanent record."

Not wanting to upset the girls before their court date, Raine refrained from pointing out that holding law enforcement officers from several counties at bay for hours undoubtedly hadn't done much for Gwen's permanent record.

"Gwen's in the running for valedictorian," Shawna revealed.

"Really?" Raine had just picked up the phone to dial the number of the school that her grandmother had written at one time on the small slate board above the wall phone.

"You don't have to look so surprised," Gwen complained. "I said I wanted to be a doctor."

"That's true. But I also seem to recall something about living on the street and panhandling on the ferry."

"Oh, that. I didn't drop out for very long. Mama Ida got me a tutor and since I was ahead of my class anyway, it didn't take me all that long to catch up."

"Well." Raine gave her a long look, seeing the girl through new eyes. This entire misadventure was turning out to be just one surprise after another.

"I'm very impressed." She wondered how, if Gwen decided to keep this baby, she thought she'd be able to keep her grades up while dealing with the demands of a newborn.

The principal passed along the word that everyone at the school was pulling for Gwen to do well in her hearing today. Obviously, Raine thought as she hung up, she'd been guilty of stereotyping yet again.

"Well, that's taken care of." She glanced around. "Where's Lilith?"

"Here I am," a silvery voice trilled from the doorway. Raine turned and viewed her mother, dressed in a flowing silk skirt, matching tunic, and ballet slippers with ribbons that laced up her still-shapely calves. The hue—a watercolor swirl of color blending through shades of blue from turquoise to cobalt—was an attractive foil for her silver hair and made her eyes appear even bluer. While not at all businesslike, Lilith's attire would do, Raine decided. Except for one thing.

"The crystals have to go." Lilith had obviously gone for broke. Pink and violet amethysts, a smoky quartz interspersed with green tourmaline, amber, and other stones Raine couldn't recognize hung from her earlobes, adorned her neck, wrists, and, Raine noticed with a glance back down at the ballet slippers, even her ankles.

"Oh, I couldn't possibly go to court without them, darling." Lilith lifted a hand, which sported a milky crystal the size of Vermont, to the sparkling gems at her throat. "They're vital for focusing my inner energy."

Raine tried not to roll her eyes. "I don't care. I

refuse to allow you to enter that courtroom looking like Carlsbad Caverns."

Lilith's ruby lips turned downward in a pouty moue. "That's not a very nice thing to say to your mother, Raine."

"That's exactly the point. I'm not your daughter today. We can't admit it to the court, but I'm acting as Gram's attorney. The deal was that everyone was to do exactly what I say."

Lilith tilted her head and studied Raine silently. "Well," she said on a little huff of breath, "far be it from me to impede our defense." With that, she flounced from the room, returning moments later without the rocks.

"I'm not taking these off, Raine," she warned as she saw Raine taking in the earrings that had replaced the crystals. The onyx beads on the right earlobe nearly brushed her shoulder while an embossed shining silver replica of a Buddhist prayer wheel hung from the left. "They're shamanistic. You may not believe in a power higher than you, but the way I see it, Ida and these poor girls are going to need all the help they can get."

"All right." They were due in court in fifteen minutes; there was simply no time to argue any further. "But if you're called to testify, I don't want you saying a single word about psychic energy, chakras, shamans, vortexes, or any of that other New Age nonsense."

"I would have expected a daughter of mine to have a more open mind," Lilith complained.

Not even wanting to get into a discussion about mothers and daughters, Raine merely shook her head, picked up her briefcase, and turned her mind to what it did best—honing her upcoming legal argument.

If Raine was nervous about the importance of this court appearance, she was downright appalled by the way her heart skipped a few vital beats when she viewed Jack O'Halloran standing outside the courtroom, talking with his cousin.

Raine and Dan exchanged a greeting. When he turned away for a brief talk with the group regarding their testimony, Raine had no choice but to acknowledge Jack.

"Good morning, Sheriff." It took an effort, but she managed to keep her tone professionally brisk even as her heart continued to go pittypat in a most unprofessional way.

"Counselor." He smiled charmingly. "Sleep well?"

"Absolutely," she lied.

"It's the fresh air," he said. "Makes you sleep like a baby." Gray eyes skimmed over her in a thoroughly masculine perusal. "Nice suit." He pushed away from the wall and moved a little closer. "Woman with a suit like that could probably conquer the world."

He took two more steps forward. Raine took one back. "It's good for taking on the road. The material is three-seasonal, and the color goes with anything."

"Mmmm." He was still looking at her in that silent, thoughtful way. "Gray flannel always makes me think of that old movie," he said. "With Gregory Peck."

"I don't think I know it." He was close. Too close for comfort. Definitely too close for courthouse propriety.

"The Man in the Gray Flannel Suit. Great flick from the fifties and one of Peck's best. It's sort of a morality play with a business plot. You should see it some time."

"I'll make a point of it," she said coolly. "What do you think you're doing?" she hissed when he rubbed her flannel lapel between his thumb and index finger.

"Yep, great flick," he repeated distractedly, making Raine wonder if he'd even heard her question or simply, in his own hardheaded way, was choosing to ignore it. "Flannel and silk." The gray in his eyes deepened as he took another unnervingly long perusal of her tailored white silk blouse. Didn't the man ever blink? "That's quite an intriguing contrast."

Reminding herself of all her late-night resolutions, she slapped his hand away. "Are you hitting on me, again, Sheriff?"

"Hitting on you?" he repeated, as if trying the words out might provide a clue to whatever was happening here. "No. I don't think so."

She heard the slight rasp of his thumb against the cloth of her lapel again and reminded herself of the way he'd placed one of his large hands on Gwen's shoulder yesterday. That gesture hadn't been the slightest bit seductive, leading her to believe that Jack O'Halloran was merely a toucher. She was not.

"Next time I hit on you, Harvard, you won't have to ask. You'll know." His smile charmed yet again, but his dark, intense eyes made her mouth go dry.

Raine was trying to think of something, anything to say to that provocative challenge when she felt a tap on her shoulder.

"What is it?" she ground out as she spun around.

Dan held up both hands. "I just thought we ought to be getting into the courtroom."

"That's a grand idea." She stalked off, causing the rest of the family to nearly run to keep up.

The two men watched her walk away, her high heels contributing to a sexy swing of her hips beneath the gray flannel skirt.

"She may still have the chips on her shoulders," Dan murmured. "But damn, the woman does have dynamite legs."

"You won't get any argument from me on that," Jack agreed.

Dan slanted a look toward his cousin. "If a man was looking for a woman—"

"Which I'm not."

"Don't you think this grieving widower act has gone on long enough?"

"It's not an act."

"Hell, I know that." Dan swiped a frustrated hand through his hair. "But it's not natural, Jack. Peg's been gone, what, two years now?"

"Twenty-two months," Jack said tightly. He'd been sitting beside her hospital bed that morning, holding her slender hand in both of his when she'd finally slipped away from him. "But, since I've recently come to the conclusion that you may have a point, you might as well know that I'm thinking of asking Jenny Winger out to dinner."

"Christ, you can't be serious. She may be gorgeous, in a big hair, big teeth sort of way, but all Jenny ever talks about is her glorious reign as Miss Teen Olympic County."

"So?" Jack shrugged. "I'm not looking for conversation."

"It's not going to work, you know," a new voice entered the conversation. Both men glanced over at Cooper Ryan, who'd obviously arrived at the courtroom in time to hear the exchange.

"What's not going to work?" Jack asked.

"Trying to hide from your feelings for one woman by spending time with another."

"That's not what I'm doing."

"Isn't it?" both Cooper and Dan said together. They exchanged knowing grins.

"Believe me," Cooper advised, "I've been where you are, Jack, and I can tell you that you're headed down a rocky road. But it can also be one helluva trip."

"So why aren't you taking it with Lilith? Since it was more than a little obvious the other night that you two left a lot unsettled."

Cooper rubbed his jaw as he watched the covey of females disappear into the courtroom. "True enough. But I have every intention of settling those issues once and for all."

"Brave man," Dan murmured. "As charming as the lady is, I imagine she'd be a handful."

"She can be that," Cooper agreed. "And more. But the way I figure it, nothing worth having comes easy. You know, though I'd hate to think that looking back is a sign of impending old age, it's damn true what they say about the things you regret being things you didn't do. I let youthful pride rule my behavior back when we were kids."

His square jaw firmed. "As she recently reminded me during that little ruckus up on Hurricane Ridge,

I was the first man in Lilith Lindstrom's life. And it doesn't matter how many guys she's known since then, or how many last names she's acquired. Because I have every intention of being the last."

Jack and Dan wished the older man luck. As they entered the courtroom of his longtime friend, Jack decided that if the sparks he'd witnessed between Cooper Ryan and Lilith Lindstrom the other night were any indication, people in Coldwater Cove weren't going to have to wait until the Fourth of July for a display of fireworks.

He may have left his ball playing days behind him, but Judge Wallace Cunningham looked like a jock. His face was darkly tanned, his brown hair had been streaked by the sun, and beneath the black robe Raine could tell that his shoulders were nearly as broad as his old teammate's.

Surprisingly, he also seemed to have a quick legal mind, rapidly cutting through the courtroom legalese to get to the bottom line.

"Well, young woman," he boomed, looking down at Gwen, who was currently standing before him. Her face was ashen and from her seat behind the railing, Raine watched the girl twisting her hands together behind her back. "While I suspect that you had every intention of leaving the store"—he glanced down at the casework his bailiff had provided—"Linda's Beads and Baubles, with those earrings, it's my guess that you also planned to get caught.

"After all, it's always easier to be the one to cut your losses, rather than wait around and have the rug pulled out from under you. Isn't it?"

"Yessir," Gwen said in a low, miserable voice that

had Raine reaching out to take her mother's hand on one side, Ida's on the other. "Your Honor," the teenager corrected quickly, obviously recalling Raine's earlier instruction.

Dan had put forth a sound defense, yet even though she doubted she could have done better, Raine worried it might not be enough. While juvenile criminal law was not her area of expertise, there had been times over the past years when she was required to appear in court to defend the rebellious offspring of one of the firm's wealthier clients.

It hadn't taken her long to discover that in big cities, with their overburdened jails, judges tended to overlook lesser juvenile offenses. While small towns, on the other hand, tended to apply the weight of the law more heavily, to send a message to other kids who might be tempted off the straight and narrow.

Raine had been relieved when Jack, looking like an outrageously macho model for a law enforcement recruiting poster in his stiffly starched uniform with the five-sided star pinned to his broad chest, managed to help their case even as he stuck to the facts. While technically Gwen hadn't been guilty of shoplifting, circumstantial evidence—like those earrings in her pocket—didn't look good. Especially for a kid who was already on probation for a series of similar charges.

"I played a little ball back when I was younger," Judge Wally was telling Gwen. "So, I know, just a bit, how it feels to be yanked from place to place. I wasn't exactly pro-quality," he confided. "I was a step too slow to make it into the Big Leagues, so I spent most of my less-than-brilliant career being traded throughout the minors—Tacoma, Springfield, Albuquerque.

"It got to be a drag, so I accepted reality and finally threw in the towel after three years when I was about to be traded to Midland, Texas. Of course that's nothing compared to the instability you've experienced."

He rubbed his chin thoughtfully. "As sorry as I am about what you've gone through over the years, I don't think I'd be sending the right message to the other kids in the county if I give you a pass on this." That earned a soft moan from Gwen and a gasp from Ida. The other girls looked on the verge of bursting into tears.

"However," Judge Wally continued, "I can't see how moving you to a juvenile detention facility would be beneficial. So, here's what we're going to do." He leaned back and began swiveling his tall black leather chair. "After your baby's born, I'm sentencing you to three months community service, the details of which you'll work out with Ms. Kelly." He nodded toward Old Fussbudget, who was seated nearby, her rigid spine making it look as if someone had put a steel rod up the back of her navy blue suit jacket. "I'm also requiring weekly counseling sessions during this time. Again, the details to be handled by your probation officer."

He leaned forward, his friendly expression turning judicially stern. "If you land back here in my courtroom, or any other of my colleague's courtrooms, I will immediately revoke these conditions and you'll find yourself down on your knees scrubbing toilets in juvie so fast your head will spin. Is that clear, young lady?"

"Yessir. Your Honor." Gwen's frail voice was choked with tears; whether from fear or relief, Raine couldn't tell.

"Fine." That matter settled, he turned to his bailiff. "So, what's the next case, Marian?"

Back in the hallway, hugs were exchanged and more than a few surreptitious tears shed. Apparently swinging on hormones, Gwen was both weeping and laughing.

"Thank you," Raine said as she shook hands with Dan. "You were terrific."

"It wasn't that big a deal."

"Not to you, perhaps. But to Gwen and my grandmother, it was more important than any Supreme Court case."

Raine had been surprised at how stressful it had proven to be to be forced to sit and watch and hope. Law school hadn't taught her the tumultuous range of emotions you suffered through as you watched a virtual stranger fight your battle for you. It was as if Dan had held their entire lives in his hands.

Raine wondered if this was how her clients felt, then decided probably not. Her cases dealt with business law and there was certainly a great deal more to life than business. When that stunning revelation struck like a blow from behind, Raine decided she was really going to have to give the idea more thought. Later, when things settled down.

"Something wrong?"

Still focused on the idea that there may actually be a world outside her legal circles, Raine realized her mind had been drifting again. A dangerous thing for it to be indulging in right before she was due to argue Ida's guardianship case.

"Not really," she said, trying to dismiss that sudden flash of insight. "I was just thinking of something."

"It must have not been all that pleasant."

"It was just a little . . . ," she searched for the word, ". . . surprising."

"That's what I love about the law," Dan said with a winning smile that was a near duplicate of his cousin's. "It's chock full of surprises." He glanced over at the little group who were headed down the hall toward the Pepsi machine, the girls trailing behind Ida like a trio of downy ducklings. "I wish I could stick around for Ida's case, but this deposition in Forks has been scheduled for a month, and—"

"Don't worry." Raine assured herself that after saving Odessa Oil millions of dollars in profits, a simple guardianship argument should be a snap. "I can handle it."

"I've not a single doubt of that." He flashed her another of those warm and winning grins that unfortunately didn't strum a single feminine chord. "Take care, Counselor. Maybe we'll bump into each other in a courtroom one of these days."

Since she was going to be returning to Manhattan on the red-eye tonight, the possibility of that was slim to none. But Raine politely agreed, thanked him again, then sat down on a bench in the hallway to go over her argument one final time.

Unfortunately, their luck didn't hold. Raine knew they were in trouble the minute they'd entered the courtroom when Lilith drew in a sharp breath.

"Oh, no."

"What?" Raine whispered, not wanting to disrupt

the proceedings going on at the front of the courtroom.

"I know the judge."

Raine thought back to the old joke Dan had tossed at her last night about a good lawyer knowing the law, but a great lawyer knowing the judge. Unfortunately, if the bleak expression on her mother's face was anything to go on, they weren't going to experience the same advantage they'd enjoyed with Judge Wally.

"And?" she asked, her sharper-than-usual tone inviting elaboration.

"We went to school together. In fact, we used to be best friends."

"Used to be?"

"Well, it's a little difficult to explain."

"Try." It was more order than request.

"It's complicated." Lilith shrugged her silk-clad shoulders. "But Barbara accused me of stealing Jimmy Young away from her."

Raine assured herself that a thirty-two-year-old teenage dispute over a boyfriend certainly wouldn't affect their case. Not after all these years. The woman in question had graduated from law school. Not only had she been well-versed in the tenets of justice, she'd achieved the honored black robe of judicial prudence. Besides, from her name—Barbara Patterson-Young—it appeared that the judge and the faithless Jimmy Young had managed to patch things up.

Unfortunately, even as Raine was giving herself that little pep talk, Judge Patterson-Young glanced up. Her gaze unerringly zeroed straight in on Lilith like a heat-seeking missile. The hatred in those hazel eyes was unmistakable.

"Great," Raine muttered as they sat down on one of the back benches. "This is just great. She hasn't forgotten you."

"Barbara always was one to hold a grudge. But I didn't exactly steal Jimmy, Raine. She'd already left him to go off to college in Hawaii."

She might not have dated all that much in high school, but even Raine understood that in the world of teenage romance, the going-away-to-college excuse was a mere technicality. The guilty look in her mother's not-so-vivid eyes told her that Lilith knew it too.

"I thought Cooper Ryan was your high school boyfriend," Raine hissed.

"This was later. After Cooper was drafted."

Terrific. The love of her life was about to be shipped off to Vietnam and Lilith was stateside, blithely stealing the boyfriend of a girl who'd grow up to be the judge who'd hear the most important case in Ida Lindstrom's life.

"This is just goddamn great," she muttered again as she retrieved the aspirin bottle from her briefcase.

The judge had returned her attention to the case in front of her. But Raine could feel her antipathy linger like heat lightning hovering on a nearby horizon.

✑10✑

Raine had barely gotten into her opening statement, when BANG!—the judge pounded her gavel, silencing her in midsentence.

"If you're going to keep using those big words, Counselor," Judge Patterson-Young said with heavy sarcasm, "I'll be forced to move this case to the city. Where they indulge in that type of legal gobbledegook."

Raine felt her blood rise, but suspecting the judge would just love to slap her with a contempt charge, she relentlessly schooled herself to calm.

Her argument hadn't been wrapped in legal jargon. Even so, Raine took extra care to keep it short, sweet, and simple. She'd also arranged for Ida's neighbors, her doctor, and the pastor of the Lutheran church Ida had attended for more than half a century to speak on her grandmother's behalf. Even Jack testified that at no time during the standoff had the girls posed a threat to themselves or others.

But as each of Coldwater Cove's sterling citizens

provided glowing testimony to Dr. Ida Lindstrom's stamina, her lifetime of community service, and her generous heart, Raine knew she could have had a choir of gilt-winged angels take that witness stand and it wouldn't make a bit of difference. Because the judge had made up her mind the moment Lilith entered the courtroom.

"It is the court's opinion," Judge Patterson-Young stated after all that testimony, "that Dr. Lindstrom, her admirable reputation for being a caregiver not withstanding, is not capable of handling three teenage girls. Especially ones who have been in trouble with the law.

"On the other hand, since two of the girls are already scheduled to move out of Dr. Lindstrom's home, I'm not inclined to take the third from what just may be one of the few stable environments she's known. Especially since she's due to deliver any day. However, if the teenager is to remain in the Lindstrom home, I'll require the presence of a responsible adult. A younger one than Dr. Lindstrom."

Ida tugged on Raine's sleeve. "You should remind that girl that age discrimination is against the law," she hissed.

"Let me handle this." Raine put a firm hand on her grandmother's shoulder to keep her from leaping up to protest.

"If the court pleases," she said carefully, "there *is* another adult living in the home."

"Good try, Counselor." If a snake could smile, Raine thought, it would look exactly like Judge Barbara Patterson-Young. "But I doubt if there's a judge in this county who'd be inclined to declare Lilith Lindstrom Cantrell Townsend"—she spat out the lengthy name as if it had a bad aftertaste—"to be a responsible adult."

Raine privately agreed. As Lilith's daughter and Ida's sort-of attorney, she felt obliged to answer the unflattering charge against her mother. "May I ask on what the court is basing that opinion?"

The cold, reptilian smile disappeared, replaced by a warning glare. "It's not your place to ask the questions, Counselor."

"I understand that, Your Honor. But if the court is judging my mother by some past behavior—"

"That's enough!"

BANG! The gavel slammed down again, making Raine decide the judge had missed her calling. The unpleasant woman would have made a terrific hanging judge back in the days of the Wild West.

"Any further argument from you, Ms. Cantrell, and I'll be forced to hold you in contempt."

"If it pleases the court," Raine spoke carefully, reminding herself that she wouldn't be able to do anyone any good if she landed behind bars in Sheriff O'Halloran's Olympic County jail, "I'm not here in the capacity of Dr. Lindstrom's attorney today. I'm merely a concerned family member, speaking on my grandmother's behalf."

"You went to law school, didn't you?"

"Yes, but—"

"Harvard, right?"

"That's right."

"And you passed the bar?"

"Yes, Your Honor." Raine suspected she knew where the judge was headed with this line of questioning.

"And you became licensed to practice?"

"In New York, yes."

The judge ignored the pointed qualification. "Well, in my book that makes you Dr. Lindstrom's attorney. Unless," she tacked on evilly, "you'd prefer to have your grandmother address the court herself?"

"No, your honor. I don't believe that's necessary in this case."

"You're right." The judge surprised Raine by agreeing on something. "Because it wouldn't change my ruling. I'm allowing the girls to stay in Dr. Lindstrom's home—"

She was interrupted by Gwen's and Renee's jubilant screams. They began jumping up and down and hugging each other.

BANG! The gavel crashed down again. "There will be no disruptions in my courtroom!"

Oh, yes, Raine confirmed, refusing to cringe even though the sharp sound felt like an ax blade to her aching head. Definitely a hanging judge. She had no problem picturing Barbara Patterson-Young smiling with grim satisfaction as a Stetson-wearing sheriff— who looked discomfortingly like Jack O'Halloran— put a thick rope around Lilith's neck.

The room instantly went silent. The girls obediently sat down again. "That's better." The judge nodded. "I'm setting a one-month trial period, during which time Dr. Lindstrom will be given an opportunity to prove herself up to the task of guardianship. I am also requiring that an adult other than Dr. Lindstrom's daughter reside in the home during this time."

As everyone turned to look directly at her, Raine had a sinking feeling she knew what adult they all had in mind.

"Your Honor," she protested, once again feeling as if she were walking across a legal minefield, "I can't possibly leave my law practice for a month."

"Fine. Then the three probationers in question are returned to Ms. Kelly's control. "

Ida was on her feet in a flash. "You can't do that! Why, in case you've forgotten, Babs Patterson, I just happen to be the doctor who treated your chicken pox when you were five."

BANG!

On a roll, Ida ignored the sharp warning crack of the gavel. "I also got rid of your acne when you came crying to me that no boy would ask you out, and don't forget that I was the one who wrote your first prescription for birth control pills when you came home for Christmas vacation your freshman year of college and wanted to sleep with Edna Young's boy Jimmy."

BANG! BANG!

"Gram!" Raine grabbed hold of Ida's shoulder once again and forced her grandmother back down onto the bench. "Shut up."

"It's not fair, Raine," Ida protested, her voice ringing out over the laughter and buzz of excited conversation in the courtroom. "The only reason she's doing this is to get back at your mother for having sex with her boyfriend the minute her back was turned."

BANG! BANG! BANG!

Raine slapped a hand over her grandmother's mouth. "I apologize, Your Honor. It's just that Dr. Lindstrom feels very strongly about this issue."

"I understand that, Counselor." Scarlet flags were waving in the judge's cheeks. Raine figured they were sunk. "And it's only because of my longtime affection for your grandmother that I'm going to overlook her outburst. This time," she tacked on, shooting Ida another icy warning glare. Ida, uncowed, set her chin and glared back.

"However," the judge continued, "there's no room for emotion in the law. The fact that your grandmother obviously cares about these teenagers has no effect on my ruling."

She couldn't do it, even if she wanted to. Three days was one thing, Raine thought. There was absolutely no way she could stay away from her caseload for an entire month.

"May I make a suggestion to the court?"

Judge Patterson-Young sighed dramatically, then waved her manicured hand in a go-ahead gesture.

"May I suggest that I stay at the house for the next fifteen days." With no court appearances scheduled during that time, by utilizing the phone, fax, and e-mail, she and the always efficient Brian should be able to manage. "After which time my sister, whom I'm certain the court will find exceptionally responsible, will take another fifteen days."

Raine knew Savannah wouldn't hesitate to help their grandmother. Oh, she might have a bit of trouble getting away from her job as chef at that *chichi* Malibu resort hotel, but since her husband was resort manager, surely he wouldn't protest his wife taking a brief leave of absence for a family emergency. Even if she suspected that he may have sensed that the family in question did not consider him the right man for Savannah. Personally Raine had always privately thought him too slick. Too smooth. Too untrustworthy.

"The court will agree with that schedule," the judge said. "On the condition your sister proves herself to be a suitable guardian."

"Thank you, Your Honor." Raine didn't bother to hide her relief.

"Thirty days. And if there's a single instance of trouble during that time, Counselor, all bets are off."

BANG! With a final, swift rap of the wooden gavel, Judge Barbara Patterson-Young signaled the guardianship hearing concluded.

"You won't have that much to do," Raine assured her sister when she phoned her after they'd all returned home. "Since the court just wants a warm, responsible body in the house until Gram proves she's up to handling things."

"The day Gram runs into something she can't handle will be the day the world comes to an end. Do you ever wonder what we would have done without her?"

"I try not to. Which is why I decided not to fight her too hard on this one. It's more than obvious that Gwen needs her. But I think Gram needs Gwen, too. I get the feeling that she misses having family around." Which was why, Raine understood, Ida had created her little flock in the first place.

"Actually, your timing couldn't be better," Savannah said. "Since I just quit my job yesterday afternoon."

"You quit? But I thought you loved working at the resort."

"I do. I did," she corrected. "But that changed."

"I'm sorry." Raine decided not to press. Savannah would fill her in on the details when she was ready.

"What does Kevin think about this change?" she asked, wondering if her sister could possibly be pregnant. Although she couldn't picture Savannah's husband as a doting father, Raine nevertheless liked the idea of being an aunt.

"Other than the fact that he has to find a new chef just before the summer tourist season really takes off, I doubt he much cares." She paused. "I've left him, Raine."

"Oh, Savannah." Raine was standing by the kitchen window, watching a pair of red-breasted robins playing musical branches in the huge monkey puzzle tree that dominated the front lawn. "I'm sorry. I'd sensed the two of you were having problems when you came to New York last fall. But I was hoping you could work things out."

"I'd hoped the same thing. But I've come to the unhappy conclusion that the resort business was the only thing we had in common. We certainly had a different view of marriage."

"Oh?"

"I thought monogamy was a given. Kevin thought he should be allowed to date. I, naturally, disagreed. When I caught him playing hide the torpedo with a female lawyer from the hotel's legal division, I decided that I'd come to the end of my rope."

"You should have put it around his neck and tossed him off the nearest pier," Raine declared heatedly. "He's a fool. And a bastard."

"That's pretty much what I told him after he admitted to what he referred to as his little indiscretion. Since this wasn't the first time he's wandered,

I threatened to hack off said little indiscretion with a rusty cleaver."

"I didn't know." Raine hated thinking that her sister had been suffering through such pain alone.

"That's because I didn't want you to. I didn't want anyone to know. I realize now that I shouldn't have hung in there for so many years, but I was trying so damn hard not to follow in Lilith's footsteps. If that makes any sense."

"Absolutely." Hadn't she spent her entire life trying to avoid the same thing?

"It was also embarrassing to admit that the perfect marriage I'd always dreamed about wasn't so perfect after all."

Raine knew all too well how Savannah had always longed for a perfect, *Leave It to Beaver* family life. Being more realistic, or perhaps more cynical than her sister, Raine had preferred to devote herself to her work, rather than depend on any man for her happiness.

Savannah sighed. "So, I moved into the Beverly Wilshire, arranged to have my calls forwarded from the resort, unless they were from the rat, and ordered a bottle of ridiculously expensive champagne to celebrate my freedom. After which I proceeded to get drunk, which took my mind off the horny, unfaithful little prick for a while. Until I woke up this morning with the mother of all hangovers. Then you called."

"I really am so sorry, Savannah. This is a horrible time to ask any favors of you."

"Don't be silly, the timing couldn't be better. I'm still so furious—and, dammit, hurt—I could use a little distance and distraction to prevent me from following through on the cleaver threat."

If nothing else, Raine decided that Ida and the girls would definitely prove a distraction.

"Not that I'd ever recommend violence, but if you were to take matters into your own hands, so to speak, I just happen to know a good lawyer who'd take your case *pro bono*."

Raine heard a throaty sound and was unable to decide whether it was a choked off laugh or a sob. "God, I miss you," Savannah said on a rush of shaky breath. "And Ida. And even Lilith, believe it or not. In fact, when I woke up this morning, I thought about going home to lick my wounds, but I didn't want to look as if I was running home to Gram at the first sign of trouble."

"That's what the family is for."

Savannah laughed again, this time with more humor. "Right. And I'll bet Coldwater Cove would be the first place you'd think of hiding out if your life crumbled beneath your feet."

"Probably not," Raine admitted.

She wanted to say something reassuring. But when words failed her, Raine assured herself that there would be time for tears and hugs later. When they didn't have all these miles between them.

"And you don't have to stick to that two weeks schedule," Savannah said. "I should be able to tie up loose ends and get up there in a few days. Then I'll take over."

"Just try to make it before we run out of frozen dinners to nuke and Gram decides to start cooking," Raine instructed.

After Raine hung up, she sat for a while, thinking

how Savannah might be a perfectionist when it came to her work, but had always been ruled by her heart. She also had the unfortunate tendency to think the best of people until she was proven wrong.

Which was why, Raine considered with a flash of hot fury, her sister hadn't picked up on the warning signals that the rest of the family had when they'd first met the groom after Savannah's sudden elopement to Monte Carlo.

During their high school years, Savannah had been the flame that drew eyes as she'd laughed and flirted and had every boy in the school falling a little bit in love with her. Her natural sexuality had left Raine feeling a bit of an observer to a play in which she'd never be the star.

Not that she'd minded. Savannah having inherited Lilith's lush feminine appeal was nothing more than a quirk of fate, a fortunate accident of genetics. To envy such beauty would be like the cool silver moon resenting the brighter, bolder sun for rising in a blaze of glory each morning. Besides, they'd each carved out individual identities early on in life.

She was, of course, the "smart, sassy one," while Savannah, everyone would agree, was "the pretty, sweet one."

But even as they followed their individual dreams down different paths, deep down inside, where it really counted, despite having different fathers, she and Savannah were sisters of the heart. When one was hurting, the other felt the pain and when they spoke, they spoke with the same voice.

Family matters taken care of, at least as well as they could be for now, Raine called her office. Brian quickly caught her up on what was happening with her cases, then transferred her to the managing partner.

"I must say, Raine," Stephen Wells complained, "I'm less than pleased to hear that you're not returning any time soon."

"It's only a few days. Fifteen at the most. Fortunately, I don't have any court dates scheduled, so as long as I have my laptop and can access the firm's mainframe, I can work anywhere."

In fact, if she wanted to, she could essentially set up her office on some faraway beach. When that all too appealing idea brought up her now familiar tropical fantasy starring Jack O'Halloran, she dragged her mind back to the droning voice on the other end of the phone.

"I understand, Stephen. Yes, it's a bit of an inconvenience, but it's nothing that can't be worked out."

More complaints, along with a pointed comment about the upcoming decision to be made on the new partnerships that caused the temper Raine usually kept on a taut leash to spike. If he thought he could make her abandon her grandmother by threatening to pass her over for promotion, he definitely had another think coming!

She swallowed hard to force down her annoyance. "I promise nothing will fall between the cracks." With effort, Raine kept the irritation from her voice. "And really, Stephen, when you come right down to it, my taking a few days to deal with a family emergency is not nearly as disruptive as if I'd taken a vacation. A long-overdue vacation," she stressed. "As I'm certain many attorneys would do after obtaining an important victory like the Odessa Oil appeals decision."

For a moment, she could hear only the *tick tick tick* of the kitchen clock. "All right," he finally said. "We'll consider this a vacation, then. And I'll assure the other partners that you'll be back at your desk no later than fifteen days from now."

His point made, rather ungraciously, Raine thought, considering the money she'd brought into the firm's coffers just this month alone, Stephen Wells brought the conversation to an abrupt close.

❦ 11 ❦

Worries filled Raine's mind, circling around and around like fallen leaves caught in a whirlpool. She worried about her work, which, despite her brave words to Stephen Wells, she knew would pile up during her absence. She worried about Ida, who while as bossy and mule-headed as ever, was obviously growing older.

As they all were, Raine thought as she crawled out of bed, pulled on a robe and a pair of thick green-and-orange-striped ski socks that she'd left behind when she'd gone to law school. But Ida wore her years more heavily.

She worried that Gwen would prove too much for her grandmother to take care of on her own. Especially if she decided to keep her baby. She worried what would happen to the teenage mother and child if that proved the case. And, finally, she couldn't stop worrying about Savannah.

What many people, who made the mistake of concentrating only on her stunning looks, missed was that Savannah Townsend had a deep-seated domestic streak. As a child she'd spent hours at her Easy-Bake oven, turning out tiny cakes and cookies for the teas she'd serve with a flourish and an eye for detail far beyond her years. The miniature plates were scrubbed and decorated sand dollars she'd collected on the beach, the paper cups always sported hand-painted motifs, and Martha Stewart would have envied the ideal simplicity of Savannah's seasonal centerpieces.

While Raine had spent hours role-playing with their scores of Barbie dolls—always opting for the career look, even as a secret part of her had been drawn to the glam gowns—Savannah had tended more toward baby dolls she could bathe and rock and pretend to feed.

"A natural born mother," Ida had often said whenever Savannah brought home yet another wounded dog or cat. She'd once rescued a hawk whose wing had been broken by some older boys throwing stones. The ungrateful bird had viciously ripped the skin on Savannah's index finger during the rescue operation, but just the memory of the sight of the hawk soaring off the cliff after its recovery was enough to give Raine goosebumps.

As she went downstairs, planning to get some air on the front porch, Raine thought about the miscarriage Savannah had suffered last summer. When her sister had visited her in New York last fall, they'd spent hours talking about her sister's lifelong desire for a large family. Now Raine considered that perhaps it was fortunate she hadn't had any children. Being a single mother like Lilith would obviously be difficult.

No. Not like Lilith, Raine amended as she went

out onto the porch. The screen door opened with a rusty creak. Her sister would never abandon her children.

And speaking of her mother . . . Raine was surprised to find Lilith sitting alone in the dark on the swing. "Looks as if I'm not the only one who can't sleep," she said.

"It's been a busy past few days." A red glow brightened the dark as Lilith drew in on a cigarette.

"That's putting it mildly." Raine chose a wicker chair. "At least Shawna's case went well."

"That was something." Lilith took another longer drag on the cigarette, then exhaled a cloud of smoke that hung between them like an acrid curtain. "I still can't believe that we were unlucky enough to get Bloody Babs Patterson for a judge.

"Bloody Babs?"

"She always was horrendously vicious whenever she felt crossed. Most of the girls were terrified of her, which is why they always voted her onto the pep squad and prom committees, even when they didn't want to."

If the judge hadn't turned out to be a major problem, Raine might have laughed at Lilith's pique. It had been thirty-two years, yet from the way her mother spoke about Judge Barbara Patterson-Young, it could have been yesterday.

"Well, she definitely found a way to get the upper hand today."

"That's true." Lilith stabbed her cigarette out in the empty cup she'd been using for an ashtray. "Did you see Cooper?"

"No. Was he in the courtroom?"

"He was sitting in the back. He came in while Babs was drilling you on your credentials. And left right about the time Mother shot off her mouth."

Raine couldn't help chuckling, just a little, at the memory. "I thought I was going to have to sit on her."

"She'd have bit your ass if you'd tried," Lilith said. "It *was* funny, though. I don't think I'll ever forget Bab's face when Mother brought up the birth control pills."

"She reminded me of St. Helens, about to blow its top again."

"Didn't she?" Lilith laughed softly. Then sighed again. "Of course, to be fair, I realize now that I never should have gone out with Jimmy. They'd just had a little spat over her deciding to go to school in Hawaii instead of Washington State, like she'd originally planned."

"Sounds as if they made up the first time she came home," Raine said mildly. "If Gram's right about the pills."

"Oh, she's right. Mother has always had a steel-trap mind."

"Perhaps not so much anymore."

Lilith glanced over at Raine. "Sometimes it's still hard for me to imagine that little girl I brought into the world as an attorney. From what Ida says, you're quite an important one, too."

"Not that important. And we all grow up."

"True. We're also all getting older." Lilith drew her knees up to her chest and rested her chin on them. "Lord, that's a damn depressing thought."

"Don't worry, Lilith." Raine couldn't quite keep the

veiled sarcasm from her tone. It was so typical that her mother would find a way to put herself in the center of the situation. "You'll never get old."

"Grow up, you mean," Lilith said.

"I suppose that's a matter of semantics."

"No." Silver hair flashed like a comet in the dark as Lilith shook her head. "You're extremely skilled in the use of words, Raine. You were avoiding the truth because you didn't want to hurt my feelings. But I notice you didn't argue when Bloody Babs ruled that I wasn't competent to care for the girls."

"She didn't exactly say you were incompetent—"

"She said I was not a responsible adult." Showing a flash of her usual spark, Lilith lifted her chin, just a little. "And with your silence, you agreed."

"I couldn't lie. Not in a court room. Not with Gwen's future at stake."

"Are you saying that you honestly don't believe I could take care of her? For four short weeks?"

"Honestly?" Tired of tap dancing around the issue, Raine decided not to mince words. "No. I do not believe you'd be a stable influence on Gwen. Even allowing that we haven't seen much of each other the past few years, Lilith, after that little New Age musical you performed in the forest, the one you invited Shawna to participate in"—she reminded her mother pointedly—"I don't see how anyone could consider you a decent role model."

"The last time I looked, the constitution granted all Americans freedom of religion."

"True. But I don't recall anything about the founding fathers writing in a clause granting the freedom to dance nude in a public park."

"We weren't in public, not really . . ."

"Dammit, Lilith!" Raine was on her feet now. "Would you just drop it? You were wrong. Your behavior was outrageous. And irresponsible, since people take their children into Olympic National Park, which makes it very, very public."

"There's nothing wrong with the human body."

"True. Until you decide to flaunt it in front of a bunch of Boy Scouts."

Lilith looked up at her in surprise. "There weren't any Boy Scouts anywhere around where we'd camped."

"Not yet. But Jack told me an entire troop of them were scheduled for a nature hike the next day."

"Really?" She tilted her head and pursed her lips as she thought that over. "I wonder why Cooper didn't mention that little fact while he was slapping the shackles on me."

"They were handcuffs, Lilith. Not shackles. Besides, he only resorted to using them after you slapped him. And to answer your question, he didn't tell you about the scouts because he was afraid once you heard about them, you'd refuse to get dressed."

"Did he actually tell you that?"

"He told Jack. Sheriff O'Halloran," Raine corrected quickly. "The sheriff told me." The less-than-pleasant subject had come up last night while they'd been planning for Gwen's hearing.

"I see." Lilith's gaze turned to look out over the rolling, dark-shadowed lawn. "It appears Cooper doesn't think very much of me."

"Would you if you were in his shoes? After what you did?"

"I admitted going out with Jimmy was a mistake, but—"

"We're not talking about some stupid, damn teen-age tryst," Raine said through clenched teeth. "I was referring to the way you resisted arrest."

"That's ridiculous. All I did was tear up his stupid ticket."

"Three times. Along with his citation book."

"Well, there was that," Lilith reluctantly agreed. She allowed a faint smile at the memory. "I hate to admit this, but I was a little embarrassed when he came in the courtroom today."

Stop the presses, Raine thought. Lilith Lindstrom may actually have regrets about her behavior. Since there was nothing reasonably safe she could say to that, she didn't respond.

"Maybe even a bit ashamed," Lilith went on to confess. The silence lingered between them, so palpable Raine imagined she could reach out and touch it. "But it was still wrong of Babs to imply that I wouldn't be a proper caretaker. After all," she said with a flare of pique, "I have two daughters of my own—"

"Whom you continually abandoned like a mother cat dumping a litter of kittens." Continued exhaustion, plus the events of the past few days, caused Raine to respond more harshly than was her nature. She regretted the words the moment she heard them come out of her mouth. Almost.

"That's not fair." Moisture glistened in Lilith's expressive eyes. "I didn't abandon you. Leaving you girls with your grandmother, whenever things got too difficult for me to handle on my own, whenever my life got disrupted, was my way of providing you with a stable home."

Raine's barked laugh held not an iota of humor. "That was your idea of stability?"

"It was the best I could do, at the time," Lilith responded defensively. "You don't know how it was for me. Ida divorced my father when I was five years old—"

"He was a gambler. He stole money from her and he hit her."

"I never saw him lift a hand to Mother, but if she says it happened, it undoubtedly did. The thing is, Raine, I never got over losing him. Which is why, I suppose, I've spent so much of my life needing men to find me attractive. To want me."

"I really don't think we should go down this road," Raine warned.

"Oh, *I* think we should. Because it's important. . . . It's not easy for me to admit this, Raine. But I've been thinking a great deal about you and your sister lately, and I've come to the conclusion that in your own way, you're the most like me."

"That's preposterous!" Raine shook her head, stunned by her mother's outrageous suggestion. "We're nothing alike."

"Oh, I think you're a great deal more like me than you care to admit," Lilith said mildly. "I saw you on television the other day. You photograph very well, by the way."

"Gee, thanks. That really puts my mind at ease."

"You don't have to be sarcastic. I was merely making an observation. You have the Lindstrom bones. They'll serve you well as you grow older.

"But despite having my features, you looked amazingly like Owen, when he held his press conference on the federal-courthouse steps after he'd gotten the Sacramento Six acquitted.

"I was pregnant with you at the time. He wasn't at all happy about that, but since he was considering a possible political future, he agreed to get married. I'd known it was merely a marriage of convenience—his convenience," she clarified with an edge to her voice. "But I honestly believed that I could get him to love me. In time."

"Which you didn't have."

"No. The day we got back from Tijuana, he moved out of our apartment and we never spent another night together."

Her parents ill-fated marriage was definitely not one of Raine's favorite topics. But there was one part of Lilith's story that had captured her attention. "I reminded you of my father?"

Lilith lit another cigarette and took her time in answering. "Unfortunately, yes."

"Unfortunately?" She couldn't help herself. Lilith had Raine wondering if, just perhaps, her father had seen her on television, speaking with the press. And if he had, whether he'd been even a little bit proud of her.

"Your father is not a nice man, Raine, dear. Oh, he's admittedly intelligent and charismatic, but he's also totally egocentric—"

"And a brilliant attorney," Raine broke in, thinking that Lilith calling Owen Cantrell egocentric was definitely a case of the pot calling the kettle black.

"True. He's both brilliant and ruthless. I do believe that all those lawyer-shark jokes were coined with Owen in mind. It was that part of him I saw in you.

That's when I knew for certain that what I've been suspecting all these years was true."

"Which was?" Raine inquired icily.

"In the same way I've spent my life trying to prove to an absent father that I was appealing enough to love, you're trying to prove yourself to *your* father by becoming even more heartless than he is."

After Jack's comments about lawyers, this accusation hit particularly hard. "That's a ridiculous assumption. It's also patently wrong."

"You were on the wrong side of that retirement issue, darling. You took the shark's side. If you're not careful, you could end up just like Owen, turning your back on morality and taking on any high-profile case that will win you big bucks and a reputation as a top hired gun. I fear that if you keep going down the path you're on, Raine, someday you may well find yourself defending someone like your father's current client. A horrible, abusive bully that everyone knows is a cold-blooded killer."

Raine was so angry she could barely push the words past the painful lump in her throat. "Not that it's pertinent to this discussion, but that same constitution that gives you the right to worship the sun or moon or a damn oak tree, if you want, also declares every defendant innocent until proven guilty."

"Are you saying that if you'd been asked, you would have defended that murderer?"

"No." Despite her claim of a defendant's right to innocence, the very idea of defending that *particular* defendant was unthinkable. "But—"

"Yet you were willing to take on Odessa Oil as a client."

"Odessa didn't kill anyone."

"Not yet," Lilith countered. "But without health-care—"

"I am not going to discuss this!" Raine's shout caused a startled bird to fly out of the monkey puzzle tree into the night sky on a whirl of wings. Preferring to leave the scene making to her mother, she immediately lowered her voice. "You have no right telling me what to do with my life."

"I'm your mother."

"No." Raine shook her head emphatically. Hot, furious moisture was welling up behind her lids but she refused to give in to tears. "You abandoned any maternal rights years ago, Lilith. When you abandoned your daughters."

Even as she saw her mother flinch, Raine didn't retract her harsh words. Or apologize.

Instead, she went back into the house on unreasonably shaky legs, managing, just barely, to keep from slamming the screen door behind her.

By the following morning, Raine felt horrendously guilty for her uncharacteristic outburst. The fact that she'd believed most of what she'd said was no excuse for having lashed out and hurt Lilith. Especially since the behavior that had caused so much pain was in the past.

Lilith opened her bedroom door at Raine's first knock. Her quick response, and the shadows beneath her eyes revealed that Raine hadn't been the only one who'd found sleep difficult after their argument.

Not that the fatigue diminished her beauty. Actually, Raine considered, it made her mother appear even more delicate, like spun glass. She'd obviously gotten Lilith out of bed, yet somehow her mother had avoided the crease marks that usually marred Raine's cheeks upon awakening, and every silver hair was in place. She was wearing a blue silk nightgown and matching robe that matched her eyes and made Raine, in her dancing-sheep pajamas, feel like a street urchin.

A long-ago memory flooded back. That of a little girl, no more than seven years old, sneaking into her mother's lingerie drawers, drawn by the brightly hued silk and satin and lace confections. Raine had loved the colors that reminded her of the shimmer of rainbows, loved the slick, but oh, so soft feel of them against her fingertips and cheeks as she'd lifted them to her face, breathing in the exotic scent of Shalimar that she'd always identified with her mother.

One time, when she sensed Lilith was about ready to take her daughters back to Coldwater Cove again, Raine had stolen a scarlet, lace-trimmed slip from the drawer and hidden it away in her suitcase. For months, as she'd lain alone in her bed in the room she shared with her sister at their grandmother's house, she slept with that silk slip, feeling as if in some way, she was sleeping with her mother.

"Would you like to come in?" Lilith asked.

"No. I haven't checked in with my office yet." Raine felt a distant pain and realized that she was digging her fingernails into her palms. "I just wanted to apologize for what I said last night."

"Oh, that's not necessary." Lilith gracefully waved the words of contrition away.

"Yes, it is." Raine took a deep breath that was meant to calm. It didn't. "You were right, Lilith. No matter how I feel about certain past aspects of our relationship, you're still my mother. I had no right to speak so disrespectfully to you."

"Well." Lilith was silent for a moment, seeming to take that in as she studied her elder daughter's grimly set face. "Thank you, darling. I appreciate your thoughtfulness."

They stood there, a few inches apart on opposite sides of the door jamb. There was an aura of expectancy in the air, as if both knew that such a circumstance demanded a hug, but each was unable to make the first move. Then Lilith lifted a hand to brush some tousled hair off Raine's face.

"As it happens, I promised your grandmother I'd take Shawna shopping for a graduation dress this morning. Ida wanted it to be a going-away gift. Perhaps we could go together. Maybe even have lunch afterwards. Sort of a girl's day on the town."

Raine fought against the flood of yearning that single, casual maternal touch seemed to trigger. She wanted to refuse Lilith's invitation, but found the words difficult.

"If you'd rather not, I'll understand," Lilith said when Raine didn't immediately respond.

Raine watched her mother fussing with the silk tie of the robe, twisting it in her hands and realized with surprise that Lilith was actually nervous. "It sounds like fun," she said, falling back on politeness as she tried to analyze her feelings.

"Doesn't it?" Lilith agreed.

As she left her mother's bedroom, Raine assured herself that the moisture that had seemed to glisten in Lilith's blue eyes had only been a trick of the morning light. Even stranger was the way she inexplicably felt like crying herself.

❧12❧

Short of traveling to Seattle, the Dancing Deer Dress Shoppe was the best—and only place—to buy women's clothing in Coldwater Cove. The store had been established by sisters Doris and Dottie Anderson, nee Jensen, identical twins who'd been married to Coldwater Cove's only other pair of twins, Harold and Halden Anderson, for nearly fifty years. For all those years the two women had lived next door to one another, worked side by side, worn their snowy hair exactly the same way, and even dressed alike, although Doris, who was elder by ten minutes, favored earth tones while Dottie, displaying an independent flair, usually chose scarlet.

"How wonderful that you've come home again," Dottie greeted Raine as the others began searching through a display of pastel prom and graduation dresses.

"I imagine Ida's on cloud nine," Doris agreed. "You and your sister are just about all she talks about. One of Savannah's recipes was featured in the *L.A. Times*, Raine just won a multimillion-dollar case," she quoted Ida. "You both certainly did your grandmother proud, that's for certain."

"Not just your grandmother," Dottie said before Raine could respond. "We're all proud of you."

"Thank you," Raine murmured. In the city, she lived in a world of anonymity. Like *Beauty and the Beast*'s castle, her life was made easier by the performance of a host of invisible servants. Her garbage was taken away, her apartment cleaned, her mail and groceries delivered. But here in Coldwater Cove, everyone not only knew each other's business, but their life histories, as well.

"We saw you on television," Doris said. "You photograph very well, dear, doesn't she, Sister?"

"You looked beautiful," Dottie agreed. "But a bit subdued. I thought I'd read that it was always preferable to wear bright colors on television."

"I didn't dress for the television cameras," Raine said mildly.

"Well, I suppose you have a point. Although it's still possible to look feminine and professional at the same time. Have you ever watched *Melrose Place?* Or *Ally McBeal?*"

"Ally McBeal is a fictional lawyer."

"Well, that may be," Dottie allowed as she fluffed her cotton-candy hair. "But that girl certainly does know how to catch a male eye with those short skirts."

"Perhaps Raine has more important things on her mind than attracting men," Doris suggested dryly.

"Well, I can't imagine what." Dottie tilted her head like a curious bird. "After all, dear, you're not getting any younger, and I know how dearly Ida is yearning for some great-grandchildren to bounce on her knee

Why she talks about it all the time, doesn't she, Sister?"

"She's mentioned it," Doris confirmed. "Ida misses both you and Savannah, dear. Now, I realize that it isn't really any of our business—"

"None at all," Dottie broke in. "But of course that never stopped Doris from handing out advice."

"Sister," Doris complained, "it was my turn to speak."

"I realize that, Sister," Dottie said. "But I'm sure Raine didn't come here today for a lecture."

"I had no intention of lecturing her," Doris said stiffly. "I was merely intending to point out how good it's been for Ida, taking in those three poor misguided girls."

"It's given her a new lease on life, that's for certain," Dottie agreed. She leaned forward and placed a plump hand on Raine's arm. "I have to admit that I did worry in the beginning that one of them might sneak into her bedroom in the middle of the night and kill her while she was sleeping."

"If the girls were killers they wouldn't be in a group home, Sister," Doris snapped. "They'd be locked up somewhere."

"You can't always tell," Dottie insisted. "Why, just last week, I was watching that Jerry Springer show and he was interviewing this handsome young man who, to look at him, you would have easily taken for a choirboy. In fact, he reminded me a little bit of Daniel O'Halloran, at least around the eyes. But of course, Daniel is older than he was. . . ."

"I assume there's a point to this?" Doris ground out.

"Of course. As I was saying, before I was interrupted," she said, shooting a censorious look at her sister, "you never would have suspected that the young man on the show was anything but a model citizen. But it turned out he's in prison for strangling women. Then, after they're dead, he sautés their hearts in a Napa Valley chardonnay with a touch of olive oil and pesto, while wearing his victims' clothing, if you can believe such a dreadful thing."

"Sister!" Doris's expression revealed her shock. "You're forgetting your manners! Didn't Mother teach us that some subjects are not meant to be discussed in public?" She shook her head in frustration as she turned back toward Raine. "Don't pay any attention to Dottie, Raine, dear. Ever since she started watching those daytime television shows, her conversation has become absolutely scandalous."

Dottie lifted both pink chins. "It's important to know what's going on in the world. Unlike some of us who are content to only pay attention to the goings-on here in Coldwater Cove."

"I doubt that cross-dressing, cannibalistic serial killers are all that common even outside our small hamlet," Doris argued. "In fact, I would imagine that you don't hear about them all that often even in the big city. Do you, Raine?"

It was all Raine could do to keep her lips from giving into the smile that was tickling at the corners of her mouth. "Not as a rule."

Doris turned back to her twin and folded her arms over the front of her olive green shirtwaist dress. "See? I told you those horrid shows are not reflective of real life. The outrageous stories are probably even made up."

"Oh, I can't believe they'd allow people to lie on television," Dottie replied vaguely. "But I'm getting off track. My initial point was that at first many of us were concerned for Ida when she took those girls in. However, I, for one, have decided to give them the benefit of the doubt."

"Still," she amended as her intense blue eyes drifted toward the little family group across the room, "I'm afraid their shenanigans the other day didn't exactly help their cause any."

"That was unfortunate," Raine agreed.

"Oh, well," Dottie said with a flare of her unsinkable optimism, "at least the standoff brought you home, Raine. So, I've no doubt that your grandmother must think all that pesky trouble was worth it. Speaking of that standoff, what did you think of the sheriff?"

Since the Anderson sisters were the closest thing Coldwater Cove had to town criers, Raine decided not to share her initial impression that he was too sexy for comfort. "He seems like a fair man."

"Oh, he is. But I wasn't talking about that. I was referring to his looks. Didn't you find him absolutely dashing?"

"I didn't really notice."

"Oh, darling, if that's truly the case, then you have been working too hard. Every single woman in town has been chasing after that man since he was widowed. I suspect that quite a few of the married ones wouldn't mind him putting his cowboy boots beside their beds, either. While just the other day I was in the market and I saw Marianne Wagner—you remember her, Raine, she's Peter and Elizabeth Garrison's youngest daughter—flirting with our sheriff over the broccoli.

"Of course I can understand how she'd be lonely, especially now that her husband had to take that timber job down in Oregon, but still, with three children to take care of, you'd think she'd be too busy to find time to pick up men in the market, not that he seemed all that interested."

"Sister!" Doris spat out. "Really, that's enough. Raine didn't come here to gossip about the sheriff. She came here to shop. So, we should just let her get to it." With that, she literally dragged her talkative sister away.

The others had already disappeared into the dressing rooms when Lilith approached with a silk dress awash with tropical flowers.

"Look, darling. Isn't this lovely?"

"Gorgeous," Raine agreed, easily picturing her mother in the vastly romantic dress.

"I'm so pleased you think so. Since I want to buy it for you."

"That's not necessary."

"It is to me." The earnest look in Lilith's eyes brought back last night's argument.

"It's not suitable for the city," Raine said in a weak attempt to resist her mother's silent appeal.

"You're not in the city now, darling."

"True. But I can't imagine needing a dress like that here in Coldwater Cove, either."

"You never know." Ignoring Raine's frown, Lilith held it up against her body. "Perhaps you'll be invited out to dinner."

Raine tried to imagine wearing the ultraromantic

dress to Oley's for barbecue and couldn't. "I didn't come home to date."

"Well, of course you didn't, dear. But it's such a lovely dress."

"It's beautiful," Gwen, who'd suddenly appeared, cajoled. "Try it on, Raine, please?"

It wasn't her style. Raine thought of all the neat little dress-for-success suits hanging in her closet. She'd never owned a dress like this in her life.

"It wouldn't hurt to try it on," Lilith said. "Unless, of course," she added slyly, "you're afraid."

"Why on earth would I be afraid of a dress?"

"I have no idea." Lilith shrugged. "Perhaps because you're afraid that you'll discover a sexy, tempestuous female lurking beneath that grim, serious legal facade you present to the world?"

It was more challenge than insult. Even knowing that her mother was pushing buttons, Raine couldn't quite resist taking her up on it.

She snatched the dress from Lilith's manicured hand. "It's not my size. It's too small."

"I don't think so." Lilith skimmed an appraising look over Raine. "Give it a try, and if you need a larger size, I'll go get one. . . . Meanwhile, I'm going to see how Shawna's coming along."

It wasn't her style, Raine repeated to herself as she stripped off her slacks and sweater. Besides, her mother was wrong. There wasn't a single tempestuous bone in her body. She was intelligent, reasonable, and cool headed. She preferred classic styles and colors—like a little basic-black dress worn with a single strand of very good pearls. The kind of dress that could go from the office out to dinner.

As she pulled the dress over her head, Raine overlooked the fact that it had been a very long time since any man had asked her out to dinner. Even longer since she'd accepted.

The dress slid over her like a silk waterfall. Raine refused to be enticed. Until she looked into the mirror and viewed the stranger who was looking straight back at her.

"Raine?" Lilith called out to her. "How does it fit?"

"I think it's a little snug." The bodice bared her shoulders and the silk hugged her curves like a lover's caress on the way down her body to swirl around her calves. It felt cool and carefree and, dammit, sexy.

Raine reminded herself that she'd never *wanted* to be sexy. That was her mother's role. While there were, admittedly days that she found her own life less than perfect, there was no way she'd want to trade places with Lilith. Not in a million years.

"Come out and let's see."

"That's not necessary—"

"Oh, Raine, don't be such a party pooper," Lilith complained as she pulled open the curtain. "Oh, darling, it's perfect."

"For you, perhaps. But it's not me." Was it her imagination, or did the brightly hued hibiscus blossoms bring out red highlights in her hair she'd never noticed?

"Of course it is. If you hadn't spent most of your life working overtime, pretending to be someone, and something you're not, you'd realize that."

"I'm not pretending." Raine turned sideways and skimmed her palm over a silk-covered hip. It really was stunning. "Not really."

"Then what would you call it?"

"Surviving."

Their eyes met. Another of those thick, uncomfortable silences settled over them. Raine viewed the hurt in her mother's expertly made-up eyes and felt a tinge of guilt for having put it there.

"Oh, Shawna, that's gorgeous!" they heard Renee exclaim. "Lilith, Raine, come see how beautiful Shawna is! She looks just like a supermodel!"

The tense mood was broken. Grateful for the interruption, Raine escaped the dressing room. And her mother.

"Oh, that is truly lovely." she breathed as she took in the seventeen-year-old standing in front of the three-way mirror just outside the dressing rooms. The white lace top, held up by slender satin ribbons, skimmed the waistband of a short tight skirt trimmed at the hem with more lace. The girl's coltish legs looked a mile long.

"Do you really think so?" the teenager asked, holding her arms out to her sides.

"It's perfect," Lilith and Raine said together. Unaccustomed to agreeing about anything, they exchanged a brief, surprised look. "Absolutely perfect," Lilith insisted.

Shawna grinned. "I love your dress, too," she said to Raine.

"It's not my dress," Raine said.

"You're not going to get it?" Renee and Shawna asked in unison. They both stared at her in disbelief. Gwen, Raine noticed, looked absolutely crestfallen.

"No. It's just not my style, it's too small, and—"

"Oh, look, girls," Lilith trilled, overrunning Raine's planned rejection of the dress that was proving too tempting for comfort. "It's the sheriff."

Terrific. This was all she needed. Raine briefly closed her eyes, then turned toward the door where he was holding the hand of the most beautiful child she had ever seen. The little girl could have been a princess who'd stepped right out of the pages of a fairy tale book.

Her heart-shaped face was the color of cream tinged with an underlying peach hue, like one of the antique roses in Ida's backyard garden. Her petal pink mouth formed a perfect cupid's bow; long, pale, sun-gilded hair the color of a palomino's tail rippled down her back.

"I'm so glad to see you, Sheriff," Lilith greeted him with one of her practiced smiles that somehow didn't cause a single crinkle at the corner of her eyes. "You left the courthouse so quickly yesterday, I didn't have an opportunity to thank you for your expert testimony in Shawna's case. Why, I do believe you saved the day for us all." She glanced over to Raine, who was edging back toward the dressing rooms. "Didn't he, Raine?"

"It meant a lot to our case," Raine agreed. Unnerved by the flare of obvious male interest she viewed in his gaze, but realizing that escape now was impossible, she turned her attention toward his daughter. "Hello. I'm Raine. And you must be Amy."

"That's right." Emerald green eyes fringed by a double row of long, curly lashes smiled up at Raine. "How did you know?"

"Your daddy told me about you. When he was taking care of your Nano Kitty."

"Puffy," Amy said with a nod of her gilt head. "He's a lot of fun, but I'd rather have a real one."

She slanted a sly look upward at her father, who laughed.

"Keep trying, kiddo," he said. "You'll wear me down one of these days."

"He's very stubborn," Amy confided in Raine.

Six going on thirty, Raine remembered Jack saying. He'd been right. "I've discovered that for myself," she agreed.

"We're here to buy underpants," Amy announced. "My old ones are too small. Gramma says I'm shooting up like a beanpole, huh, Daddy?"

"That's what she said, all right," Jack agreed.

"Daddy brought some home last week, but they were little-kid ones. They had Barney on them." She wrinkled her nose in childish displeasure. "But I'm too old for Barney, so we brought them back. To exchange."

That settled, Amy turned her attention to Shawna. "You look really pretty in that dress. Like when Brandy played Cinderella on TV. Do those earrings hurt?" she asked as she took in the trio of gold hoops adorning each earlobe.

"Nah," the older girl said.

"I really really want to get my ears pierced. But Daddy says I'm too young."

"I was just a baby when I got my first holes," Shawna revealed. "I can't even remember getting them."

"Really?" Amy looked up at her father. "Did you hear that, Daddy?"

"I heard. But it doesn't make any difference because my mind is made up, my feet are set in concrete, and the subject is not even up for discussion until you're at least twelve."

"I told you he was stubborn," Amy said to Raine on a huge, dramatic sigh that had Raine smiling.

"I've got a belly-button ring, too," Shawna announced.

"Really?" Amy's eyes widened. "Can I see it?"

"Sure." As Shawna lifted the lacy top, Amy slipped free of her father's hand and moved closer to investigate.

"Christ," Jack muttered under his breath as he watched the avid discussion going on a few feet away, "that's just what I need, to have her wanting to get holes punched into her body. Next she'll be wanting a tattoo."

"I doubt that. She's a stunningly beautiful little girl," Raine said as the group of girls discussed the pros and cons of body piercing. Even as she told herself that she wasn't interested in any personal way, she couldn't help wondering how closely Amy took after her mother. "You're definitely right about her being mature for her age."

"I know. It's bad enough to discover that she's already outgrowing kid underwear."

"Perhaps she merely doesn't appreciate purple dinosaurs," Raine suggested.

"She made that more than clear." He dragged his hand through his dark hair. "What I know about raising a daughter could fit on the head of a pin. I think the safest thing to do is to just lock her in a closet until she's thirty-five."

Although he looked honestly distressed, Raine laughed at the idea of this teenage Lothario growing up to be the father of a daughter who was bound to attract a new generation of sex-crazed boys. "It appears you're doing just fine."

"Thanks. But I'm keeping that closet idea as an option for when she becomes a teenager and wants to start dating." His gaze intensified a bit as he studied her. Then he reached out, took off the dark-framed glasses she was wearing again today and traced the smudged lines beneath her eyes. "You're carrying a lot of luggage here, Harvard."

"I have a lot on my mind." She plucked the glasses from his hand and shoved them back onto her face. They weren't much protection from that steady, searching cop stare, but they were better than nothing.

"Now that I'll believe."

"Daddy," Amy called to him. "I'm going to help Shawna pick out some earrings to go with her new dress, okay?"

He glanced back over at the family group again. "I'll keep an eye on her," Lilith answered his unspoken question.

"Thanks," he answered. "Go ahead, Pumpkin," he said to Amy. "We're not in that much of a hurry."

Amy took off, holding Lilith's hand as she practically skipped across the store to where the jewelry displays had been set up. Jack watched her for a moment, sighed again as envisioning his little girl growing up before his eyes, then turned back to Raine.

"That's one dynamite dress."

"I was just trying it on. Lilith insisted. In her own way," Raine said dryly, "my mother can be every bit as stubborn as Ida. If you don't stand up to her, you'll suddenly find yourself being run over by a velvet bulldozer. "

"I've always gotten a kick out of Lilith. But I can

understand how she could become a bit tiring on a day to day basis," he allowed. "Sounds as if the two of you are having problems."

"Is it that obvious?"

"When I walked in this place, the tension between you was downright palpable."

"Only to someone who's looking," she pointed out.

"True enough."

"It's my fault," she admitted on a sigh. "Both of us had trouble sleeping last night, so we ended up outside talking. Naturally we started discussing both of the court appearances, and one thing led to another, and well"—she shrugged her shoulders, her face as miserable as he'd seen it—"I was overly harsh and said some things I shouldn't have."

Obviously a man comfortable with touching, he rubbed at the lines etching their way into her forehead. "Things you didn't mean?"

"No." She briefly closed her eyes, allowing herself to enjoy the soothing touch. "They were true. But also hurtful."

"Mothers and daughters argue. Even grown daughters."

She opened her eyes again. "Lilith and I have never argued before." She didn't add that she'd always been too afraid to rock an already leaky boat.

He lifted a brow. "Never?"

"Never."

"Well, if that's really the case, it sounds as if this tiff was long overdue. Did it ever occur to you to just lay your cards on the table and tell your mother how you felt?"

"Is that what you'd do?"

"Absolutely. I'm not into playing games. Partly because they're a waste of time and partly because I'm not very good at them."

"Neither am I," Raine found herself admitting. "One of the reasons I've never spoken up before is because there really isn't any point. Accusing Lilith of being Lilith is a lot like scolding a butterfly for being flighty."

"Nevertheless, you can't deny that the situation has you tense." His thumbs skimmed a path from her temples, down her face, to her jaw. "Too tense." He brushed a light caress in the silky hollow between lips and chin.

Raine backed away. "You really shouldn't touch me like that."

"I like touching you."

"Doris and Dottie Anderson just happen to be the biggest gossips in Coldwater Cove," she reminded him. "If you keep it up, it'll be all over town by nightfall that we're lovers."

"Would that be so bad?"

"That it would be all over town?"

"No." Because she was finding his touch impossibly alluring, Raine was relieved when he dipped his hands into his pockets. "That we were lovers."

She felt the color flood into her cheeks. "You shouldn't be talking to me like that, either.

"You started it." When she lifted a brow, he said, "When you put on that dress."

"I certainly didn't put it on for you."

"Perhaps not. But you'd make me the most grateful man in Coldwater Cove if you'd go ahead and buy it."

It was at that moment that Raine belatedly recog-

nized the dress Lilith had challenged her to try on.
It was the one in her tropical hallucination. The very
same one she was wearing on that moon-spangled
beach when a man—this man—kissed her. Heaven
help her, the unbidden romantic fantasies had been
unsettling enough before they'd somehow become
intertwined with her real life.

"I don't want this," she complained.

"What makes you think I do?"

"*You're* the one who keeps looking at me that way.
Talking to me that way." She drew in a ragged
breath that had the silk pulling against her breasts
and caused heat to flash in his eyes. "Touching me."

"I can't help it. I like looking at you, Harvard. I
like talking with you. I especially like touching you.
In fact, since you brought it up, I suppose this is
where I warn you that I'd like to do a whole lot
more of it."

She held out a hand like a traffic cop. "You're hitting on me again."

"Absolutely."

Electricity was arcing around them once again.
Raine felt as if a thunderstorm was hovering on the
horizon, about to hit with a vengeance at any moment, while they were standing at ground zero. Her
nerves strung nearly to the breaking point, she
nearly wept with relief when a small bundle of gold
hair and tanned arms and legs came hurtling into
Jack, shattering the expectant, intimate mood.

∽ 13 ∽

"Daddy!" Amy said, "I just had the most wonderful, scintillating idea.

She'd always been a talkative child, constantly picking up new words like other kids might pick up pretty sea shells on the beach, which gave her a vocabulary beyond her age. *Scintillating* seemed to be her new word this week, gleaned from the remake of *The Parent Trap* they'd watched on video the other night.

"Did you, now?" Jack scooped her into his arms.

"Yes. I was telling everybody about the farm, and Renee said she's never seen a Christmas tree growing out in the woods, so I invited them to our planting party. That's okay, right?"

"I think it sounds like a dandy idea. The more hands the better."

"Planting party?" Raine asked.

"Every spring we plant new trees to make up for the ones we harvested the previous Christmas season. Peg started inviting friends and family and Amy and I've continued the tradition."

"It's bunches and bunches of fun," Amy said. "Isn't it, Daddy?"

"Bunches," Jack agreed with a smile for his daughter.

"That's why Mommy wanted the farm in the first place," Amy divulged with childish candor. "So whenever we felt bad because she died, Daddy and I could watch the new trees grow and think about the future. Instead of the sad times."

"I see." Raine risked a glance at Jack, who gave her a chagrined kids-what-can-you-do-with-them? look in return. "That's a lovely idea."

"Trees take a very long time to grow," Amy said matter-of-factly. "Daddy says I'll be a big kid, in high school even, before we can cut the ones we planted last year." Her expression revealed that to her six-year-old mind, that waiting time may as well be forever.

"That should be fun, though," Raine said. "You can invite all your teenage friends to the party."

Amy chewed on her thumbnail as she considered that suggestion. "Big kids like parties. I saw that on an *After School Special* at Gramma's. So, I guess it'll be fun, too."

"Bunches and bunches." Raine smiled.

"That's a pretty dress," Amy said suddenly.

"Thank you."

"You're pretty, too. Are you married?"

Raine exchanged another brief look with Jack. "No."

"Neither is my daddy, anymore."

Jack rubbed the bridge of his nose at that heavy-handed announcement. His mother and cousin weren't the only ones who thought he should be moving on with his life. His daughter had, in the past few months, become relentless in her campaign for a new mother.

If she'd had her way, he'd be married to her teacher, or Kelli Cheney, a pretty blond nurse in the doctor's office, or Marilyn Foster, a single mom who tended bar at the Log Cabin nights and picked up much-needed extra cash working mornings and afternoons as the school crossing guard.

"Lilith said Dr. Lindstrom wouldn't mind if Shawna, Renee, and Gwen came," Amy was saying when Jack dragged his mind back to the potentially hazardous conversation. He was tempted to remind her that she shouldn't call adults by their first names, then realized he didn't know which last name Lilith was going by these days.

"I'm sure she wouldn't," Raine said with another warm smile. "I'm also positive they'd love it."

"Oh, they would. But you have to come along, too."

"Me?" Her smile deflated like a hot-air balloon that had just sprung a leak.

"As the court ordered, darling," Lilith, who'd joined them, reminded Raine pointedly. "I'm sure, if she were asked, Judge Babs would insist that you accompany the girls on any outing. To make certain they don't get into any more trouble."

Jack was enjoying the way Amy and Lilith had essentially boxed Raine into a corner. "A little physical work outside in the fresh air will probably be good for the girls," he pointed out. "Gwen should probably take it easy, though."

"Definitely." Raine's mind was scrambling for a way out.

"Then you'll come?" If his daughter's wide eyes had been brown rather than green, she would have looked like a cocker spaniel, begging its owner to come out and play. Jack had had that look aimed at him enough times to know how difficult it was to resist.

Raine shrugged, as if knowing when she was licked. "Okay. I'll come."

"Oh, goodie!" Amy clapped her hands. "Hey everybody," she called out as Jack lowered her back to the floor. "Raine says you can all come to our planting party."

She ran back to the girls, followed by Lilith, who had obviously decided that her work was done.

"Well." Raine breathed out a frustrated breath. "Obviously subtlety is not my mother's strong point."

Jack laughed at that, finding himself actually looking forward to the weekend. "Nor my daughter's. I'm sorry if Amy embarrassed you. If it's any consolation, it isn't exactly personal. She's been on a campaign to get her old man married for months." He gave her his best grin, the one he hadn't tried out for nearly two years. "I guess she's getting tired of my spaghetti."

Raine smiled at that, as he'd intended her to.

Damn, the woman was downright gorgeous when she smiled. She had him feeling things he hadn't for a very long time. Thinking things that he probably shouldn't.

"It'll be fun." Because he couldn't be this close to her without touching, Jack skimmed his fingertips up her face. "Put some sun in that city pallor." When she batted at his hand, he caught hold of hers and linked their fingers together.

"You really have to stop this touching, Sheriff," she insisted, returning to that cool-as-frost court-room voice that instead of annoying or intimidating him, only made Jack want to kiss the breath out of her.

"Now that you're on my daughter's candidate list, you may as well drop the *sheriff* and call me Jack," he reminded her mildly. "I'm just checking."

"Checking what?"

"If they fit. They do." He touched palm to palm, ignoring the fact that his hand dwarfed her smaller, whiter ones. "I thought they might." His smile was slow, arrogant, and designed to seduce.

"That's definitely hitting." She tugged her hand free, spun around on her heel and made a beeline toward the dressing rooms. Jack watched the sexy sway of her hips beneath that flowered silk and re-sisted, just barely, the urge to tackle her.

"Hey, Harvard," he called.

"What now?" She turned half toward him, her fists planted on her hips in a way that pulled the material even tighter.

Amused, and more interested than he should be, Jack grinned. "The party's informal—old jeans and T-shirts. But buy the dress anyway. It's definitely you."

"It's definitely you," Raine mimicked later. After finally finishing their shopping, they'd had lunch at the Timberline Café, and were now headed back to the house. "The nerve of some people."

"Did you say something, darling?" Lilith asked with a feigned innocence that Raine didn't buy for a minute.

"Nothing that can be repeated in front of children," she answered through gritted teeth.

"You're angry at me again."

"Angry? Why should I be angry?" Raine asked with a calm she was a very long way from feeling.

"I have no idea. But you definitely seem upset about something."

"How about the way you practically threw me at Jack O'Halloran?"

"I didn't do any such thing."

Raine shot her an accusatory glare. "Didn't you?"

"Not at all," Lilith lied blithely. "However, to be perfectly honest, darling, I think the tree-planting outing could do you a world of good. Living in the city has you looking much too pale."

"I wish people would quit saying I look pale, because I'm not. I'm merely fair skinned." Raine frowned as she remembered Jack O'Halloran's cocky grin. It had been slow, arrogant, and undeniably charming. "As for that that dress . . ."

"It's stunning," Lilith filled in when Raine's voice dropped off.

"It's not my style," Raine insisted yet again.

"Of course not, dear," Lilith agreed.

Neither one of them mentioned that the dress in question was currently covered in a green-and-white-striped plastic bag, hanging on a hook behind the driver's seat,

"Now, a chat about"—Peg wiggled her nose—"boys."

Jack was sitting with Amy, watching one of the tapes. Peg's hair had begun to grow in when she'd taped this one; he remembered how surprised and pleased she'd been when she'd discovered that the debilitating chemo that had almost killed her had left her with curls.

"One of these days," Peg was saying, "if you haven't already, you're going to meet a boy you really like. Probably at school, which is where I met your father, although we were older than you. If you're lucky, he'll like you, too.

"Now the problem is," she said, leaning back in the wing chair and steepling her slender fingers, "boys aren't as mature as we girls. They get nervous when they realize that they're starting to like us. Most of the time that has them acting a little goofy." She turned and seemed to be grinning at someone offscreen. Jack knew that someone had been himself. "Okay, a lot goofy."

"Put it on pause, Daddy," Amy said suddenly. Jack did as instructed, freezing his wife's image onto the screen.

"What's the matter, Pumpkin?"

"Is that true? Do boys act goofy? Did you?"

"Absolutely." Jack smiled at the memory that was so clear it could have been yesterday. "I offered to carry your mother's library books back to her dorm."

"But you were so busy staring at her, thinking how pretty she was, that you tripped over a sprinkler head and dropped them in the fountain. And they got all wet." Amy had heard this story before.

"Soaking wet. They ballooned up to about ten times their original size."

"Then you paid the library fine so Mommy wouldn't have to."

"It was my fault." He'd gotten a second job busing

tables at a sorority to pay the bill for the ruined books. "It was only right that I take responsibility."

"Then you fell in love. And got married. And adopted me."

"That's exactly how it happened," he agreed. "Except you forgot the part about how we loved you to pieces."

"I know that. . . . Okay." Amy nodded, satisfied. "You can start it again, Daddy."

It was not the first time they'd watched this particular tape. In fact, it had become such a favorite over the past month, that Jack figured he could probably say the words right along with Peg. As his wife went on to talk about boys chasing girls on the school ground, and how, in the third grade, Jimmy Hazlett had washed her face in the snow, and then, that same day, had given her a lace-trimmed valentine with a puffy red satin heart, Jack's mind wandered, as it had been doing far too often these past three days, to Raine Cantrell.

There's no future in this, pal; a nagging voice in the back of his mind pointed out what he'd already decided.

Having given the matter a great deal of thought, he'd come to the conclusion that the kind of men the lady usually went out with were undoubtedly sophisticated, cultured guys who'd take her to the ballet and the opera. Guys who could whisper sweet nothings in at least one foreign language. Guys who, if not at the pinnacle of their profession, would at least be on the fast track up to that lofty peak.

She's city, you're country. You arrest the bad guys and put them in jail; she gets them out. She's French champagne, you're whatever beer's on sale. It would never work out.

On that point, both Jack and his internal voice agreed. But he wasn't interested in forever. He'd gone into his marriage with Peg with that goal, only to discover that real life wasn't anything like the fairy tales Amy loved to have him read at bedtime.

In fairy tales, the beautiful princess never got ovarian cancer; the princess's hair stayed long and shiny and strong enough for the prince to climb up, and when she did die, or go to sleep for a hundred years, she could always be awakened by the prince's kiss and they both lived happily ever after. Whenever the princess's life was threatened, the prince would come charging in on a white steed, armor gleaming in the sun, and save the day.

Which just went to show what a flop he was as a knight in shining armor, Jack thought grimly.

The following day, while Amy was at school, Jack called in to dispatch that he was turning his radio off for the rest of the afternoon. Then he drove out of town, up into the mountains.

The meadow was ablaze in wildflowers, just as it had been when he'd first made love to Peg on a blue-and-black plaid blanket beneath a buttery spring sun. As it had been, years later, when he'd scattered the ashes of the woman he'd thought he was going to grow old with in this very same spot.

He sat on a flat rock which offered a breath-stealing view of green forests and water. Clouds formed overhead, blocking out the sun.

"I don't know what to do," he admitted out loud. "Ever since you"—he couldn't say the word *died*, not

in this place that held so many bittersweet memories—"went away," he said instead, "I've been so
busy trying to stay sane and take care of our daughter and fill Dad's shoes, that I haven't had any time
to even think about a woman."

He plucked some spring green grass from beside
the rock. It was not the first time he'd come up here
to talk with his wife. In the beginning he'd cried,
sobbing like a baby, releasing tears that he hadn't
dared shed in front of his friends, his parents, his
daughter. Especially his daughter. Later, after he
couldn't cry anymore, the anger had come out and
he'd stomped over the alpine meadow, screaming at
the top of his lungs. The only witnesses to his an-
guish were the marmots and a red-tailed hawk that
lived in a nearby tree.

Finally, he'd moved past the pain and the anger
to a point where he could come here to find comfort—even a strange sort of companionship—when
he got too lonely. Jack knew that some people
might think him nuts for talking this way to his dead
wife. He didn't care.

"Then Ida's damn granddaughter came roaring
into town with all guns blazing," he said.

He couldn't help smiling at the memory of her,
marching through the rain and mire on that long-
legged stride. Even soaked to the skin, she'd reminded him of some amazing female warrior princess. Like the one Amy liked to watch on TV. Xena,
he recalled after a moment's thought.

"She can be a real pain in the ass. But there's
another side to her. A gentler, caring side that I
think she's tried real hard to bury over the years.

Which, if you'd ever met her mother, you'd probably understand."

Peg had always been much more forgiving of human failings than he was. Then again, until she'd gotten sick, she'd taught kindergarten, which had sheltered her from the daily examples of man's inhumanity to man that he'd witnessed on Seattle's mean streets.

"Of course there's no future in it. She's only going to be here for a couple more weeks, then she'll go back to her fancy, high-rise office in New York."

If what Dan had told him about Raine's win for Odessa Oil was even half-true, she was a power player in a city that defined high stakes. He had no trouble picturing her in a corner-window office that looked out over the city and made the cars on the street below look like Hot Wheels toys.

"Get this—she's a lawyer." He shook his head. Despite his affection for his cousin, Jack was having trouble getting past this one. "At first I thought it was just hormones. Which wasn't any big deal. . . . But I'm beginning to think it's more than that. And that scares the hell out of me."

Peg didn't answer, of course. But when he felt a soft breeze against his cheek, Jack was reminded of yet another tape she'd left behind. One she'd given to his mother for safekeeping until after she'd gone.

He'd first viewed what turned out to be her final goodbye in the early hours of the morning the day after her memorial service. Or at least he'd tried to watch it. It had taken three attempts before he was able to get all the way through it.

"Darling Jack," she'd soothed, her soft voice and her liquid blue eyes filled with warm comfort. "I know how horrible you must be feeling now. But I don't want you mourning me. Because I'm not gone. Not really."

That was when he'd turned off the VCR the first time. If she wasn't really gone, then why the hell wasn't she upstairs in their bed where she belonged?

"I'll always be in your heart, Jack," the farewell had continued when he'd tried again a week or so later. "In our daughter's heart. I'll be with the both of you always, for all eternity. I'll watch over you while you honor your oath to keep our friends and neighbors safe. I'll be with you on the sunniest summer days and the darkest winter nights.

"When you hear the breeze in the treetops, it will be my breath whispering your name, and whenever you feel a soft rain cooling your skin, it'll be my spirit passing by."

This was where he'd stopped on that second attempt. Then proceeded to drink himself into temporary oblivion.

Finally, nearly six months after he'd kissed his wife for the last time, he'd worked up the courage to watch the tape to the end.

"I know you love me, Jack. As I love you. Truly, madly, deeply. Forever. But sometimes forever on earth isn't as long as we'd hoped and it would break my heart to think of you alone, mourning my death instead of celebrating the wonderful life we had together and the blessings that brought us our darling daughter."

Jack heard a moan and realized it had been torn from his own throat. He felt the moisture on his cheeks, looked up, and while the gunmetal gray sky was getting increasingly lower, it hadn't yet begun to rain.

"Now I know this will make you angry, Jack," Peg said, in that sweet, cajoling way that he'd always found impossible to resist. "But I want you to marry again. Partly for Amy's sake, so she'll have more of a mother than this mountain of video tapes I've created can provide. She needs a real Mommy, Jack. A living, breathing one who can make Jell-O when she has a tummy ache and help soothe teenage broken hearts.

"A mother who'll someday watch you walk her down the aisle to begin a new life with a young man, who if she's very, very lucky, will love her the way you always loved me."

Her voice choked up at this point. Her blue eyes shimmered with tears. She bit her lip, drew in a ragged breath and combed her graceful fingers through her short blond cap of curls.

"I'm sorry," she murmured. "I just need a minute." She drew in another breath. This one more shallow than the first. Then, demonstrating the same strength of will he'd witnessed during the two years she'd valiantly fought off death, she forged on to the end.

"But I also want you to get married again for yourself. Because you have such an amazing capacity for caring, Jack, it would be a sin not to open your heart to someone else. Someone who needs you as much as you need her. Someone who loves you the way you will her.

"Now, I know how your mind works." She'd sniffled away the tears that had threatened earlier, now sounding more like the Peg who could keep a class of two dozen rambunctious five-year-olds in line. "I know how you feel about honor and loyalty, but you mustn't ever feel guilty about loving again, or even think you're abandoning me or my memory."

Her voice and her eyes gentled again. Offering reassurance. "Because I believe, with every fiber of my being, that someday, darling Jack, we'll meet again in a beautiful place where love is infinite and there will be plenty for all of us to share."

Alone on the mountain, in the meadow they'd laughingly once claimed as their own, Jack closed his eyes and pictured the way her wedding band had gleamed in the sun slanting through the hospice window as she'd touched her fingertips first to her lips and then to the camera lens.

Fade to black.

The sky overhead opened up and the rain that had been threatening began to fall. But as he sat there, remembering, Jack didn't notice.

∾ 14 ∾

Raine had come to expect the unexpected from Lilith. But it appeared her mother had found a new way to drive her crazy.

For as long as she could remember, her mother had glowed with an internal light. But after Ida's guardianship hearing—and their argument—it was if that inner light had been snuffed out by an icy wind. Lilith became uncharacteristically subdued. She seldom spoke, and when she did it was in a listless voice lacking its customary music. She'd twisted her flowing silver hair into a decidedly unglamourous knot at the nape of her neck and exchanged her rainbow of colorful silks for clothing that could have come from Raine's own closet. Everything was now charcoal gray, bark brown, or black.

When Raine entered the kitchen a week after the hearing and found her mother clad in black slacks and a matching cotton shirt, it crossed her mind that in this new camouflage clothing Lilith could blend in quite well on the streets of Manhattan.

Even more surprising was the sight of her dropping cookie dough onto a greased aluminum sheet.

"Hello, darling." Lilith smiled a bit uncertainly. "I hope you like chocolate chip cookies."

"Of course I do." Raine tried to remember a previous time she'd seen her mother engaged in any domestic activity and came up blank. Obviously Lilith had been working for some time; there were spatters on the cupboard doors, the counter was covered with flour, and there were enough mixing bowls, measuring cups, and assorted utensils piled up in the sink to create an eight-course dinner.

"I decided baking cookies to welcome Savannah home this evening would be a nice, maternal thing to do." Atypical worry lines bracketed her mouth. "I do hope she likes chocolate chip. Perhaps I should have made oatmeal instead. I forgot to buy raisins when I was at the store, but I could always go back, and—"

"Don't worry. Everyone loves chocolate chip," Raine assured her, feeling strangely as if she'd walked through some unseen psychic curtain and landed in *The Twilight Zone*. That was the only excuse she could think of for Lilith Lindstrom Cantrell Townsend wearing an apron. "Savannah's going to be pleased you went to the trouble." *And surprised as hell.*

"I also bought some pancake mix while I was at the market. I thought they might be a nice change from cold cereal tomorrow morning."

"Sounds great." If it wasn't *The Twilight Zone*, she must have somehow entered a parallel universe, Raine decided.

"I couldn't make up my mind whether to buy the

buttermilk or the blueberry." Lilith wiped her hands distractedly on the front of the apron. "So I bought both."

"Good idea." Or perhaps, Raine considered, some aliens had landed in Coldwater Cove, snatched her mother up to the Mother Ship for some sort of strange medical experiments and left a Stepford Wife in her place.

"Of course, I realize that Savannah would never, in a million years, use a mix," Lilith continued as she returned to filling the cookie sheet with mounds of dough. They were eerily the same size, precisely the way a programed Stepford Wife might form them. "But I hoped that . . . Oh, no!"

Smoke was billowing from around the edges of the oven door. While Lilith twisted her hands together and made little wailing sounds, Raine grabbed the quilted oven mitt from the counter, opened the oven, pulled out the cookie sheet, and dropped it into the sink.

"Oh no." Lilith repeated bleakly, staring in abject dismay at the rounded black mounds. "They're burned."

More like cremated, Raine thought but did not say. "They are a bit crisp," she agreed carefully.

"They're ruined!" Her mother's pansy blue eyes were swimming with moisture.

"It's no big deal. You can just bake more."

"I'll ruin them, too." The tears that had been threatening began to fall, streaming down Lilith's face in wet, mascara-darkened trails. "I'm such a mess. I can't do anything right!"

"We're only talking cookies." The smoke alarm began to blare; Raine opened a window.

"I was thinking about what you said the other night, about how selfish I'd been, and decided that you were right. I truly didn't mean to cause you pain, Raine, but obviously I did. So I decided that I was going to turn over a new leaf and try to make things up to you and Savannah." The tears began to flow faster. "But those damn burned cookies are a metaphor for my entire life."

This display of dramatics was the most emotion her mother had shown in days. It was also surprisingly welcome. "If that's the truth, then we're in trouble," Raine said soothingly. "Because, with the exception of Savannah, none of the Lindstrom women have ever been able to cook."

"We've always had better things to do," Ida, drawn by the smoke and the alarm to the kitchen, pronounced from the doorway. "More important things than spending our lives in an apron and standing in front of a hot stove."

"That's just the point," Lilith wailed. "I've never done anything even the slightest bit important with my life." She sank onto one of the ladderback chairs, buried her face in her hands, and wept copiously.

Raine exchanged a distressed look with Ida, who shrugged. "Nonsense," the elderly woman said. "Don't go talking such foolishness, Lilith. Your singing has obviously given a lot of people pleasure."

"They only put up with me because I still look good in short skirts and leather and they're waiting for the star performer."

"Now, you know that's not true. You've always had a lovely voice.

"And you were a good actress," Raine said encouragingly.

"I was a terrible actress."

"Well, you weren't exactly Bette Davis or Kate Hepburn," Ida allowed. "But I'll bet there wasn't anybody in the horror movie business who could scream louder than you. Or who looked better in a wet nightgown."

Raine knew things were serious when her mother didn't agree with the nightgown assessment.

"And you've given birth to two exceptional young women," Ida continued. "That in itself is an accomplishment."

Lilith lifted her head. "Even an alley cat can give birth," she said, reminding Raine uncomfortably of the words she'd flung at her mother in anger. "That doesn't mean that she's capable of taking care of her kittens."

"You did the best you could at the time," Ida said briskly. "That's all any of us can do."

The words seemed to have a settling effect. Lilith's weeping trailed off to ragged, gulping sobs, and the flood of tears began to subside.

"What a mess." Her bleak eyes looked around the kitchen. Her shoulders slumped. No longer a Stepford Wife, she looked like a dejected fifty-year-old woman who'd just discovered that real life wasn't always fun. "I'd better start cleaning up before Savannah arrives." She pushed herself out of the chair, tipped the blackened mounds into the wastebasket and returned the cookie sheet to the sink. When she turned on the tap, water sizzled on the still-hot aluminum.

The sight of her mother with her rubber-gloved hands in soapsuds was even stranger than Lilith

baking. Raine was about to suggest she take over
when Gwen and Renee came into the room.

"Wow," Renee said.

"I know." Lilith's voice threatened renewed tears.
"It's a mess." Soapy water sloshed over the rim of
the sink onto the pine floor, which, like the counter,
was dusted with flour. The resulting mixture resembled library paste.

"Why don't you let us help?" Gwen grabbed a dish-
rag. "I'll clean up while Renee finishes baking the
cookies."

"It's my mess." More water sloshed onto the floor
as Lilith energetically scrubbed at a Pyrex mixing
bowl. "I'm going to clean it up."

Realizing that her mother's efforts were only making things worse, Raine decided to attempt to dis-
tract her.

"You know," she suggested, "as much as Savannah's going to enjoy those cookies, I'll bet she'd love
some fresh flowers in the bedroom. None of us have
the marvelous eye for color and design you do,
Mother."

Lilith spun toward her, billowy soapsuds dripping
unnoticed from the yellow rubber gloves. "What did
you call me?"

Raine was as surprised to have said the word out
loud as Lilith was to have heard it. "Mother."
Strangely, it sounded almost right. "Does that
bother you?"

"Oh, no, darling! Of course not!" There was a renewed flood of tears as Lilith threw her arms around
Raine. "It sounds wonderful. Does this mean you've
forgiven me?"

Her T-shirt was getting soaked by dishwater and

tears. "There's nothing to forgive," Raine said, not quite truthfully. Grateful to have the old Lilith back, she was nevertheless discomfited by the emotional display. "Now, why don't you let the girls finish up and go take care of those flowers?"

"That's a grand idea." Lilith released Raine from the tight embrace. "I think hyacinths might be nice. Or sweetpeas." She nodded. "Definitely sweetpeas." She peeled off the gloves, untied the apron, and threw it uncaringly onto one of the kitchen chairs, seeming not to notice when it slid onto the gummy floor. "They're perfect for spring."

"Well," Ida said, after Lilith left the room with renewed purpose in both her step and her eyes, "I never thought I'd say it, but it's a relief to have the old Lilith back with us."

The others murmured heartfelt agreement.

"You know," Ida mused, "she did have a good idea, making those cookies for Savannah. Family coming home is cause for a celebration. I believe, since we're being so domestic, I'll make my meatloaf."

As Raine exchanged a fatalistic look with the girls, she hoped Savannah stopped for dinner before she arrived in Coldwater Cove.

Savannah Townsend's late-night arrival in Coldwater Cove might just as well have been accompanied by a flourish of trumpets. Looking at her younger sister, if she hadn't known better, Raine would have thought nothing had gone wrong in her life. Indeed, she resembled Alexander the Great entering Babylon for the first time—strong, bold, invincible.

"It's about time you came back home where you belonged," Ida said with her usual bluntness.

"It's good to be here," Savannah agreed as she hugged her grandmother.

"Of course it is. Everyone knows that home is where the hearth is."

Savannah laughed. "Now I know I'm home." She bestowed a smile on her mother. "Lilith, I swear you look younger every day."

"It's the clean life your grandmother makes me lead whenever I come back to Coldwater Cove." More laughter, hugs were exchanged.

After embracing Raine, Savannah leaned back and observed her sister more closely. "You've lost weight."

"Not that much."

"You've also got circles beneath your eyes and you're too pale. If I didn't know better, I'd think that you were the one getting a divorce."

"I've been busy." Raine was getting tired of people's negative comments on her looks. She also couldn't help marveling at the way her sister could have her marriage collapse, give up a job she'd worked like hell to achieve, move out of her home, drive for three long days, and still arrive looking like some supermodel in a white jumpsuit trimmed in gold braid that didn't have a single wrinkle or stain. There were times, and this was definitely one of them, that Raine was forced to wonder if Savannah sprayed herself with Teflon before leaving the house each morning. "I just finished a big case."

"I know. I saw you on television. That took a lot of guts."

"Making myself a target for egg throwers?"

"No. Taking Odessa Oil's side in the first place."

"They're a client."

"They're also an oil company."

Raine glanced at the sporty red BMW illuminated by the spreading glow of the porch light. "Try running those snazzy wheels on tap water and you may just develop a different view of oil companies."

"Touché," Savannah said with a dazzling smile that was a twin to Lilith's. "I also realize that you don't always have a choice which of your firm's clients you represent, so—"

"Actually, I'm the one who brought Odessa to Choate, Plimpton, Wells & Sullivan in the first place. The revenues it's already generated have about guaranteed my partnership."

"Well, isn't that wonderful. You must be on cloud nine."

Ever loyal, Savannah gave Raine another big hug and the subject was dropped. But as they went into the house, Raine couldn't help thinking how her sister's take on the case echoed that of seemingly everyone around her.

As they gathered around the table while the girls slept upstairs, it occurred to Raine that this was almost like old times. Except in the past, Lilith had seldom been part of the family group.

"I knew that Kevin was trouble the first time I met him," Lilith said heatedly. "He was too slick and too smooth for my taste."

"Heaven knows, your track record with men is terrific," Ida said beneath her breath.

"I heard that." Lilith tossed her head. Raine had been relieved this afternoon when her mother had finally pulled her hair loose of that ugly bun she'd been wearing it in these past days. "That's exactly how I recognized that he was wrong for our Savannah. Because he reminded me of exactly the type of man I've always tended to get involved with. Smooth and charming and handsome as sin."

"Ha!" Ida scoffed. "That kind of charm is the oily kind that you can wash off in the shower with a bar of Lava soap. As for him being handsome, I suppose he wasn't all that hard on the eyes," she admitted grudgingly. "But to be perfectly honest, Savannah, dear, I always felt that *his* eyes were a bit too close together. And did any of the rest of you ever notice that he squinted?"

"That was because of his contacts," Savannah said. "He had dry eyes."

Ida was not to be deterred. "They were squinty. Just the type of eyes a man who'd run around on his wife would have. So, I suppose the gal's some bikini-clad beach bunny bimbette half his age?"

"Bimbette?" Despite the seriousness of the topic, Savannah exchanged an amused look with Raine. "Where on earth did you pick up that one?"

"I have lunch with Dottie Anderson in the back office of the Dancing Deer once a month," Ida said. "We watch television while we eat. Last month we watched a show where new mothers confronted the bimbette babysitters who were sleeping with their husbands. Well, needless to say, things got wild. I'll tell you, there's more violence on some of those shows than on the wrestling programs."

"You watch wrestling?" Raine asked.

"At times. No matter what people say about it being staged, it's great entertainment. Gwen and I like to make popcorn and root for Hulk Hogan." Ida jutted out her Lindstrom chin. "Do you have any problem with that?"

"None at all," Raine said quickly. "I was just surprised."

"It's important to try new things. Getting old is kind of like being a salmon. . . . If you don't keep moving forward you die."

"It's a shark that has to keep moving," Raine murmured.

"Whatever." Ida turned back to her younger granddaughter, "So is she a bimbette?"

"Actually, she's an attorney from the resort's legal department. One of those hard-edged, ice-water-in-the-veins, career Amazons with brass balls." The moment she heard the words come out of her mouth, Savannah cringed. "I'm sorry, Raine. I certainly didn't mean to imply that *you* were anything like that."

Raine managed a smile. "I know." But she was a lot like that. And everyone in the kitchen knew it. Cream puffs did not become Xena, Warrior Princess.

"I'll bet she keeps them in her fancy briefcase," Ida decided.

"Keeps what, Mother?" Lilith asked.

"Her brass balls."

They shared a laugh at that.

Savannah sighed and poured more wine from the bottle Lilith had placed in the middle of the table. "When I first moved out, Kevin insisted he didn't want a divorce. But now he's playing hardball."

She combed her fingers through her long auburn hair. The California sun had brightened the red curls with gold streaks. Looking at all that lush hair, the

Malibu tan, and bright emerald eyes, Raine thought that Savannah resembled some glorious goddess created by a master alchemist, rather than a mortal woman.

"He called me on my car phone about the time I crossed the California-Oregon border to warn me that the company considered any recipes I created while I'd worked there to be the resort's intellectual property."

Lilith lifted a beringed hand to her throat. "Surely you're not serious, darling?"

"That's what he's claiming."

"We can take care of that," Raine assured her briskly. "We'll get you a good lawyer and make the squinty-eyed, cheating bastard regret that he ever messed with a Lindstrom woman." Sometimes being a take-no-prisoner warrior woman could be a good thing.

When they'd been young, she and Savannah had shared M&Ms, popsicles, chicken pox, Barbie dolls, and the absence of a beautiful, but flawed mother. Later, they fought over bathroom time and hair dryers, even as they shared teenage confidences, secrets, and dreams. Now, during this trying time, Raine vowed to stand by her sister, just as Savannah would have stood by her, with the solidarity of the March sisters.

"I'd hoped we could end things civilly." Savannah rubbed her temples, momentarily letting down her guard long enough for Raine to see the incredible stress her sister was feeling. "But since I also refuse to cave in and let Kevin keep making money off my creations, I guess that's going to be impossible."

"Well, of course it is, dear." Lilith leaned forward

to pat her daughter's knee before refilling her own glass. "If God had intended for us to be friends with our ex-husbands, She wouldn't have made them such bastards in the first place."

Ida retrieved a second bottle of wine from the refrigerator. "He'll get his comeuppance," she predicted. "Everyone knows that time wounds all heels."

As the full, white moon outside the window sailed across a star-studded jet night sky, and both the chardonnay and the conversation continued to flow, Raine couldn't help thinking how good it felt to be home.

After another restless night spent chasing sleep, the first thing Raine noticed the next morning was that Savannah's bed was empty. Which was a bit surprising since Raine doubted that her sister had gotten all that much sleep.

It had been sometime after midnight when Raine had realized that the weeping ghost woman in her dream wasn't a ghost at all, but her sister, crying softly in the adjoining bathroom.

She'd slipped soundlessly out of bed and stood outside the door for a long, hesitant time, torn between trying to offer comfort and allowing her sister privacy. She'd even lifted her hand to knock, then, at the last moment, turned away and returned to bed.

It was a full twenty minutes more before Savannah returned to bed. Once again, Raine considered saying something. Anything. She might be a whiz at coming up with exactly the right words to sway a judge or jury, but personal matters were another story. Try as she might, she couldn't think of a single thing to say that might ease Savannah's obviously wounded heart. So, she'd kept silent.

But more than once during the long night, Raine was all too aware of her sister, lying awake in the next bed, only a few feet away, and wished that she could be, just for this one instance, as open and uninhibited as Lilith.

Thinking back on her sisterly failure now, Raine sighed and looked around the pretty little room. The curtains were white priscillas, the lace hand-tatted in a floral pattern. More flowers bloomed on the cream-colored wallpaper, reminding Raine of the day Ida had taken her young granddaughters shopping. Raine had wanted a muted white on white stripe, while Savannah, unsurprisingly, had opted for blindingly red poppies. The delicate purple violets had been a compromise. One that, in time, they'd both come to appreciate.

When she'd first returned to Coldwater Cove, after the clamor of the city, Raine had found the silence of the rural little town unnerving. But over the past days, she'd gradually come to realize that it wasn't silent at all. The window was halfway open, allowing her to hear the sweet morning song of birds, the rhythmic clang of a buoy out in the bay, and a *click click click* she could almost, but not quite recognize.

She went over to the window and looked out just in time to see the neighbor's eight-year-old son ride by on his bicycle, playing cards clipped to the spokes. Raine smiled, remembering having done the same thing so many years ago. Unfortunately, that was the week Ida had hosted her bridge club luncheon. Needless to say, her grandmother had not been pleased to discover the face cards missing.

The town was alive with signs of seasonal renewal: the watercolor colors of the flower beds in Pioneer Park could have washed off an Impressionist painting, and the blossoming fruit trees lining Harbor Street looked like giant pink-and-white lollipops. Looking out over the quaint town that resembled a Charles Wysocki painting of spring in New England, Raine thought that if there was a prettier place on the planet, she certainly hadn't seen it. If she were ever to choose somewhere other than New York to live, she could do far worse than come home to Coldwater Cove.

Not that she wanted to, Raine reminded herself. Turning one's back on the fast life and a lucrative urban law practice might be fine for Daniel O'Halloran, but not for her.

With that thought firmly etched in her mind, she took a quick shower, dried her hair, and went downstairs to the kitchen that smelled cheerily of just-brewed coffee. Her sister's head was inside the refrigerator door.

"Good morning," Raine greeted her.

"Good morning." Savannah turned around. Her smile was as warm as ever, but smudges beneath her eyes hinted at a sleepless night. "Gram's already out and about by the way. She said something about running by a friend's to pick up some plant cuttings that Gwen was all excited about planting out back. She took the girls with her."

"I assume Lilith's still sleeping?" So much for her mother's plan to make pancakes. Raine couldn't quite keep the note of censure from her voice.

"We were up late. Besides, you know Lilith and her beauty sleep."

"I know it certainly seems to have worked. Other than her hair, I don't think she looks any different than she did when we were kids."

"She may look the same, but she seemed less flamboyant than usual last night."

Raine sighed and poured some coffee from the carafe into an earthenware mug handpainted with sunflowers. "That's my fault. I got angry after the hearing and accused her of being selfish and irresponsible."

"Of course she is," Savannah said easily. "So, what else is new? Your problem is, Sister dear, that you've always expected her to suddenly turn into Mrs. Cleaver. Which isn't going to happen in this lifetime. . . . You've got your choice between French toast or an omelet."

"An omelet sounds great." Raine couldn't argue with Savannah's perception of their mother. "But you don't have to go to the trouble."

"It's no trouble." She took a carton of eggs and a wedge of cheese out of the refrigerator. "Normally, I'd be cooking for a lot larger crowd than just family. Especially on the weekend."

"It's not fair," Raine muttered. She took a sip of coffee and tasted cinnamon. "Having to give up a job you love because your husband was unfaithful."

"I can always get another one." Savannah began breaking eggs into a bright blue bowl.

"But you shouldn't have to. You lost more than your marriage, Savannah. You lost your livelihood, a generous benefit plan, profit sharing. Not to mention that without you in the kitchen, the resort undoubtedly wouldn't have earned nearly the profits, which makes you a valuable corporate asset. You know, you could always sue to keep your job. Since the company would undoubtedly settle just to avoid the negative publicity, the case wouldn't even come to court."

Savannah laughed at that. "Spoken like a born lawyer. I'm not going to fight Kevin to stay at a place where I'd have to work with him everyday."

"I imagine that would be hard." Since her sister didn't seem eager to pursue legal measures, Raine didn't mention that they could undoubtedly force the company to transfer the cheating rat to another resort. Preferably somewhere far away, like Timbuktu. Or Mars. When she found herself comparing her sister's rat of a husband with Jack, Raine decided there was no comparison.

"It would certainly be difficult to resist throwing all my pots and pans at his head." Savannah whisked the eggs with a bit more force than necessary.

"How are you doing? Really?" Raine asked carefully, remembering last night's weeping.

"As well as can be expected. Actually, my pride is a lot more wounded than my heart. I mean, it's not as if his sleeping around came as any great surprise." She sighed as she sprinkled crushed dill into the eggs. "Our marriage has been rocky for a long time. I think the only thing keeping us together, other than my determination not to repeat our mother's mistakes, was inertia."

She began grating the cheese into the egg-and-dill mixture. "I knew if I left him that it'd cost me my job at Las Casitas. But since I haven't exactly been happy there, either—"

"You haven't?" This was one more surprise in a week of surprises. "I thought you loved your work."

"I love cooking for people." Savannah smiled back over her shoulder. "But the resort was so large and impersonal that it wasn't what I'd imagined back when I went off to Paris for cooking school." She opened a cupboard and found a shiny, copper-bottomed omelet pan that looked as if it had never been used. Given Ida's lack of domestic skills, Raine suspected it hadn't. "I've always had a fantasy of something more intimate."

"Like our teas."

Savannah flashed another of those smiles that was a twin of their glamorous mother's. "Exactly." Butter sizzled fragrantly in the pan, making Raine's mouth water. "The past year I've been thinking of leaving the resort and opening up a small inn. Perhaps a bed-and-breakfast. I even looked for a building, but of course the real estate prices in Los Angeles were beyond my budget."

She tilted the eggs from the bowl into the pan with a twist of the wrist. "So, on the drive home, it occurred to me that I should just look around here."

"In Coldwater Cove?"

"Sure. The last couple times I've been back, I've been amazed at the amount of tourist business the town's been getting during the summer, now that the Pacific Northwest's become such a popular vacation spot. I was looking at the real estate ads in the paper before you came down and did some quick number crunching and I think, once Kevin and I divide up our assets, I should be able to swing buying a fixer-upper."

Life was getting stranger and stranger. Raine was becoming more and more convinced that she'd tum-

bled down a rabbit hole and instead of landing in
Coldwater Cove, had ended up in Wonderland.

"Do you even know *how* to renovate a house?"

"No. But I figure I can learn. The same way I
learned to cook. The same way you learned to be
a lawyer."

"Your point," Raine allowed, watching with admiration as her sister deftly flipped the omelet onto a
plate. "I'd just never pictured you living in Coldwater Cove."

"We're not all cut out for big-city life." Savannah
cut the omelet, slid the halves onto two pottery
plates, placed the plates on the table and refilled
both their coffee cups. "I'm almost afraid to mention
it, but if those dark circles under your eyes are any
indication, it doesn't look as if you are, either."

"It's been a rough few months," Raine hedged. Not
eager to have to defend herself yet again, she took
a bite of omelet and nearly wept. "This is delicious."
It was also so light and fluffy it could have floated
off the plate.

Savannah shrugged. "An omelet's easy."

"For you, maybe. Newsflash, baby sister, more
Americans eat a Pop Tart or Egg McMuffin for
breakfast than dill-and-cheese omelets."

"All the more reason they'll want to stay at my
inn," Savannah pointed out. "As flattered as I admittedly am by your appreciation of my culinary skills,
I believe we were discussing your life?"

"There's nothing to discuss. At least it doesn't
make me cry at night." Not yet, anyway.

"You heard." Savannah didn't look all that
surprised.

"I heard." Raine put down her fork with a sigh

that was directed inward, reached out and linked their fingers together atop the table. "I was a rotten sister not to try to do something about it."

"There's nothing you could have done." Savannah looked down at their joined hands. "I was just so angry. Angry at Kevin. But angrier at myself. For avoiding the truth all these years." Her smile was less brilliant and more than a little chagrined. "But I suppose I shouldn't be surprised. Since you and I are both queens of denial."

Raine's first thought was that perhaps that description fit Savannah, who tended to look at life through rose-colored lenses, but she'd always been unflinchingly honest with herself. When that idea caused a little twinge somewhere deep in the far recesses of her mind, Raine's second thought was that she didn't want to think about this.

"This conversation is getting depressing," she said. "Why don't you tell me what kind of house you have in mind?"

Savannah did not need a second invitation. As she shared her rosy, if a bit overly optimistic, plans for her future, her face lit up with enthusiasm. Raine felt a quick, unexpected stab of envy.

Which was, of course, ridiculous. In spite of the good face her sister was trying to put on it, Savannah's life had just crumbled down around her. While Raine's own, on the other hand, was right on course. After all the years of personal sacrifice, of long hours, take-out meals eaten at her desk, and restless nights anticipating or rerunning trials in her dreams, partnership was finally in sight.

When she finally achieved that long-sought-after objective, she could afford to kick back and relax a little. She could begin eating more healthily and return to the running that had burned off the excess tension during her law school days. Perhaps she'd even take up meditation. Heaven knows, Brian swore by the practice, claiming it soothed both his mind and body.

Of course she currently didn't have the twenty minutes to spare each morning and evening Brian spent chanting his mantra or whatever one did while meditating. But she would soon. Once she made partner.

"Enough about me," Savannah said, drawing Raine's attention back to their conversation. "Gram's told me you're about to make partner. Which didn't surprise me, since when he was reporting your oil story, Peter Jennings actually referred to you as the up-and-coming attorney of choice for the high-powered corporate world. I think it's wonderful and I couldn't be more proud of you. But what I really want to know about is your personal life."

"What personal life?" Raine's laugh lacked humor.

"Well, to cut it down to one word—men. Since my love life's turned to mud, why don't you cheer me up by telling me that you're having a mad, passionate affair with some eccentric, bearded SoHo-artist type who adorns your hot naked flesh with edible body paint, then spends all night licking it off."

This time Raine's laugh was genuine. "A bearded artist type?"

"It's always an artist in the movies."

"That proves it. You've definitely been living in LaLa Land too long."

"Well, you may be right about that," Savannah allowed with a little laugh of her own. "But you're dodging the question."

"I don't have time to think about men. At least not in that way."

Raine didn't dare admit that since arriving back home, she'd been thinking about one man *that way*. Too much for comfort.

❧15❧

Now that her sister had arrived, Raine could return to New York. After helping Savannah with the breakfast dishes, then spending an hour on the phone with Brian and another two hours catching up on e-mail and some brief-writing that needed to be done, she went upstairs to begin packing.

As she went to open the drawer, her attention was drawn to a photograph atop the bureau. She remembered the day as if it were yesterday. It had been the summer of her eleventh year and she and her mother and sister had spent a rare, carefree day at the beach. She held the photo up to her face, pulled her hair back, tried to see any part of her mother in the reflection looking back at her from the mirror, and with the exception of a possible faint resemblance around the eyes couldn't see anything that declared her to be Lilith's daughter.

Driven by feelings that had been simmering on the surface since she'd first arrived home, Raine put the photo back, then went into the closet beneath the eaves and took down the box she'd hidden beneath another box of blankets. She placed the box on the bed, opened the lid, and pulled out a scrapbook. The yellowed newspaper clippings were as crisp as dried autumn leaves. As she ran her fingertips over one, the edges that had come loose from the Scotch tape crumbled beneath her touch.

Sighing, she returned to the mirror and held the book up, this time comparing her reflection with a photo of her father that she'd cut out of *Newsweek* so many years ago. Again, nothing. She could have been a changeling.

Which was just fine with her, since she preferred to think of herself as her own woman. A self-made woman who was intelligent and self-confident. A woman capable of fighting her own battles. A woman who didn't need anyone.

Liar.

Raine thought back on those hurtful words Lilith had thrown at her the other night, the accusation that her entire life had been nothing but an attempt to gain her famous father's attention. That wasn't true. Oh, perhaps it had been in the beginning, but most of the time Raine was resigned to the idea that she and Owen Cantrell would never have any sort of father-daughter relationship.

She stared into the mirror, looking hard and deep, now searching for Xena. But the Warrior Princess appeared to have abandoned her.

"Just like Lilith," she murmured, beginning to understand that her personal armor had first been donned to protect a child against feelings of anger, confusion, and fear. And it had done its job well, for so many years. But now it was beginning to unravel and Raine realized that if she wanted to finally heal her relationship with her mother, she was going to have to discard it entirely.

That idea was more terrifying than any court case she'd ever presented. Even more frightening than facing that mob on the federal courthouse steps last week. Feeling as if she were suffocating, Raine practically ran down the stairs, fleeing old ghosts and ancient hurts.

She didn't know how long she sat on the porch swing, vaguely aware, on some level, of the distant buzz of a lawnmower. As she breathed in the scent of newly mown grass, Raine reminded herself that in contrast to her flighty mother, she preferred an orderly life. Since she didn't like leaving things undone, it was time to try to resolve her rocky relationship with her mother.

Knowing that this could take time, Raine decided that if Stephen Wells wouldn't allow her to continue to work away from the office, at least until after Gwen's baby was born, she'd just take advantage of the firm's generous family leave policy.

Not that she knew anyone who actually ever had taken precious work time off for family. But there had to be a first time, Raine thought. Why not her?

Jack's mind kept wandering on the morning of the planting party, making it difficult to keep his mind on his daughter's conversation.

"Gramma made cakes for the party," she revealed as they cleared the table. "One's devil's food." She was carrying the plates over to the counter. When the stack tilted precariously, Jack managed to refrain from reaching out to take it away from her. "The other's carrot cake. With her special frosting."

"Your favorite."

"Even better than strawberry shortcake with whipped cream," Her youthful brow furrowed. "Do you think Raine will like it?"

"I can't imagine anyone not liking your grand-mother's carrot cake."

"Yeah. It's really good. That's why she always wins the blue ribbon at the fair. Grandpa always said that Gramma is the best baker in the county."

"Your grandfather knew what he was talking about. Since he had the biggest sweet tooth in the county."

"I know. He always carried those M&Ms around in his pocket and let me have the red ones . . . . I wonder if Raine can make cakes."

"She's Ms. Cantrell to you, Pumpkin," Jack corrected, "I have no idea if she can bake or not." However, if he were to hazard a guess, he'd say no.

"I know you said I should always call adults by their last name, but when we were in the Dancing Deer, she told me I could call her Raine," Amy reminded him as they stacked the plates in the dishwasher. "Maybe you could ask her today."

Jack dragged himself back from a fantasy of licking fluffy clouds of whipped cream off Raine Cantrell's slender, but eminently appealing body. "Ask her what?"

"About if she knows how to bake."

"Maybe we should just mind our own business," he suggested on a mild tone that invited no further discussion. "How about bringing me your milk glass?"

"I don't see what the big deal is. It's just a question." Amy's frustrated sigh ruffled her pale gold bangs as she returned to the table. "Don't you always tell me that if I want to know something, I should just ask?"

Jack was extremely grateful that the citizens of Coldwater Cove were more inclined than his daughter to view him as a symbol of authority.

"Whether or not *Ms. Cantrell*"—he stressed again—"bakes is not only none of our business, it's beside the point. Since she's going back to New York soon."

"Maybe if she has a good enough time at the party, she'll decide to stay here. I'll bet she doesn't ever plant Christmas trees in New York." She put the glass in the top rack and gave him a guileless smile Jack didn't buy for a minute. His daughter was many delightful things. Subtle definitely wasn't one of them.

"They sell Christmas trees in the city."

"I know that. But if she stayed here, she could just cut one of ours. Or you could cut it for her."

"She's not staying in Coldwater Cove." Less than pleased by the memory of allowing himself to think along much the same lines somewhere just before dawn, he poured the detergent in the machine and slammed the door with more force than necessary. "Her job is in New York."

A job he realized was immensely important to her. It had only taken Dan a few calls to learn that Raine Cantrell was definitely on the fast track to partnership in an old, established practice Dan had described as a "white shoe" firm. How many people would be willing to turn their back on that? Especially to come home to Coldwater Cove, where her biggest case could involve a dispute over a parking spot?

How many people would be willing to turn their backs on a career that undoubtedly paid in the mid--six figures, for the type of practice where clients occasionally paid their bills with fresh-caught fish, poultry, or baked goods? Not many he'd guess. And not her.

"*Your* job used to be in Seattle," Amy reminded him. "But now we live here."

"That's us." He smoothed his hand over the top of her head. "It doesn't work that way for everyone, kiddo."

Jack had always vowed to keep his daughter out of his personal life, when and if he ever got around to having one. Unfortunately, it appeared he wasn't doing a very good job where Raine was concerned.

"Maybe if we asked her to stay, she would."

"We're not going to ask. Because Ms. Cantrell's life is none of our business," he reminded her yet again.

"It is if you like her." She paused a beat, then looked up at him through a fringe of thick lashes. As impossible as it was, since she was still a child, she almost reminded him of the way Vivien Leigh had looked at Clark Gable when she'd put on drapes and gone to coax Rhett Butler into giving her the money to save Tara. "You do like Raine, don't you, Daddy?"

Wondering where on earth his six-year-old daughter had picked up such a blatantly female seductive look, it took Jack a stunned minute to answer. "Well, yeah. Sure I do, but—"

"I do, too," Amy said quickly, before he could add a qualifier. "I think she'd make a neat Mommy. And besides, you're not getting any younger, Daddy. If you don't stop being so particular, you'll be too old for anyone to marry you."

With that pronouncement hanging in the morning air, she swept out of the kitchen, leaving Jack more than a little bemused and feeling as if he were growing more ancient by the minute.

Although Shawna and Renee had moved to their aunt and uncle's home in Bremerton, there'd been no thought of going to the planting party without them. Raine had picked them up earlier, then taken them back to the house to join the others. She'd been relieved when they'd assured her that they were fitting into their new home just fine.

"Oh, look at that!" Gwen said as they drove past the acres of conical blue-green fir and spruce trees. "They look exactly like Christmas trees."

"Duh," Shawna responded with teenage disdain. "Maybe that's why they call it a Christmas tree farm."

"I knew that," Gwen said with a toss of her Orphan Annie curls. "I just never imagined that they'd look so . . . well, finished."

"They've been shaped," Raine revealed. "Even though the spruce and fir trees are trained to grow in more of a pyramid shape than pine trees, they still need to be trimmed at least once a year to shape them." Gwen was right in a way, though, she thought. The only thing missing were gilt angels smiling benevolently atop the trees and some lights and colored glass balls.

"How in the world do you know that?" Ida, sitting beside Raine in the front seat, shot her a curious glance. "I wouldn't think there'd be much need for you to be an expert on growing Christmas trees in New York."

"No. There's not." Raine kept both her expression and her tone casual. "And I'm far from an expert. I just happened to wander across a few sites on the Internet while I was retrieving my e-mail last night."

"I can see how that might happen," Ida agreed dryly. "Cyberspace being such a small, intimate place, I'll bet it's almost impossible not to stumble across Christmas-tree-growing tips. Especially in May."

"All right." If she hadn't been driving, Raine would have thrown up her hands. "So I did a little research. But only so I wouldn't appear too clueless today."

Lilith leaned over from the back seat to give her daughter a knowing look. "Raine, darling, believe me, Jack O'Halloran doesn't give two hoots whether you know anything about his silly old trees. As for being clueless, surely you're aware that the sheriff is head over heels over cowboy hat over you.

"As a matter of fact, Mother and I were talking about that just this morning, and we both agreed that we're feeling a bit guilty for keeping you so occupied solving our problems."

"That's what I came back for."

"True. And we all appreciate it, don't we girls?" Lilith asked, drawing a heartfelt response from the three teenagers. "But we've had a little meeting and decided that we're going to pitch in so you'll have more time with Jack. You've no idea how pleased everyone is that he's finally dating again."

"We're not dating," Raine said firmly, wondering

which one of them she was trying to convince. Herself or her mother. Another thought occurred to her. "And what do you mean by everyone?"

"Why, all of us, of course. When I stopped in at the market to pick up some coffee yesterday, Olivia Brown was working the cash register, and she mentioned it. Then, Ingrid, from the Viking Café, was standing in line behind me and she said she thought it was high time Jack paid some personal attention to someone besides his daughter. Not that Amy isn't a delightful child, but—"

"Wait a minute." Raine held up a hand. "Are you telling me that my relationship with Jack O'Halloran, not that we even have one," she insisted yet again, "is the talk of the town?"

"Of course. Coldwater Cove's a small community, Raine. Everyone cares about each other."

"About each other's business," Raine complained. "I may admittedly be a little rusty on the logistics, but I'm positive that you don't take your entire family along on a date."

"I don't know," Lilith argued. "You just might. If you were dating the kind of man who puts family first."

"It's not a date." Raine's expression was firm, her voice was not.

"Well, then, darling," Lilith drawled as they approached the farmhouse. "Someone should have remembered to tell Jack. Because I doubt if the man is going to stand outside to greet every one of his guests today."

Oh God, Raine groaned inwardly. Just the sight of him, tall and rangy, leaning against a porch pillar, looking a lot like a young Gary Cooper in his work-weathered jeans, plaid shirt, and spring-straw Stetson, was enough to make any woman suffer an estrogen meltdown.

With her heart thudding like a foolish schoolgirl's, she somehow managed to park the Jeep between a white Chevy pickup and a forest green Explorer. As the rest of the family clamored out of the Jeep, she stayed where she was, her gaze transfixed on his face. Although the day had dawned a bright one, Raine imagined she heard the rumble of thunder in the distance. And when his mouth curved in a welcoming smile, she felt as if a bolt of lightning had suddenly struck from out of the robin's egg blue sky.

Her own mouth went dry and her suddenly damp hands tightened on the steering wheel as if to tether her to the planet which had begun spinning out of control. She was vastly relieved when, after another suspended second, he merely touched his fingers to the brim of his hat and left the porch, joining the group of friends and family who'd shown up for the planting.

A surprising number of townspeople were present—including, Raine noticed with surprise, Judge Barbara Patterson-Young. She guessed that the slightly pudgy, bespectacled, balding man with the judge was Jimmy Young, whose brief teenage indiscretion so many years ago was still causing problems. The way he was going out of his way to avoid Lilith, who was decked out in teal cowboy boots, a teal-and-purple broomstick-pleated skirt, and a purple western-cut shirt adorned with silver studs, suggested that he'd heard about the confrontation in court. And was desperately trying to prevent Round Two.

The fact that so many people turned out gave testimony to the fact that Jack was as well-liked in Coldwater Cove as he'd been when he'd been a high school star jock.

He was also, Raine noted, obviously respected. Which didn't come as the surprise it might have her first night home, having already witnessed firsthand how fair-minded he could be. How kind. Watching him organize the work teams, she also couldn't help contrasting him with the men she was used to—brash, arrogant, domineering, win-at-any-cost males who brandished their control like Barbary Coast pirates brandishing cutlasses.

The sheriff was neither brash nor domineering. But without raising his voice, he had everyone doing exactly what he wanted them to. Willingly, even eagerly. For the first time she understood why he'd always been voted football team captain. Jack O'Halloran may have raised hell in his younger days, but he was a born leader. The type of male who could lead men on the gridiron, into battle, or even into fields of freshly tilled earth.

She was relieved when the information she'd gleaned about tree farms from her lengthy Internet search proved to be accurate. The work itself turned out to be relatively simple. Planting strings, with knots tied at five-foot intervals, marked off the fields.

"When the first tree in each row is planted straight," Jack explained to the first-timers, "subsequent trees will all be in straight rows, up and down, back and forth, and diagonally. It makes it a lot easier to mow between the rows." Then he'd grinned and seemed to be looking straight at her. "It also just looks prettier."

Raine smiled back and decided that while the detail-oriented part of her appreciated the exacting layout, another, more instinctive part of her agreed that the seemingly endless rows of deep green trees were indeed lovely.

They were divided into groups, Raine assigned to work with Lilith and Shawna, while Ida, Savannah, and Renee made up another team. The work went quickly as Raine used a short-handled spade to dig slits in the fragrant freshly turned soil, Lilith plunked in the transplanted seedlings which had spent their first two years in a greenhouse on the property, and Shawna tamped the soil down around it. It took Raine a few times to get a hole straight rather than digging at a slant, which would, Jack had warned, leave the tree roots too near the surface, allowing the roots to dry out too quickly and weaken the tree. But they soon developed a rhythm and were planting nearly as fast as they could walk.

From time to time, whenever they'd take a break while Renee ran back to get more transplants, Raine would glance around, watch the others working in the dark brown fields, and be reminded of the reproduction of *The Gleaners* she'd bought for her office wall. There was something about the painting that had both emotionally moved and relaxed her when she'd spotted it on the wall at the SoHo gallery. She was enjoying those same feelings now as she worked beneath the cloud-scudded sky, breathed in the pungent scent of fir and earth and the faint tinge of salt riding on the air.

Since so many people had turned out, it didn't take long to complete the planting. Which signaled the beginning of the party phase of the day. The mood was unabashedly festive. Meat, salmon, and oysters sizzled on barbecue grills, tables covered in red-and-white-checked paper cloths were groaning beneath bowls of colorful salads, casseroles, pots of vegetables, and myriad desserts. Fortunately, Savannah had provided the contribution for their family—a Tex-Mex shrimp salad with flavor that burst on the tongue, a chickpea burger topped with fennel-olive relish for Renee, and a plate of rich fudge brownies that disappeared almost as soon as the plate had been placed on the table.

Ida had brought along her infamous meatloaf in a casserole dish decorated with perky daisies. And while more than a few people, Jack included, put it on their paper plates, Raine noticed that no one was actually eating it. Not that she blamed them. But it did say something about the close-knit community that so many people went out of their way to avoid hurting an elderly lady's feelings.

"Are you going to keep your baby?" Amy, who was sitting across the table from Raine, asked Gwen.

"Amy, darling," Eleanor O'Halloran chided, "that's a very personal question. And none of your business."

When she'd first been introduced to Jack's mother shortly after arriving, Raine had found her to be a gracious, pleasant woman. Her smooth complexion, short blond hair and still-lithe figure that looked terrific in a pair of faded Wranglers suggested she must have been stunning in her youth. She was, in a less flamboyant way, Raine decided, every bit as beautiful as Lilith. Having shared a casual conversation with her over grilled salmon and Savannah's salad, she'd also proven to be intelligent, with a lively wit.

"That's okay," Gwen answered with a shrug. "It's not as if my being pregnant is a secret, or anything." She glanced down at her bulging belly, which Raine could have sworn had grown even larger in the past days. "And I haven't decided yet." She sighed. "Sometimes I really want to keep her, because it's so hard to imagine giving her away to strangers after having her inside me for so long.

"But other times I think I should give her up for adoption, so she'll have a Mom and Dad who'll take care of her better than I can."

She sighed again and looked out over the freshly planted fields. But Raine suspected it was not the bright green seedlings she was seeing, but some idyllic *Father Knows Best* family that only existed in fiction.

"I went to some adoption agencies last month with Lilith, and—"

"With Lilith?" Raine interrupted, exchanging a glance with Savannah, who was sitting beside Gwen and appeared equally surprised. "My mother went with you to interview prospective adoption agencies?" If Raine had given any thought to the matter, which she hadn't, she would have guessed that Ida would have been the logical one to take on that responsibility.

"Yeah. She's real easy to talk to," Gwen said. "A lot easier than most adults and she doesn't tell me what she thinks I should do. Like Mama Ida . . . Not that I don't really appreciate Mama Ida's advice," she assured Raine quickly as a hectic blush stained her cheeks.

"Don't worry, Gwen," Savannah said with a reassuring smile. "Raine and I know firsthand how bossy Gram can be."

"Of course, the problem is she's usually right," Raine said.

"True." It was Savannah's turn to sigh. "She certainly never liked Kevin. That should have been my first clue as to what a rat he was." Her emerald eyes sparked with a hint of lingering anger. And determination. "But it's too lovely a day and we're having too good a time to think about him. . . . So, how did the interviews go?" she asked Gwen.

"Okay, I guess." Despite her positive assessment, the teenager's expression was gloomier than Raine had witnessed during her visit. "I was nervous, but Lilith asked some great questions. Ones I never would have thought of. At first I was surprised, but she said that since she'd been such a failure at being a mother, she could spot a bad one a mile away."

That remark brought Raine's mind back to her vow to attempt to bridge the gap between them. Working together today had been a good start, but eventually they were going to have to have a real talk. Soon, Raine vowed.

She glanced over at a neighboring table, where, a few seats down from Ida, who was engaged in a lively conversation with Dottie and Doris Anderson, her mother was sitting with Cooper Ryan. Not only were they not arguing, they seemed to be miles away in their own private world. The chemistry was more than obvious, even from this distance. But there was something else there, too, Raine considered. Something that appeared to be affection.

"It sounds as if they left you depressed," she suggested carefully, returning her mind to the conversation.

"Yeah. I guess they kind of did. Though most of the people were nice and the offices were real fancy with Oriental rugs and paintings and stuff. But that was part of the problem."

"The paintings?" Eleanor O'Halloran asked gently.

"No. I just kept feeling like they were places just for rich people, and I didn't really belong there. I'll bet if I wasn't having this baby they all want so bad, they wouldn't have even let me in the door in the first place."

"Oh, I'm sure that's not the case," Raine assured her.

"You didn't see them," Gwen argued. "Besides, you're probably used to all that fancy stuff, having an office in New York City and all, but it made me real uncomfortable. Like, though everyone was smiling, they were secretly afraid I was going to knock over a lamp or something. I kept thinking about my baby in a place like that, never being allowed to touch anything, always having to worry about being on her best behavior, and, though it's kinda hard to explain, it made me feel real bad."

Lilith paused as she passed the table. Raine was surprised to see her holding two glasses of lemonade. Her mother's usual role at functions like this was that of Scarlett O'Hara being waited on by the Tarleton twins.

"Gwen felt as if the agencies, and, by extension, their clients, were more concerned with buying a child to complete their perfect lives than the baby's happiness," she explained. "Isn't that right, dear?" Both her tone and her gaze were solicitous.

Gwen nodded. "Yeah. It felt as if I was selling my baby."

"I was adopted," Amy volunteered. "Wasn't I, Gramma?"

"You certainly were," Eleanor agreed with a warm smile. She gave the little girl a brief hug. "And there's not a day that goes by I'm not grateful for that."

"Me, too," Amy agreed, returning the hug. Then she turned back to Gwen. "Mommy and Daddy weren't poor. Not like those homeless kids Daddy took me to buy Christmas presents for last winter. But we weren't rich, either. Not even when Mommy was working. Before she got sick.

"Daddy says it's just the same as if I was their born child." Six-year-old eyes widened earnestly. "Even better. Because out of all the babies in the world, they chose me."

"That's very special," Savannah agreed quietly.

Remembering her sister's miscarriage last year, Raine understood the undertone of sadness she heard in Savannah's voice.

"Oh! I have the most wonderful, scintillating idea," Amy said suddenly. She leaped up from the table and went running back toward the house.

"You raised a wonderful son," Lilith said to Eleanor. "It's such a shame his daughter has to grow up without a mother's guiding hand."

"Isn't it?" Eleanor agreed.

Everyone was suddenly looking at Raine, who was madly trying to think of something, anything to say to deflect attention from herself, when she was saved by Amy's return.

"Here." She held up an orange egg, shaped like the green nano Kitty that had been driving Jack to such distraction. "It's a Nano Baby. Daddy just bought it for me yesterday, because I've been wanting one more than anything. But you can borrow it," she said to Gwen.

"I think it's more for little kids," Gwen demurred.

"But it'll be perfect," Amy insisted. "Because there are all sorts of things you have to do. Like, see that," she said, pointing out the digital droppings that suddenly appeared on the screen. "When you see those, or tiny little footprints, you have to clean the baby up."

She pressed a button, selected a cleaning icon, and wiped away the mess. "You also have to play with her. The game where you help her crawl is my favorite, and she has to get plenty of sleep, so when you hear her snoring, you have to turn out the lights. But you have to remember to turn them on again when the baby wakes up and then you have to feed her."

A serious frown furrowed the childish brow. "But not too many snacks, or she'll get sick and then you have to give her medicine. You also have to teach her to behave, but Daddy says that's not really important because newborn babies don't know about being good or bad.

"It's a lot like a real baby, but if you forget to take care of it, all that happens is that the game ends. Then you can start a new Nano Baby. Daddy says that's a lot easier than in real life, but this way you'll be able to practice. Maybe it'll help you decide if you can take care of a real baby by yourself."

"From the mouths of babes," Lilith murmured as Gwen, seeming intrigued, accepted the gift.

Raine didn't say anything. But it didn't escape her notice that for the first time in her life, she and her mother were in perfect agreement.

❧16❧

The day grew longer. The sun began casting long shadows across the back lawn and the acres of Christmas trees beyond. Gradually, some people wandered away, back to their homes, their lives. But most stayed, laughing and eating and enjoying the company and the evening. The yard was illuminated with glowing Japanese lanterns and warmed by the fragrant applewood fire Jack had started in an outdoor clay fireplace.

Sometime after sunset, to the obvious delight of his guests, he, Dan, and Cooper Ryan pulled out guitars and began playing a medley of country songs. When they segued from a rockabilly tune to a slow, romantic ballad about a lost love reclaimed, Raine watched the way Cooper seemed to be singing directly to Lilith. In turn, Lilith only had eyes for him. They could have been the only two people in Coldwater Cove. The only two in the world.

That idea caused a vision of being alone on a raft, in the middle of a storm-tossed ocean while the sky poured down icy water, to flash through Raine's mind. It faded quickly, leaving behind a profound sense of loneliness.

She belatedly realized someone was talking to her. "I'm sorry, Amy. My mind was drifting. What did you say?"

"I was wondering if you'd like to see my room," Amy, who was standing beside the redwood chair, invited. "Maybe you can watch a video with me, too. Daddy and I usually watch one together after supper, but he's out by the pond teaching my cousin John how to cast with his new fishing rod."

She was wearing a pair of red jeans, a T-shirt bearing a drawing of a Disney mermaid, and a pair of sneakers. She had a smudge of dirt on one cheek; a bit of chocolate from the homemade ice cream Eleanor O'Halloran had contributed to the party was smeared at one corner of her mouth. But neither detracted from the fact that she was going to grow up to be a beauty. Her thickly fringed eyes were wide and innocent, her smile, persuasive. Raine wondered how Jack managed to deny this golden child anything.

Raine bent down and tied one of Amy's loose sneaker laces. "I'd love to watch a video."

"Have you ever seen *The Little Mermaid?*"

"No, I missed that one."

"You'll like it a lot. It's the best." With that promise, Amy streaked off toward the house. A little bit in love, Raine followed.

"And Ariel and Prince Eric got married and they lived happily ever after," Amy announced as the tape ended. "That's my favorite story. Even better than

Pocohontas or *Snow White*. But they're good, too. Would you like to watch another tape?"

"If you'd like," Raine said, trying not to reveal she'd been more than a little discomfited by the fact that the television turned out to be in Jack's bedroom.

The first thing she'd noticed when Amy had practically dragged her into the room by the hand was the sterling-silver-framed photograph on the bedside table. Time had tarnished the silver a bit, but the smiles on the faces of the bride and groom hadn't faded in wattage a bit.

"That's Daddy," Amy said when she saw the direction of Raine's gaze. "And Mommy."

"I can see that."

"It was on the day they were married. They hadn't adopted me yet," she said matter-of-factly. "Isn't Daddy handsome?"

"He certainly is." Having grown accustomed to seeing him in jeans, Raine wouldn't have pictured him in a tux. But if she had, even her vivid imagination couldn't have made him look any better. "And your Mommy's pretty, too."

"She was sooo beautiful. Like a princess in a fairy tale." Amy slid off the bed, went over to the dresser, picked up a silver-backed hand mirror and studied her reflection. "Daddy says that even though I'm adopted, I'm going to grow up to look just like her. That I'll be beautiful, too."

"Your daddy's right. You're already a very pretty little girl."

"That's what Daddy says." Again, this was said with a complete lack of guile or pride, suggesting that Jack had done an excellent job building his daughter's ego. "Would you like to see a tape about when I was still a baby?"

"Sure."

"I'll be right back!" The little girl left the room and Raine could hear her flying down the stairs.

Feeling as if she were snooping into personal things that were none of her business, Raine couldn't resist the lure of the wedding photograph. She picked the frame up to study it closer.

Peg O'Halloran looked like a fairy princess, dressed in a froth of white satin and beaded lace that must have weighed almost as much as she did. Her train was beaded as well, her veil, topped by a band of white roses, was fingertip length, drawing a viewer's eye to the gold band she was wearing on her left hand. Her billowy cloud of long blond hair was so pale and so shiny it could only have been natural. She literally glowed with life.

Jack, on the other hand, looked poleaxed. But in an endearing way, Raine decided. The way he was staring down at his bride suggested that he couldn't quite believe his good fortune. It was obvious that they'd been so in love. So optimistic. So unaware of the tragedy that was lurking just around the corner.

"Here it is!" Amy announced, holding up the black videotape case. "It's one of my very favorites. But I don't remember that day because I was just a tiny baby."

She switched tapes, then crawled back up onto the queen-size sleigh bed beside Raine, whose instincts, which had kicked in of late, were already telling her this was a mistake.

That proved to be an understatement. As she sat there, in the bedroom Peg and Jack had shared, on the bed where they'd made love, watching one of the most intimate acts a man and woman can share— bringing their new infant home from the hospital— she felt like the worst kind of voyeur.

"See, that was my old room. Before we moved to this house." Amy's voice managed to penetrate the white noise filling Raine's head. "Mommy hung that wallpaper with the storks on it all by herself. Daddy painted the crib. They got it secondhand from one of Daddy's cousins, but they fixed it up so it was just like new."

Raine suspected Amy was parroting what her parents had told her about that day. That seemingly endless day. The joy was almost painful to watch, especially knowing how short-lived it would be. Amy, on the other hand, didn't seem at all distraught as she kept on a running commentary of every little thing that was happening on screen.

"And that's when Daddy gave me my bath. And splashed Mommy and got her blouse all wet. Then she splashed Daddy back. And we all laughed and laughed," Amy was saying when Raine became aware of a third person standing in the open doorway.

"Amy." Jack's voice was low, but intense. "I thought we had an agreement about you not watching those tapes alone."

"I'm not watching those tapes, Daddy." She turned to Raine. "He's talking about the tapes Mommy made me. So I'd always feel like she was here with me."

A painful lump had risen in her throat. Raine swallowed, then forced her words past it. "That was a very special thing for her to do."

"I know." The lamplight haloed Amy's blond hair as she nodded. "It's my legacy."

She looked back up at her father, who was now standing beside the bed, arms folded, the remote in his hand. He'd stopped the tape, Raine noticed when she saw the news footage of tonight's Seattle Mariners baseball game appear on the television screen in place of the seemingly perfect, picture-book family.

"Raine said I was pretty. Like Mommy. Then she said she wanted to see the tape of when I was a baby."

"After you asked her first, I'll bet."

"It wasn't one of Mommy's tapes," she stressed again, sounding perilously close to tears. "Besides, Raine liked it, didn't you?"

The distressed face looking up at her tugged at Raine's heartstrings. She gathered Jack's daughter to her and began rocking in an instinctive motion she hadn't even realized she knew how to do. "I thought it was a wonderful video. And I'm glad you shared it with me."

"Daddy and Gramma say I'm supposed to share." Her voice was muffled against Raine's sweater. Feeling somehow to blame, and more than a little helpless, Raine stroked her hair and looked up to Jack for guidance.

"Gwen's looking for you, Amy," he said gently. "She needs some help with the Nano Baby you gave her."

"Okay." Proving that recovery came fast for the young, she wiggled out of Raine's embrace, slid off the bed, gave her father's legs a quick hug, and took off down the hall. Moments later they could hear her footfalls on the stairs.

The mattress gave as Jack slumped down beside her. "I'm sorry." He put his arm around her in that way she was beginning to enjoy far too much.

"It's all right. She's right. She was a beautiful baby. She's a beautiful little girl, too."

"Modest, too," he said dryly.

"A strong ego is a good thing. I think you have a lot to do with that."

"Don't make me out to be something I'm not, Raine." His voice was tight, offering her as much of a warning as the foghorn tolling somewhere in the bay. "I'm just a regular guy. An ordinary guy who went through some tough times. There are people handling worse every day."

"You can protest all you want, Jack," Raine said. Slipping free of his light embrace, she stood up. "But I've gone through enough jury selections to know that the trick is to ignore what people say, and concentrate on what they do. And what you've done with your daughter is far from ordinary."

Because she found being alone with him in his bedroom too tempting for comfort, Raine brushed her lips against his, then left to rejoin the party.

Because he wanted more than that light, sweet kiss, Jack followed Raine, intending to steal more. Unfortunately, he was sidetracked by an aunt, who professed that she had met the nicest young woman at her widows survival group at church and since the lady in question and Jack had so much in common, she was certain they'd be perfect for one another.

Deciding that it would do no good to explain that

compatibility required more than the loss of a spouse, he dodged the matchmaking with the excuse that right now his work was keeping him too busy to enter into a relationship. Although it was obviously not the response she'd been seeking, he managed to get away before she could press her case.

It took a few minutes, but he found Raine in the driveway, leaning against Ida's Jeep, gazing up at the sky.

"I've forgotten how many stars there are," she murmured, seeming not all that surprised by his appearance. "You never see stars like this in the city."

"True. But we don't have the bright lights."

"No." She turned her gaze from the sky toward him. "I was listening to you play the guitar with Dan and Cooper after dinner. You're very good."

"I made a few bucks playing at some country bars while I was in college."

"So, is it true what they say about musicians and women?"

"I don't know. What do they say?"

"You know." She shrugged. "That you all have harems of groupies."

"I don't know about other guys. But I didn't." He half smiled at the bittersweet memory of Peg sitting at a front table, drinking cherry cokes while he did his best to entertain a bunch of hard-drinking cowboys who hadn't come there to listen to the music. "I've always been pretty much a one-woman-at-a-time kind of guy."

"That's nice. And unusual."

"Monogamy's not all that unusual," he said mildly. "Perhaps you've just run into some bad apples."

"Perhaps." Her tone sounded unconvinced.

"Which brings up something I've been meaning to ask you."

"What's that?"

"Is there a man in your life, Harvard? Some guy in a fifteen-hundred-dollar pinstriped suit and gold cufflinks waiting for you back in New York?"

"Would it matter if there was?"

"Would you like me to say it would?" he asked, moving still closer, encouraged when she didn't back away. "Do you want me to say that I'd back off and leave you alone if you belonged to some other man?"

"I'll never *belong* to any man."

"Objection sustained." He was close enough to touch. Nearly close enough to taste. "Let's not waste time on semantics, Counselor." When he reached up to touch her cheek, she stepped back. "I told you I wasn't into playing games, so I'm going to say this straight out."

Knowing he was pressing his advantage, but not feeling a bit guilty, since she'd already caused him more sleepless nights than any woman he'd ever encountered, Jack took another step, trapping her between Ida's Jeep and him.

"You've riled me up from the beginning. At first I figured that it was just sex. That'd I'd been too long without a woman and you came along and stirred up my juices."

"Charmingly put. Once again you flatter me, Sheriff."

"The flattery part comes later," he promised. "After I get this out of the way. Now, like I said, at first I thought it was only a case of runaway hormones. Which a woman like you could give any man, even one who hadn't been celibate for the past three years."

"Three?" She seemed surprised by that.

"I told you, I'm a one-woman man. There was no way I was going to fool around on my wife. Then she got sick. And I haven't wanted any other woman since she died. Until now."

He skimmed his fingers up her cheek into her hair. "Until you. I'm not going to apologize for wanting you, Raine. Especially since, unless every instinct I have has gone on the blink, I think you want me, too."

When she didn't argue, he bent his head and brushed his lips against her temple. "But the thing is, since I keep getting the feeling there's something else going on here. I figure we'd be cheating ourselves not to test it out."

A ghost of a smile hovered at the corners of her lips. "That's some seduction line."

"Is it working?"

"I don't know." She closed her eyes and took a deep breath that did intriguing things to her breasts beneath her T-shirt.

"How long has it been since you've been on a picnic?"

Her eyes flew open. "A picnic?"

"Yeah. A picnic. You know, where you go out into the woods, spread a tablecloth on the ground, sit on a blanket, and fight off ants while you share a loaf of bread and a jug of wine. The forecast calls for blue skies tomorrow. Come play with me."

"Surely you need to work."

"Since I'm sheriff, that makes me the boss. So I'll give myself the day off."

"How convenient."

"Isn't it?" He watched her sliding into her lawyer skin and found himself enjoying the anticipation of stripping it back off again with her clothes.

"If you're taking me out into the woods to have sex with me, you should know that it's not going to happen."

"Actually, I believe I mentioned taking you out into the wilderness to feed you," he said mildly. "Having sex would, admittedly be icing on the cake, speaking metaphorically." He wondered if she'd run away if he told her that he was beginning to think that when it did happen, they'd be making love rather than having sex. "But I'm willing to settle for a few hot kisses and some groping that's bound to leave us both hot and frustrated. If that's what you really want."

"A picnic sounds lovely." Her tone was cool, designed to deter a less-determined man. Jack had never backed down from a challenge and he wasn't about to start with her. "But without the groping," she insisted unsteadily as he rubbed his cheek against the silk of her hair.

"Fine. We'll settle for the kissing."

"That sounds an awful lot like just sex."

"Hey." He curled his fingers around the nape of her neck. "Sex isn't such a bad start. Besides, you can't deny that all this chemistry has been a distraction. For both of us." He nibbled on her lower lip, satisfied when he drew a soft, ragged moan from her throat. "Once we get the sex part out of the way, we can see if there's anything more going on here."

"What if there is?" She was tempted. Jack could taste it on her lips. See it in her soft-focused eyes as she tilted her head back to look up at him. "Something more than sex?"

Although he suspected that she'd throw herself off Mount Olympus before admitting it, she was afraid, Jack realized. He knew the feeling all too well.

"Then we'll jump off that bridge—together—when we get to it."

"You have to understand . . ." Her planned protest faded away as he began nuzzling at her fragrant neck. "I've never . . ." When he caught her earlobe in his teeth and tugged, she expelled a long, shuddering breath. "Oh, God." She put both hands against his chest and pushed. Not hard, but enough to put a little distance between them. "What I'm trying to say is, that I've never taken sex casually."

"Then you don't have to worry. Because believe me, sweetheart, there's nothing casual about the way I feel about you."

"Oh, God," she repeated, lifting her hands from the front of his shirt to drag them through her hair "I think I've just run out of arguments."

"A lawyer without arguments." He caught her distressed face in his hand. "Now that's gotta be a first."

Deciding that he'd been patient long enough, he lowered his head, watching her lips part in anticipation. A soft, yielding sigh slipped from between her lips to his. The night air had turned cool, but her lips were warm and moist and generous. She welcomed his tongue with a breathless moan that burned through him like wildfire and when his teeth scraped at her bottom lip, she went up onto her toes and twined her arms around his neck and clung.

Her body strained against Jack's. Her hot, avid mouth was as urgent and impatient as his. The way she was moving her body against his was causing all the blood to rush from his head to his groin and with the last vestige of coherent thought he possessed, Jack realized that he'd miscalculated.

He hadn't intended for things to get so hot so quick. Nor had he intended to ache. Not just the physical ache that had him as hard as a damn boulder, but a deep, grinding ache that went all the way to the bone. Some deep primal urge had him wanting to drag her into the backseat of the Jeep, never mind that nearly half the town could stumble across them at any minute. He forced himself to break the exquisite contact.

"Oh, no." She was staring up at him, giving him the impression that she shared the disorientation that had him feeling as if someone had just informed him that the law of physics had been suspended, that down was now up, up down, and gravity no longer existed. "I was afraid of that."

He watched her take a deep, ragged breath and felt a renewed slap of lust. "Of what?"

"Of what just happened." She dragged a trembling hand through her hair. "Of how you'd make me feel."

"I'm admittedly out of practice, but if it was that bad, perhaps I'd better work on polishing my technique."

"No." She wrapped her arms around herself in an unconscious gesture of self-protection that made him want to hold her close, this time to soothe rather than arouse. With effort, Jack stayed where he was. "Your technique was fine." She sighed. "Better than fine," she admitted. "It was terrific. And that's the problem."

"We can try again," he suggested helpfully. "I'll try to do worse, if it'll make you feel any better."

"Dammit, Jack." This time she dragged both hands through her hair. "I'm serious." Even as her eyes brightened with a wet sheen, a reluctant smile tugged at the corners of her mouth. That lush, sweet mouth he could still taste.

"I know." Because he couldn't be this close to her without touching, he caught hold of one of those slender hands and brushed his thumb over her knuckles. "But perhaps you're overanalyzing things again, Raine. Didn't you ever just go with the flow?"

"No."

She looked so miserable, like a little girl who'd just had her dog die on her; Jack's heart went out to her. "It's getting late. Why don't I go get the rest of the family, and—"

"That's not necessary." She was looking past him, over his shoulder. Jack didn't need to turn around to know that they were no longer alone. The sound of female voices drifted on the night-cooled air. "Well," she drew in another breath. "I guess I'll be calling it a night. Thank you for the invitation. I had a lovely time. Please tell Amy I enjoyed watching *The Little Mermaid* with her. And seeing her baby video."

Her tone had turned so impersonal, she could have been asking a judge for a sidebar. Suspecting the ploy was more for the others' sake than his, he didn't call her on it.

"I'll tell her." Still tempted to touch, he stuck his hands deep into his pockets. "I'll see you tomorrow, then. How's ten sound?"

"Oh, do you have plans, darling?" Ida asked, proving that although she may be nearly eighty, her hearing was working just fine.

"We're going on a picnic," Jack said, before Raine could respond.

"Oh, what a wonderful idea," Lilith declared, obviously pleased by this idea. Then again, Jack thought, having watched Cooper and her, he suspected the lady had romance on the mind tonight.

The three girls concurred.

"I'll make a lunch," Savannah said.

"That's not necessary," Raine protested.

"Don't be silly. What's the point of having a Paris trained chef in the family if you don't take advantage of her?" Savannah was obviously as pleased with this development as her mother was. The wattage of her dazzling smile was enough to light up Coldwater Cove for a year.

When she'd shown up at the farm tonight, Jack had taken one look at the lushly built, red-haired goddess and understood all too well how his cousin had been scared spitless of her back in their high school days. The funny thing was, as gorgeous as Savannah Townsend admittedly was, and as genuinely nice as she seemed to be, she still couldn't cause his testosterone to spike the way her sister could.

As if realizing she was outnumbered, Raine surrendered the skirmish. "I have some work to do in the morning," she said to Jack. "Eleven would be better."

"Eleven it is."

That taken care of to everyone's satisfaction, with the possible exception of Raine, whose mind he had every intention of changing, Jack watched the family of females climb into the Jeep.

He stood in the driveway, watching the taillights as they disappeared down the long driveway out to the road, until they'd finally disappeared around a corner. Then whistled as he walked back to the house.

❧ 17 ❧

A silvery pink light was slipping around the edges of the window curtain. In a desperate attempt at control, Raine told herself that the only reason she'd woken up at dawn was that her internal clock had somehow reset itself back to New York time.

Liar. She was, Raine told herself as she tossed back the quilt, pitiful. It was expectation, pure and simple. No, she corrected as she stealthily slipped into her robe, trying not to wake her sleeping sister. Not simple at all.

Although she still had several hours before Jack showed up, Raine wasn't in the mood to start work. Instead, rather than take the time for real coffee, she nuked a mug of instant in the microwave and carried it out onto the front porch. Then stopped in her tracks when she viewed the Greek god leaning against the white porch railing.

"Good morning, Cooper." She wondered idly if he was coming or going then reminded herself that her mother's sex life was none of her business. "Can I get you some coffee? It's instant, but—"

"Thanks anyway. But I've got a thermos in the truck."

"Oh." She glanced past him at the park service pickup. Then up at her mother's bedroom window.

"We're going to drown some worms." His answer to her unasked question only gave birth to more.

"You're drowning worms?"

He grinned. "Fishing, Raine. Lilith and I are going out to see if we can catch some brook trout for Savannah. Seems she has this new recipe she's been wanting to try out."

"My mother's going fishing?" She looked up at the window again and wondered if she was still asleep. Surely this must be a dream. Or yet another hallucination.

He rubbed his chin. His grin widened. "Well, to tell the truth, she's probably going to spend most of the day sitting on a rock prettying up the scenery."

She sat down in the swing. "That's one of her strongest talents."

"Have you ever taken any martial arts?" he asked.

Raine blinked at the seemingly sudden change of subject. "No. I've been thinking about taking up yoga, though."

"Good idea. It's supposed to be great for relaxation." She was grateful when he didn't point out what everyone else had since her arrival home. That she looked as if she needed relaxation. "I've studied aikido since I was a kid."

"Oh. Is that like karate?"

"In a way. It's one of the martial arts that teaches self-defense without weapons. It teaches you to neutralize any attack by learning to blend with the opposing energy. Or redirect it. To put it simply, once you know the right techniques, you can be empowered by staying in your center."

Raine grasped his analogy immediately. "Lilith never attacks." That she would have been able to handle. After all, she was an expert on the battlefield. It was her own feelings that she'd never been able to quite vanquish.

"No, that's never been her style," he agreed mildly. "Another thing aikido teaches is the ability to sense openings in your opponent. When we're working on the mat, we learn to sense our practice partner's strengths and weaknesses and honor and blend with them, to create harmony."

Lilith and harmony were two words Raine never would have used in the same sentence.

When she didn't respond to that, Cooper seemed to sense her vulnerability. He also seemed to possess mind-reading ability. "Your mother didn't try to make your life tougher than perhaps it should have been, Raine," he said gently. "She was only a girl, a decade younger than you are now when she became a mother for the first time with no real support system of her own."

"She could have come home."

"True. But between that glossy exterior and a very warm heart, Lilith definitely possesses her share of the Lindstrom female pride. She hadn't wanted to admit to your grandmother that she'd failed."

"Time and time again."

"True. But she was only human, honey. Playing the cards she'd been dealt as best she knew how. Also, don't forget that she swallowed that pride every single time she brought you and Savannah back to Ida. Because she was trying, in her own, admittedly flawed way, to do right by her daughters."

His take on the situation left her feeling even more guilty than she had the morning after the blowup. Raine bit her bottom lip and looked out over the bay, which was draped in a light layer of white fog, like the angel hair she remembered Savannah draping over the limbs of the Christmas tree one year.

Like Jack, he was a man comfortable with silence. For a long time there was only the morning sound of the birds and the creak of the swing chain.

"Well, you've definitely given me something to think about," she said finally.

"I'm glad. For both your and Lilith's sake. Would you mind one more piece of unsolicited advice?"

"Of course not."

"When I first started my training, I was young and stubborn. My sensei didn't think I'd ever learn how to let go enough to follow the rhythm and the movement, rather than my expectations. It took me a very long time to discover that I got hurt a lot more when I'd think I knew what my practice partner's next move was. Because by planning for it, I allowed myself to become more vulnerable to a different move."

She took a sip of the cooling coffee. "Go with the flow, you mean."

"It's a bit more complicated than that. But yeah, it's the general idea."

She thought some more. About her mother. Herself. And, this man who seemed so comfortable on Ida's porch. Raine suspected he'd spent a great deal of time on this very same swing in the past.

"May I ask you something?"

"Anything," he said promptly.

"Are you going to be my new stepfather?"

"You bet." He smiled at her. With his mouth and his eyes and as she smiled back, Raine wondered if here was something in the air here on the peninsula that made the male population so self-confident.

She smiled back. "I'm glad."

At that moment the screen door opened and Lilith came out, dressed in a designer version of fishing chic. Her blouse was a washable silk the color of mountain streams, her jeans had obviously been custom-tailored to fit her lush curves like a glove, and the sneakers on her feet were snowy white, suggesting they were new. Her gold earrings resembled fishing lures and flowers the same color as her blouse bloomed on the baseball cap atop her head.

"Good morning," she greeted them. "Gracious Raine, darling, I was wondering who Cooper was speaking with. Whatever are you doing up so early?"

"It was a lovely morning. I thought I'd sit out here and enjoy it."

"You couldn't have found a better place. I know I always feel ever so much better whenever I come home." Her smile, as she looked over at Cooper, was overbrimming with private meaning. "Especially this time."

He smiled back and once again the air was so charged, Raine felt as if she couldn't breathe. Deciding that if Savannah was actually counting on these two returning home with any fish, she'd be disappointed, Raine rose from the swing.

"Have a good time, you two." She brushed a kiss against her mother's cheek and felt another little stab of guilt at the surprise and pleasure that

sparked in Lilith's eyes. Raine couldn't recall the las
time she'd initiated kissing her mother.

A week ago she never would have thought of goin
up on her toes to kiss Cooper's cheek as well, bu
as she did so, Raine decided that it felt eminentl
right. "Good luck," she murmured,

Then, feeling even more heady anticipation that
she had when she'd first awakened, she took her cu
and went back into the house, counting the hour
until eleven o'clock.

The Suburban was not exactly designed for tigh
cornering, but Raine was not surprised by the wa
Jack maneuvered around the twisting switchback
leading deep into the forest. He seemed to do every
thing well. When that thought caused a little spik
in her heartbeat, she turned her attention to the sce
nery in an attempt to tamp down rampaging
hormones.

The sky had turned a tarnished silver hue tha
hinted at a storm lying somewhere out to sea, while
a pale sun latticed the landscape with a tapestry o
green. The willows wore their bright spring coats o
goldish green leaves, while bolder, red-green maple
leaves unfolded from newly burst buds. Scattered
amidst blushing meadows dotted with Indian paint-
brush, bracken ferns were uncurling new, frothy,
delicate pale fronds.

Growing more and more comfortable with each
other, despite the sexual tension that still lingered
as strong as ever, they allowed the silence to settle.
For a long time the only sound was that of falling
water, as crystal streams born in melting glaciers
fed the roaring rivers that ran into the sea.

"Are you going to tell me where we're going?" Raine asked finally.

"A little place I know out by Lake Crescent."

Set dramatically amidst the majestic Olympic Mountains, the dazzling blue-green lake was considered by many to be the gem of the peninsula.

"Not the lodge?"

"No." He glanced over at her. "I thought we'd go someplace off by ourselves. Unless you'd like to go to the lodge."

Knowing that he had definitely not planned on sharing the stolen day with tourists, Raine appreciated him giving her a choice. "No. I get enough of people in the city. I'm starting to enjoy the peace and quiet."

"Better be careful," he said easily as he turned off onto another even narrower road that twisted like a snarled fishing line unreeling through the mountain passes in a series of sharp zigzags that defied compass reckoning. "This place can get in your blood if you let it. You might have a hard time getting away again."

"I'll admit that I'm seeing the town with new eyes. But I am going back to New York." She wondered which of them she was reminding—him or her.

"All the more reason to make the most of the time you have here."

They passed a waving green sea of meadow on which white Sitka valerium bobbed like whitecaps atop cresting waves. "You must spend a lot of time at this place, wherever it is." She'd been lost for the past half hour. "To be able to find it so easily."

"I haven't been here for years, so I may not. We may end up getting hopelessly lost and forced to live

off the land. Which, I suppose, could turn out to [
an adventure."

"Obviously we have different definitions [
adventure."

"You just need to use your imagination."

"I was. I was imagining icy rain, hurricane ga
winds, and mountain lions. Not to mention bear
So, if you don't mind, I think I'll pass on playir
Grizzly Adams with you."

"You've got the wrong adventure story." H
reached out, caught her hand and linked their fir
gers together. "It'd be more like Adam and Eve. Ju
you and I, Harvard, alone in a lush green Garde
of Eden."

"I don't like snakes."

"Fine. Since it's our imaginary game, we won
have any."

"What about clothes?"

"Only if you insist."

"I do."

He sighed heavily. "I was afraid you were goin
to say that. Well, I suppose you can whip somethin
up out of some leaves while I build our log cabin.

"You're going to build a cabin? With what?"

"My bare hands. And, of course, my handy-dand
Swiss Army knife."

"I didn't realize those came with a chain sav
feature."

"Never underestimate the Swiss. Then, when I ge
it all constructed, you can make us a comfy bed ou
of pine needles."

"Two beds."

He shot her a sideways glance and another o

those boyish grins that Raine kept telling herself shouldn't affect her so strongly, but did. "Spoilsport."

He made a sharp left turn that, even with her seat belt fastened, almost had her sliding into his lap. They passed a herd of deer peacefully grazing in yet another meadow awash in color.

"Lucky for us these woods are filled with game, so we won't have to go hungry," he said.

Raine folded her arms. "I categorically refuse to eat Bambi."

"How about fish?"

She thought about that. "I suppose that would be preferable to starving."

"Absolutely. Then we don't have any problem. I'll catch some tasty salmon with the pointed stick I whittle with my knife then smoke them over a fire, just like I learned when I was a Boy Scout."

"You were a Boy Scout?"

"You don't have to sound all that surprised. As a matter of fact, I earned a merit badge in survivalist skills."

"I knew you were a hell-raiser. But I had no idea you were also training to be one of those antigovernment militia types." Her faint smile took the accusation from her tone.

"That was before those nutty guys who like to blow things up gave the term a bad name," he said mildly. "We learned all sorts of handy stuff I'd almost made Eagle Scout when I got kicked out."

"Now that I believe. What did you do? Row across the lake in the middle of the night and lead a panty raid on the Girl Scout camp?"

"You can be a sharp-tongued woman, Harvard.

Fortunately for you, I like a woman with spunk. And, as a matter of fact, I put a skunk in the counselor's tent."

"Once again I'm not surprised. What does strain credulity is the idea of you actually growing up to serve as the symbol of law and order in Olympic County."

"Hey, the guy deserved it. There was this kid, Kenny Woods, who was packing a few too many pounds. The damn jock counselor wouldn't let up on him. Not even after Kenny almost passed out from heat exhaustion on a five-mile hike. Someone had to do something."

"And that someone was you?"

"I was the one who was there at the time."

"What about other counselors? Parents? Camp authorities?"

He laughed at that. "I would have thought all those years in the city would have made you a realist. In the undemocratic world of kids and counselors, the counselors reign supreme. Which means the kid was on his own."

"So you took the law into your own hands."

"Yeah. And before you tell me that you can't condone that, as sheriff, I'll admit I don't recommend the policy as a habit. But I'd do it again. In a New York minute."

Raine thought about that. "I have to admire you for sticking up for that boy. Even if I don't approve of your solution."

"Hey, it worked. The guy was a pariah for days. You can't imagine the cans of tomato juice he went through trying to bathe out the eau de skunk.

"And getting back to our little survivalist game,

while I'm impressing you with my manly food-acquiring skills, you can play domestic by gathering up wild berries for our dessert."

"In the little basket I've woven from reeds while you've been spearing poor unsuspecting fish," she guessed.

"Nah. I figure you can gather them up in that skirt you insisted on sewing out of leaves."

"Giving you a look at my legs."

He let go of her hand and ruffled her hair. "I knew you were a perceptive woman."

Moments later, he pulled off into a secluded glen that could have served as a model for paradise. A crystal waterfall tumbled over moss-covered rocks into a sapphire blue pool at one end of the lush green chamber; in the far distance, the sun glinted off the waters of Lake Crescent.

"Oh!" Raine drew in a breath as she climbed out of the truck and surveyed the pristine scene. "It's lovely. Like a secret garden."

"Dan and I used to come here when we were kids to play Tarzan." He touched his canted nose. "I broke this when he dared me to ride the waterfall face first while we were searching for the jewels of Opar."

"You could have died. That was foolishly reckless." A wayward breeze fluttered her hair across her eyes. She brushed it away.

"Yeah." Another whispery gust blew the hair back; this time Jack pushed it away. His hand stayed on her cheek. "But I've always had a tendency for recklessness."

They both knew that he was no longer talking about some childhood accident. Electricity sparked in the air like heat lightning and Raine found herself holding her breath, waiting for the kiss she kept insisting she didn't want.

"I promised you lunch."

"Yes." If she were to make a list of needs and desires right now, food wouldn't even make the top ten.

He gave her another of those long enigmatic looks that gave Raine the uncomfortable feeling that he could see inside her heart. Then he dropped his hand and backed away. "I'd better get the basket out of the truck."

Unable to respond, with her words clogged in her throat, Raine merely nodded.

Savannah had outdone herself, preparing crudités shaped like flowers, a grilled-chicken salad with goat cheese and fresh raspberries, a loaf of crunchy, homemade sourdough bread, a key lime cheesecake so light it seemed to melt in Raine's mouth, and iced tea sprigged with mint.

The conversation stayed light during lunch. As if by mutual agreement, they stuck to family anecdotes and career stories before somehow moving on to all the places around the world they'd visited, or wanted to.

"I've been planning to go to the islands," Raine admitted.

"Which ones?"

She shrugged. "It doesn't really matter. Any one with tropical breezes, lagoons as clear as aquamarines, and white sugar beaches. Oh, and a steel band and mai tais would be nice, too."

"Maybe we should take a trip to one for our second date."

Even knowing he was kidding, Raine felt her

nerves tangle at his casual mention of a future when she hadn't allowed herself to think beyond today. Which, given her penchant for planning every last detail of her life just went to show how crazy the man made her.

"This isn't a date. Not really."

"Okay." He leaned back on his elbows and crossed his long legs at the ankles. "What would you call it, then?"

Good point. "I suppose"—she shrugged, trying to appear nonchalant—"two friends having lunch."

His smile was slow, seductive, and openly skeptical. Raine wasn't surprised he didn't believe her. She didn't believe her flimsy definition either. He looked at her again, hard and deep, then, apparently deciding not to push, reached out and snagged another piece of cheesecake. "Your sister's a dynamite cook."

"She's always had a magic touch in the kitchen." Raine couldn't decide whether or not to be relieved that he was backing away yet again, allowing—no, forcing—her to be the one to make the decision how serious this would get. "She's also the only woman in our family who can do more than boil water or nuke a frozen dinner in the microwave."

"There's always Ida's meatloaf."

They shared a laugh over that. Then sat in comfortable silence for a time. Clouds continued to gather over the mountaintops and the air was growing cooler, but Raine was in no hurry to leave. A bright blue jay fluttered down from an overhead branch, stole a bit of crumb crust that had dropped onto the blanket, and disappeared back into the trees again.

Raine realized, with some surprise, that she was

beginning to get used to the quiet. That first morning, alone in the kitchen, the lack of noise had made her edgy. Now, as she drank in a landscape created to soothe the soul, she reveled in the exquisite serenity. She also realized that it had been nearly a day since she'd worried about what was happening at work. Which had to be a record.

"Your mother looks as if she'd be a good cook," she said.

"Mom's real good, but she doesn't fix fancy stuff like Savannah. Dad was more of a meat-and-potatoes kind of guy."

There was no mistaking the warmth in his voice at the mention of his father. "You must miss him."

"A bunch. It's been six months and there are times when I walk into the office and am surprised not to see him sitting behind the desk. He always seemed larger than life to me, not just when I was a kid, but even after I'd grown up. It wasn't just because he was a big man, but because he was strong in a way that made people trust him."

"I'd imagine that would be important in his line of work, especially since it's an elected position."

"He won eight straight elections," Jack divulged. "The last two no one even bothered to run against him. I always figured that wasn't so much that a would-be opponent was afraid of losing, as much as the fact that no one in the county could think of a better man for the job."

"That's quite a legacy."

"You can say that again. And one that's not always easy to live up to."

"Actually, I think you're doing a very good job. If it hadn't been for you, I'm afraid to think what could have happened the night the girls locked themselves in the house."

His lips curved a bit. "Is that a compliment I hear coming from those delectable lips, Harvard?"

Delectable. Even as her nerves skittered at him bringing an intimacy back into the conversation, a lovely warmth flowed through Raine. She couldn't remember the last time a man had described her lips as delectable. Probably because none ever had.

She moved her shoulders, pretended vast interest in a chipmunk gathering berries at the edge of the blue pool, and avoided what she knew would be a teasing look. "I've always believed in giving credit where credit is due."

"Me too." He skimmed a hand down her hair. When his arm settled casually around her shoulder, she did not shrug it away. "Who would have thought a big city lawyer and a country sheriff would have anything in common?"

Because his touch was so inviting, his smile so seductive, because once again she was finding herself on a steep precipice that she was struggling not to fall over, Raine decided to turn the subject back to something safer.

"When I was in the eighth grade, my class took a tour of your dad's jail. Everyone else had a great time. I had nightmares of being locked away in one of those cells for weeks."

"He caught me playing chicken with log trucks in my Trans Am when I was sixteen," Jack divulged. "Locked me up for twenty-four horrible hours. Fortunately, the jail was empty that weekend, so I didn't have a roommate."

"He sounds strict."

"He was. But fair. He made sure I knew what the rules were, and the penalty for breaking them. Then nothing on God's green earth would get him to give in." He shook his head, but his expression was one of affection. "He was a man of his word. A man who could be trusted. . . .

"Another time, when I was eight, I got a bellyache while we were backpacking deep in the Olympics, in a wilderness area. I didn't say anything because I didn't want him to think he had a sissy for a son. But finally he noticed that I was sweating more than I should be, even for a kid who was carrying a twenty-five pound pack up a mountainside. He immediately dumped both our packs, put me on his back, and carried me out, ten miles to the trailhead where we'd parked the truck.

"The entire time he kept assuring me that I was going to be all right. And I believed him. Because he was my pop."

"What was wrong with you?"

"Appendicitis. They had me in the operating room five minutes after we got to the hospital. Afterwards, they told my dad that I was minutes away from having it burst."

"That was lucky. That he got you there when he did."

"Real lucky," he agreed. "The doc gave me the appendix. I kept it in a jar of formaldehyde in my room until I went off to college."

"You realize that's gross."

"Not to an eight-year-old boy. I kept it for a trophy, but also because it reminded me of one of the more eventful trips Pop and I took together."

Compared to these stories of his childhood, Raine

could have grown up on Jupiter. "It must have been wonderful," she murmured wistfully. "Knowing that you could always count on someone like that."

"Like I said, Pop was special. I always knew that, on some abstract level. It was only after Peg and I adopted Amy that I realized how he'd been the rock of the family, while Mom has always been the heart."

"I envy you such a strong family bond."

His arm tightened around her shoulder, pulling her a little closer. He skimmed his lips against the top of her head. "You have that, too. With Ida and Savannah. And Lilith."

She thought about that for a moment. "With Ida and Savannah. But Lilith . . ." Not wanting to ruin a lovely afternoon with negative thoughts about her mother, Raine's voice drifted off.

"You know, when I was still toddling around in diapers, my folks figured every boy should have a dog," he said conversationally. "So, they went to the animal shelter and adopted a springer spaniel–sheltie mix, figuring we could grow up together.

"That's sweet."

"I've always thought so. She was a dynamite dog. And loyal to a fault. She loved to go duck hunting with Dan and me, but we'd have to take her home at lunchtime, because the damn mutt would've kept diving into that icy water all day long. Partly because she loved fetching ducks. But mostly because she wanted, more than anything, to please me. She died when I was fifteen."

"I'm sorry."

"So was I. Even if she did live a helluva long time

for a dog. After a couple days, Dad took me down to the animal shelter and I suppose there were some pretty good candidates, but I was determined to get a dog exactly like Cleo."

"Cleo?"

"Because she had these dark lines around her eyes, kinda like Elizabeth Taylor when she played Cleopatra. . . . Hey"—he complained when she grinned—"I didn't name her. My mother did. If you'll recall, I was too young to be making such weighty decisions."

"Point taken."

"Okay. So, bein' a stubborn sort of kid, I kept trying to find a replacement for Cleo. It took six months, but I finally found a dead ringer. Right down to her crazy, brown nose with its black racing stripe down the center. I took her down to the beach to start training her for hunting season and must've thrown a hundred pieces of driftwood, but this new Cleo just sat there, looking up at me with a cockeyed adoring dog look, wagging her stub of a tail.

"After about a month, I finally got her to chase the damn sticks, but she never did figure out that she was supposed to bring them back. For a while I was so ticked off at the dog, I didn't even want to look at her. Because she didn't live up to my expectations."

Raine was silent for a moment, taking in the parable that was so similar to what Cooper had said earlier. "You think I'm too hard on Lilith."

"I think you're trying to make her into something she isn't," he said gently. "Because you've got some idealized beliefs about what a mother should be and anyone who doesn't live up to your high standard is bound to prove a failure in your eyes."

"That's not a very attractive picture." But painfully close to the truth, she secretly admitted. "If you truly believe I'm so judgmental, I can't imagine why you'd want anything to do with me."

"That's easy. You've got a great ass and the best legs I've ever seen on a female. And you taste pretty good, too."

Despite her discomfort with the topic, Raine smiled at that, just, as she suspected, he'd meant her to. "You realize, of course, that my mother would not be pleased to hear you compare her to a dog. Especially a mongrel."

"You're right. So, we'll just have to let that be our little secret." He pulled her closer. Then lowered his head, until his mouth was a whisper away from hers. "If you don't want this to happen, Raine, tell me now. Because while we're sharing secrets, I gotta tell you, sweetheart, I'm dying here."

His voice was rough. Pained. Thrilling. "Me, too," Raine whispered.

"Thank God." Jack's words exploded on a rush of air as he covered her lips with his and lowered her down to the blanket.

❧ 18 ❧

He wanted her. Really wanted her. The idea was as terrifying as it was thrilling. What if she couldn't satisfy him? Raine worried. What if she did something wrong and disappointed both of them? What if . . .

"Jack . . ." Her mind fogged, her voice drifted off and her body arched instinctively as he skimmed a hot kiss down her neck. "I think this is . . . Oh, God," she murmured when he touched the hollow of her throat with the tip of his tongue and sent her pulse hammering. "I have to tell you . . ." She could barely speak. Barely breathe. "It's been a long time since I've done this."

"Don't worry." He began unbuttoning her blouse while kissing his way back up to her mouth. "It's like riding a bicycle. It'll come back to you."

Her body arched when his hand closed over her breast. "It already has." Waves of pleasures flowed through her, as warm and liquid as a tropical sea. "More than I . . . Oh!" Raine gasped, then shuddered as he nipped at an erogenous zone on her neck she'd never even known she possessed. "More than I ever thought possible," she said on a quick rush of tangled breath. "But I'm not on the pill, and I don't have anything. . . ."

Her voice trailed as another wave, this time of embarrassment, threatened to engulf her. What was she thinking? To go so far without having given any thought to the consequences? She was behaving no more intelligently than poor, needy, lovesick Gwen had behaved with the faithless Randy. And look how that had turned out.

"Don't worry. I do." He lifted his hips just enough to dig into a pocket and pull out a handful of condoms.

From somewhere, a sense of humor she thought the intense world of corporate litigation had burned out of her years ago rose to ease what had proven to be an embarrassing moment. "Are you sure you brought enough?"

"For starters." As his mouth returned to hers, Raine could feel his smile against her lips.

She looked up at him, positive he was joking. "You're very sure of yourself, Sheriff." With good reason, she suspected as she watched the sexy glint flash in his midnight dark eyes.

"Nah. I'm just pretty damn sure of us, Counselor."

Her heart hitched. Then tumbled dangerously. She could lose it to this man, she realized in a blinding flash of realization. So easily. If she was smart, if she knew what was good for her, she'd back away now, even if she would go through life knowing she'd earned one of the most unflattering words used to describe a woman.

"May I ask one more question?"

His laugh was rough. "Could I stop you?"

Raine couldn't decide whether his gritty humor was directed at her, himself, or their situation. She knew she was talking too much, which could undoubtedly be blamed on nerves. But there was one more thing she needed to know.

"Did you ever bring . . ." she couldn't quite bring herself to say Jack's wife's name. Not when she was about to make love with him. Have sex, she corrected. "Bring anyone else here?"

His teasing grin faded and his expression was as sober as she'd ever seen it. "You're the only woman I've ever brought here, Raine. In fact, I'd forgotten it even existed. Until sometime in the middle of last night, when I was trying to think of a place I could get you alone and do this."

One hand tangled her hair as his mouth captured her tingling lips again, his kisses growing deeper. More drugging. The other was doing glorious things to her breasts that sent a sweet pleasure humming through her veins even as the caressing touch made her want more.

"And this." He pushed the cotton blouse aside and lightly bit her shoulder, then soothed the flesh with his tongue. Her breathing quickened as he unfastened her bra with a quick flick of the wrist and began torturing her unfettered breast with first his hands, then his mouth. Raine shivered as his teeth tugged on a taut nipple, causing sparks that shot straight down to that warm, moist place between her legs. Her head spun, her body craved. Desire rose so high and so hot it stunned.

"Please, Jack." Her fingers turned unusually

clumsy as she fumbled with the metal button on his jeans. "I need you." It was not an easy admission. Raine had never been one to give up control. She'd never wanted to surrender power. Until now. Until Jack.

"And I need you, too, sweetheart." He captured her hand and pulled it away, lifting it to his lips. When he began sucking on her fingers, one at a time, she felt a strong, corresponding pull deep inside her. "But it's been a while for me." His free hand opened her jeans, as she'd been planning to do to him, but with a great deal more finesse. "I don't want things to go too fast."

When he trailed a lazy fingertip down her stomach, through the nest of soft curls into the aching, dark warmth below, Raine heard a whimper and realized that it had come from between her own ravished lips.

"Fast would be okay," she managed as she bucked against his intimate touch. *Need* was too weak a word. She craved him. With every burning atom in her body. "In fact, fast would be fine."

He laughed at that, a deep, rich sound that rumbled through her. "Next time," he promised. "But I've been waiting too long for this not to at least try to make it last."

"Not that long." Desperate to touch, she pulled her hand free, ripped open his shirt and pressed first her palms, then her lips against the hard wall of his chest. His heart was pounding like a jackhammer, vivid proof that she was not the only one so harshly affected. His skin was hot and moist, and as she touched her tongue to it, Raine tasted a faint tang of salt. "I've only been home a few days."

"Ah, but I've been waiting for you longer than that." When he grabbed hold of her wrists and held her hands above her head, an edgy excitement crackled along her skin like flashfire.

"You couldn't have been," she managed to argue on a gasp as he touched his open mouth to that surprisingly sensitive spot at the base of her throat. "There was no way you'd know I'd be coming back to town."

"True enough." He continued his tender torture, skimming a trail of wet kisses down her rib cage. When he got to the waist of her jeans, he released her hands and slid them slowly down her legs, then followed the denim with his mouth in a slow, erotic journey that had her writhing on the blanket. "I didn't know you'd be coming. Hell, I didn't even know that I was waiting for you to come back. Until you showed up one rainy night and triggered something inside me I'd thought had died."

Lilith might endorse New Age beliefs, but Raine had never been one to accept the idea of fate. Or destiny. She'd never given credence to the idea of the Easter Bunny or the tooth fairy, and had stopped believing in Santa Claus when she was three years old and had gotten up on Christmas morning to discover that he hadn't shown up.

A week later, she was back at her grandmother's house, unwrapping gifts Ida assured her that Santa had delivered to Coldwater Cove by mistake. But Raine had known the truth. And that was the year trust had died.

But now, as she surrendered to Jack's murmured words, his tender touches, his devastating kisses, Raine wondered, through the rosy haze clouding her mind, if perhaps she'd been waiting for him, too. Without knowing she'd been waiting. Wanting him, without knowing she'd been wanting.

The idea was as thrilling as it was terrifying.

A sound that was half gasp, half sob was ripped from her throat as he licked his way back up her legs again, creating a sizzling pleasure-pain at the inside of her thighs. "Please," she moaned again. She'd never begged for anything in her life. But she was willing to now if that's what it took to end this exquisite torture.

"Not yet." He lifted his fingers to his mouth, touched his tongue to them, then slipped the wet tips beneath the elastic leg band of her panties. "Not nearly."

Hot, heavy moisture had soaked the cotton crotch. Raine tossed her head back and forth as he stripped the panties off and eased one of those treacherous fingers deep inside her. When his thumb parted the sensitive pink folds, she was certain she could feel her bones melt. When the rough pad of his seeking thumb stroked a swathe across the nub that was aching for his touch, sensation after sensation tore through her. Then, before she could catch her breath, he was lifting her to his mouth, feasting on her, claiming her, ravishing her.

Raine's eyes, which had been squeezed shut against the devastating assault on her senses flew open, wide with shock as she felt her body explode into a fireball, like a new sun being born.

She was boneless. Limp. Helpless. The entire forest could suddenly follow her up in flame and she wouldn't be able to move a muscle to save herself.

"That was," she gasped on a labored breath as he

held her in his arms while she tumbled back to earth. "Amazing."

"No." He touched his mouth to hers in a kiss that was surprisingly tender compared to his earlier hunger. "It's just the beginning."

As the afternoon lengthened and silver-edged clouds swept by overhead, Jack proved to be a man of his word as he drew out their lovemaking, treating her to a pleasure so sublime it nearly made her weep and a renewed passion so intense she feared it would make her shatter.

And when he finally took her over that final peak, Raine's last coherent thought was she felt as if she'd dived off the towering cliff above Neah Bay into a storm-tossed sea. Then risen from the waves again, exactly where she was fated to be. In his arms.

A light fog was skimming along the ground, like little gray ghosts as they drove in thoughtful silence back to town. He'd been afraid of this. While Jack had no idea what was going through Raine's mind at the moment, his own was rerunning every minute from that fateful moment he'd first seen her, wet and furious and sexy as hell. He hadn't lied when he'd told her that he'd wanted her from the beginning. Since he was, after all, human, he wasn't going to apologize for an all too human craving. The only problem was that he'd miscalculated.

He'd tried to tell himself that his only problem was he'd been celibate too long. And, although he wasn't the type of man to hop into the sack with the first available woman, he'd also tried assuring himself that Raine Cantrell wasn't the only attractive, intelligent, desirable woman in Coldwater Cove. Unfortunately, she was the only one he'd wanted.

Since they were, after all, both single, unattached adults, he'd decided there was no reason to deny themselves what they both wanted. He'd hoped that once he made love to Raine, once he satisfied the hunger that had tormented his daytime hours and haunted his sleep, he'd be satisfied. Ready to move on. Ready to let her move on.

But there had been a moment there, when he'd been deep inside her, just before his own climax, that his head had begun to swim and all the air seemed to have been sucked out of his lungs. It had felt as if he were drowning; and the crazy thing about it was that he couldn't even care.

This was ridiculous. Nothing could come of it; any relationship between them was a dead-end street. She lived in the fast lane a continent away; the life he'd made for himself and his daughter in Coldwater Cove was so laid back the lady lawyer would probably get more excitement from watching paint dry. She was rich—not Manhattan megamogul rich, but she sure as hell brought in a bigger paycheck than a civil servant. Jack figured she probably earned about three times what he did. That idea didn't really bother him, but it might her, since it could prove a bit difficult to explain to high-living friends that she'd married a small-town Western sheriff.

Marry? The idea hit with the force of a sledgehammer at the back of his head. Christ, talk about getting carried away just because of a couple hours of good sex. Okay, make that *great* sex. But it was still important to keep it in perspective. Raine may have spent a great deal of her childhood in Coldwater

Cove, but she'd moved on. She was city; he was country. She was Chateaubriand; he was ground chuck.

"Tomato, tomahto." He murmured the old song lyric as the fog lights cut through the mist rising from the damp pavement. A light sprinkle dotted the windshield, causing him to turn on the wipers.

She glanced over at him. "What did you say?"

He shrugged. "It's not important. I was just talking to myself."

"Oh."

Her voice invited elaboration he wasn't yet prepared to share. "I was thinking that it was too bad you had to run off so quick."

"I was thinking the same thing." she murmured. Since he'd already determined that Raine Cantrell was not a woman who was comfortable with touching, the foolishly romantic part of him that Jack thought had died was encouraged when she placed her hand gently, almost casually, on his thigh. "Talk about your rotten timing."

He covered her slender hand with his. "Hey, at least we'll always have Coldwater Cove."

Her laugh was light and warm and made him want to pull over to the side of the road and take her again in the back of the Suburban. "That's the difference between us. I'm always looking for the catch while you manage to find a bright side to everything."

"You make optimism sound like a flaw."

"I didn't mean it that way." Turning her hand beneath his, she linked their fingers together. "To tell the truth, I rather envy you your positive outlook on life. Especially after . . ." Her voice drifted off.

"Peg's death," he finished for her.

"It must have been difficult."

"It wasn't exactly a walk in the park."

"I imagine not." She paused again, as if choosing her words carefully. For a time the only sound was the intermittent *swish swish* of the windshield wipers. "If you don't want to talk about it—"

"I don't mind. I don't talk much about those days since the role of a grieving widower definitely isn't all that appealing. To me or anyone who has to put up with it. But after this afternoon, I'd say you're entitled to ask anything you want."

Her fingers tensed in his. She was silent and thoughtful in that way that he suspected would prove advantageous in a courtroom situation. She was a woman who used words carefully. Except, Jack thought with a very primitive male satisfaction, when she'd been bucking beneath him.

Sensing that she was curious, but uncomfortable with the topic, he decided to help her out. "It was bad. It took a very long time, and, though she fought like a trooper, I knew she was in a lot more pain than she ever let on."

"She was lucky to have you."

"Not always," he confessed. "In the beginning, during the initial treatment stage, we were a team. Granted, I hated having to stand on the sidelines while she fought the battle, and there were times when the role reversal was hard to take."

"But she knew you were in her corner. Supporting her, urging her on, putting your own pain aside to concentrate on reassuring her that everything would be okay. That she'd be okay."

"I'm not sure she always knew that. Not after we

ran out of options." Because that memory still hurt, he drew in a breath. "Peg accepted things even when I wanted her to keep fighting. There were still a lot of experimental treatments we could have tried. Granted, they hadn't proven effective in clinical trials, but it was damn well better than the alternative." At least that's what he'd argued at the time.

"But she put her foot down, insisting she wanted to be at home, with her family instead of in some Mexican or Swiss clinic. She said she wanted to enjoy her last months with her daughter and die in peace."

He released Raine's hand to drag his down his face. "From the first day I met her, she was unrelentingly easygoing, eager to do whatever she thought would make me happy. But then, just when it really mattered, she dug in her heels and refused to budge."

"That must have been difficult," Raine said.

Jack hated the pity he thought he heard in her voice. "I was furious that she was willing to give up; I yelled at her that if she loved me she'd keep on fighting." The guilt still hurt. Jack figured it always would. "What kind of man yells at his dying wife?"

"A human one," Raine suggested quietly. She caught hold of his hand again. "You're being too hard on yourself."

"Perhaps you're being too easy."

"No, I'm not." She lifted their joined hands and touched his knuckles to her lips. "There was a time in my life when I would have given away everything I owned, for even a little bit of that commitment you gave Peg."

Having figured out that she seldom said anything

she didn't mean, Jack immediately noticed her use of the past tense. "And now?"

Another pause. "And now," she said slowly, and a little regretfully, he thought, "I've learned not to count on anyone except myself."

"That's sad."

"No," she corrected, lowering their hands and releasing his. "It's safe."

"Safe can be a close cousin to boring," he said mildly. He reached out and put his arm around her shoulder. "And believe me, Harvard, you are anything but boring."

She smiled at that, as he'd intended. "I believe I'll take that as a compliment."

"Oh, I've got a lot more where that one came from."

Deciding that self-restraint was definitely overrated, he pulled off the highway again onto an unmarked logging skid road, cut the engine, unfastened their seatbelts, and hauled her onto his lap.

"Did I mention that your hair reminds me of silk?" He fisted his hand in the dark strands.

"I vaguely recall something along those lines."

He kissed her. Hard. "How about the fact that the color in your cheeks after I kiss you reminds me of strawberries on new snow?"

"Oh, I like that one." The smile was shining in her eyes again. "But maybe you ought to kiss me again. Just to be sure."

"Absolutely." Light, quick nibbles turned longer, deeper. "And your eyes." Her lids fluttered obediently shut as he dropped a kiss on each one. "Are like antique gold coins."

"They're hazel." She twined her fingers around his neck and arched her back, inviting his lips to continue their sensual quest.

After a few more deep, drugging kisses, he obliged, pleased when her pulse began to thrum wildly in the fragrant hollow of her throat.

As Jack worked his way down her body, fog thickened around the Suburban, sheltering them in a private, sensual world of their own making.

❧ 19 ❧

Raine had suspected that making love with Jack would complicate her life. It was more than just the sex, as wonderful as that was. Their earlier conversation, comparing her upbringing with his, had gotten her thinking about families and loyalty and commitment again.

She hated to admit it, even to herself, but suspected that he may have been right about Lilith. About so much of her unhappiness over the years having been because she'd been hoping for something that her mother had not been able to give. Granted, Lilith had not been a rock of stability, but as Cooper had pointed out, she'd at least admitted her own faults enough to take her daughters back to Coldwater Cove whenever her own life had spiraled out of control.

The problem was, Raine had always only thought of her mother as a flawed parent. Not a woman with dreams and hopes and disappointments of her own. And certainly never as a friend.

Yet with all her faults, despite her flaws, Lilith had

displayed an honest willingness to at least attempt to change during the time Raine had been back in Coldwater Cove. Some people might feel that fifty years old was a bit late to be deciding to grow up. But, Raine thought, better late than never.

These thoughts led uncomfortably to another. Over the past years, whenever Ida had complained that her eldest granddaughter didn't come home often enough, Raine had used work as an excuse. That had been partly true. But she also couldn't deny that she'd always felt more comfortable at work; it was one place where she felt in control. While family matters, on the other hand, tended to become emotionally sticky. Which was why she tried to ignore them.

Which brought her to the realization that in one small but important way, she was more like her mother than she'd tried to pretend all these years. Lilith had been infamous for thinking of herself first and last. Now Raine was forced to concede that she'd been guilty of exactly the same behavior.

She hadn't even known the names of the girls whom Ida obviously cared deeply about. It had been so long since she'd spent any time with her sister, she hadn't known how bad the trouble in Savannah's marriage had become. Just as her mother hadn't been there for her while she'd been growing up, Raine now was faced with the possibility that she'd developed her own form of abandonment. Her legal work, while important, was only that. Work. It shouldn't be her life. Should it?

She was also forced to consider that what she'd viewed all these years as independence, was, in a way, a form of solitude that had cut her off from her family ties, a symbolic cutting of the cord connecting the generations of females.

The father she'd never known may have been the role model for her success, but Lilith was the mile marker she used to measure her own personal travels.

Dammit, she wasn't used to this. This need to balance her own needs and desires with anyone else's. She wasn't any good at it. Especially when compared to Jack, who somehow managed to balance his duties as sheriff with his even more important responsibility to his daughter. Raine tried to picture any attorney she knew—including herself—pausing during an argument in court to keep a toy kitten alive for a little girl who'd already lost too many people she loved, and failed.

"I hope I'm not the cause of that frown." Jack's mild voice infiltrated her turmoiled thoughts.

"No. I was just thinking of something." The afternoon's peace and sublime pleasure began to fade away as if it had never been. Almost as if she'd imagined it.

"Want to talk about it?"

Raine believed in keeping her life neatly compartmentalized. There was her career. And everything else. The two tracks ran parallel, never crossing. Until three little girls had locked themselves in her grandmother's house, setting up a confrontation with this man. Accustomed to keeping her private thoughts strictly to herself, she found it difficult to share them now.

Her careless shrug was as fake as her smile. "It's not that important."

It was a lie and they both knew it. Jack didn't

immediately answer. Instead he slanted her one of those deep looks that made her once again think that he'd be a whiz at interrogation. She hadn't had much occasion to handle criminal work, but understood that cops, like attorneys, knew how to use silence to their advantage. Raine had always considered herself pretty good at this tactic. She was beginning to realize Jack just might possibly be even better.

"Your confession rate must have been the highest in the city," she muttered, switching her irritation at herself to him.

He turned his attention back to the wet, slick road. But that didn't stop his continued silence from making her even more edgy. Oh yes, any criminal unfortunate enough to end on the wrong side of the interrogation table with this man would undoubtedly soon find himself on a one-way trip up the river.

He glanced at her again, brow lifted. "That's what you were thinking about?"

"I was just picturing you in the box."

"The box?" His lips quirked.

"That's what it's called, right?" Feeling challenged, her voice turned as cool as the rain falling outside the truck. "Where you drill a suspect to win a confession?"

"Yeah. The box." She could hear the repressed laughter in his deep voice. "And if that's what you were thinking about, Harvard, I sure as hell must not have done a very good job of relaxing you this afternoon."

Just the mention of their shared lovemaking was all it took to cause a wave of desire that hit as quick and hard as a spring squall. Furious pride warred with an equally furious need inside Raine. Eventually pride won out.

"As I said, it's not that important."

He shrugged. "Whatever you say." His tone remained casual, but Raine wasn't fooled for a moment. She wasn't completely off the hook. And they both well knew it.

Jack and Raine had no sooner entered the house when a blood-curdling scream came from somewhere upstairs. A moment later Gwen came clattering down the stairs. She was wearing her *Lucy* maternity outfit, but there was absolutely nothing humorous about her appearance.

"What's wrong?" Ida, who'd rushed in from the front parlor, caught the trembling teenager by the upper arms. "What happened? Are you in labor?"

"No-o-o! I k-k-killed it!"

"What?" Savannah asked, as she joined them. From the white cotton chef's apron she was wearing over her jeans and T-shirt, Raine figured her sister had been saving them from another night of takeout or meatloaf.

"The baby."

"The baby?" Ida ran her hand over the teenager's swollen belly. "Are you cramping? Bleeding?"

"Not that baby!" Tears were streaming down Gwen's cheeks. "The N-N-Nano Baby. I was studying for my chemistry final and didn't hear it beeping and it s-s-starved to death!"

"Oh, darling." Ever the nurturer, Savannah gathered the tearful girl into her arms. "It's okay. It's just a toy."

"I know it's just a toy!" The teenager's words were muffled against Savannah's shoulders. "But don't you see?" When she lifted her head, her face was twisted in a very real agony that pulled painfully at Raine's heart. "It c-c-could have been a real baby."

"Oh, pooh," Ida scoffed. "You're a levelheaded young lady, Gwendolyn. And even if you weren't, your maternal instincts will kick in once you give birth. You'd never forget to feed your own child."

"That's not necessarily true," a new voice entered the conversation. Raine turned to see her mother standing in the arched doorway of the parlor, Cooper right behind her.

"This doesn't really have anything to do with you, Lilith," Ida said, her sharp tone declaring the matter settled.

"Perhaps not. But in a few days Gwen's going to have to make the most important decision of her life. And I think she deserves to hear more than the Pollyanna side of the story."

Lilith took a deep breath and briefly closed her eyes in a way that suggested she was garnering strength. Which, Raine figured, she undoubtedly was. Motherhood had never been Lilith's favorite subject. Especially since it had never been her forte.

"I was only a few years older than you when I had Raine, Gwen, dear," she said. "I hadn't intended to get pregnant, and while abortion was illegal in those days, everyone knew someone who could, I was assured, 'take care of the problem.' But while I suppose that would have been an easy solution, the practical solution, I was stunned by the depth of my feelings for the child I was carrying."

She turned to Ida. "Now I know, you'll say it's

impossible, but I knew, the moment after I'd made love with Raine's father, that I was pregnant."

"It *is* impossible," Ida muttered. "Owen Cantrell may have turned out to be some big-name hotshot attorney, but he doesn't have supersperm. It would have taken those guys a while to swim upstream. And even longer to penetrate an egg. So you weren't pregnant."

"Perhaps not physically. But emotionally, my heart somehow knew that Owen and I had made a baby. Of course there wasn't any way to tell whether I was carrying a girl or a boy in those days, but I knew I was going to have a daughter. I also knew that I loved her more than life itself."

"That's nice," Gwen sniffled.

"It's the truth." Lilith exchanged a glance with Raine. Her pansy blue eyes swam with moisture. Raine's own eyes stung. "The thing is, Gwen, darling, that as much as I was looking forward to being a mother, insisting on keeping Raine was selfish. Because I was incapable of taking care of a child. I was flighty, selfish, and there would be times that I'd be out having fun, like young girls will, and would actually forget I had a baby at home."

She wasn't surprised. Still, hearing her mother voice those words out loud made Raine flinch. Without a word, Jack reached out and took hold of her hand, linking their fingers together in the same intimate way he had when he'd so wondrously filled her earlier.

"You left Raine alone?" Gwen asked disbelievingly. "When she was a baby?"

"No. Of course she wasn't alone." Lilith shook her head. Then combed her fingers through the tousled silver strands. Raine couldn't help noting how her mother's hand was shaking. "Fortunately even I was never that irresponsible. And, thanks to Mother, Raine survived. But she might not have. Because, while I dearly loved both you girls to pieces"—she directed her words to Savannah and Raine—"my maternal instincts were, at best, lousy. At worst, nil."

"You weren't that bad," Ida insisted.

"Yes, I was," Lilith said, her voice low, but just as firm. "As you well remember."

"Well."

Raine could recall very few times when her grandmother had been at a loss for words. This was one of them. As the silence hovered, she saw Cooper slip a supportive arm around Lilith's waist in a move that appeared entirely natural.

"You're comparing oranges and orangutans," Ida said finally. "Because you and Gwendolyn are not at all alike. Gwen's a steady, studious girl and—"

"That's just the point," Gwen broke in again. Hectic red flags flew in her paper white cheeks. "I forgot to feed Amy's Nano Baby because I was studying so hard I didn't even hear it beeping."

"That's alright, kiddo," Jack assured her. "Amy won't mind."

"Maybe not. But I do." She bit her bottom lip. Tears filled her anguished eyes. "I've wanted to be a doctor ever since I was a little kid. I even wanted Doctor Barbie, when all the other girls were going crazy over Malibu Barbie. And maybe I'm being selfish, but how can I do that if I'm trying to take care of a baby while I'm still in high school?"

Not one person in the room could give her a good answer.

"Wanting to care for people isn't at all selfish," Raine tried. "But you're right. You still have another year of high school, then college, then medical school, which is even more difficult than law school. And I know I never could have juggled a baby and school. But some people do."

"Adults," Gwen suggested. "So." She took a deep breath. "I guess I don't have any choice but to go back to one of those adoption agencies and let one of those rich people adopt my baby."

"Oh, darling." Lilith's eyes filled with empathetic tears again. "I know how unhappy you were with those prospective parents. Surely there's another solution?"

She looked toward Raine, as if expecting her eldest daughter to pull one out of her legal bag of tricks. Which, of course, was impossible. Raine suspected mothers-to-be had been forced to make such decisions since the beginning of time. She doubted it ever got any easier. Or less painful.

Another silence settled like thick, wet morning fog.

"May I make a suggestion?" Savannah asked hesitantly.

"Okay," Gwen said, looking more forlorn than Raine had ever seen her. She looked even more depressed than she had that first night, when she'd watched Raine sign Old Fussbudget's custody forms from the backseat of Jack's Suburban.

"I have some friends who have been trying to adopt a child for years, since Terri can't have any herself, but the waiting lists for public agencies are terribly long, and they can't afford private adoption.

"Not that they're poor," she hastened to add. "It's

just that they have all their liquid assets tied up in their business. It's a winery. And it's not that far away. In Sequim, as a matter of fact. They make a marvelous, reasonably priced selection of red wines. During the three years I've been buying wine from them for the resort, we've become friends, and I can certainly vouch that no two people could love a child more than Terri and Bill. Or take better care of one."

"A winery?" Gwen asked on a sniffle. She rubbed her nose with the back of her hand.

"One that's becoming more successful every year," Savannah said. "I've no doubt that someday they could be rich. But right now, they're merely comfortable."

"Comfortable's okay." Gwen sniffled again, then wiped her nose on the Kleenex Lilith silently handed her. "Do they live at the winery?"

"Right on the grounds, in a wonderful old turn-of-the-century home that they're restoring." Savannah's smile was warm and reminiscent. "The nursery was the first room they completed. It's been sitting empty for the past five years."

"Five years is a long time to wait for a baby." Gwen looked thoughtful. And, Raine thought she could see the worry lift. Just a bit.

"Yes," Savannah agreed quietly. "It is."

"Do you think they might want my baby?"

"I know they'd love it as if it were their own natural-born child. Perhaps even more," Savannah said, glancing over toward Jack in a way that suggested she was remembering Amy's declaration at the party.

Gwen blew her nose. A more normal color was

returning to her complexion. "Do you think I could meet them?"

"Absolutely. Whenever you like."

"Maybe you can call them now?"

"I'll do that. But I won't make the appointment until the weekend. That way you won't have to miss finals. And you'll have more time to think things over. To make certain this is really what you want to do.

"Not that agreeing to meet with Terri and Bill means that you'd be agreeing to let them adopt your baby," Savannah hastened to assure the teenager. "We'll just consider it a getting-acquainted meeting."

"Okay." Gwen's relief was more-than-a-little obvious. She turned to Lilith. "Will you come? To help ask the questions, like you did before?"

Although her eyes were still swimming, Lilith's smile only wobbled slightly. "Of course, darling. I'd love to."

Gwen turned to Raine. "Will you come, too?"

"Oh, Gwen, I'm afraid I can't draw up any papers—"

"No. Not as a lawyer. As family."

Family. Raine reminded herself of all the years she'd spent wishing for a traditional, Ozzie-and-Harriet family. What she'd belatedly discovered might not fit the two-parent, two-point-five-children model, but somehow, when she hadn't been looking, it appeared she'd landed smack into the middle of one.

"I'll be there. And I'll stay here until your baby's born."

While the others, including, Raine noticed, Cooper Ryan, followed Savannah back into the kitchen to be present for the important call, Raine wandered back out onto the front porch with Jack.

"That was a nice thing to do," he said.

"I didn't have a choice." It was a foolish thing, perhaps, but she was inordinately pleased by his compliment.

He cupped her face with his hand and gave her a long look. "That's not exactly true," he said eventually, "Between Savannah and Dan, Gwen's in good hands. Even before you factor in Ida's common sense and Lilith's empathy. I'm not the least bit surprised by your decision, but I'll bet dollars to dentures that you are, just a little."

Hearing him repeat one of Ida's malapropisms made her smile at the same time the light touch of his fingertips on her cheek caused a renewed rise of desire. Had it only been desire, Raine figured she could have handled it. After having experienced Jack's exquisite lovemaking, it would only be natural to want more. Any woman would. It was the realization that she needed him, needed him in ways that had nothing to do with sex, that had her shaken.

"Perhaps, just a little," she admitted in a voice she wished was stronger.

His fingertips skimmed up her cheek and into her hair. "You just need to spend a little more time getting in touch with your inner Raine."

His lips were smiling; his eyes were smoldering in a way that created a spike in her hormones. Since looking into those eyes had her wanting to pull him down onto the swing, Raine concentrated on his lips. Which proved a big mistake when she could recall their taste in exact, glorious detail.

"Perhaps I do." Her legs were turning as shaky as her voice. "Are you offering to help?"

"Absolutely." When his mouth covered hers, Raine could feel his smile broaden. As she twined her arms around his neck and went up on her toes to kiss him back, Raine's answering smile broke free.

∾20∾

"How would you like to have dinner at the farm?" Jack asked after the blissful kiss finally ended.

"I'd love to have dinner with you." After this afternoon, Raine saw no point in being coy. Besides, she wanted to spend as much time as she could with Jack before she went back to New York. "But what about Amy?"

"Well, that's kind of the thing." He rubbed his cheek. "I've pulled a couple nights I don't usually do the past couple weeks, and I'd just as soon not leave her alone again tonight. I was thinking that if you don't mind the drive and you're willing to trust my cooking, we could have dinner at the farm."

"I like spaghetti," she said, recalling an earlier invitation she'd turned down.

"Hey, I can cook more than that. In fact, I'm also a whiz at steaks, lasagna, and grilled salmon."

"Ah, yes. You mentioned something about grilled fish in your little survival fantasy."

"Our *lovemaking* fantasy," he corrected.

"Lovemaking? I don't remember anything about

that. In the fantasy I heard, you were sharpening sticks and building log cabins with your Swiss Army chain saw while I made beds and sewed skirts."

"The skirts were your idea," he reminded her. "And didn't I mention the lovemaking part?"

"No."

"Damn. And that's the best part." He looped his arms around her waist and pulled her toward him. "After dinner, I take that skirt off you, leaf by leaf—"

"Sounds a lot like peeling an artichoke."

He shook his head. "Anyone ever tell you that you can—at times—be a bit too literal?"

"I'm an attorney. It goes with the territory."

"With you, perhaps. Most lawyers I've met tend to be verbally creative types. Creative with the truth, anyway."

"Truth is a bit like beauty. It's in the eye of the beholder."

"Objection sustained." He drew her a little closer. "And speaking of beauty, I strip those banana leaves off you, one at a time—"

"Banana leaves? I thought this fantasy took place here on the peninsula."

"There you go, getting bogged down in details again. Besides, Coldwater Cove is in the Pacific Northwest's banana belt."

"A banana belt, like beauty and truth, is relative. We happen to be across the Strait of Juan de Fuca from Canada. That's not exactly the tropics. We grow Douglas firs here. Not bananas."

"Yeah, but you ever try to wear a skirt made out of prickly fir needles?"

Raine shook her head. "This is ridiculous. And irrelevant. Salmon sounds terrific. Lasagna is great. Heck, I'll even settle for a peanut butter sandwich."

"Peanut butter was one of my specialties even before I had a six-year-old." He lowered his head and kissed her. Lightly, quickly. The kiss caused Raine's heart to turn cartwheels even as it left her wanting more. Much, much more. "Is that the only reason you're taking me up on my invitation?"

On some level, she knew that at least waffling a bit would be prudent. But Raine couldn't lie. Not after their brief discussion of truth, not about this. Not when her heart was still spinning. And her body felt all tingly. She smiled faintly when she remembered reading that people who were about to be struck by lightning felt the same sort of beneath-the-skin sensation.

Too late. The little voice of reason she'd steadfastly ignored earlier managed to make itself heard in the far reaches of her mind. *You've already been struck.*

"No," she said, smiling up at Jack, wondering if he could read her foolish, reckless heart in her eyes and oddly not caring if he could. "I'm not going to feel guilty about taking time away from work, because I've earned it. But I will have to go back to New York as soon as Gwen's had her baby. Meanwhile"—she framed his face with her hands—"what time do you want me?"

"Anytime. All the time."

How was it that those few little words could send her heart into another series of somersaults? "I meant what time you wanted me at the farm."

"Anytime," he repeated. "You're the one having to do the driving, which I'm sorry about—"

"That's okay. The drive to the farm should be especially lovely this time of evening. I'll start out in about an hour. That way you can have some private time with your daughter."

"Sounds like a plan."

He kissed her again. Neither of them saw the family, standing at the front parlor window, barely concealed by the white lace curtains.

"I knew it," Ida crowed. "There'll be a summer wedding or I'll eat my shoes."

"Some kisses don't necessarily make a marriage," Savannah said.

"True," Lilith agreed. "But their auras are nearly blinding, they're so bright. It's obvious that Raine and the sheriff are destined to be with one another."

"You don't have to see auras or any of that other New Age folderol to see that they're in love," Ida said. "If that kiss got any hotter, they'd be setting the porch on fire."

"I don't think we should be watching," Gwen murmured.

"If you're that uncomfortable, dear, why don't you just go on upstairs," Lilith suggested.

"And miss this?" Gwen pressed her nose against the glass. "It'll be so neat."

"What darling?" Lilith asked absently.

"Raine and Jack getting married. It'll be fun having Amy for a sister. And boy, we could really use a man in this family."

"Women need men like fish need rollerskates," Ida stated her oft-repeated opinion firmly.

"Speak for yourself, Mother," Lilith drawled as she exchanged a warm smile with Cooper, who'd chosen to stay across the room. "I think Jack O'Halloran is going to be a marvelous addition to our little family."

Gwen murmured instantaneous agreement. Ida didn't respond. But, uncharacteristically, she didn't argue, either.

Jack had already put the lasagna in the oven by the time Raine arrived at the farm. The rich aromas of basil, oregano, and tomato sauce filled the air.

"If that tastes half as good as it smells," she said as she shrugged out of the jacket she'd worn in deference to the cool evening air, "you could quit the cop job and go into the inn and restaurant business with Savannah."

"Guests might get a little bit tired of four things on the menu." Jack hung the jacket on the antique coatrack.

"Five." She smiled. "Don't forget the peanut butter."

"I think I'd better stick to the things I do well." He skimmed an appreciative gaze over her. "You look so lovely."

"Oh, you definitely do that well." Raine felt the color rise in her cheeks again and thought that she hadn't blushed as much in her entire life as she had since returning home. "The sweater is Lilith's. I was afraid cashmere might be a little much for a dinner at home, but—"

"It's perfect." The soft ivory-hued sweater's neckline cut across her collarbone in a way that encouraged it to slide off a shoulder, as it was now. Drawn by the fragrance, Jack skimmed first his fingertip, then his lips over the bared skin that was gleaming like porcelain in the spreading glow of the overhead light fixture. "And, in case I get hungry while I'm waiting for the lasagna to heat up, I can always nibble on you."

"Surely you wouldn't want to set a bad example for Amy."

"That's something we need to talk about. I tried to call you and see if you wanted to cancel, but you'd already left the house and—"

"Cancel? Why would I want to do that?" She'd no sooner said the words when an unpalatable thought occurred to her. "If she doesn't want me to be here—"

"No." It was his turn to interrupt. "Of course she wants you. Hell, if you'd come planning to set up housekeeping, she'd be tickled pink. The problem is, she's sick."

"Oh, no." She experienced a sharp, unbidden need to run upstairs and check on the little girl herself. "I hope it's nothing serious. Has she seen a doctor?"

"No, it's not serious, and I called the doctor as soon as I picked her up at Mom's. It's just one of those stomach virus things that all the kids in her class apparently have come down with. It's not bad. But, it's not real pretty, either. In fact, if Hollywood decides to remake *The Exorcist*, Ariel'll be a shoe-in for the role of the pea soup kid."

"Oh, the poor thing." Something else he said belatedly sunk in. "Ariel?"

"She woke up this morning and informed all of us—me, my mom, her teacher, the other kids at school—that we're supposed to call her Ariel. I'm hoping this will be a short-lived stage."

Raine laughed. "When I was in the second grade, I changed my name to Jane."

"Well. That's, uh, very down to earth," he decided.

"Certainly more than Raine. You can't imagine the jokes I used to get—Raine, Raine, go away; come again another day." She shrugged. "Stuff like that."

"I can see how that might have been tough. So, when did you change it back?"

"When Lanny Davis told me that he thought Raine was prettier. You might remember him. He was three years older and delivered the paper every afternoon. He had a maroon mountain bike with jet striping, black hair, and a pouty scowl that seemed incredibly sexy when I was ten years old. He tended to wear white T-shirts, jeans, and a black motorcycle jacket. Even in the summer."

"Yeah, I remember him. Coldwater Cove's own James Dean."

"I suppose that was his appeal. Since girls tend to have a tendency for falling for bad boys."

"So I've heard, and your little story only confirms my decision that if I'm smart, I'll just lock Amy—"

"Ariel," Raine reminded him.

"Right. I'll just lock the little mermaid in the closet—preferably one located in a nunnery—and not let her out until she's at least thirty-five."

"That's a bit drastic," she said, enjoying the conversation. And him. "Besides, I'm not certain reaching adulthood is any guarantee of choosing the right man."

Since Dan's calls hadn't uncovered anything about a boyfriend, Jack suspected the shadow in her eyes had something to do with her sister. "Is Savannah home for good?"

"I don't know." The laughter had faded from her voice and her eyes. "She says so. I hate to see any marriage break up, yet in this case, I suppose it's for the best."

"Guess she got one of those bad boys by default."

"Yeah. She sure as hell did." Raine shook her head. And tossed the somber mood off. "Do you think it'd be okay if I went upstairs and said hi to Ariel?"

"She'd love to see you, but I have to warn you. She's not in the best of moods."

"I believe I can handle one ill, cranky six-year-old," Raine assured him.

She was nearly to the landing when Jack called out to her. "Hey, Harvard. What about you?"

"What about me, what?"

"Are you the type of woman who falls for bad boys?"

"The past couple years I haven't had any time to think about it. But since you brought it up, I think if I were looking for a man, he wouldn't be a bad boy, but a good man. He'd be strong enough to be sensitive, and confident enough not to be threatened by a woman. Oh yeah, and he'd be a wonderful lover."

"What about money?"

"What about it?"

"Would he have to be rich?"

"Of course not. Besides, we'll be too busy making love and celebrating all we have to pay any attention to what we might not have."

"Sounds as if tangling the sheets is pretty high on the list."

"Oh, it is." Raine shot him a blatantly flirtatious,

from beneath-the-lashes glance. "Because, as Ida always says"—her voice turned Marilyn Monroe breathy—"a hard man is good to find."

With a toss of her head, she resumed climbing the stairs, pleased by the way her behavior had caused that wicked gleam in his eyes. No wonder her mother was such a flirt, Raine thought. It was more fun than she could have ever imagined.

The child formerly known as Amy was propped up in bed with a trio of pillows. Mermaids and various forms of colorful sea life swam over her sheets and comforters and she was surrounded by enough stuffed animals to start her own plush zoo.

"I'm sick," she announced when Raine appeared in the doorway. She was wearing a pink nightgown that matched the bedclothes.

"I know. Your daddy told me." Raine crossed the room, pushed aside a purple polka-dot elephant dressed in a rainbow-hued tutu and a tiger with one ear missing, then sat on the edge of the narrow bed. "I'm so sorry." She pressed the back of her hand against a forehead that felt unnaturally warm.

"I have a fever." Her eyes were dull, her cheeks pink. "It's one hundred degrees. Daddy gave me some medicine, but then I threw up again, so he was afraid to give me any more for a while."

"Sounds as if your Daddy has everything under control."

"Oh, he always does. That's why he's sheriff." She pulled the Lion King from the pile and hugged it to her chest. "I threw up at school, too. In the cafeteria. Johnny McNeil said it was because the cafeteria ladies put dog food in the tacos. But the school nurse said it's just something that's going around.

"Daddy said I'll only feel bad for a few days. Then, when I get better, we can go to the aquarium in Seattle. That's my favorite place," she confided.

"That sounds like a very good favorite place for a little girl named Ariel."

"That's not my name any more." If the child's bottom lip sank any lower, it'd be resting on the bright comforter. "When I was Amy, I didn't get sick. Then I was Ariel for just one morning and I threw up. So I changed it back."

"Amy's a very pretty name." Raine brushed some damp flaxen hair from her forehead.

"I know." She sighed. A moment later, her eyes got saucer wide and her skin took on a faint green tinge.

Sensing what was about to come, Raine grabbed the copper-bottom Dutch oven Jack had placed on the white-enamel-painted bedside table and stuck it in front of Amy just in time.

Fortunately, after having been sick all day, there wasn't much left to come up, although the painful retching nearly broke Raine's heart.

"I hate that," Amy muttered as she flopped back against the pillow.

"I know." Touched, Raine smoothed her fingers across the forehead that she thought might feel a bit cooler. "I'll be right back with a cool cloth."

"Daddy brought me one." She waved a small hand toward the Winnie-the-Pooh and Tigger washcloth on the table. "But then it got hot. Like me."

"Well, sounds as if it's time for a new one." Raine washed out the pan in the bathroom across the hall, dampened the washcloth again with cool water, then returned to the bedroom where Amy, lying back against all those pillows again, was pulling off a fair impression of Camille.

"Thank you," she said in something perilously close to a whimper as Raine wiped the small face and placed the folded cloth on her forehead.

"You're welcome." Raine picked up the members of the menagerie that had fallen onto the pink carpeting during the excitement and rearranged them around the little girl again.

"The cloth feels good." Her eyes were closed, the gilt tipped lashes looking like gold dust against her fair cheeks.

"I'm glad." Raine perched on the edge of the bed again and began finger-combing the long, tousled curls.

A faint purring sound slipped from between the childish lips. "It's not true, is it?"

"What, darling?" Raine asked absently, as she struggled with an overwhelming urge to hold Jack's daughter close.

"About the dog food."

"No. I think Johnny McNeil must have an overactive imagination."

"I knew he was lying. I told him that if the cafeteria ladies put dog food in the tacos, Daddy would put them in jail."

"They certainly would be in trouble," Raine agreed carefully.

"I wish he'd put Johnny in jail." She breathed a frustrated sigh. "He's not very nice. Last week he got a Time Out for calling the teacher a bad name. . . . You're nice," she said, displaying a child's ability to switch topics on a dime.

"So are you."

The blue eyes opened, spearing Raine with a direct look. "Do you like aquariums?"

Raine knew where this was headed and was vaguely surprised that she wasn't bothered. "They're one of my favorite things."

"Mine, too. I like the saltwater fish best, because they're so pretty. Like jewels. But the sharks are neat, too." One hand was busying playing with an errant curl, the other absently stroking a stuffed red lobster. "Maybe you can go with Daddy and me when I get better."

Raine smiled, bent her head and kissed the feverish brow. "I'd like that. Bunches and bunches."

"Hey, Pumpkin," a deep voice called from the doorway. "I brought you a bowl of orange Jell-O, a glass of 7 Up, and some crackers. It's what my Mom always gave me when I was sick."

He looked a little weary, somewhat frazzled, and, Raine thought, absolutely wonderful.

"I threw up again," Amy informed him. "But Raine took care of me."

His expression as he looked over at her was apologetic. Raine shrugged it off. "We've been having a nice visit," she said mildly.

"Raine said the same thing you and the nurse did. That it wasn't dog food that made me sick. And guess what, Daddy?"

"What, sweetheart?"

"When I get better, Raine's coming to the aquarium with us. I asked her and she said yes. Isn't that the best thing?"

"Absolutely the very best," he agreed.

Jack's dark eyes met Raine's and held. The intimate look, while not overtly sexual, nevertheless possessed the power to send rivers of warmth flowing through her and had her thinking, for one wild, wonderfully irrational moment, that if the gods were to suddenly grant her the power to stop time, she might very well choose this moment.

❧21❧

Three days later, Raine was sitting on the swing, answering e-mail when Ida came out of the house.

"We've got to get going," she announced.

Raine glanced up. "Where?"

"To those friends of Savannah's who might be adopting Gwen's baby."

Wondering if she could have gotten so laid back since returning to Coldwater Cove that she might have lost track of what day of the week it was, Raine glanced down at her watch.

"The meeting's still another four days away."

"It was four days. Until Gwen asked Lilith to read her tarot cards. Apparently, according to your mother, the girl's going to give birth within the next forty-eight hours."

"Oh, for heaven's sake." Raine hit *save* in order not to lose the message she'd been composing. "You're a doctor. Didn't you explain to Gwen that those cards are merely superstition?"

"Of course I did. But she's insisting on going out

to that winery to meet the Stevensons before she goes into labor."

"Does she look as if she's about to go into labor?"

"It's impossible to tell." Her grandmother shrugged shoulders clad in a T-shirt that told the world *Where There's Smoke, There's Toast*. "I know Savannah and Dan wanted to give her more time to think it over, but since she's so determined, it's probably best to try to get the adoption issue settled before the baby's born."

Raine called Dan, who fortunately had a free morning and agreed to meet them at the Stevensons' winery in Sequim.

"Oh, it's so pretty," Gwen breathed at her first glimpse of her unborn child's possible future home. It's like out of a fairy tale book."

"I certainly wouldn't mind growing up here, if I were your little girl," Lilith told Gwen.

Savannah, Ida, and Raine all agreed that it was indeed one of the most scenic spots on the peninsula. Situated on the hilltop former summer estate of a Seattle lumber baron, Blue Mountain Winery overlooked a vast sweep of spring green vineyards set in dark soil that stretched nearly to the Strait of Juan de Fuca. The winery itself was located in a century-old stone-castle-like building, while the nineteenth-century house with its sharp spires revealed the original owner's roots in Germany's Rhine Valley.

Dazzling gardens curled through an emerald lawn; the waters of a duck pond glistened in the spring sunshine. The scent of lilacs perfumed air alive with birdsongs. Serving as a glorious backdrop for the scene were, as always, the snow-capped spines of the Olympic Mountains.

The current owners were refugees from California's Napa Valley, where, Terri offered with unmistakable pride, Bill had worked as a wine master. When she named the winery, even Raine, who certainly didn't have her sister's knowledge of such things, was impressed.

"A person should never go into the wine business to get rich," Bill Stevenson said. A soft-spoken man whose gentle brown eyes were a contrast to his wife's dancing blue ones, he'd spoken little during the tour of the winery, only interjecting the occasional technical explanation into Terri's enthusiastic spiel. "So much depends on the weather, and the soil, and wine drinkers' personal tastes."

"Which is why it's so wonderful that people like you are willing to put your love of wine before the demands of the accountants," Savannah said.

His smile was slow, a little shy, but Raine, who'd been watching the couple closely, had decided he was a kind and gentle man who'd undoubtedly make a wonderful father. "It's a little easier to take risks when you don't have all that much to lose." He looked out over the rolling green hills. "Unfortunately, in the larger wineries, the accountants tend to be winning."

"Are you saying your business could fail?" Gwen asked. She'd said little during the tour, but this, apparently concerned her. "And lose all this?"

"Of course we won't," Terri hastened to assure her. "We were fortunate enough to receive a nice inheritance from my great-grandmother. We used that, along with our savings to put a large enough down

payment on Blue Mountain that even if we do have
a few lean years we won't have to leave. This is our
home, Gwen. A home where we hope to be able to
raise children and someday sit on the lawn and
watch our grandchildren feeding pieces of bread to
the ducks on the pond."

"That sounds nice." Gwen's tone was wistful. Although she'd never considered herself a very fanciful
person until recently, Raine found herself wishing
that she possessed a magic wand she could use to
make the teenager's troubles disappear.

They'd gathered together on a little patio overlooking the duck pond, protected by a wide overhang
from the misty rain that had begun to fall. Raine
couldn't help noticing that Lilith had prepared Gwen
well. She was a font of questions, all of which the
Stevensons answered openly and honestly.

"What if there's something wrong with the baby?"
Gwen asked. "I've tried to take good care of myself.
I don't drink and I've never done drugs or smoked
any kind of cigarettes, regular ones or pot. Mama
Ida makes sure I eat right and exercise and get regular checkups, but all the books still say that things
can go wrong. Would you still want the baby if she
wasn't perfect?"

"Of course we would," Terri said.

"We have insurance that would cover any health
expenses, so that wouldn't be a concern," Bill added.

"And since a child would be the answer to all our
prayers, we'd love any one God might bless us with."
Terri's response was too heartfelt not to be sincere.

"What if she turns out to be gay? Would you kick
her out?"

Terri laughed a little at that. "Darling, I grew up

in San Francisco. Bill and I both have gay friends. There's no way we'd turn any child of ours away."

"Not even if she gets pregnant when she's a teenager?"

"Not even then."

Gwen valiantly blinked back tears. "It's too bad you don't want a teenager," she said with a forced, wobbly smile. "Then you could adopt me."

Even as they all shared a little laugh at that, Raine found the mood decidedly bittersweet. Then Terri sobered. "Bill and I have given a great deal of thought to this and have decided that we're proponents of open adoption. You're welcome to be part of your daughter's life, if you'd like."

"I don't know." Gwen bit her teeth into her lower lip, as if to stop it from quivering. "It might be too hard."

"Well, the final decision is up to you." Terri reached across the wrought-iron table and covered Gwen's hand with one tanned from days spent working in gardens and vineyards. "The amount of involvement in her life is up to you to choose."

A single tear escaped to trail down the teenager's cheek. Then another. She wiped them away with the backs of her hands, looking like a forlorn urchin. The funereal black dress she'd worn for this important occasion only made her face appear paler.

"What if I want her back?"

It was the Stevenson's turn to look concerned. They exchanged a look. "Of course you're given time to change your mind," Terri assured her.

"Do you think you might want to call the adoption off?" Bill asked in his quiet way.

Gwen swallowed visibly. Then turned her swimming gaze out over the strait where a cruise boat, with *Midnight Sun* painted in black script on gleaming white, was heading out to the sea.

"No." It was a ragged whisper. The teenager closed her eyes and took a long breath that had the rest of them taking one right along with her. "No," she said more firmly. "You can give her more than I ever could. You can keep her safe and she'll live in this nice house, and you'll be able to send her to college." She took another deep, obviously painful breath that caused Raine to bite her own lip.

"I know I'll always miss her, and probably feel bad on her birthday and on Mother's Day for a long time, but Lilith is right when she says that this isn't about me. It's about my baby. And what's right for her."

The tears were flowing openly now. Streaming not just down Gwen's cheeks, Terri's, Savannah's, and Raine's as well. Lilith, too, was weeping silently, Bill blew his nose, and as she pressed a Kleenex beneath her eyes, Raine noticed that even Ida's eyes were unnaturally bright.

"There's just one thing," Gwen said from the comforting protection of the arm Lilith had put around her shoulder.

"Anything," Terri said without hesitation.

"If she ever needs anything, like a blood transfusion, or a kidney, or a bone-marrow transplant, or anything like that you might not be able to give her, will you promise to call me first?"

"Absolutely," Terri and Bill promised together.

There were more tears. More hugs. Finally, the papers Dan had brought with him were signed and they left the winery headed back to Coldwater Cove.

"I think you did the right thing, Gwen," Raine said into the silence. "For both you and your baby."

"I know," the teenager sniffled as she huddled against the window in the back seat. "But it's still so hard."

"Of course it is," Ida said. She glanced into the rearview mirror. "Which is only partly why I'm proud to know you."

"Really?"

"You bet. You're definitely one of the bravest, most unselfish people I've ever met."

"That's a nice thing to say."

"It's the truth."

"Oh, look, darling." Lilith said suddenly. In the distance, rising from a silvery mist, a rainbow arced over the mountains. "It's a sign. From the Goddess that everything is going to turn out all right."

Gwen didn't answer. But as she cast a glance up into the rearview mirror, Raine thought the teenager looked a bit more hopeful about her future.

All too aware that they'd become a subject of speculation in Coldwater Cove, Raine hadn't hesitated to accept Jack's invitation to escape to Seattle so they could spend an entire night together.

"Don't be foolish," Ida said briskly when she suggested canceling in case Gwen went into labor. "First births take several hours. In the off chance she does have to go to the hospital, you'll have plenty of time to get there."

"If you're sure."

"Oh, for heaven's sake, darling," Lilith said. "I'll be the first to admit that I haven't exactly been a model of propriety over the years, but it is possible to carry duty too far."

"One of the reasons I stayed here was to be around when Gwen had her baby," Raine reminded her mother. But not the only reason. During the past days the tensions had eased between them as Raine tried to focus on the positive things about Lilith—her zest for living life to the fullest, her humor, her ability to always look for that silver lining no matter how dark the cloud—and not take the negative so personally. They were still at the baby-step stage. But in the past two weeks they'd made more progress than in the entire previous thirty years of Raine's life.

"Please, Raine," Gwen said. "I'd feel horribly guilty if you stayed home just for me."

Raine hesitated, even as she longed to accept their permission to go. "If you're sure."

"We're sure!" all three shouted at once just as Jack pulled into the driveway.

Feeling as free as Savannah's hawk when it soared into the sky, Raine picked up her overnight bag and ran out to meet him.

Four hours later, Raine was sitting across from Jack in the Lighthouse Restaurant, high atop the Seattle Windsor Palace hotel.

"God, you are gorgeous." He lifted a glass of the champagne he'd ordered in a silent toast. "Beauty, intelligence, and courage, all wrapped up in one package. The gods were definitely generous to you when they were handing out gifts, Harvard."

She'd never had a man talk to her the way Jack did. Never would she have believed any other man if he had. "While you obviously received the gift of blarney." She smiled at him over the rim of the crystal flute.

"It's not blarney if it's true." He leaned across the table and skimmed a fingertip beneath her eyes. "The shadows are gone. And you seem more relaxed."

"I am." It was the truth. She belatedly realized that she hadn't had a headache for days. "However, if you keep touching me that way, my nerves are going to get all tangled."

"No problem. We'll just go back downstairs to our room and untangle them again."

The memory of their predinner lovemaking caused that now-familiar warmth to flood into her cheeks, making Raine wonder why it was that she'd never blushed before knowing Jack. Because, she answered her own rhetorical question, she hadn't had all that much to blush about before Jack.

"You promised me crab cakes."

"True." He leaned back in his chair and lifted his own glass of champagne to his lips, the long-stemmed crystal flute looking even more flimsy in his large hand. "But you can't blame me for being distracted." Desire thickened his voice, causing a thrill to skim up her spine. "I suppose it would damage your hard-earned professional reputation if I were to drag you beneath the table and have my way with you."

"Is that what you feel like doing? Dragging me beneath the table?"

"For starters."

Raine had never flirted; had never known how to flirt. But she was discovering that Jack made it easy.

"I don't believe you'd actually do it." She stroked the stem of the champagne glass with her fingers in a blatantly seductive way that, from the way his eyes darkened, she knew wasn't lost on him.

"You don't?"

"No. Because you have your own sterling reputation to protect. Everyone knows that Dudley Doright would never ravish a woman in a public restaurant."

"Maybe Sweet Nell never tempted him the way you are me." He tossed back his wine. "How hungry are you?"

"Not very. Not now."

"How does ordering something up from room service later sound? Much, much later."

"It sounds glorious." She took the snowy damask napkin from her lap, placed it on the table, and stood up.

On his feet in a flash, Jack tossed some bills onto the table, placed his hand on her back in a proprietary way, and led her out of the restaurant.

"Have I thanked you for buying that dress?" he asked as the elevator doors closed behind them.

It was the flowered one she'd been trying on at The Dancing Deer when he'd brought his daughter to the store in order to exchange underwear. The one she'd sworn she was not going to buy. But had, with him in mind.

"Yes. But not in the last twenty minutes." Dizzy with an appetite that had nothing to do with any need for French food, Raine twined her arms around his neck and leaned against his hard body.

"Then I've definitely been remiss." When he lowered his mouth to within a breath from hers, Raine held on tighter, bracing herself for his kiss. But instead he began nibbling at her neck. "But don't worry, sweetheart. I have every intention of making it up to you."

The woman in her was turning weak and woozy. The lawyer couldn't resist a challenge. "I suppose I'll just have to take a wait-and-see attitude on that." Her voice, which had started out courtroom cool, skimmed up the scale when he nipped her ear.

"Lord, I never would have guessed that I'd find contrariness in a female such a turn-on." He switched targets and gave her chin a teasing nip. "As for waiting, now that you bring it up, it sounds like a pretty good idea. After all, I've already proven I can make you scream." His hand slipped between them and cupped her breast. "Perhaps this time I'll see if I can make you beg."

"I could have you on your knees." Her voice was half moan, half laugh.

"In a heartbeat." When his thumb brushed against a nipple, Raine heard the rasp of roughened skin against scarlet silk. "Especially since that was already in the game plan."

He released her breast to capture her chin between his fingers, holding her gaze to his. His eyes burned in his rugged face like two hot coals; a nerve jumped in his cheek. Raine had never seen him looking so dangerous. So uncivilized.

A need rose up inside her—so huge, so powerful, that it took her breath away. She drew in a deep gulp of air, and then his mouth was on hers, his kiss hot and greedy and wonderful. The thought that they were in a public elevator briefly flashed through her mind, but then he lifted her off her feet and pulled her even tighter against him and caution spun away. He was a hot, fully aroused male and dear heavens, how she wanted him.

"I need you." Teeth scraped as she gasped the admission out. "I've never needed any one like I need you."

His rough laugh vibrated against her lips as the elevator dinged. "Believe me, darlin', I know the feeling."

Behaving as if carrying women through hotels was a common occurrence, Jack nodded to the elderly couple dressed in formal wear who'd been waiting for the elevator. "Good evening," he said.

"Oh, God," Raine giggled as he strode down the hallway toward their room. That was another thing that had changed. She *never* giggled. "I think we shocked them."

"If that's all it takes, then it's a good thing they're not going to witness the rest of the night." He deftly managed to unlock the door with the key card while still holding her in his arms.

After carrying her over the threshold, he lowered her to the floor. Her high heels sank into the plush carpeting. He shrugged off his suit jacket and tossed it onto a nearby chair, then backed a few feet away.

"Don't move," he murmured huskily. "I just want to look at you." When he silently twirled a finger, Raine turned. After she'd gone full circle and faced him again, the heat in Jack's dark eyes made her a little wobbly in the impossibly impractical and outrageously sexy and dangerously spindly hibiscus red high heels Savannah had pressed on her before she'd left the house.

"That really is one dynamite dress," he said finally. "Too bad you're not going to get to wear it all that long." He drew her back into his arms. The zipper slid down, exposing her back to the air.

"Are you cold?" he asked when she shivered.

"No." She lifted her eyes to his. "Actually, I think I'm burning up."

His answering laugh skimmed beneath her heated flesh, stimulating nerve endings in erogenous zones she'd never known she possessed until she'd made love with Jack. "The trick," he said, as he pushed the silk off her shoulders, allowing it to skim down her body, "is not to put the fires out too soon."

The dress fell to the floor in a pool of crimson silk. Still in the unaccustomed heels, Raine managed to step out of it, relieved when she didn't destroy the sensual mood by toppling over. The heat in his gaze rose even higher when he viewed the strapless ivory lace teddy and thigh-high stockings, making Raine vastly grateful that she'd surrendered when her mother and sister had insisted on raiding their lingerie drawers.

She watched his Adam's apple bob viciously as he swallowed. "I see you pulled out the heavy artillery."

"It's not often I have an opportunity to have you at a disadvantage." Feminine instincts kicked in. "I decided I may as well make the most of it."

Removing his tie didn't go quite as smoothly as it had in all her fantasies, but Jack didn't seem to notice her slight clumsiness. She slipped her fingers under the buttons of his shirt and reveled in the warmth of his skin.

"Are you seducing me?"

"Absolutely." His shirt proved easier than the tie, and Raine loved the way he sucked in his stomach as her fingers skimmed over his flesh. "Is it working?"

When she reached his belt, Jack caught hold of her wrist and pressed her hand against the front of his dress slacks. "What do you think?"

He stirred against her palm, huge and full and ready. The knowledge that she was responsible for such a powerful male response caused another thrill of female power to rush through her.

"I think you're magnificent," she murmured as she unfastened his belt buckle. She pulled the belt through the loops, then tossed it aside. It landed on top of his discarded jacket, then slid to the carpeting. Neither Jack nor Raine noticed.

"You're going to have to take your shoes off," she instructed as she moved to the button at the top of his dress slacks. "To make this work."

"Had a lot of practice undressing men, have you?" he asked blandly as he nevertheless toed off the cordovan loafers she was extremely grateful he'd chosen to wear in place of the usual boots.

"Actually, there's not all that much to it," Raine responded blithely. "Unlike women's clothing, there aren't any hidden fasteners to get caught or delicate lace to tear. Just durable white cotton—"

"You haven't finished yet. You'd think all those years in the courtroom would have taught you not to leap to judgement."

"Ah, but a good attorney factors in previous evidence." Although it was a little tricky, she managed to lower the zipper without causing any dire damage, then began sliding the charcoal gray slacks down his legs. "See? Just as I said. White briefs."

"You mean *boring* white briefs."

"You could never be boring." Her sultry voice was part honey, part smoke.

Expectation pounded hot and heavy in Jack's blood, and when she pressed her open mouth against the placket of those ordinary Jockey briefs, he bit the inside of his cheek, afraid he'd explode before things even got started.

"Sweet Jesus." His fingers tangled in her hair, but when he would have pulled her away, she murmured a refusal and tightened her hands around his thighs. She was on her knees, looking up at him, her amber eyes as earnest as he'd ever seen them.

"Every time we've made love, you've been the one doing all the work."

"You haven't exactly been passive, sweetheart." Jack knew, when he was an old man, looking back on the golden moments of his life, the memory of this woman writhing on the backseat of the Suburban, short, utilitarian nails raking down his back, would remain as crystal clear as it was today.

"I know." The color he loved to watch bloomed on her cheeks. Then spread across her chest like a fever rash. "But you've always been the one to initiate things. Not that I'm complaining," she said quickly. "I just want you to feel as wonderful and as crazy as I do, when I surrender all my control to you."

Jack had known, from the beginning, how important control was to Raine. But for the first time, he truly understood the value of the gift she'd given him. How could he give her any less?

He held both hands out to his sides. "I'm all yours."

That proved to be an understatement as Raine quickly proved herself to be fully in command. Of his body, his senses, and his heart. As they lay on the bed, her hands were never still, fluttering over him with the light teasing touch of butterfly wings. Then, just when he least expected it, they turned stronger, searching out and exploiting hidden centers of passion so intense it skimmed the edge of pain.

His flesh turned hot and damp beneath her roving touch; his muscles tensed as her lips followed the flaming path her hands were burning into him. As his stomach muscles clenched, then quivered, he reached for her, but it felt as if he were caught in a dream; his arms were heavy, his movements, slow. Too slow to catch her as she moved over the mattress, over him.

Their room was situated high above Seattle, allowing privacy even though they hadn't taken time to close the drapes. Far below, city lights, sparkling like fallen stars, stretched out to the mysterious indigo darkness of Elliot Bay.

Through his dazed senses, Jack realized Raine was quickening the pace, her hands streaking faster, her mouth hotter, and more greedy. His breath clogged in his lungs, smoke clouded his mind. He couldn't speak. Couldn't think. There was nothing to do but to feel.

Bathed in silvery moondust that made her flesh gleam like pearls, she was straddling him, rocking against him, causing the last bit of blood to rush from his head to his groin. Desperate for the feel of flesh against flesh, to be deep inside her, he tore the frothy bit of ivory silk and lace away. His hands dug into her waist.

"Now." His voice was rough with a pent up need bordering on the violent.

Her eyes flashed, her moist lips were parted; her hair was damp, her body, hot. "Now," she agreed breathlessly.

Raine cried out as he pulled her down onto him at the same time he arched off the mattress, impaling her, claiming her.

She froze, her expression stunned. Jack's last thought, before she rode them both into the flames, was that the sight of Raine astride him, cast in molten silver by the streaming moonlight, was the sexiest thing he'd ever seen.

❧ 22 ❧

Raine woke slowly, reluctant to leave the cozy little hut that her dream lover had built from palm fronds at the edge of the sugar white sand. The first thing she saw when she opened her eyes was Jack, sprawled in a wing chair beside the window. He was wearing jeans and a chambray shirt he hadn't bothered to button. All it took was the sight of that broad chest to assure her that last night's passion had been neither hallucination nor dream. The warmth in his eyes only reconfirmed that fact.

"How long have you been awake?"

"A while. I ordered breakfast, but you were sleeping so soundly, I didn't want to wake you."

"Oh." She glanced over at the clock radio, amazed at the time. "I'm sorry. I can't remember ever sleeping in so late."

"You were probably worn out by all the exercise."

She felt the heat flood into her cheeks again. "Perhaps."

The friendly sensuality gleaming in his eyes had her wanting to drag him back to bed. Every nerve in her body felt wonderfully alive. She felt wonderfully alive. It was all she could do not to stretch like a lazy cat. Raine couldn't recall ever feeling so exquisite after a night of hot, unbridled sex. Actually, she couldn't recall ever experiencing a night of such hot, unbridled sex, but that wasn't the point.

"I'm not exactly at my best in the morning."

"If I remember correctly, and I do, the last time we made love was just before dawn. And you were terrific."

His grin was a wicked slash that had her imagining him as a pirate, standing, legs braced, on the deck of his ship, the Jolly Roger flying overhead in a stiff ocean breeze, cutlass in hand. Dear heavens, she really was crazy. Crazy about him, she admitted.

"I think I'll take a shower."

"Sounds like a plan." He stood up, crossed over to the bed, lifted her from the love-tangled sheets, and carried her into the bathroom, where they spent a very long time driving each other crazy.

Somehow, when he realized that they could be in danger of drowning, Jack managed to get the water turned off and Raine wrapped in a thick terry cloth robe with the gold hotel crown insignia. Since he'd always felt a little silly wearing a bathrobe—the last time had been when he'd been recovering from being shot and the nurse, who'd he'd decided had been Atilla the Hun in a previous life, insisted—he put his jeans and shirt back on.

They were drinking coffee, engaged in the type of morning-after small talk that lovers who have begun to grow comfortable with each other do, when Jack decided that the time had come just to lay his cards on the table.

He stood up, took hold of her hands, brought her to her feet as well, touched his lips to her temple, and felt her heartbeat, a stepped up rhythm that echoed his own. That's what he wanted—that unity of heart and body. Of mind and soul.

"I love you."

Jack was not surprised when she stiffened in his arms. Disappointed, but not surprised. "You can't."

"Sure I can." Despite her discomfort, he was determined to forge on. "You may have been a bit of a pain in the butt in the beginning," he said in a teasing tone designed to calm her nerves, "but you're certainly not unlovable."

"It's too soon."

"Just because it happened fast doesn't mean that it isn't right."

"Falling in love wasn't part of the deal."

"I don't remember making any deal."

"Well, perhaps we didn't state the terms out loud," Raine allowed. "But it was certainly implied that we were going to have an affair. A brief affair," she stressed. "Just while I was in Coldwater Cove. I don't want you to love me."

"Too bad. And too late."

Raine pulled away and went over to the window, where she pressed her forehead against the glass and stared out at Elliot Bay. Wishing he possessed the power to read minds, Jack folded his arms and waited. Since a cop had to learn patience or turn in his badge, Jack forced himself to let the silence spin out.

Finally, she turned back toward him. "I don't know what to say."

"You don't have to say anything."

"Yes. I do. But I've got so many thoughts going through my head right now, I can't sort them all out."

Jack was about to let her off the hook when the phone rang. Frustrated at the interruption, he scooped up the receiver.

"O'Halloran," he ground out. "Oh, hi Ida." He exchanged a look with Raine. "Sure. She's right here."

Raine took the receiver he was holding out toward her. "What's wrong? . . . Oh, no. Are you certain she's all right? Of course we'll take the first ferry back. And give her my love."

After exchanging goodbyes, she hung up.

"Lilith will be impossible to live with now," she said with a faint smile. "I know she'll insist she predicted this with those damn tarot cards."

"Maybe she did. How is the kid?"

"Fine. She's only a couple centimeters dilated, so Ida says we have plenty of time to get there."

He pulled the schedule out of the front pocket of his jeans. "Looks as if we've got a couple hours to kill before the ferry to Coldwater Cove leaves. You know what you said that first time? About fast being okay?"

"I wasn't thinking very clearly at the time, but the words do ring a bell."

"So, how serious were you?"

Momentarily putting aside all concerns about the future, Raine smiled, with her lips and with her eyes. "Fast sounds terrific."

*   *   *

As they packed to leave Seattle after making love one last time, neither Jack nor Raine spoke of his earlier declaration. Finally, standing on the deck of the ferry on their way home, Raine broke the silence.

"What would happen," she asked cautiously, "if, just hypothetically speaking, I were to say I loved you?"

"Why don't you try it?" he suggested mildly. "And see what happens."

When she didn't answer, he sighed. "You, of all people should know that life doesn't come with gold-plated guarantees, Harvard. Every time you go into a courtroom, you don't really have any idea how things are going to turn out. You might win. Or you might lose. Life's a gamble, darlin'. Even getting out of bed in the morning is taking a risk."

"That's a very neat analogy. But there's one thing wrong with it. When I go into a courtroom, I have *some* power over my own destiny. My client's destiny. I'm a good lawyer—"

"I never doubted that for a minute."

"Thank you. But my point is that I know how to play the legal game. I know the rules."

When her obvious vulnerability brought out his protective side, Jack was forced to wonder if a modern man of the '90s should even want the woman he loved, a woman more than capable of slaying her own dragons, to need him. *Hell yes*, he decided.

"After Peg died, I drove my family nuts because I kept turning down their efforts to set me up," he said quietly. "Because I didn't believe I'd ever be lucky enough to find another woman I could love with all my heart. Like I do you. A woman I wanted to spend the rest of my life with. Like I do you."

She drew in a deep, hitching breath. "I don't have any experience with love, Jack. I'm afraid of doing something wrong. Something that will ruin it."

Knowing how much that admission cost her only made Jack love her more. "It isn't that easy to screw up if it's meant to be. And this is."

A gust of wind coming off the water blew her hair across her cheek. Her hand trembled as she brushed it away. "Let's also say, hypothetically speaking again, that we got married. Where would we live?"

"Is that a prerequisite to you falling in love with me?"

"No. Of course not. I just like to know where I'm going."

"Sometimes it's not the destination, but the journey."

"You sound just like Lilith." she complained, the frown now carving canyons into her forehead. "You have to understand. . . . I'm not that way. I don't *think* that way." Her eyes glistened with suspicious moisture. "I've never been a person to trust fate or believe in destiny, or to just go with the flow. I need to know where I'm going to be next week. Next year. Five years from now."

"I can understand that." Given her unstable child-hood, Jack could, indeed, understand her need for guideposts. But that didn't mean he was willing to stand by and let her fear of the unknown keep them apart.

"If there's one thing that Peg's death taught me it's that we never really know what's around the corner. We thought we had our life all figured out, too. I was going to make detective, which would get me off the streets, because she worried about me being killed. And, to tell the truth, so did I. Just a little.

"We never talked about it, but I think that in the back of both our minds, we figured I'd be the one to go first. Meanwhile, since she couldn't have children, we were planning to adopt more kids—at least one, maybe two. But then we discovered the hard way that the old cliché about God laughing when you make plans is all too true."

She bit her lip and turned away again, staring out over the water that the setting sun was turning a brilliant copper and gold. Jack waited.

"Everything I've ever wanted, everything I am, is tied up with being a lawyer," she said in a quiet voice that was barely audible over the hum of the ferry's engines.

"If that were true, it'd be the most pitiful thing I've ever heard. But as good an attorney as you are, you're more than that, Raine. A great deal more."

"Would you move to New York?"

"Would you ask me to?"

"No." She turned back toward him and shook her head. "I can't imagine you being happy in New York. Though Harriet would probably be thrilled," she added on an afterthought.

"Who's Harriet?"

"A woman in our office. She's got a thing for alpha males."

"And you consider me an alpha male?"

"Absolutely." A faint smile shone through the moisture brimming in her eyes. Her lovely, distressed eyes.

"Hypothetically speaking," Jack qualified, wanting to see her smile again.

"No. That's the absolute truth."

In the distance, Jack could begin to make out Coldwater Cove's green hills and decided they'd spent enough precious time on hypothetical conversations.

"I sure don't have all the answers, Raine. Hell, I don't even know all the questions. But I do know we shouldn't be wasting whatever time we have left together. So, why don't you come over here?"

She hesitated only a moment. Then went into his arms.

By the time Raine arrived at the hospital, Gwen had been settled into bed in the birthing room, a fetal monitor strapped about her belly, an IV of saline solution placed in the back of her hand, and was well into labor.

Having always felt the need for control, Raine hated feeling so helpless as she took her turn comforting Gwen. What if something went wrong? Granted, contrary to what could have happened if Ida hadn't taken her home from the ferry so many months ago, the teenager was strong and healthy. And, between Ida and the doctor, she'd had excellent prenatal care.

Still, even in modern times things could go wrong. Terrible, frightening things that hovered in Raine's mind like monsters in a night closet. In an odd twist of roles, she was a nervous wreck, while Lilith remained absolutely calm, soothing the mother-to-be with encouraging words and gentle hands. Yet more proof, Raine thought, that her formerly orderly world had turned upside down.

Since they didn't want to overwhelm Gwen, the family took turns sitting with her throughout the labor. Savannah had gone to call the Stevensons again, to update them on the situation, when Gwen went into transition. As she moistened the teenagers chapped lips with pieces of ice, and allowed fingernails to dig into the back of her hand, instead of feeling queasy, as she feared she might, Raine found herself thinking of Jack, who'd been patiently waiting, taking her downstairs to the cafeteria for coffee breaks and offering the reassurance she'd come to expect from him.

She thought about how her life had changed in such a short time, thought about how much more little things—like the sunshine glistening on a field of wildflowers, a mother's touch, a little girl's carefree laughter, and a man's warm smile—had come to mean to her. And most of all, she imagined herself in Gwen's place, carrying Jack's child. Giving birth to a brother or sister for Amy. Remarkably, rather than terrifying her, the fantasy was eminently appealing.

"The baby's crowning, Gwen." Ida's voice broke into Raine's thoughts. Although Ida wasn't officially Gwen's obstetrician, nothing could have kept her from being with the at-risk teenager she'd rescued from the streets.

"Just a little bit more, Gwen," the doctor said encouragingly. "A couple more really strong pushes should do it."

Panting harshly in a way that had Raine worrying she was on the verge of hyperventilating, Gwen pushed again. As the infant girl slid from Gwen's womb into the world, Raine suddenly knew what it was to witness a miracle. When the expected cry didn't come, she understood true terror.

The nurse quickly, deftly, suctioned the baby's nose and mouth, and an instant later the screech that escaped the rosebud lips shattered the hushed, expectant stillness. The baby was placed on Gwen's stomach while the doctor clamped the umbilical cord.

"As perfect a moment as this is, unfortunately you've still got a little bit of work left to do," the doctor told Gwen.

Assured that the new mother was in good hands, and more than a little overwhelmed by the emotional impact of what she'd witnessed, Raine escaped to the waiting room in order to regain her composure.

Jack stood up as she entered, took one look at her face, and nodded in understanding. "Nothing like it, is there? Since we had an open adoption, we were able to be there when Amy was born. I decided at the time that short of having a bush suddenly start burning in front of us, it's probably as close as any of us mortals will come to witnessing a miracle."

"That's pretty much what I was thinking."

He drew her into his arms, brushed away an errant tear that had escaped, and lowered his forehead to hers. "I love you, Raine."

"I know." Shouldn't a woman be thrilled when a man like this professed his love? Especially after she'd spent a good part of the day fantasizing about having his children? "I love you, too, Jack." She drew in a deep, shuddering breath. "So much."

He drew back, put a finger beneath her chin, and tipped her face up to his. Rather than the irritation she feared, or the frustration she knew he had a right to feel, his expression was one of infinite patience. The kind of patience a man who'd stand in the rain for hours to protect three teenage girls would need to have. "You don't sound all that happy about it."

"I think what I am is scared."

"Don't feel like the Lone Ranger." His hands were stroking her back in a soothing way that caused smoldering embers to flare.

Raine told herself that she should feel better knowing that she wasn't the only one of them who felt as if she were on the verge of leaping out of a plane without a parachute. She should. But she didn't.

"I don't know if I can give you what you want. What you need." She drew in a deep, painful breath. What you deserve, she thought but did not say.

"Now there you go, underestimating yourself again." He brushed a finger across her downturned lips. "You're everything I want, Harvard. Everything I need."

"You don't understand." Instead of backing away, she clung tighter, hating herself for giving him such mixed messages, but needing his strength. "The woman you think you love." Another breath, more painful than the first. "She isn't really me."

She felt his deep, rumbling chuckle as he rested his chin atop her head. "I've always admired your intelligence, Harvard. But that statement just flew right by me."

"I don't do things like this." Because she feared

that if she didn't let go now, she never would, she forced herself to back away. In a vain attempt to work off the nerves that were tangling inside her, she began to pace.

"Like what? Kiss in hospital waiting rooms? Because if that's the only problem, I promise we'll just stay out of hospital. How do you feel about home births?"

She'd reached the window, spun around, fisted her hands on her hips, and gave him a frustrated look. "You're not taking this seriously."

"I told you. I take everything about you seriously, Raine. Now, I understand that under normal conditions, you probably wouldn't have made love with a guy you only knew a few days—"

"Of course I wouldn't." She cut him off as she began to pace again. "Never in a million years. Unless . . ." She stopped in midstride and shut her eyes.

He was standing in front of her. She felt him. Wanted him. Oh, God, so much.

"Unless you loved him," Jack finished her statement up for her, "and were sure, not in your head, which can perform all sorts of fancy mental gymnastics, but deep down in your heart where it really counts, that he loved you, too."

She pressed her hand against his chest, unable to decide whether she wanted to push him away or pull him to her. Raine figured she'd probably suffered more episodes of indecision in the past two weeks than during her entire six years practicing law.

"Oh, dear. I'm sorry to interrupt." At the familiar voice, Raine spun toward the waiting-room doorway, never so glad to see her mother as she was at this minute. "That's all right. We were just wrapping up anyway." She ignored Jack's faint chuckle behind her. "How's Gwen doing?"

"Physically, she's fine. The baby's all cleaned up and looking like a little blue-eyed doll. The Stevensons are on their way."

"How's she doing emotionally?"

"As well as can be expected. According to Savannah, the Stevensons are floating on air."

"I can imagine." Raine sighed. "It's so wonderful. And so sad."

"It's also for the best," Lilith reminded her.

"I suppose so. . . . I'll be right there."

Lilith's gaze went from Raine to Jack and back to Raine again. "Take your time."

"Speaking of time, I need some," Raine told Jack when they were alone again. "To think."

"I suppose, under the circumstances, that's reasonable."

Before she could thank him for being so understanding, he ducked his head and kissed her—a quick, hard kiss that ended too soon and left her head spinning. "Think fast."

With that he left. But as she leaned against the wall and closed her eyes, she could hear the tap of his boots on the tile floor of the hallway. And the unmistakably cheery sound of him whistling *My Girl.*

❦ 23 ❧

The Stevensons returned to the hospital the following day, arriving at the same time the family arrived to take Gwen home. The couple's mood was appropriately subdued, but their joy radiated so brightly, Raine almost understood her mother's alleged ability to read auras.

They were exchanging slightly stilted greetings when a hospital volunteer showed up in the room with the camera. "Would you like a picture taken with your baby?" she asked with a perkiness ill-suited to the occasion. The sudden silence her question created was thick enough to be cut with a knife.

"I don't know." The desperately needy look on Gwen's face nearly broke Raine's heart. The girl was sitting on the edge of the bed, the suitcase Lilith had brought to the hospital last night at her feet.

"I think you should." Taking charge of the uncomfortable situation, Terri placed the infant girl in Gwen's arms. She was wearing a pink knitted cap that was a gift from the hospital and a pink drawstring nightgown covered with white hearts. "In fact, we should take two. One for you and one for your baby, so she'll always have a picture of the mommy whose tummy she grew in for her first nine months."

Gwen looked more than a little nervous as she held the wobbly little pink-capped head steady and managed a faint, equally wobbly smile for the camera. There was another strained silence as they all waited for the image to appear on the Polaroid film.

"Whatever you ultimately decide about keeping in touch, I'll make certain Lily gets this when we tell her about how she was adopted," Terri promised.

"Thank you." Gwen's voice was soft, but, Raine was relieved to see, surprisingly steady. "I wrote her a letter last night. So she'll know how much I loved her." She took the envelope from the pocket of her oversize denim top and, since Terri's arms were filled with the baby again, handed it to Bill.

After tearfully thanking Gwen again, Terri left with her new daughter and husband.

"Well." Gwen exhaled a long shuddering breath. "I guess that's that." Her eyes were swimming, but Raine thought she seemed at peace with her decision. "They're going to make good parents."

"Absolutely," Savannah promised.

Although the mood was not exactly festive as they drove home to Coldwater Cove, Raine could sense the burden that had been lifted from Gwen's shoulders. And when she began discussing medical schools with Ida, Raine knew that the teenager had begun to move on with her life.

Raine spent the next three days taking a long, hard look at her life. Her options. If she didn't have her career to think of, she'd stay here in Coldwater Cove with her family. With Jack.

But the problem was, while she might honestly wish differently, Raine knew she needed more of a challenge than small-town law could offer. However, whenever she thought about returning to New York, which, compared to Coldwater Cove, was as user-friendly as a convertible submarine, she'd experience the twinges of a headache and was forced to stop by the market and buy a new bottle of Maalox.

In a perfect world, she wouldn't be forced to make these choices. Unfortunately, Raine had discovered at a very young age that there was no such thing as a perfect world. There had to be a solution, she kept assuring herself as she walked in the lush spring garden Gwen had planted and continued to tend in Ida's backyard, rocked endless miles in the porch swing, and paced the kitchen, as she went over and over the options with Savannah, always ending back at the same place. Jack and a family she'd never dared dream she could have, or her career. Coldwater Cove or New York. She was an intelligent woman, she kept reminding herself. There had to be a solution. Finally, early one morning, just when she thought she'd go crazy from wandering through her mental maze all day and most of the nights, a possible solution occurred to her. She leaped out of bed and made two calls. One to Oliver Choate. The second to the man who held the final piece of her life's puzzle.

After dropping Amy off at her best friend Sarah Young's house, where the two girls were going to spend the day playing Barbies, Jack drove to Port

Angeles. He arrived home just as a new fire engine red Ford Expedition pulled into his driveway. He climbed out of the Suburban, folded his arms, and enjoyed the view of those long, slender legs climbing out of the driver's seat.

"Nice truck."

"Thank you. It's new."

"I figured that from the temporary tags. So, who does it belong to?"

"Me."

"Isn't four-wheel drive overkill for the city?"

"I have no idea. Since I don't intend to drive it in the city."

"I see." He was beginning to. Or at least he hoped he was.

Raine closed the distance between them. "I'm not going to be driving it in New York because I'm not going back. As it turns out, Dan has quite a few deals pending between old friends from the Silicon Valley and Seattle-area computer companies. In fact, thanks to referrals, he's got more business than he can handle alone. Which is why he jumped at the idea of taking on a partner."

"That partner being you."

"None other."

"What about your job back east? Are you saying you walked away from that?"

"Not exactly. I called Oliver Choate this morning. He's the founder of Choate, Plimpton, Wells & Sullivan. The firm has been wanting to get into Eastern Rim business, but it's been difficult from the East Coast. We worked out a deal where I'll work for them on a consulting basis. Dan thought it was a great idea."

"I'm sure he did. Sounds as if you've got everything figured out."

"Not quite." He watched her take a deep breath. "So, were you serious about getting married?"

"I suppose that depends on whether you want me to be serious or not." It was going to be okay, Jack thought. They were going to be okay.

"You're ducking the question, Sheriff. If you refuse to answer, I may have to go track down Judge Wally and have him hold you in contempt."

"Never happen. Wally's wife just happens to be my second cousin on my daddy's side."

"And you O'Hallorans stick together."

"Like glue. . . . You know what they say about a picture being worth a thousand words?"

"Yes, but you're out of order. And you still haven't answered my question."

"I'm getting there. If you're going to move home to Coldwater Cove, you're going to have to learn patience, Harvard. Since we country boys tend to like to take things a little slow. Sorta heightens the anticipation." He took a folder from his denim-jacket pocket and handed it to her. "Here's exhibit one. I picked it up in Port Angeles this morning."

The cover of the folder featured a lush, romantic palm-tree-fringed white beach. Adding a splash of brilliant color to the travel poster scene, a shimmering rainbow arced over an aquamarine lagoon.

"Tickets?"

"To Bora Bora. You said you've always wanted to go to some tropical island. I figured this one might not be such a bad spot for a honeymoon."

"A honeymoon implies marriage."

"Smart and sexy. That's definitely an irresistible

combination. . . . Next, I'd like the record to show that I, too, made a few calls to some old-friends-turned-small-town-police-chiefs who professed to be more than willing to hire me onto their police forces. All within commuting distance of Manhattan."

"You were willing to do that? For me?"

"For us. However, since you seemed to have come up with an equally clever solution, we may as well move on so I can put my next exhibit into evidence. The one that goes to relevance."

He dragged her up against him and kissed her so hard and so long that by the time they finally came up for air, Raine had nearly forgotten her plan to make him suffer.

"Well." She had to fight to catch her breath. "That certainly rules out reasonable doubt."

"God, I love it when you talk like a lawyer." He nipped at her ear and turned her into a puddle of need.

"I am a lawyer," she managed as he stroked his finger down her throat, lingering where her pulse was beating furiously.

"I know." His caressing touch continued downward, slipping below the neckline of her blouse. "A cop and a lawyer. The gods must be having one helluva laugh over that one." He tormented her with kisses as he unbuttoned her blouse. "So, Counselor, what would you say to playing a little stop and frisk?"

He'd pressed her against the side of her new truck, effectively trapping her as he slipped his knee between her legs and made her ache. "I'd say a change of venue is definitely in order."

"Good idea." Without taking his mouth from hers, he carried her into the house and up the stairs, where he dropped her onto the bed.

It was on her second bounce that she noticed the photograph was gone. She'd come to terms with Peg's place in Jack's life. In Amy's life. Still, this proof that she wouldn't have to live with the ghost of his wife between them caused a glorious sense of joy melded with relief.

"So," he said, as he lay down beside her and slid her blouse down her arms. "What's the verdict? Are you going to marry me?"

"Of course I am." She pressed her hands against his chest, where his heart was beating as wildly as her own. "I'll want us to have more children." She pressed her mouth against his. "One would be a nice start. Two would be even better."

He tangled his hands in her hair and tilted her head back. "Are you sure? What about your career?"

"Having a career doesn't preclude having babies. In fact, impatient city girl that I am, I was hoping we might get started on that project today."

He closed his eyes briefly. Then opened them and grinned, that cocky, masculine grin that Raine knew would still have the power to thrill her when she was ninety. "I'm sure as hell not going to argue with that."

This time their lovemaking was different. As if committing to a future together had moved it to a higher plane. When Jack braced himself on his elbows and fixed his dark gaze on hers, Raine looked up into his ruggedly handsome face and knew she'd be forever grateful that fate, and three teenage girls, had brought her to this place in time with this passionate, patient, wonderful man.

As if reading her mind, he smiled as he linked their fingers together. "Welcome home." Then he slipped into her, filling her, loving her.

Home. Having finally discovered her heart's own true place, Raine vowed to never, ever leave again.

~Epilogue~

The weddings took place in the garden. A garden that Gwen had tended with increased devotion these past two weeks, resulting in a riotous explosion of color. The day dawned bright and sunny and warm, a gift that Lilith attributed to several ancient Celtic goddesses and a complex spell involving star power that Raine didn't even try to understand.

Not wanting to ruin this perfect day, she wasn't about to challenge her mother's belief system. Besides, there was a part of her who, when she thought about all the ways her life had changed—her homecoming, her reconciliation with her mother, being blessed with a man who loved her and a daughter she already adored—couldn't help but wonder if perhaps magic had played a part.

Folding chairs had been set up on the lawn, claimed by various O'Hallorans, Lindstroms, Dottie and Doris Anderson, and so many others who'd come to the house to share the family's joy.

"Don't lock your knees," Cooper Ryan advised as the flutist who'd been at the Beltane ceremony at the Heart of the Hills began to play a traditional wedding march. The music was one of the many compromises Lilith and Raine had managed to achieve. "Or you'll pass out."

"I may anyway," Jack muttered. He put his hand against the front of his white shirtfront. "In fact, I think I might be having a heart attack. Maybe I should have had Ida check me out before the ceremony."

"Well, it's too late now," Cooper said as Amy, clad in a pink dress she'd picked out herself at The Dancing Deer and a new pair of white patent leather Mary Janes, skipped down the white satin runner, energetically throwing rose petals into the air from a white wicker basket. "Lord, she's a doll, Jack. You're a lucky man."

"I know." About this Jack's tone was firm and sure. "Okay. That's it. I can't have a heart attack in front of my own daughter. It'd scar her for life."

"You're both cops," Dan said, laughter in his low voice. "I can't believe you're this scared of getting married."

"It's not the marrying part," Cooper said. "It's all this." He motioned surreptitiously toward the lilac arbor, the puffy white satin bows on the chairs, and all the guests dressed in their Sunday best.

"Just wait until it's your turn." Jack shot him a warning sideways glance. "I'm going to remind you of this."

The best man to both grooms grinned. "I figure we'll just elope to Vegas and get hitched by some Elvis impersonator. It's easier and faster."

"Try telling that to your bride," Cooper advised sagely.

"I will," Dan agreed. "At the first opportunity." He glanced over toward Savannah, who, in her role as maid of honor to her mother and sister was standing on the other side of the aisle. Their eyes met and any guests who might have been looking at either of them would have caught the quick flash of remembered heat.

There was a strum of harp strings. "Jesus, Lilith looks gorgeous, doesn't she?" Cooper asked beneath his breath.

"Gorgeous," both men agreed as the first bride walked down the aisle behind the three teenage bridesmaids.

She was wearing a flowing gown made of some material that caught the sun and looked as if it had been spun from spiderwebs and then dipped in dew. She'd explained that the gown was cut on the bias, and although Cooper had no idea what that meant, it draped over her curvaceous body like a dream. She'd brought out the crystals, but she'd left her left hand bare, awaiting the ring he'd been carrying around in his pocket since the day after he'd arrested her in the park.

When she reached him, her smile, filled with love and a lust for life he knew she'd still possess when she was a hundred, dazzled as it always had.

Another strum of harp strings had the guests turning behind them again. There was a collective intake of breath as Raine appeared, dressed in a white lacy froth of a wedding gown that, had Jack not already discovered that his bride was a closet romantic, would have surprised the hell out of him.

"Oh, Raine looks just like a fairy princess, Daddy." Amy's voice, ringing out above the flute, caused laughter to ring through the assembled guests. "She's even prettier than Ariel, isn't she?"

"Absolutely," Jack said, his words directed to his daughter, but his eyes on the stunning woman who seemed to be floating toward him. Her eyes, shimmering with love, stayed on his as she approached.

As she walked toward Jack, Raine felt as if she were walking on air. Listening to him repeat the words that she'd never expected to hear, let alone say, Raine knew how solemnly he took those vows. He was the most loving, honorable man she'd ever met. And now, wondrously, he was hers. For ever and ever. Amen. When she held out her hand for him to slip the woven gold band onto her finger, she felt the unwavering warmth of his love flow straight to her heart.

"You may kiss your brides," the minister announced.

"It's about time," Cooper and Jack said at the same time.

Afraid that she might float straight up into that clear blue June sky, Raine held on to Jack's shoulders as she lifted her face for her husband's kiss.